THE SINFUL STARS

Tales of the Fading Suns

OTHER FADING SUNS BOOKS
Fading Suns roleplaying game rulebook
Fading Suns Players Companion
Lords of the Known Worlds
Priests of the Celestial Sun
Merchants of the Jumpweb
Byzantium Secundus
Weird Places
Forbidden Lore: Technology
The Dark Between the Stars
Children of the Gods: Obun & Ukar
Sinners & Saints

STARSHIP MINIATURES GAME
Noble Armada

COMPUTER GAMES
Emperor of the Fading Suns (Segasoft)
Fading Suns: Starship Diplomacy (Ripcord Games; forthcoming)

The Sinful Stars
is a product of Holistic Design Inc.

Editor: Bill Bridges
Cover art: John Bridges

First edition/October 1998

FADING SUNS™ created by Bill Bridges and Andrew Greenberg

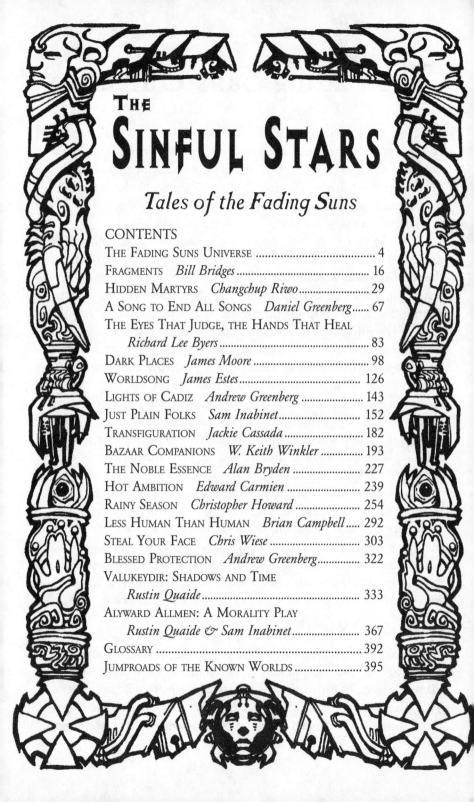

THE
SINFUL STARS

Tales of the Fading Suns

CONTENTS

The Fading Suns Universe

Once the suns shone brightly, beacons in the vast night of space, calling humanity onward. The stars were symbols of humanity's vast potential, a purpose and destiny revealed in progress, inciting an exodus of unlimited growth to the distant stars. Once people looked to the heavens with hope and longing in their eyes.

Then the suns — and the hope — began to fade.

It is the year 4998 and history has come to an end. Humanity's greatest civilization has fallen, leaving ignorance and fear scattered among the ruins of many worlds. A new Dark Age is upon humanity and few believe in renewal and progress anymore. Now there is only waiting. Waiting for a slow death as the age-old stars fade to cinders and the souls of the sinful are called to Final Judgment.

But not all believe in this destiny. A leader has arisen, an Emperor sworn to unite the worlds of Human Space together again under one banner. To ignite hope once more in people's hearts.

It is a monumental task, for most people have already given up and fallen into the ways of the past, playing serfs to feudal lords. What is hope to them now but a falsehood which leads to pain? Better to leave the hard decisions to their masters and let the Church console their souls.

There are enemies everywhere, those who seek to selfishly profit from humanity's demise: vain nobles ruling far-flung worlds, power-hungry priests who seek dominion over the lives of men, the greedy merchant guilds growing rich from bartering humanity's needs and wants. They are not alone. Others are out there among the darkening stars, alien races angry with humankind for age-old slavery, and enigmatic alien empires with agendas too paradoxical to fathom.

History

The chronicle of humanity's history among the stars is a long one, stretching over two millennia. It is not a quiet story. From the greedy planet-grabbing of early colonists to the bloody battles of the Emperor Wars, humans have rarely slept peacefully in the void. They have prospered, suffered defeat, and dared to hope again. And they have not traveled down the paths of history alone; aliens walk among them, with long histories and destinies of their own to complete.

First Republic

Humanity first reached the stars under the auspices of the First Republic, a one-world government run by the "zaibatsu": greedy mercantile barons whose corporate states replaced the nations of the earth. The zaibatsu colonized the solar system in search of new sources of wealth and mineral resources. At the edge of the solar system they found the jumpgate.

This ancient artifact of alien manufacture baffled and awed humanity. It took many years of research to unlock even the most basic secrets of its technology, but its main function was clear: it opened portals to distant star systems. Diligent scientists constructed the first jump drive, an engine installed on a spaceship which could propel the ship through the gate, transporting it instantly into foreign space light years away.

The exodus began.

At first, the zaibatsu carefully controlled the manufacture and ownership of jump ships and reaped the resources of the new worlds and solar systems. Additionally, they outlawed and suppressed a religious movement which grew around the jump experience, based on a mystical experience common to many jump pilots: the Sathra Effect, so called because of the first words from the lips of the ecstatic pilots. The zaibatsu installed dampers on ships that ended the communion and halted the rebellious religion.

But repression was not long suffered. After anarchists leaked the secret of the technology to all, nobody could keep back the vast wave of people seeking to escape corporate tyranny and claim worlds of their own. The First Republic collapsed in a civil war over ever-expanding territory and diminishing loyalties.

Diaspora

The new universe of Human Space was made up of fractured, planetary nations, some democratic, some totalitarian. Many of the original rulers of these worlds created dynasties which would last for millennia: the first noble houses to rule the stars. But years of political and social experiments yielded only chaos and strife between worlds. Into this dangerous universe came the Prophet, a man with a vision of Creation he claimed was gifted to him by God, whom he called the Pancreator. The Prophet gathered disciples and followers about him and performed many miracles. A humanity desperate for unity and hope looked to the Prophet for their answers.

During this time, humanity met its first sentient race, the ungulate Shantor. At first, they were thought to be merely clever horselike beings. But it was soon realized how intelligent they were — and how dangerous. Another sentient race, the Ukar, were gifted with psychic powers — powers which they used to goad the Shantor into a bloody revolt. By the time the truth behind the Shantor's rage was discovered, it was too late to reform the beasts in humanity's eyes: the "dangerous and uncontrollable" Shantor were enslaved and moved to reservations across the Known Worlds, breaking up their families and culture.

The following Ukar War united humanity against another star-faring race, one inimicable to human interests. With the aid of the Ukar's cousin race, the Obun, humanity gained ground in their galactic war. Finally, Palamedes Alecto, follower of the Prophet, led the newly formed Universal Church of the Celestial Sun against the Ukari on their homeworld. Humanity was victorious, and the place of the Church in future politics and martial power was cemented.

Humanity marched across new worlds and subjugated the sentients living upon them, most of whom were incapable of star travel and thus considered inferior.

Until the Vau.

Humanity met more than its match when it subjugated a peaceful race of gardeners known as the G'nesh. When their overlords arrived from unknown worlds in vastly superior starships with devastating energy weapons, humans had no choice but to fall back and go no further. Luckily, the Vau were non-expansionistic, and pursued no vendetta against humanity. As long as they were left alone, they would cause no trouble — or so most humans believed. But enigmatic "gifts" and lore from the Vau over the centuries have been curiously effective at starting conflicts among humans.

Second Republic

Eventually, with the unity provided by the Church and economic interests heralded by mercantile leaders, the Second Republic was born, a democratic government which eventually spanned all the worlds of

Human Space. Under its auspices, an unprecedented era of prosperity and high technology was initiated. It seemed that there were no limits to human development, no secrets which could not be unlocked by the power of the human mind, along with a little ingenuity and grit. Scientists even tapped into the very genetic code of humanity, creating mutated beings later known as the Changed.

But power eventually seems to coalesce into the hands of a few, especially when the people are no longer vigilant. The noble houses of the Diaspora, still rich but now relegated to meaningless roles, hungered for the vast power they once had and plotted against the Republic. They were aided by a new milleniallism and apocalyptic fever, for scientists had discovered a new, dread phenomenon: the suns were fading. The stars grew dim and no one knew why.

The government could not calm the fears of all the worlds, and the untimely crash of the welfare computer system caused riots in every major city on every planet. Rebels rose up and with lightning speed, claimed the central government on Byzantium Secundus. The nobles joined together with the Church to free the capital. Victorious, they refused to return power to the senators and instead seized power for themselves. This ushered in a new age for humanity: a Dark Age of feudal lords, fanatic priests and scheming guilds.

New Dark Ages

The new lords of the Known Worlds quickly began to war upon one another, with only the largest, most cunning or richest houses rising to prominence, while many others were destroyed. In this chaos, the common people were left defenseless. In desperation, many signed generational contracts with the noble houses, swearing fealty to their local lords for themselves and their children to come. At first, the Church fought such indenture, but it eventually adopted such contracts itself when they proved the only reliable means to raise armies against rivals — and the Church was just as combative and martial as the nobles.

The corporations of the Second Republic were left with little of the spoils. With their holdings seized or signed over forcefully, they had little overt power. But a conglomeration of these corporation banded together to form the Merchant League, and rewrote their charters to form guilds rather than corporations. Guilds could more easily control membership and advancement within their ranks. In addition, the League maintained their secret technological patents, often paying for this privilege with the death of many agents charged with wiping such data from computers the universe over lest it fall into the hands of the noble lords.

Without the means to repair their starships and high-tech weaponry, the nobles and the Church could not long stand. After a vicious campaign against the guilds failed to free the League's secrets, the lords had little choice but to admit the merchant guilds into the halls of power. Even the Church was forced to concede their power, and issued a Patriarchal Bull allowing only them (along with the nobles and priests) to use certain proscribed high-technologies. Once these scientific secrets were kept from the people, the Known Worlds' descent into a feudal society was complete: only the upper classes moved among the stars; the peasants lived and died on the planets where they were born.

But the Known Worlds were not the only words of Human Space. During the Fall of the Second Republic, many planets were lost, their jump coordinates stolen or the jumpgates sealed. After centuries of absence, some of these worlds reappeared, heralded by barbarian hordes who swept into the Known Worlds, wreaking havoc and looting noble lands.

Only a powerful coalition of nobles could defend against the scattered barbarian clans, and only a master tactician could form such a coalition. This man was Vladimir, whose campaign against the barbarians propelled him to power. After his victory against the raiders, he declared himself the first Emperor of the Known Worlds. A campaign of pacification convinced the noble houses to accept his rule.

But upon his coronation day, when he placed the crown upon his head, he mysteriously died in a sudden conflagration. His coalition fell apart, and house fell upon house, each blaming the others for the death of Vladimir. Eventually, peace was secured again, sealed with Vladimir's reforms: all the houses, sects and guilds would vote equally to choose a noble to become Regent, to rule until a new Emperor could be decided upon.

It would be nearly half a millennium before an Emperor was again chosen, and only after nearly 40 years of violent war. The Emperor Wars lasted for two generations, and saw a greater rise in technology than any time since the Second Republic. But it was war tech: powerful killing machines, chemical weapons, fusion bombs and other means of destruction. Finally, one man was victorious: Alexius Hawkwood, the new Emperor of the Fading Suns.

In his newly forged reign — now but three years old — peace has finally come. The jumproutes are open again, and pilgrims can travel safely to other worlds. Merchants can once more ply the starlanes, selling exotic goods to people who have not seen them within their grandfather's lifetimes. And adventure awaits, for Alexius has called for a great quest: to explore the stars, discover the lost worlds of the Second Republic, and solve the mystery of the fading suns.

The Noble Houses

Of the many noble houses throughout the Known Worlds, five have achieved prominence and effectively rule most of the Human Space — under their new Emperor, of course. The Emperor Wars took a toll on many of these houses: the losers now struggle to regain lost lands or power, while the victors fight to ensure that their rivals stay down.

The life of a noble is not the leisurely idyll one might expect: there are fiefs to manage, rivals to crush and wars to wage. While there is much power to be gained, there is always the risk of humiliation or loss of holdings and position. It is no wonder that they know how to party: their gala affairs are lavish and awe-inspiring — but also rife with intrigue, innuendo, back-stabbing and even sword dueling. To escape such pressures, noble sons and daughters often take to the stars with only a small entourage of friends and retainers, to better know the worlds they wish to one day rule.

The five major houses (called the Royal Houses) are:

House Hawkwood: Prideful yet honorable, the Hawkwoods have seen one of their own take the Emperor's throne. While Alexius Hawkwood has since distanced himself from his family to appear more impartial, the Hawkwoods take such political setbacks with stoicism — the same fierce perseverance with which they beat back the barbarian raiders to their worlds. A Hawkwood does not give up. House Hawkwood is more beloved by its vassals than any other house, for they treat them fairly and with justice.

House Decados: Slimy, cunning and extremely successful, the Decados have risen to power through treachery and an uncanny understanding of their rivals — helped in no small part, no doubt, by their vast, invisible intelligence network. While the other families accuse them of a number of crimes, the Decados are here to stay and thus must be dealt with on their own terms. Decados vassals despise their lords but are kept in line through fear or the promise of power for those who make good quislings.

The Hazat: Hot-blooded and intense, the martial Hazat know how to field an army but are also no strangers to intrigue. When they can calm the vicious infighting from family to family, they can present a formidable front against rivals from other houses. Left with less land after the wars than they began with, they now pursue a campaign against a barbarian world, seeking new lands outside of the Empire. Hazat vassals are loyal, for they know that sacrifices for their lords are often rewarded.

House Li Halan: This pious and disciplined family was once the worst behaved of all nobles. Their immoral exploits are legendary, as is the tale of their overnight conversion to the Church. They now pursue the scriptures as fanatically as they once chased pleasure. While other nobles may snicker at the faithful lords, they more often fear the Li Halan, for this family has proved implacable on both the battlefield and at court. Their vassals are fiercely loyal, for they know their place as vassals in the Pancreator's plan.

House al-Malik: The exotic and inscrutable al-Malik are often accused of being mere merchants, for their ties to the League are well known. But they have proven their noble legerdemain many times, through the acquisition of land and a unique understanding of human nature and politics. It is very hard to pull one over on an al-Malik, but it is likewise hard for them to resist the lure of a good adventure or challenge. Vassals of this family are well-treated and return the respect with solid service.

The Church

Although the Universal Church of the Celestial Sun may present a unified front for the faithful of the Known Worlds, its cathedrals are rife with sectarianism. While the Patriarch has rule over all aspects of the Church, it is often difficult to manage the actions of priests the universe over. Many sects and orders have arisen, powerful enough to earn official status from a reluctant Orthodoxy. Even more heresies have arisen, forcing the Patriarch to spend his time hunting heretics rather than unifying the present sects.

A priest's life is often a trying one: If it's not local disasters or famines they must try to relieve, it's occult threats to the faith, from demon possessions, zombie plagues or malicious psychics. Church magical rites are effective, regardless of whether they are considered merely a form of psychic power by the more skeptical.

The five major sects/orders ordained by the Church are:

Urth Orthodox: The largest sect, it is the Orthodoxy that most people associate with the Church. Its priests can be found on all worlds, from the ostentatious bishops of the capital cities to the more humble parish priests in the most poverty-stricken fiefs. While the Orthodoxy has gained a reputation for their cunning political maneuvers, most priests know little of such things, being entirely too busy protecting the souls of the simple faithful. While many may spurn the Orthodoxy for its martial role in the Emperor Wars, when tragedy strikes, it is the Orthodoxy they return to for consolation.

Brother Battle: This order of monk knights is the most elite fighting unit in the Known Worlds, surpassing even the Emperor's Phoenix Guard in martial prowess. Originally initiated to protect pilgrims and pursue heretics, the order is now chartered by noble houses, Church sects and even guilds to perform elite military operations on many worlds, including the deadly Stigmata Front against the Symbiot alien invaders. Despite rumors of heresy and usury within their ranks, everyone wants a Brother Battle monk by their side in times of trouble.

Eskatonic Order: These hermetic sages are often thought of as wizards by the common folk, but the nobles and guildsmen know them for the kooks they often are. While there are many within the order who possess profound wisdom and learning, there are just as many who are obsessed with the end of the universe and who stand on street corners telling everyone about it. Once considered a heresy by the Orthodoxy, the Eskatonics were admitted into the fold when their theurgical rites proved effective against the Symbiots.

Temple Avesti: Dreaded inquisitors. The Avestites long ago seized most of the seats on the Inquisitorial Synod, and have since then made it their duty to search the Known Worlds for signs of heresy, demonism and any other threat to the faithful. Their illiteracy, fear of learning and dogmatic adherence to certain extreme scriptures makes them feared and hated throughout Human Space. But they are obeyed nonetheless. Only the most fanatic and ascetic initiates are admitted to this sect.

Sanctuary Aeon: Healers and compassionate mystics. Everybody loves the priests and priestesses of Sanctuary Aeon, followers of Saint Amalthea. When an Amalthean comes to town, there is always someone willing to provide hospitality for her. Indeed, so beloved by the commoners are they that when one was once accused of witchcraft by an Avestite, the Avestite was seized by the populace and burned at the stake instead.

The Merchant League

The remnants of the Second Republic mega-corporations can be found among the many guilds of the Merchant League. It is the League which controls high-technology: invention, manufacture and distribution. It is the guilds who pilot noble starships or repair Church think machines. If any one of these factions were to anger them, a League blockade would quickly end the argument.

The guilds gladly accept their role as second-class citizens at the royal soirees, for they know that there is little profit to be made arguing over the best or worst dressed. They instead charge high dollar for the privilege of hiring a guild specialist — and their enforcers ensure that only the guild specializes in certain skills and tech; black marketers and tech counterfeiters are thrown from airlocks.

While the guilds are numerous, only five have risen to intergalactic prominence and regularly travel the jumpweb in the employ of nobles, priests or other guildsmen:

Charioteers: Star pilots and merchants marine, this intrepid guild is what most people think of when they imagine the Merchant League, for it is the Charioteer merchants with their exotic, traveling medicine shows who are most often seen by the commoners. They own the star lanes — literally. Without their secret jumpcode technology, travel through jumpgates would be impossible. In addition, the best pilots come from this guild.

Engineers: High technology is rare in the Dark Ages, and most people fear it, for as the Church teaches, it is the symbol of human hubris which brought down the Republic. Few dare to delve into its secrets anymore, and those that do are considered mad — like the Engineers. These strange technicians often modify their bodies with cybertech, becoming more machine than human. While they creep out the commoners and disgust the priests, everyone knows just how valuable their lore is in maintaining intergalactic power and communication.

Scravers: If you can't find what you're looking for legally, chances are the Scravers can get it — for a price. Scravers specialize in all sorts of activities normally viewed as anti-social (but often fun): gambling, black market goods and even thievery. Of course, they deny it all, hiding behind the guise of a salvage and reclamation guild. Since they possess blackmail on just about every major official — even bishops — little is done against them.

The Muster: Professional soldiers, these mercenaries are essential to most military operations throughout the Known Worlds. Even the Brothers Battle rely on their orbital artillery support, and most noble houses have hired them to either assault their rivals or quell rebellions. But soldiery is not the only labor this guild contracts; they specialize in all sorts of trained help: cooks, technicians, animal trainers, butlers, etc. In fact, it's very dangerous to hire trained labor without contracting this guild — their enforcers ensure that they get the largest and juiciest contracts.

Reeves: Somebody's got to do the paperwork, and this job is left to the Reeves. They do it quite well. So well that they are the de facto bankers of the Known Worlds and probably one of the richest factions in the universe — although few realize just how rich they've become through their loans to noble houses. Just about everybody owes the Reeves, and when one comes calling on favors, few dare deny him.

Aliens

There are a number of sentient races within the Known Worlds: the simian Gannok, the ungulate Shantor, the avian Etyri, amphibian Oro'ym, insectoid Ascorbites and the reptilian Hironem. But three other races have achieved the most freedom of movement and self-determination:

Ur-Obun: This peaceful, philosophical race, like their Ur-Ukar cousins, claim deep Anunnaki involvement in their history. The Anunnaki (the ancient race who built the jumpgates) apparently engineered the two races' fates, separating them onto different worlds before they disappeared from history. The Obun are given positions of respect as councilors and advisors in Known Worlds society. However, while they are treated politely, their advice is often considered naive by the militant human culture. Nonetheless, an Ur-Obun became one of the Prophet's disciples, and is honored by an Obun sect of the Church.

Ur-Ukar: Due to their initial hostile dealings with humanity, the Ukari are now a broken race. Their homeworld is owned by the League, who reap it for its mineral resources, selling the spoils off-world to noble houses. The have been removed from their ancestral, subterranean lands and herded into tight caves in poverty. Few humans care what happens to them. A resistance movement has responded with terrorist tactics, and has taken its war of hatred to other worlds. Nonetheless, the League values them for their shady, underworld skills.

Vorox: Huge carnivorous, multi-limbed beasts, the Vorox are new to civilization. That they achieved sentience at all on their toxic jungle world is a wonder. That they have come as far as they have since is a tribute to their adaptability and powerful attributes — valuable qualities in the Known Worlds. They are most often trained as elite shock troops by noble houses, but many have joined the League to see the stars firsthand.

Enemies

There are many dangers in the universe of the **Fading Suns,** not the least of which are humans themselves. The intrigues and conspiracies of the noble houses, Church and League are enough to keep most people occupied for a lifetime. The post-war years have seen an increase in such covert activity, for few dare to openly disturb the peace. The Emperor has his hands full trying to cement his rule against internal malcontents and external alien and barbarian empires.

Barbarians: Of the hundreds of worlds once part of the Second Republic, a handful remain in reach of the empire. Many more still exist in space, waiting for some intrepid adventurer to rediscover the jumpcodes. Some of these have new civilizations of their own, from the loose and fractious Vuldrok Star-Nation, whose raiders harry the Hawkwood worlds and to whom loyalty is only as good as the value of booty, to the regal Kurgan Caliphate, whose disciplined people follow the latest in a long succession of prophet-kings. Both of these cultures are labeled "barbarian" by the empire, and declared heretical by the Church. The spectre of a crusade looms over the Known Worlds...

Among the more dangerous, non-human threats out there are:

The Vau: This technologically superior alien empire has so far-proved little threat — as long as humans stay on their side of the border.

The few times Vau ambassadors have parleyed with humans, trouble has resulted, although in forms hard to trace back to the Vau. For instance, the Vau "gifted" humanity with the jumpcoordinates to reach a previously lost world called Pandemonium. This world in turn revealed coordinates to another lost world called Iver. A cold war for the spoils of these new worlds began; the Vau's present has proven most troublesome.

If the Vau were to expand into Human Space, no one is sure if they could be halted, for their tech is impressive. Human's stole their own knowledge about energy shields and blasters from early Vau encounters. It is theorized that the Vau know far more about these fields than has been revealed.

Symbiots: A greater threat to Known Worlds hegemony, however, are the Symbiots, parasitic entities attempting to break through into Human Space and possess its inhabitants, turning them into hive mind slaves — or so the propaganda goes. In truth, nobody really knows what the Symbiots want or even just what they are. Everybody does know that they are dangerous and inimicable to human goals. Rumor of a Symbiot infestation is enough to bring a squad of Church inquisitors with flameguns, ready to burn first and ask questions later.

Demons: The Church claims that demons exist and can possess people to perform their nefarious deeds in this world. The sad thing is that this seems to be true. Even the most rational scientists must admit to the reality of *something* out there, something often unseen but seemingly hostile. These entities, demons or aliens or whatever, can so far only be combated by Church theurgy and miracles of faith.

Fragments
Bill Bridges

From the journals of Provost Guisseppe Alustro, Eskatonic Order, in the service of Lady Erian Li Halan.

Night on Hira is bright when the bombs go off. The sky is lit with the fiery, short-lived glow of munitions. The Hazat and Kurgan Caliphate forces never seem to tire of war.

But the lights and the sounds eventually fade as the night grows older and the soldiers tire, and peace settles over the broken land. The rubble of countless villages lies as a no-man's land between the forces' current embattlements, with only long-range missiles, aerial fly-bys and the occasional theurgic rite forming any contact between the enemies.

We are safe here for now. In the ruins of Matanto city, in the blasted basement labyrinth of the former ruler's palace, we have taken shelter to search the past for our future. This building, constructed during the Second Republic of strong maxicrete and plasteel, has lasted through a millennia of erosion only to be torn open and exposed to the sky by a series of direct artillery barrages.

It wasn't even looted. Once the ruling family escaped the burning town, the Hazat and Kurgan forces moved on, fighting over new lands not yet sworn to either side. Why they mutually assaulted this city, I don't really understand. My lady Erian says it had something to do with the ruler's neutrality, an increasingly rare and dangerous thing to both Hazat and Kurgan — it is a tactical mistake to let anybody live who could later ally with an enemy. Tactical mistake, perhaps, but a moral gesture, something lacking in the behavior of both sides. I am ashamed at the way one of our own, a royal family of the Known Worlds, attempts to bring the civilized rule of the empire to this barbarian world. I am even more ashamed of the Patriarch's complaisant role in this. Were he here to witness the atrocities, he would surely move to reign them in with all the powers at his command. Or so I like to believe.

I don't even know who is winning the war. From our vantage, it is impossible to tell who is gaining ground. It seems that no one is. Well, little matter. As long as the fighting does not make its way back here, our mission can proceed without interruption.

Consul Darok Rohmer is our neighbor in the palace. We did not expect to find anyone when we arrived, but he was already here, the only one in the city who did not flee when the war reached the town. His fellows in the Reeves guild surely believed him dead. A great loss, for Consul Rohmer was one of the foremost authorities on the Anunnaki, the precursor race who left behind the jumpgates. His studies brought him here, to this old Second Republic museum, once a treasure trove of Ur artifacts, then a noble palace, and now ruins.

It is our reason for coming here, too. Clues on our quest to resolve the great vision given Erian by the Gargoyle of Nowhere — a foreboding Ur artifact in itself — led us here, to this war-torn planet just outside of the Known Worlds. Something was here for us, some ancient piece in a present-day puzzle that, once assembled, would spell the fate and duty of my noble lady. Thus, I, my liege Erian Li Halan, her bodyguard Cardanzo, pilot Julia Abrams, friend Onganggorak (a Vorox) and associate Sanjuk oj Kaval (an Ur-Ukar), arrived in the *Resurgent* to resolve our quest.

We hid our ship under camouflage tarp in the nearby hills and set up camp in the ruins of the palace. It did not take long for Ong to sniff out Rohmer, who hid in the lowest level, evading all patrols that passed through. At first, Rohmer feared we were scavengers or Hazat conscription forces, and he led Ong a chase through the seemingly endless corridors below. But once caught by our over-eager friend and presented to Erian, he realized that we were independents, unaligned (or, at least not working) with any side in the war.

Since then, he has been gracious enough to show us about the museum in return for our aid in lifting and removing rubble, and for cooked meals. His rations were running rather low by the time we arrived; it was a blessing for him that we were well-stocked.

Cardanzo spent most of his time patrolling the region, making sure nobody came near to our camp. On two occasions he chased away local refugees — starving bandits, by his report — who came too near. He had wisely prepared for such a role before we had embarked on this journey, and now wore Hazat military garb. Anyone who saw him feared he was a ranger for a greater force nearby.

As the others tended mainly to logistical or defense matters, Erian and I combed the ruins for the sculpture seen in her dream: an Ur mandala. This item was carved from the same alloy as the jumpgates

(the copperish-purple metal no one has ever identified) and was studded with glowing jewels. More importantly, Erian believed that the
mandala pattern itself was a key of sorts, some sort of clue into... what?
She did not know, but we all knew it was important, part of the greater
tapestry of visions she had experienced since her coming-of-age on
Midian.

So we spent the days searching the museum. Rohmer had not seen
the piece, but helped us search whenever he could. He had research of
his own here was trying to finish, a search for the lost Anunnaki culture
as revealed in their language and art. This was a monumentally hard
task, for what clues they left behind are mere fragments; the whole only
came together after study over far-flung worlds, and even then provided
only a hazy image, a warped imperfection in stained glass.

"No, we don't know what they looked like," he told me, "but we do
know something of their behavior as revealed in the myths of the Obun
and Ukar, the Oro'ym and the ancient legends of Urth itself. Yes, Urth,
cradle of humanity. I believe, as did the xenologists of the Second Republic, that the Anunnaki visited Urth in its infancy and guided the
early footsteps of humankind. The fact that a jumpgate exists there, and
the known ruins on Mars, is proof enough. But there are sites on Holy
Terra itself, although they are not acknowledged as such. Ancient places
where only vague traces remain, a stray rock here, a carving there."

"Have you seen any of these?" I asked. "Where are they?"

"All over the planet. If there's one good the Church has done, it's
to keep Holy Terra pristine, a living museum. Certainly, many complain when their request to emigrate to the Cradle is denied, but thank
the Pancreator for it! The world was once trampled with too many feet
– as Byzantium Secundus and Leagueheim are now – and they kick
away the footprints of those who went before."

I noticed that he was not specific in naming a site, but chose not to
question him further. As he began to open up more, he would perhaps
tell me one or two of these places.

"See this?" he said, pointing to a cylinder sealed behind a see-through
case, lit by an everlight, glowing since its Second Republic maker set it
to burning a thousand years ago. "What do you think that is?"

I looked carefully at it, walking around its case to see it from all
angles. It was smooth, with carvings all over, abstract designs with a
hint of anthropomorphism in certain swirls. Carved from the unearthly

alloy common to Ur artifacts, it had no opening: a perfectly sealed rod. Yet, somehow, in some strange way, I *knew* it was hollow, that some unspeakable space was enclosed within it, an otherworldly place sharing our space, our dimension.

"A king's scepter, perhaps?" I said, noticing his look of disappointment. "Or a phallus? Perhaps a fertility sculpture?"

"You apply modern concepts to the distant past," he said shaking his head. "But don't feel stupid: your answers are the same as Crafter Oncales at the Academy Interatta. You see, there is an exact duplicate of this cylinder at that school. Indeed, I bet you could find at least one in every system of the Known Worlds. Do you know why?"

I shook my head.

"Because it comes from a jumpgate. This one was removed from the jumpgate of this very system. I don't know where the academy's is from. This one's removal, I believe, is what caused this planet to disappear from Human Space for many years."

"This? This is the reason Hira's jumpgate shut down, keeping all ships out of the system for centuries?"

"I believe so. But I don't think the scientists who took it knew. It is one of the last additions to the collection."

"Then why did the gate open again? If this item is here, why does the gate now respond to codes it ignored for years?"

"I'm not sure about that. If I was, I would be the most celebrated man in the Known Worlds, wouldn't I? The Emperor surely has need of such lore to open all the closed gates to all the Lost Worlds of Human Space. Perhaps it's like a fuse; when removed, no circuits can complete themselves. The jumpgates have already shown signs of self-repair. It is no great leap to imagine that, over the years, the jumpgate rerouted itself so that energy could flow again."

"A machine that repairs itself? How can such a thing be? That would imply life."

"The genius of its manufacture eludes us, as does the genius of all Anunnaki science. All of it built on unknown scientific principles. The line between animate life and mere matter — mind and matter — grows indistinct the more one studies the Ur races. Nothing lasts. Nothing but Ur tech," he said wistfully.

I stared in awe at the cylinder. He looked at me and smiled, shaking his head again.

"Don't go worshipping it, now. I could be wrong, you know. It may be a simple antenna, or a strut meant to help maintain structural integrity. We can't really know for sure. It's all just theory."

"Unknown principles..." I said, looking away from it. "Well, I must continue the search. Thank you for your time again."

"Think nothing of it. Any more questions, feel free to ask. By the way, what's for dinner tonight? Are you going to fix another of those Ukari dishes? I rather enjoy the way the worms squirm as you bite them."

I thought he was being sarcastic at first, but he seemed to genuinely like Ukari cuisine. I had fixed some the previous night, based on a recipe Sanjuk had provided, attempting to use as much local resources as possible rather than our sealed stores. Ukari cuisine is a subterranean dining experience: mushrooms and earthworms.

"Perhaps," I said, turning to go. "I shall have to poll the others about their responses to last night's meal..."

Erian was not where I had left her, so I went up the stairs to the level above, coming out into the night air, now still and quiet after the nightly artillery died. Erian was there, whispering to Julia and Sanjuk. I came close and coughed to announce myself.

"Alustro," Erian said. "I don't want to alarm you, but Cardanzo believes soldiers are approaching the town. We may have to evacuate."

"Now? But we haven't found the object of our quest yet!" I complained.

"Keep your voice down," Julia said. "That thing ain't worth our lives." She looked to Erian as she said this, hoping for confirmation.

"Alustro and I will keep searching. Sanjuk, will you help? There's a large room with no lights and your upbringing in the dark may help us."

Sanjuk sighed. "I have lived in the light for twenty years. Only five were spent in the dark, and even then, my clan was not traditional. I knew what a fusion torch was at two. But yes, I will help you. I'm still surely better at moving in darkness than you blind humans."

Erian frowned but said nothing. She was used to Sanjuk's manner by now, and knew better than to press royal rules of intercourse here. She turned to the stairs, and Sanjuk and I followed. Julia remained above, watching for Cardanzo and Ong's return from their patrol.

The room was indeed dark. Our fusion torches seemed to penetrate only slightly into the gloom, and a thin mist could be felt and barely seen in the air. Consul Rohmer, who had joined us on our way down, coughed.

"Eternair..." he muttered.

"Excuse me, consul?" Erian said. "What did you say?"

"It's Eternair. Eternal Air. A preservative atmosphere devised by Second Republic archivists to use when sealing things in cases. It's meant to keep those items unchanged over time. It's near miraculous. A canister must have broken somewhere in the room. With little ventilation, the stuff stays in the air here."

"Is it dangerous to breath?" I asked.

"I hope not," he replied.

We continued on into the room, navigating the cases and shelves. This did appear to be an archivist's room, for many items were displayed on tables with tags clearly showing that they were not yet ready for public display. Most of the items were reproductions of actual Ur items, made from extensive drawings and holograms. A few items were genuine, however. Consul Rohmer's obvious interest in these told me which were real and which fake.

"You know," Sanjuk said from somewhere up ahead, unseen in the darkness. "I really think we should set up some of the camp lights down here. We're not going to find anything in this light."

Erian sighed. "You are right. We will set them up during the day tomorrow, once we've heard from Cardanzo about the approaching troops."

"If the troops don't get here first," Sanjuk said.

We left the room and returned to our camp in the servant's quarters on the first level of the palace. This section was in the rear of the building, its back entrance now blocked by rubble. Anybody entering would have to come through the main hall, where we could see them well before they saw us. Cardanzo had led a search through the upper levels, now open to the elements, and had identified a number of sniper points he could assume if necessary. One of these, the remaining high tower, part of the original architecture, we used as a watchpost. Looking up at it from the street below, I could barely make out the old museum sign, now partially covered with the local ruler's torn and dirty flag: "Museum of the Ancients, Estab—" I wondered what date it read.

Cardanzo and Ong had returned from their patrol. The approaching troops were rangers, teams from both sides of the conflict. They each entered the market section of town, a few miles from us, and left soon after encountering each other (with no shots fired, apparently).

"I think now that each knows the other was here, they will move troops in force, each believing the other is trying to claim this ground," Cardanzo said. "With luck, it'll take them two days to get back here. We need to be gone by then."

"We will spend another day searching," Erian said. "Then leave."

"No later," Cardanzo said, looking into his liege's eyes. "We still need time to escape atmosphere before any fighters take to the skies."

"That's all we need!" Julia said. "A dogfight between Hazat and Kurgans. Oh, yeah, I can fly through that no problem!"

"Point taken," Erian said. "We leave tomorrow evening then. No later."

I was relieved to know we'd be out of danger soon, but nervous that we would leave without our prize. As I prepared dinner (chorro steaks, courtesy of Ong, who came back from his patrol with a catch, saving us from another Ukari dinner), I cast my mind into the museum and walked through every room I knew, trying to divine where the curators would have kept the mandala. The smell of burnt steak woke me from my musings, and I consented to have the spoiled meat for my plate while I paid greater attention to the others' preparations.

As I served the steaks and finally sat down to eat myself, a loud chiming sound broke the silence. Everyone looked at me.

"Uhm... sorry," I said, placing my plate on the scuffed table and running to my bags nearby. I pulled the small, hand-held think machine from its pouch and touched the power stud, shutting off the chimes.

"Why does that thing always go off?" Julia said, glaring at me. "I hate it. Can't you tell time like the rest of us?"

"It's not for telling time," I explained. "And that alarm was to remind me that it is only a number of hours till Renewal Day, the anniversary of Zebulon's healing by Saint Amalthea."

"That's nice and all, but what's it got to do with us here? There's far better uses to put a rare think machine, you know. Can't you just pray at dawn like most priests?"

"Dawn on Hira is not dawn on Grail. My think machine is set to automatically begin a recitation of the Thankful Exaltation, the Latin chorus as delivered by Zebulon to Amalthea, on exactly the proper moment: when dawn breaks over Mount Siddik."

Julia rolled her eyes. "And what the heck does it matter if you miss the exact moment? I'm sure Saint Amalthea will forgive you; she's certainly forgiven much worse."

"That's not the point. I am an Eskatonic; the energetic correspondences are very important. By opening a channel in our hearts and minds at the proper moment, we cast our light back to Grail, and it is in turn reflected back to us. In this way, we partake of the divine moment as if we were on Grail itself. The theurgic significance is incredible."

"Whatever," Julia said, finishing her steak and then rising to stretch. "Just don't let that racket wake me before my watch!" She left for her sleeping bag in the garret directly above us.

I checked the program again to be sure its clock was correct and set the liturgy to play upon the appointed hour. After cleaning and storing the cookware, I crawled into my own sleeping bag by the kitchen.

That evening, I did not dream. This is not unusual except that I had dreamed every night since we arrived on Hira, dreams of ruins and combat.

We spent the following afternoon searching the darkened room. We moved all our portable lights there and found the illumination enough for a cursory search. Consul Rohmer idly examined the Ur artifacts and replicas.

"I had hoped to make my fortune here," he said. "To build my life. I doubt anything can come of this now. I don't dare alert anyone, or the Hazat will storm in seeking war-tech. Best to leave it be for now until I can get others to come. So little of this can be moved."

"Can't we just remove the artifacts from the cases?" I asked.

"Have you ever tried cracking one of those things? Near impossible, not without shipyard grade tools. And the cases themselves are likewise immovable, meant to deter thieves in an era where such criminals had high tech means to steal. No, most of this will remain here as it has for centuries."

"But that means... If the mandala is in a case, we'll never get it out!"

He looked at me sympathetically. "Well, we can always take holograms of it. I have a camera with me."

Sanjuk came over. "A holocamera? That must of set you back a few firebirds."

"Not really," Rohmer said, continuing his idle search. "I took it in return for a bad debt, in my younger days in Collections. The debtor paid up eventually anyway, but I kept the camera."

"There is nothing here!" Erian said from a few shelves away, frustrated. "Surely we would have found it by now if they kept it in this room."

"Perhaps we should try elsewhere," I suggested. "There's still the back wing..."

"It's strictly Diaspora era," Rohmer said. "I checked when I first arrived."

"What if the mandala was discovered then?" Erian said. "Wouldn't it be kept there?"

"Well, I suppose it's possible," Rohmer said. "I wasn't looking for it in my search, since I hadn't met you yet. It's at least worth another look."

"Sanjuk, would you come with me?" Erian said, heading for the door. "Alustro, please keep searching here, just in case."

"But I'd like to see some Diaspora artifacts!"

"Just dioramas mainly," Rohmer said. "Images the Second Republic believed were true of life during humanity's first spread to the stars. Rather boring, actually."

Erian was already gone, so I resigned myself to a continued search. I had worked my way down the far left aisle and was ready to traverse the back wall when a rumble shook the building.

"They can't be shelling this early," Rohmer said, confused, looking at the ceiling as if he could see through it to the skies above.

"I think we should leave, consul," I said, moving toward the door. "If they are shelling, it may mean troops are advancing already."

He sighed. "Alright, but let's go back through the east wing. I want one last look at—"

The air exploded and the ceiling collapsed, burying me under a pile of tiles. I coughed, singed from the fire that had momentarily engulfed me. The Eternair must have ignited, I thought. But the mist still swirled around me, so it had not all gone up.

I pushed the tiles off and crawled to my feet. Half of the room was gone, blocked by a wall of rock, dirt and furniture from the levels above. "Consul?" I yelled.

"Here..." a weak voice answered. I worked my way over to him across the sliding tiles and rock. Consul Rohmer was half buried under a maxicrete strut, his head bleeding, his hand clutching his chest.

"It's finally over..." he moaned.

"I can heal you!" I cried, trying to lift the maxicrete that pinned him. "But we have to move this strut!"

"No..." he said, his eyes glazing. "It doesn't matter. Your faith can't heal plastic."

"What? I don't understand," I said, trying to raise the strut but failing completely. It was too heavy. If Ong were here—

"Don't... don't bother." He coughed blood. "My heart... it's cybernetic. My third one. The others failed. I knew this would, too. That's why I came. To make something of myself, to complete my work."

"But... maybe we... Julia... can fix it," I stammered.

"Leave me here," he said, weaker, barely audible. "Among... the Ur. Close... the door... on your way... out. Air will... preserve me." His eyes closed and a final breath escaped his body.

I now understood his respect for the artifacts around him. They were the only things to last in a world of entropy. Everything died — people, culture, even the stars. But the Anunnaki had crafted with their unknown principles things immune to the laws of decay.

I felt for a pulse but could find none, then placed my hand on his false heart, tears welling in my eyes. I said the Prayer to the Departed, asking the Pancreator to draw Consul Rohmer's illuminate soul to its reward, to protect it as it traversed the dim and dying spaces. And then I switched off all the camp lights in the room and closed the door, leaving him in the peaceful, preserved dark.

I looked about, trying to get my bearings in the aftermath of death. My survival was important now, and I feared for my liege and companions. Had they been buried, too? The hall was a mess; my way was blocked on all sides. Only a thin ray of light from atop a pile of stone (a later addition to the palace, not a part of the original structure) promised a way of escape. I climbed and began to pull dirt and rock aside. I soon had a small hole through which I could squeeze. It was tight but I was soon on the ground floor again.

I stood, scraping dust off and surveying the area. The walls no longer existed, and gaping holes into the museum could be seen the length of the palace. I had no idea where I was standing. Was it the main hall or the dining room?

The sun was setting on the horizon and it was growing dark very quickly. As I stepped forward to search for my liege, praying she was still alive and well, a footstep sounded behind me. I turned and stared into the eyes of a Kurgan ranger, his rifle pointed straight at me.

He should have shot me on sight. But something was wrong. I could see fear in his eyes. Not fear of me, but fear of death. His arm bled profusely, although it still seemed usable. His face was one of near shock, a man too long on the front lines.

But courage returned, and he slowly raised his rifle to aim.

Then the Prophet sang.

He paused, confused. From nearby, under a thin shale of tile, came the chorus of the Thankful Exaltation. My think machine. It was now dawn on Grail: the divine moment had arrived.

He looked at me and then at the sky, as if shocked to realize the time and the day. He slowly lowered his rifle, looking into my eyes to see what I would do, and brought his hands together in prayer.

I joined him. We both closed our eyes and answered the chorus.

"And the light that burns, burns away poison.

And the hands that heal tend the flame..."

He knew the Latin words. Our cultures, separated by time and the gulfs between the stars, still each remembered the deeds of the Prophet and knew them to be holy. Tears ran down my face as I answered the chorus line by line, unfearful, for I heard his voice singing, too.

When the program ended, and silence fell, we each slowly opened our eyes and looked at the other. Before anything further could pass between us, he stood and clambered over the stones. He was out of sight before I could think to yell to him, to offer to heal his wound.

I stood there for a time, thinking upon the wonders revealed amid the horror. Eventually, Onganggorak shook my shoulder, startling me. He had crept through the ruins silently, a great Vorox hunter.

"Alustro, are you well? I smell no injury," he said tenderly.

"I am fine, Ong. Where are the others? Is Erian okay?"

"She is wounded, but will live. Cardanzo guards her at the *Resurgent* and Julia prepares to leave. I came to find you, little confessor."

I smiled. "That was foolhardy. Kurgans are here. You could have been caught."

"Hmmph. We cannot leave without you. Ong's life is little next to yours," he said, tugging me to leave with him.

I made to disagree but finally assented and went over to the pile of shale that hid my bags and my think machine, the device which had saved my life today. "I'm ready."

"Where is the consul? I cannot find his scent. He should leave with us," Ong said.

"He... died," I said. "He rests with his artifacts."

Ong nodded and made a grunting noise, a statement of some sort in his own tongue, but before I could ask what he meant, he turned to go, motioning me with one of his four arms to follow.

As we began our trek to the ship, the sky thundered and glowed. Bombs flew once more. The flickering light of the deadly fireworks lit the area, and I saw the remains of the high tower, now scattered across the ground. The ruler's flag was gone and the museum sign stood bare. I could now read it:

Museum of the Ancients. Established 3973. "And the Anunnaki fashioned their individual shrines, the 300 younger gods of heaven and the Anunnaki of the Apsu all assembled."

I stood in shock, staring at the sign. "Ong!" I cried, and he came running, sniffing the air and casting his eyes all about. "There!" I pointed to the sign.

Underneath the ancient quote from some long-forgotten Urth text was a beautiful mandala.

Our mandala.

I rushed over to the sign to examine it. It was the very same seen in Erian's dream — copperish-purple alloy, four images quartered around a central star. "This is it, Ong. Our artifact."

I tugged at it, and it snapped right off its base. We both stared at each other, chills traveling up our spines. Of all the Ur artifacts in the museum, why was this one so easily removed? I looked at the base it had rested on and realized that it had taken a direct artillery hit. The ceramsteel was melted and pitted, blackened every place but where the mandala had rested. The metal and magnetic glue had given out, but the artifact was unblemished.

I decided that enough was enough. Placing the mandala in my bag, we headed off to the ship. Ong blazed the trail, taking small paths through the ruins. I heard voices from afar, and radio chatter, but Ong's path avoided all patrols.

We finally arrived at the ship. As I entered the hatch and Ong closed it behind me, I heard Erian call to me from her cabin. I ran quickly and saw her lying on the bed, her leg wrapped in red bandages.

"My lady!" I yelled, and immediately set to examining her wound.

Cardanzo put his hand on my shoulder.

"She is fine, Alustro. I staunched the blood flow."

Erian looked tired but she was awake. I reached into my bag and produced the artifact, holding it up to show her.

"The mandala!" she cried, trying to rise to her feet. Cardanzo and I both rushed to keep her down, slowly lowering her back into bed. She gazed at it wondrously. "Where did you find it?"

"The sign. The museum sign covered by the flag, the one on the tower. All this time, right above us."

She looked at me and a I felt a rush of pride. "Well done, my priest. Well done."

I nodded and rose. "Get your rest, lady. We can examine it later." I left the artifact with her as I headed to my cabin to change out of my filthy clothes. I would tell her about Consul Rohmer later, when there was time to reflect on a life now past. I felt the rumble of the engines and knew the ship was taking off.

As I entered my cabin, I heard Sanjuk and Julia talking in the cockpit.

"I can't believe he found it," Sanjuk said. "Of all the dumb luck."

"I knew he would," Julia said. "It's not luck. The boy's got a track record."

I smiled, knowing that her comment was not meant for me to hear.

The next few hours were rough, as Julia encountered two squadrons of Hazat troops demanding we land to be examined by their military generals. Of course she denied all requests in Erian's name, knowing our ship would be conscripted if it fell into their hands, and flew us out of the way of most conflict. Our ship's shield easily deflected the few shots we took.

As I write this, we have not yet reached the jumpgate. Julia intends to hide behind the last planet until the jumpgate is clear, or until the few ships there engage enemies coming or going. Then we'll slip over as quickly as possible, activate the gate, and be gone from this place.

I am confident that we will encounter little problem. We have come too far, and the fates have been too kind. Why would they mean us disaster now? The pattern is clearer now, fragments assembled by some principle whose meaning is as yet unknown.

Hidden Martyrs

Changchup Riwo

Far out in icy space, where the light of the stars is dim, a cold wind blows. It is called by Eskatonic mystics the Ghost Wind, and is said to come from the Darkness Between the Stars. It has blown for as long as space has been navigated, coming from blackness and howling silently for the death of the burning, glowing stars which illuminate the nebulas and galaxies, stars giving hope to sentients in the dark nights of a thousand thousand worlds.

Recognizing this wind as the *Heain Kuai Su*, or Dark Wind of Furious Speed, some have attempted to join their power with the icy darkness of its origin, and to extinguish, under the command of ghostly voices, the illuminated lights of the universe. *The Great Commentary* of Yumin Lu Chou mentions that the wind has its origin in the 27th unreflected realm of Samghata, ruled over by the demon Aksana Kou-Ch'ien, representative of the principle of violent, unreflected energy.

In the Year of the Red Ox, Alexius Hawkwood became Emperor of the Known Worlds. His Hazat and Decados enemies sued for mercy. It was an auspicious year, ushering in the Imperial Ascendancy that cast shadows on the Five Noble Families. The Yellow Ideogram, drawn by Obun soothsayers on the Emperor's coronation, signified reduction of chaos to order, anchoring fate's ascendancy under a victorious forest of spears. The splintering slashes off the protective middle of the ideogram, representing birds in flight, foretold an escaping enemy of great cunning, fleeing from the field, bringing pearl on a distant day.

In the Year of the Red Ox, a young Li Halan poet, Rakai, produced his book, *Cantos to the Red Emperor*. Fortuitous signs greeted the young poet of the School of Twenty Three Cranes, and his name began to glow in the popular imagination like a rising harvest moon. His future embellished a character denoting success through sacrifice, harmony with the vicissitudes, rash courage, destroyer and painter of patterns.

In the Year of the Baleful Dog, Prince Hyram Decados, upon the pretext of space exploration, took his trusted security detail and advisors aboard his flagship, the *Nicholas and Alexander*. He placed his mas-

sive stellar warship in proximity of the Ghost Wind, while an ancient
Ukar Taudwon drew designs in colored sand and uttered prayers of
welcoming to the stygian gale. Pictograms representing Wind Above
The Stars and the Shadow Court of Nine Thousand Nine Hundred and
Ninety Nine-Notable Spirits Who Rule the Night were drawn to exact-
ing detail. Chanting ancient intonations, a slumbering mood fell across
the witnesses. Occasionally, high-pitched notes of great length and startling clarity startled them.

And there came an answer from beyond the Ghost Wind, wailing
up from forgotten regions off uncharted maps.

Also in the year of the Baleful Dog, the young poet Rakai Li Halan
completed his second book, *Vorox Dreams,* further enhancing his name,
bringing good fortune and the grave respect of the house elders. Rakai
fought with Vorox Commandos during the Emperor Wars, and their
oral songs, deep and sorrowful, inspired the poetry. People placed him
above the six notables, whose number included the reclusive and inspired poet SSu Shih, whose name envelopes the changing seasons like
a whirling wind.

In the Year of the Shantor, in the month of Siyue, a Vorox was
found dead, curled up behind the ducal gardens of the Pavilion of Red
Blossoms, on Icon. Two arrow tips containing minute amounts of
Seddipin, or "Vorox Killer," were found lodged in his throat, fired by
an unknown assailant with a powerful crossbow. The Vorox, Umon
Grondta, "Tiktik," was assigned to the bodyguard of Duke Tan Fou
Maximino Li Halan, younger brother of Prince Flavius Yue Se Chou
Kung Li Halan, Head of the Most Serene and August Family. Symbols
forecasting Extinguished Harvesting, a Weed in the Chrysanthemum
Garden, and Hints of Mist Concealing Autumn Moon interpreted by
his astrologers alarmed the duke, who looked askance at his court, contemplating where the assailant came from.

Tiktik's four arms were folded gently over his weapons, and his
body was covered in cherry blossoms while Duke Maximino said the
funeral rites before his court. His priests chanted prayers for his safe
passage under the bright and decorative banners of the four winds.
Duke Maximino wept openly, forgetting composure, and demanded an
investigation to the insult. It was bad form, he grumbled, to slay a noble
man's bodyguard and go unpunished.

In the Year of the Shantor, Rakai Li Halan wed Sidera Torenson, taking on the responsibilities of estate and family, according to ancient custom. Jade dragonflies, signifying duty, adorned her marriage robes.

The three events, the meetings of Prince Hyram Decados with certain intelligences, the death of the much decorated Tiktik of Duke Maximino's Vorox Guard, and the growing reputation of the poet Rakai are interrelated. But then again, certain poets and philosophers maintain that all things are interrelated, and that there are no casual relationships. Triads are easier then dualities in explaining events, according to the ancient house philosopher Miyamoto of the Dragon Arm.

The Decados, known for one of the best spy networks in the Known Worlds, successfully hid the meeting from all rivals. Still, information of the event escaped, for many intelligences observe the physical universe.

Some of those intelligences answer to the Li Halan.

The Li Halan Worlds, or the Middle Principality, consisting of the planets of Kish, Midian, Icon, Rampart and Vorox, lie between the jumpgates bordering the Vau Hegemony, the worlds of the merchant princes, who worship technological wonder over the Order of Heaven, and the barbarous calamity of the bandit Decados worlds. Thus, the Li Halan stand under the Mandate of the Reflective Heavens as the only true civilizing force in the region, a remark attributed to Prince Tai Chung Li Halan, one hundred years ago, on the Canal of Velvet Bells, where he read from the *Book of the Middle Doctrine*.

The Li Halan have two official intelligence services, the cumbersome and spy-ridden *Jingcha*, and the military intelligence networks which compose the *Yüan Men*, the Guardians of the Garden Worlds. Their spies watch the frontiers, and test the strength of the house's enemies. There is a third intelligence service, never mentioned and not supported by official revenue, called the Hidden Martyrs, who watch over the cultural, domestic and interplanetary affairs of House Li Halan. They report directly to the ruling prince, and are the eyes and ears of the Most Exalted Family of Illustrious Merit.

By a curious question relating to poetic form, the secret meeting of Prince Hyram Decados became known to the most shadowy of spy networks. Delving into the origins of certain Ur pictograms and characters, a Li Halan noble contracted the ancestral spiritual rites of Countess Amita Li Halan, the most gifted Manja practitioner of her age.

The Li Halan noble was the young poet Rakai.

Manja was an alteration of the Ukari death rituals, the *Sukara Manja,* by the ancient Li Halan. While the Ukari performed the rites' fearsome rituals to keep the ancestral spirits away from the shores of the living, the decadent Li Halan of old changed the rituals to summon the departed ancestral spirits, turning a religious rite into a necromancy cult. The paths to the dead became a revolving door, and ancient rasping voices' spoke prophecies to those practitioners hungry for knowledge. Officially banned after Cardano Li Halan's conversion to the Path of Zebulon, it remained in the shadows, still practiced by secret adherents within the Most Illustrious Family.

Rakai Li Halan sought out Countess Amita Li Halan, posing questions for the ancestral spirits on certain Ur pictograms. One night, in the Year of the Baleful Dog, the old Countess agreed to his request.

Buildings like the bones of the earth jutted before Rakai Li Halan, and in the moonlight the crumbling towers of Mwerrid Mwonna cast a skeletal appearance, taunting the heavens with their macabre, twisted grotesqueries.

The young poet wrapped his cloak for protection from the icy breath of the north wind, staring at the old, scarecrow woman in front of him. His dark hair fell in curls, and his deep eyes reflected the flickering light of the wind-blown embers from thirty and seven torches placed about them.

Countess Amita Li Halan's cats frothed about her like bubbles in fresh cream.

"The spirits are pleased with your poetry," she said, regarding the young man before her.

"Thank you, kinswoman," Rakai bowed. This meeting was secret, as was Amita's visit to her old estates on Kish. The silver-haired woman picked up a young black cat, who briefly struggled before her gray hand set it to purring.

Their shadows flickered like ghosts in a harsh wind.

"There is another thing the ancestors would tell you," the old woman said, piercing her cold blue eyes into his.

"Yes," he whispered, shaking.

"When recalling the hidden language of the Old Gods, named Chiu Kuei, you must tread warily and keep your senses alert. The lunar triple goddess, Yue Liang or Sapa, worshipped by the Ur races, cannot lie flat on the poet's pen. Three lines depicting her above a circle denote her wisdom and power. You must intone her, young cousin, with an artist's conviction, or she will not hear you — Wait! The spirit of our ancestor, Yu Ch'ien, Duke of Midian, informs me that the old pictograms are currently being painted in a ritual! He lets me see, allied with the wind spirit Gorgwerrid, known as Yu-Len, a place where new summons breathes life into the old symbols..."

The old woman shut her eyes. Her voice rasped out, as from a great distance, sights invisible to all but her. The cat struggled, finally leaping out of her arms and scurrying into the stygian darkness of shadows and concealment.

"It is being spoken now by an old Ukar shaman, the spirits tell me, to summon the Old Dark Ones before the throne of Prince Hyram Decados, in his flagship beyond the stars. The old Ukar shifts the Ur ideographs in a most untraditional way, changing the ancient Ur pictogram representing feast to a more modern tense, graphically depicting spirits eating on souls in the present — oh, how barbaric for one interested in the pure Ur poetry of the ancients. The symmetrical, geometric pattern of the feast symbol is combined with a horribly simplified pictogram representing 'soul,' or 'spirit,' drastically losing the upper, pointed umbrella shape, which connotes escape from the physical, usually an earth-bound symbol of four vertical lines. How intolerable! And Prince Hyram Decados intones for the blasphemous destroyer of pictograms to continue... "

Her eyes glazed over, and her words began to slow, as she spoke in the present tense to the young poet. Quickly Rakai realized that his kinswoman was describing an event much more important than pictogram evolution, and asked Amita to repeat verbatim what the spirits told her, producing his ink brush and scroll, and copying her remarks.

For three hours she continued, and her servants placed salt incense under her nose, and Rakai wiped the perspiration off her lined and furrowed forehead. A strange meeting, akin to those which occurred in the Pre-Conversion Li Halan courts, was taking place. Were the Decados allying themselves with the ancient protectors of the Li Halan? Oh, it was bad form, Countess Amita kept repeating as if talking to a naughty child — the crude Ukar Taudwon had no artistic skill and took horrendous liberties with the ancient aesthetics of Ur ideograms.

After a time, the spirit voices lessened. Countess Amita collapsed at the end, and Rakai placed a cool, water drenched cloth on her forehead, and ordered moon tea from a servant. When the Countess revived, she had little memory of the event, save for the placement of the ritualistic Ur pictograms. Rakai asked her to draw them. She did. The reproduction, in her hand, of such dreadfully ruined symbols, depressed her.

Rakai understood. It was dangerous asking his relative Manja secrets, but the countess' advice never failed him. His first book, combining modern poetic themes with the rarefied style of the Pre-Conversion Li Halan, took research. Rakai's genius was in incorporating the older styles into modern themes, thus culturally uniting the house's rich poetic history, while dropping the odes to Ukari deities that the ancient Li Halan were partial to. No one had attempted to bridge this gap before.

Rakai was a loyal son of the Church, despite his reliance on Amita's Manja practices. He had learned, while in battle during the Emperor Wars, to use whatever tools ensured his survival. Now twenty-eight, his facial features and eyes spoke of the aristocratic blood of his mother's family, the Justinians, but he had the nimble artistic hands of the Li Halan. His delving into poetic mysteries had revealed, from the countess, far richer secrets than he had dared hope for.

In short, Rakai believed in Universal Harmony, and the Order Under the Empyrean Heavens. Deeply conservative and aristocratic, he was troubled by the chaos emanating from beyond the Garden Worlds. Indeed, it was almost expected that the Decados, living in the uncertain realms beyond the frontiers, would behave like children playing with swords and injuring themselves.

Two days later, in Escoral, at the Academy, where he taught Literature and History to young Li Halan knights, Rakai placed a call into the office of Hikado Li Halan, Doctor of Letters and Head of the Department. The gray-haired, sad-eyed Hikado was a teacher of military history, and dabbled in calligraphy. Hikado was the only one Rakai trusted with the information.

Having served in active duty during the Emperor Wars, Rakai mistrusted the intelligence networks to keep his information secret. Decados agents had infiltrated the Jingcha. This was common knowledge to the house.

"Rakai," the older man said, his soft tones breaking the silence of a hot afternoon. Hikado's office slept in the streams of light pouring through dull red drapes, and the musky odor of crumbling books mingled with the drowsiness of the day.

Rakai bowed to the gaunt, silver haired man before him, dressed in the long robe of the gentlemen caste.

"You have called me in here today for a very special reason. Some tea?"

Rakai nodded.

Hikado clapped his hands, and a young woman briefly entered, wearing the dull white and tan outfit of the peasantry, and swiftly poured two cups of spice tea. Bowing twice, she disappeared behind the wooden door.

The older man gently sipped his tea, and Rakai followed ceremoniously.

After some minutes, Hikado placed the tea cup down on a low lying table and waited.

"I am sorry to break convention and form, but I must share this knowledge with you," Rakai said. "It contains notes on a meeting which might be of interest to the family."

Rakai placed his papers before Hikado.

Hikado stood up, brushing a dying fly away. He took the notes, and began reading them. His left hand, clutching the paper, began to shake.

"Young cousin, where did you get this?"

Rakai bowed, and told him of his dealings in Manja to revive old poetic secrets. Hikado listened, and then asked when the event occurred, and who knew of it.

Rakai said no one but himself, and the countess, who fell into a trance and retained only fragments on waking.

"Do you have any copies?"

"No," Rakai admitted.

Hikado began to sweat, murmuring, as if to himself, "This is hard to verify. I must get reports on ship movements in the Decados space, and must test Manja to see if this is true or simply an induced trance producing strange fancies. But the countess does not trade in inaccuracies, may the illustrious fortune of the Empyrean heavens guard her!"

Hikado broke into nervous coughing, losing composure. Rakai looked at the prints on the wall, embarrassed for the old man, attempting to let him save face. Hikado poured some more tea into his cup embellished with frolicking red and gold dragons, and shot Rakai a stern glance.

"I am commanding you, Rakai, as a man of faith, not to use Manja again. You have performed faithfully as Warden of the Six Gates of the Mist Covered Frontier, so I shall overlook the sin this time. Manja is dangerous, cousin. I know you take your craft seriously, but be careful."

Hikado glanced up, squinting in Rakai's direction while his hand nervously caressed the tea cup before him. He cleared his throat twice, and then wiped his brow with a prayer scarf.

A slight breeze rattled the drapes. Outside, the bells of the nearby cathedral began tolling. Hikado looked at a painting of swans reflected in a river, and then motioned that the meeting was over. Clearly, the old man had something in mind, but the hour of clarification would wait.

Rakai thought of their relationship, both friendly and elusive. Count Hikado first contacted him in the Year of the Contemplative Ox, when he returned from the Emperor Wars. Rakai's war record was exceptional, twice decorated with the Cardano Cross for personal bravery, and granted an estate by the prince in Zhou Gouyan. Rare for one of the royal family, Rakai trained to be a Ranger, and served on Malignatius. He had personally begged Prince Flavius to be allowed to serve. Many at court saw his poetry as excellent propaganda for morale. "We can't let our great poet die in some bombing raid," the Prince's mother, Princess Melissa Hiao Li Halan, stated to the agreement of most the court.

His Ranger training was hard, but at the end of a tough six month's regimen of demolition, espionage and martial arts, he mustered into the elite Jian Bing Corps. Underwater and space training thinned out most of his comrades, but the young poet was determined to make it.

On Malignatius, he lead men against the Decados war machine, but was captured in the route of Ghost Mountain. Miraculously, he managed to escape Colonel Kolya's infamous Jakovian prison camp, Gulag 3, disguised in the robes of an Amalthean healer. Hooking up with the Vorox commandos, Rakai spent the remainder of the war performing guerrilla warfare. When hostilities ended, Rakai had mastered enough Vorox oral tales for a second book of poetry, heavily influenced by their traditions.

After completing *Vorox Dreams*, Rakai was offered a teaching position in the Li Halan Capitol of Escoral by Count Hikado, an expert scholar of ancient warfare. This meant easy access to the family archives, and life near court. Rakai accepted. He was from a distant, rural branch of the Li Halan family, sinking by general degrees to freeman status. His father, a noted geologist, urged him to make his life useful.

After seven months, Hikado approached him again with a more elite offer: the chance to join the Hidden Martyrs, whose reputation came as a shadow, a midnight wind, suggestive by the lack of presence, whose power was in rumor and the unseen hold the name had on the hearts of men. An ideogram depicting removal, mist, combined with the symbol for protection, warding off harmful elements, was drawn at the meeting.

"Honored Cousin, why do you need me?" Rakai asked then.

"To protect the cultural ways of the house, in line with Orthodox philosophy. You are the new poet. Even the old royal poet, Jing Ti, recognizes your superiority and proclaims that there has been no one like you since Tuquan of blessed memory. The responsibility of upholding the house's cultural purity, in line with the Fortune of Heaven, now rests upon you. "

Those words he remembered well.

Rakai recalled them, leaving Hikado's office, tasting the hot arid wind that blew through Escoral. He remembered the older man tutoring him in the art of information gathering, poisons, languages and codes, as well as fighting techniques. Hikado was a harsh master, but Rakai's military training and own experiences made him a swift learner. In four months he had mastered Hikado's techniques and was ready for initiation.

The young man glanced about, observing young buds, thick and heavy, awaiting birth. Rakai thought back on his five months at an old monastery fortress, whose location was secret. Remembering his father's geological talks, he guessed it to be in the Shan Mai mountains by the chalk deposits. The young man slept in a cold cell, and could feel the wind seeping through at night. Meditating eased the cold as he recited lists of Empyrean saints, and in his head composed verses of light-filled imagery, translucent and pure, burning off the temporal corruption of the flesh. This was called the Doctrine of Reflective Luminosity.

Walking to his apartment on the academy grounds, he found himself recalling the long philosophical and theological litanies infused into the heads of hearts of new recruits. The Hidden Martyrs were part of the *Mystikos* of the natural order, selflessly sacrificing themselves for the most holy of noble houses, the Li Halan, and the correct theology of the Orthodox branch of Zebulon's Universal Church. Planting herself as a spiritual seed in the physical universe, the Church took on the guardianship of sentient souls, signified by the primal harmony presented in Zebulon's teachings, which permeated the physical universe as a soft, luminous rain. This was called the Doctrine of Descending Luminosity.

Still, Rakai reflected, a certain fatalistic outlook prevailed their thought. They were an invisible force, wholly loyal to Li Halan and Church, waiting for the summons to battle against agents of the Outer Darkness. Rakai felt proud to be so honored. He passed training, and resumed his teaching post.

Then came the Night of Blood Baptism. Rakai never spoke of this to anyone. To do so meant death. Back in Escoral, he received a summons and a box containing the black robes and hood of peasant cenobites who came out on Feast Days in religious parades, lashing themselves. A note told him to go to the old west section of Escoral. He was to proceed to the Church of St. Maya the Scorned Woman, on the Avenue of the Jade Dragon, and enter the Church. Making his way down twisting labyrinths, dressed in the black robe and hood, he came to a large inner chamber with a domed roof, lit with torches. In the catacombs beyond, statues of the saints stood motionless, peeking behind nave columns, representing the dim glory of the Universal Church of the Celestial Sun. Other black and hooded figures, unseen except for the eyes piercing the dark hoods, formed a wide circle around a standing hooded figure.

The central figure removed the hood, and Prince Flavius Li Halan stood before them.

They presented themselves to Prince Flavius and received, individually, their hidden names. These the prince whispered, and the identity of all the other figures remained a secret. Rakai received the title, "Xin Jaio, Believer, Saint Blood of Memory."

After the naming ceremony was completed, the prince drank from the Grail of Martyrs, which contained the blood of St. Rurik. He then passed it around, uniting the new initiates by the sacred blood of the martyr who perished preaching to the Pre-Conversion Li Halan. Two figures by the Prince chanted "Hunc elegi meo servitio; hunc elegi nostro consortio..."

The chanting echoed off the old frescos depicting the martyrdom of the Church's faithful, and disappeared into the depths of darkness.

Rakai reflected on this, climbing the stone steps to his apartment, recalling the elusive and ghostly figures, phantoms reflected in still waters, clouds of mysterious fog before the moon.

Then he laughed, exorcising heavy moods with lightness.

For a year the only service Rakai saw was in editing poetic magazines to Orthodox standards. Rakai also read foreign works, deciding on their merit. Some were cheap pornography, and proscribed, but a curious poem, *Istakhr Labyrinth*, by a promising al-Malik poet of rare refinement, caught his attention. Rakai read it again and again. That it was subversive he had no doubt, but stylistically it aimed at a high metaphor of reality, with the Pancreator's secrets disguised in overlooked market stalls displaying cheap wares. The Third Republic sympathies made it banned to the public at large, but Rakai allowed a few copies to be displayed in the House Library for any interested house members, decided on artistic merit alone.

Rakai opened the wooden door, and sighed. He did not forget about the strange message of the Decados meeting he brought Count Hikado, but life went on. If anything, it was out of his hands, and others were deciphering the symbols and planning strategy. He prepared to meditate, arranging the flowers in a vase. His apartment was sparse, with his personal belongings concealed.

In the month of Wuyue, in the Year of the Shantor, when the short rains were over and the fragrance of the desert flowers bloomed, he wed Sidera Torenson in the Prophet's Cathedral. The following month, he received a summons from Hikado. Events moved in a circular pattern, although Rakai did not guess the meeting had anything to do with the copied Ur pictograms and Amita's Manja report, given months before.

They met deep in the Li Halan archives. Dusty stacks of books reached to the ceiling, and the only sound was the cold air pouring in through distant vents. Rare works, enshrined in Second Republic air-vacuum cases, lined the further walls. Distortion devices were set up, to alter any bugging or visual transmitters.

Hikado displayed a card with an alien pictogram upon it. "What does this mean?"

"It is the sign of a dark Ur deity, representing the Sons of Rillos."

Hikado nodded, laughing. "You see, scratch a Li Halan, and we remember the dark deities we use to worship before Cardano's conversion."

"I do not understand, Hikado."

"Your first report to me has been confirmed. The Decados have made contact with one, or some, of the Dark Deities or Powers we use to worship. Information was exchanged, perhaps some sort of alliance tentatively struck." Count Hikado made a curious clucking sound, like he was scolding an ignorant child.

"Our family knows that you have to be cautious in dealing with these powers from beyond the Reflective light. The Decados? One cannot say. Mere imitators of the Li Halan Principality, descended from the pale northern barbarians of Old Urth. Evidently Prince Hyram returned from the meeting quite pleased, and has hatched his plots anew. He sends agents to contact Duke Maximino."

"Prince Flavius's brother?"

Hikado nodded. "Why not? Maximino has made it no secret that he believes Flavius should hold the Imperial throne and August Title of Sole Emperor Under the Reflective Heavens. Hence, Duke Maximino is perfect for Decados plots against the Emperor."

"And this must be stopped."

"No," Hikado said. "We have to let the Decados through. We must stop any Imperial Eye agents from infiltrating the meeting."

A wave of cold fear swept over Rakai. He looked at Hikado, and wondered if the moment was really happening. The Li Halan had aided the Hawkwood in placing Alexius on the throne of the Known Worlds. The Emperor was the leader of all the Known Worlds. The old man before him spoke treason, the breaking of the imperial line into chaotic fragments. Hikado's gaunt fingers interlocked, and the old man spoke again.

"In time you will learn," Hikado said sympathetically, "allies spy on allies. And we must glean as much information from the Decados as we can. What are they offering Duke Maximino? What can we get from their aims, the better to secure House Li Halan against the Decados plan, whether it aids or harm us? The Jincha has all but ensured that a meeting will take place, on Maximino's Estate on Icon. You will go there, and keep your eyes open for imperial agents. I will give you a file on the old Hawkwood and Decados spy networks across our worlds, with an update on the Imperial Eye network."

The old man pulled out a small book, leather bound with curious symbols denoting simple serf tasks, threshing and ox-plowing.

"I am giving you this," he said. "It is not complete; the Imperial Eye often uses Hawkwood merchants to gain intelligence. Even tourists, mainly to collect geographic information. They have the best maps in the Known Worlds. Also, it is suspected that they keep an eye on Duke Maximino, from a close source, perhaps his wife. Too many security leaks."

"What should we expect?" asked Rakai.

"Horrible things," muttered Hikado, rubbing his temples. "It is blasphemous to ally with such beings, or the power within the *Heain Kuai Su*, the Ghost Wind, bringing on Soul Death. I do not have to state that the Decados Prince is in danger of losing his reflective humanity, becoming a host for devouring viruses sent by hungering gods long fallen. Long fallen."

Hikado rolled a pen absently between his long fingers, perspiring.

"My guess is that Prince Hyram had a loyal underling infected, bearing the seed of the demon Askana Kou-Ch'in, or Bad'ha-Hohd, to summon the power of the great icy winds of death. I have made inquiries with the Church," he continued, "but so far withheld information from the Emperor's spy service. We are in a quandary, Rakai. Our agents on Icon are busy, moving unseen. If it can be proved that Prince Hyram is indulging himself with dark alliances, he can be excommunicated. A political disaster for him. The pale Decados prince is wise and cunning, and will cover his tracks."

"Does Maximino know?" Rakai asked.

"Yes and no. This strange power Prince Hyram Decados summoned he has placed in the hands of his trusted agent, Baroness Ninochka, whose history involves heavy espionage against the Hawkwood and Li Halan worlds. She is extremely capable. The notes will explain her drug smuggling and intelligence gathering activities on Malignatius. I believe she willingly bears the spores of the Ghost Wind's demiurgic origins, beyond the light of the Empyrean and reflected stars. In short, Baroness Ninochka is a host virus, willingly, of the fallen intelligences from the 27th hell, where the *Heain Kuai* originates, in ice cold regions of contemplative and cold demons."

When he mentioned the Baroness Rakai noticed that Hikado's face went white, and he steadied his breathing. He moved to say more about her, but cleared his throat and went on to other matters.

"We have two goals, Rakai: to see what this power is, if any good can come of it, and to record it. For this reason we have not consulted the Emperor or the other houses. It is too dangerous, and our house, with its blasphemous past, knows something of what the pale prince is attempting. If the Decados propose an alliance, we must know Hyram's mind. The Decados have been too silent since the wars died down. If he barters power with the fallen ones, let us display it before the Known Worlds. But if he has something of interest to Prince Flavius and our house, let us consider."

Hikado brushed a long dust web, shattering it. Motes settled on old stacks of leather bound volumes. Rakai bowed, each movement uncertain, and a feeling of vertigo shot through him.

"I would go myself," Hikado said, "but I am too old. I have to trust you. You see, Rakai, all alliances become entangled. Elements within the Imperial Eye think some of us want to return to our Pre-Conversion ways and ally with the Decados. Not the Hidden Martyrs! We are the guardians of Orthodoxy! There is a price, Rakai, paid to living in the shadows, concealed, while doing the work of light. Ah, it is sad to hear the whispers beyond the mist-shrouded frontier. I will urge Prince Flavius to send the young Emperor the old Urth works on governing, from Zhong Guo, to civilize these Hawkwoods into acceptable noble behavior."

Three weeks later, the escort ship descended from space orbit, carrying Rakai and Sidera down to the seaport city of Shan Tao on Icon, the resort city near Duke Maximino's winter palace. Sidera clutched his hand; she hated space travel, but kept her fears to herself. This was to be their honeymoon, suddenly provided for by a wealthy friend of her father's. Sidera herself was from the minor Torenson noble house, and brought up in their graceful style.

Wrapped in Rakai's belongings was a small calligraphy pen, able to act as an image scrambler and electronic countermeasure device, distorting enemy transmissions. Rakai also brought, in his personnel baggage, a sword, a handgun (a Mitchau .40 Ripper), an energy shield concealed in an amulet, and the black robes and hood of the Hidden Martyrs. His luggage would not be checked. A contact on Icon made sure of that.

The spaceport of Shan Tao on Icon was primitive; a chalk board announced incoming space flights. Old-fashioned security guards ushered the people through customs, stamping papers and inspecting luggage. Since the flight was from Kish it did not receive the arduous inspection that foreign ships did, and soon two members of the household staff met Rakai and Sidera. The servants were women, with thick peasant accents. They negotiated the couple to a waiting solar car, which slowly moved them into the estate awaiting beyond the mountains.

Shan Tao was tropical and hot, and beyond the lush palms and trees the blue-green ocean beckoned. Unlike Escoral, the humidity was thick, and the poverty more visible, small adobe houses smashed next to guarded compound estates, and a visible Li Halan military presence on the highway, halting cars and horses, checking papers. Rakai noticed that the people were brown skinned, resembling somewhat the peoples of the Ishwin Confederacy on Kish.

"It is difficult," his wife said, giving up on understanding their assigned servants, who babbled on about night spots and dancing and rich racing tracks. Knowing Rakai for one of the Li Halan, whom they had never seen up close, caused them to laugh in self-conscious embarrassment.

The car took them over a primitive two-lane highway into the mountains where tropical birds cried out and peasant graveyards lay on the road side, richly decorated and exposed in white tombstones and sepulchers. Their guest house loomed over a small fishing village, and was a compound with iron electric fences guarding a beautiful adobe house done in the old arched style of the Ascendancy. Outside, bulls wandered the streets and roosters crowed constantly, and below the hill where happy dogs scratched themselves in the noon sun the waves of the ocean could be heard, a constant crashing rhythm inducing sleep in old men and adolescents alike.

After walking to the beach down a winding dirt road, and passing herds of pigs and farmers harvesting mangos, and one lone horse happily galloping past them, they swam in the warm clear ocean by an empty beach. Beyond, the breezes swept through the palm leaves in a lazy pattern, reminiscent of crickets singing.

That night, Rakai studied what he could on Duke Maximino. The local magic lantern transmission (rare on many worlds, a sign of the Garden Worlds' higher standards) showed a popular soap opera, "Nobles Also Weep," which Rakai found oddly disconcerting, although he could not pinpoint why. Not uplifting enough for the peasantry? Sidera sighed in her sleep and Rakai studied the file.

Duke Maximino was the second son of Princess Melissa Li Halan and her husband, Count Stefano Hazat of Aragon. Unlike his brother, Prince Flavius, who took to the controlled manner and mood of the Li Halan, Maximino's Hazat blood produced a powerful, erratic figure, known for his intense passions. He took part in the military conquest of Rampart, but became angered when the house's drive to make Flavius Emperor ran up against the military genius of Alexius Hawkwood.

Brooding on Icon, he took over the office of Planetary Governor by forcing his studious and contemplative cousin, Masao, out by gun point, and then promptly sent messengers to Flavius telling of the change in administration. It was a change Flavius had previously agreed to, and it was hoped that the responsibilities of running a planet would induce a more mature attitude in the duke.

Maximino ran the planet in his personalized style. Granting favors to his friends, gambling and running with women, helped produce the wild tales that enthralled the Known Worlds. Maximino's first wife, Qi Shi, died upon birth of their daughter, Melissa Shu Miao. His second wife was the exotic and beautiful Lady Fatima al-Malik. Even her charms couldn't keep the duke's roving eye from wandering. When a famous Ravenna actress caught his eye, he had his retainers beat up her husband and send him off planet while he wined and dined her.

Still, he proved an able administrator, improving the planet's transportation system and lessening corruption in social services. The people loved his flamboyant character, and he was, despite his rebellious streak, fiercely loyal to his brother. Word would get to him that the famous poet of Kish was present, and since the duke liked to have lively parties, it was only a matter of time before an invitation found Rakai out.

Rakai silently burned the file, committing it to memory. He began a poem, but grew tired, and went to sleep by his wife.

The next day a lisping servant of the duke extended the formal invitation to join the Duke's company in two days, for the week leading up to the Festival of Moon Blossoms.

On the beach that day, they met a couple from Lyonesse province, planet Midian, who were staying at the duke's estate. They introduced themselves as Stefan and Julia Milio, and were from the small class of freemen technocrats of Lyonesse. "You must try the duke's beach; it is but fifteen minutes drive from here, and the peasants will take you on the Jade Islands, for a small fee," Stefan said, bowing.

"husband and I enjoy your poetry," Julia said. "I never thought

I would meet you in person!" Their brisk manner and unfamiliarity with court etiquette marked them as crass social climbers, but Sidera later reminded Rakai that Lyonesse customs, of all the Li Halan holdings, were the most different, having little history of native royalty there.

"A mistake," Rakai replied. "People flourish happier under the Mandate of the Illustrious Families. Ours is to set by example. But still, despite a briskness bordering on the hasty, they're not entirely disagreeable, no?"

The Milios were involved in engineering in the naval shipyards, and spoke with a thick Lyonesse accent. Stefan designed paint pigments that bonded with ship hulls and could withstand glancing energy bolts. They were vacationing here, a luxury few non-nobles could afford on the Li Halan worlds. Julia spoke of a passion for oceanography and marine life. They took Rakai and Sidera out in a glass-bottomed boat, and despite the discomfort of being in the company of *giu jian*, commoners, they enjoyed the experience. Rakai spotted an Icon striped eel, and they left the clear blue-green waters for refreshments under the shade of majestic palms.

"Really, nothing like that until you see the Fleshing Eels of the Borachio Sea on Byzantium Secundus," Stefan remarked. Stefan was a thin man, brown hair graying at the temples, whose eyes sparkled in a friendly manner.

"Native to that world?" Sidera asked about the eel.

"Yes, although sea life from Old Urth was introduced there. Some took. Mollusks, for example, almost destroyed the native marine insects. Bad ecological planning."

Still, Rakai was glad to be rid of them. It was not good form to befriend technocrats, and while Lyonesse had its place in the Li Halan Garden, it was carefully placed apart, so as not to cross-pollinate with the other fiefs.

The following day the duke's servants took them to Casaverda, the Castle of the Duke, overlooking the turquoise ocean from a majestic hill. Armed guards in livery opened the Great East Gate, and an army of servants beyond tended to the rare gardens that lead to the castle entrance. They were presented a small guest cottage to dwell in.

Maximino's estate was elaborate: ornate architecture and rare gardens and trees gave a regal aesthetic to the place. The elaborate Garden of a Thousand Pictograms, famous throughout the Known Worlds, was

here. Pools with ancient statues glistened in the noon sun, and inside
the larger buildings tapestries from ancient days covered the golden
walls. That night, they would meet Duke Maximino.

Rakai instinctively noted that security was tight, spotting sharp
shooters behind the trees. There was no laxity with the duke's safety.
Characters denoting vigilance, a spearlike lance equipped with hook
and crossbar, were carved on the walls.

Duke Maximino invited them to his table that night. A powerful
man with a large head and jet black hair, he wore a white Hazat military
outfit, being an honorary commander of the Aragon Knights. By his
side his al-Malik wife smiled, briefly nodding her head.

"The poet, eh, enjoying his honeymoon," the duke laughed. "And
of course, your beautiful wife." Sidera bowed.

"You know, cousin, I know a young man has other ideas when he
weds, but I insist that you no longer act as a stranger on Icon," Duke
Maximino said. "My home is yours. I hear you conducted yourself well
on Malignatius, against those Decados upstarts!"

"If the duke says, it is so. I but did my duty." Rakai bowed and
begged permission to recite two poems before the dinner. This was
granted, and Rakai recited his new composition, in honor of Duke
Maximino's victories on Rampart, and the three hundred guests clapped
in applause. Then he recited the customary poetic greetings to the duke's
wife, but placing it in elegant, short verses:

"Her hand releases the Western Wind
A star falls in the sea, and the lone heron
Sends ripples through his rising sun's reflection
Beyond, the sun, her heart, kisses the morning trees."

Afterwards, they ate roasted duck, jellied shark meat, and rich millirice
harvested on Icon, flavored with moon jelly. The duke was an agreeable,
affable companion, often joking with his Torenson advisor or yelling to
his servants to bring over various guests to meet his cousin, the poet.
Rakai met representatives on business from the al-Malik worlds, many
local nobility, as well as an out-of-place, lone Oro'ym, its amphibious
scales reflecting the torch lights in rich hues. The Oro'ym, Too'kara,
asked him questions of poetry, and agreed to later recite his own ancestral poems to the poet. Rakai couldn't get over the water retaining
environmental suit the amphibian wore, or the colorful patterns of the
Madoc native's skin.

Entertainment went far into the night, until the duke excused himself, not to bed, but to race horses. Rakai accompanied him, winning a small amount after watching his fortunes rise and fall at the duke's stables, before finding bed, exhausted, at sunrise.

The next day, as evening shadows covered the large estate, Rakai and Sidera walked through the Ducal Gardens. Spraying fountains and sand and rock designs allowed for a simple pattern to roll aesthetically before the eye, and bright goldfish darted in dark ponds. Beyond, layered steps in the lawn lead to the labyrinths which composed the Garden of a Thousand Pictograms, crafted into chaotic mazes a century ago by Countess Katrina Quan Shui Madagan Li Halan.

These mazes lead to spiraling confusion, and from a vantage point up the hill the duke watched his retainers get lost in the shifting shrubbery, placing bets on which one would discover the exit. Adding to the confusion was that underneath the shrubs the mobile *galisp,* large fungus-like organisms from the depths of the Ukari home world, constantly shifted, so that the ordered gardens were constantly changing form. Galisp grew in huge colonies, and the Ukari created garden cities from them. Here the galisp had been conditioned to grow and shape itself in one thousand pictogram patterns, and each day a new pattern in the garden greeted the visitor.

Reading the ever-changing garden pictograms was an exercise in constantly shifting symbols and poetic metaphor. It was believed that the countess used a rare Second Republic bioengineering method to condition the mobile galisp to take on the various shapes. On any given day, the garden possessed a different appearance. Pentagon shaped, with five entrances, it contained numerous statues and fountains, covering eight acres.

Rakai and Sidera read the long pictograms, laughing, because the pictogram for grain field was metamorphosing into the one for "plain" or "whiteness," thus altering the long string of interconnected meanings. Holding her hand, Rakai said, "Enough poetic confusion for one day. Let us go."

They walked into the more simple gardens of hill, brook and sand.

"Rakai!" a cry went out, as the couple silently drank in the wondrous beauty of the setting, and a giant Vorox came bounding over to them, a huge four armed gigantic feral beast of surprising speed. Rakai was caught. Squeezing Rakai's breath out in four massive arms, clasping

Rakai's head to a musky, hair covered hide, huge laughter erupted in the Garden of Earth Harmony.

"Tamothog?" Rakai said.

"Tamothog, Angerak Brother! Vada ji, nomo quanhoom!"

"Release me, Angerak brother," Rakai begged, but the Vorox threw him up in the air and caught him with four arms. At the edge of the garden, two other Vorox stood watching, puzzled. Tamothog waved them over, laughing, until his eyes moistened and a tear ran down his great face.

"Three years we fight on Malignatius, brothers! Three years Rakai Li Halan lived with us, Pratho, Vent, Nogguine, Tamothog, Ren-Donda and Himk-lonjer, since gone to Malashtra with Ancestors. There was one other human, Musashi. O happy are the forest eves, when an Angerak Brother returns!"

"You are Tamothog," Sidera said, feeling calm at last, wondering at first if a crazed Vorox was loose. "Rakai speaks highly of you. I am Sidera, Rakai's wife." She extended her hand, and the giant Vorox enclosed her hand in his giant one, and slightly bowed.

"Vaddak Voroxio Vaddquin! May your joint hunts be successful for you and the little Vorox to come."

Rakai regarded Sidera, dark hair and luminous skin, and prided himself on her ability to calm his friend with a single greeting. She slipped her arm in Tamothog's and he put Rakai down, with a huge hand affectionately on the poet's head.

"Tell us your life here, brother," she addressed him, and the two other Vorox smiled. Tamothog introduced them as Vragan and Dworr, fellow guards, also decorated veterans. Vragan looked down at the couple and said, "We had heard much about you, little brother, in the place of snows," They exchanged pleasantries.

Then the two Vorox excused themselves, and went about their duties, granting Tamothog time with an Angerak Brother. Tamothog smiled, proud, and told them of his life after the Emperor Wars, and being chosen, due to his loyalty and service, for the Duke's Bodyguard.

Long evening shadows stretched before them, and small gnats danced above the fish pools, when Tamothog told of the mysterious slaying of TikTik.

"It was sad, Brother, very sad, for TikTik was a great tracker. We think —" and here he tossed his great lupine head about, squinting into the setting sun, "— we think he smelled a spy, caught a scent, and was killed for it. Strange things are tracking here on the duke's ground, Rakai Angerak Brother. We fought a known enemy in bitter snows, but here, in warm jungles, a hidden enemy strikes at us."

Rakai had Tamothog list off anything suspicious, including sights, scents or unusual gatherings. Tamothog slowly answered. People from Lyonesse, and here he indicated the Milios, had the scent of Byzantium Secundus about them. "Throne world scent is wet, and you cannot hide it by change of clothes and accent," Tamothog said. "Watery worlds give off smell of strong skin and decay. Today I noticed it."

Rakai's eyes widened. That's how Stefan had been able to describe the details of marine biology on Byzantium Secundus. The obvious had escaped him. The only other incident Tamothog reported was the familiar Decados scent, when some servants of Baroness Ninochka arrived, preparing the way for their mistress in three days time. "Hate the scent, but war is over, they tell me," his Vorox comrade said thoughtfully. "But war is never over until life is over."

Rakai wrote his suspicions about the Milios in a letter, in code, to be picked up by his invisible handler. The cryptography was in an unrecorded Vorox tongue, unstudied by other worlds, but known to the linguists in the Hidden Martyrs, Rakai among them. Rakai never met or knew his Hidden Martyrs handlers in his location. This was on purpose. If caught, he had little to reveal.

Rakai, by previous design, had placed his notes in an urn (with a picture of a Shantor and a fleeing, laughing youth) in the garden, the dead drop, to be picked up by an unknown contact. Just in case, the young poet concealed himself in a heavy cloak and activated the scrambling device in his pen to blur any features taken by audio surveillance. The night air and heavy trees concealed him visually, but the duke's estates possessed many guards.

The following day a large contingent of the visitors from Maximino's court, including Rakai, Sidera and the lone Oro'ym, went to the small town of Oros that hugged the beach. Old ruins on the outside of town announced its former splendor; a portrait of Maximino was painted on maxicrete walls. Another maxicrete building, ancient, in ruins, possessed an old Second Republic hologram campaign poster, still active. "Porque Icon Eres Tu, Porque Icon Es Primera," appealing to a voting block in a language long extinct. A 3-D hologram of a Li Halan politician, in strange blue close-fitting clothing, smiling and waving, shown at odd angels under the sun. Called "The Happy Ghost Ancestor" by locals, they gave him cakes on holy feast days.

Two units of the local Li Halan army put up road blocks at the edge of town, ensuring the duke's guests' privacy. Eighteen-year-old boys, some fifteen, conscripted peasants, held machine guns while older captains waved the duke's guests by.

The beach party hired peasant fishermen to ferry them to the Jade Islands, where the greater island, Xi Dao, awaited. Xi Dao island was lush in purple flowers twining around trees, and horses were provided for the aristocrats to ride trails into the jungles. Local vendors came out to greet them, selling wares, frolicking around them. Some haggled (something Rakai's wife was surprising good at, although he considered it bad form), and then the party rode off with local guides to explore the wildlife of the island. Old Urth deer could be found on the trails, as well as pumas and some six-legged reptilian giant lizards imported generations ago from Grail.

The Oro'ym found riding hard, and begged to go swimming, and the afternoon ended with the party watching the amphibious visitor diving underwater and emerging with fish in his hands, frightening the native children with his swift tail and curious voice. By unanimous agreement, the party declared him their mascot, and placed wreaths of flowers about the astonished amphibian, declaring him King Too'kara The First of the Isles and Outer Banks, and carried him on their shoulders back to the waiting boats.

That afternoon, after returning to Oros and retiring at a restaurant provided for the duke's guests, Rakai noticed the streets were strangely empty. Inside, the tables were full of people eating, but outside on the patio all was quiet. Vendors had vanished. Even the serving staff was suddenly gone. Rakai moved to mention this to Sidera when two figures walked into the restaurant, dressed in black robes with hoods.

Before anyone reacted, they strode to the Milios' table, pulled out small handguns, and shot them both in the head with six successive shots.

A lady screamed, and the man and woman slumped over, dead.

Blood splattered across the white table cloths, creating chaotic patterns before astonished diners. The two robed and hooded figures calmly departed, black ghosts descended again into the unseen world of terror and fable. Rakai stared in horror, scarcely comprehending the turn of events. Had his actions brought this about?

A few minutes later the sound of the vendors returned, with street cries and music and babies wailing. Guards were visible, patrolling the streets.

The restaurant staff reappeared, serving wine. Two older servants calmly picked up the bodies and removed them, placing them under covers on a wooden supply cart. Young boys with mops and water buckets hurried to the floor, wiping away the red blood.

"What just happened here?" Rakai demanded in an authoritarian tone, smashing his fist on the table.

"Nothing, illustrious one," replied the middle-aged, balding proprietor of the establishment. "Nothing happened."

"Two people were shot in the middle of their dinner," Rakai said. "Look, your staff are wiping away the mess."

"I did not see such a thing," the man said, with a sphinx-like face, but beads of sweat began forming on his forehead.

Rakai slumped down. The murderers were wearing the robes of the Hidden Martyrs. Was this their noble calling? Brutal slaying before a cowed populace. Maybe events called for it, maybe the Imperial Eye agents were flushed out. But something nagged him. Rakai had monitored the couple's activities all day upon the island. The Milios seemed out of their element in this line of work, and he suspected that whoever lead the local Imperial Eye network was panicking.

Sighing, he decided to question the sweating man before him about local conditions. Sidera's face was ashen white, and Rakai escorted her to the verandah, where other witnesses gathered, drinking in the fresh air. Rakai made sure she was all right (the event gave her recurring nightmares for months), then strode back inside.

"I want to know about the local people," he said, approaching the valet in the kitchen. "How many generations have people been here, in the palace region?"

"My family, Romideo, has been in Oros for seven generations," he replied, polishing the eating utensils frantically, his breathing frightened and uneven.

"Any new residents? Speak, serf." Hatred hissed between the poet's teeth, and he seized the man's hand in a strong grip and began pressing.

"Yes," the man replied, sputtering. "The Apothecary Guild Doctor, from Malignatius, Brodering, lives on the island. Manuel De Rue came from Famater, in the North, a freeman who follows the fishing trade. Ji Sci is from Guastaildao, a good four days from here by trail. She once worked on the duke's staff, but married our local Jordun ni Chan, the Shoe and Clothes Master. And the duke's people, sir . . . "

Rakai listened while the inhabitants of the local villages were listed off, one by one, with rumors of off-world connections ("Her cousin, Feliz, was in good with the Scravers, until Duke Maximino cracked down...").

That night, the Baroness Ninochka arrived at the Palace. Wearing a tight black bodysuit of thin synthsilk, she competed in exotic beauty with the duke's wife, and confirmed immediately everybody's prejudices about Decados women: alluring and decadent. Long red hair flowed behind her, a crimson waterfall, and sky-blue eyes pierced all observers, making people giddy and uncomfortable under her gaze.

Beneath that gaze, something swam, beyond the blue a darkness pierced, slits into reality, revealing a universe of liquid madness, howling beyond the parameters of hearing, a virus screaming from elsewhere and elsewhen. For an instant a disembodied being flashed behind her smile, predatory and watching with eldritch sight, multitudinous insectoid eyes, glazed the color of lilacs.

Then, with the blink of her eyes, her humanity dispersed all terrors away to the land of childish fears and nightmares.

Baroness Ninochka was also extremely cultivated and charming, and the duke found excuses to remain at her side. In short, she was an effortlessly flawless creature, much more beautiful at forty than she had been at twenty, a fluent student of human nature, her facial expression always verging on wry amusement. Among other accomplishments, she had a studied inflection in her voice, learned with an actress's precision.

The duke introduced her to Rakai.

Ninochka smiled and bent back her hand for Rakai to kiss, and said she was an admirer of his poetry, and hoped he had forgiven the recent misunderstandings between House Decados and Li Halan, who were, after all, ancient friends spanning the centuries.

"I see no reason that our Two Houses, once allied in culture and understanding, should not seek to enrich themselves by inclusion of the other," she said. Rakai bowed. A shiver shot down his spine, and he felt that he engaged in a duel with a deadly intelligence, shifting and hungry.

"I find all of breeding and culture to be my friends, baroness," he replied, and smiled when she recited some of his lines:
"Duckling glides to shore
ripples break moon's reflection
lapping gander's legs."
Ostensibly, the baroness was representing Decados business concerns and was a collector of butterflies, which brought her to Icon. Behind her smiles and dark eyes was a message for Duke Maximino from Prince Hyram Decados, and a message from those realms beyond living and death, where spirits twisted in the cold Winds of Pain, slavering for release into the physical realms, where they could feast and grow.

Most lists of suspected Hawkwood agents (some provided by the Decados), were rounded up swiftly. Only the more recent Eye agents, planted after Alexius took the throne, escaped. The ones rounded up were known Hawkwood agents from the old days, lingering on Icon for reasons long forgotten. They weren't, as the Baroness later slyly told the Duke in private, the cream of the crop. Maximino laughed. He told her the old joke: You always know Hawkwood agents, because they're in a respectable line of work.

The next night Rakai again greeted the baroness with poetry, marking her visit and opening the costumed festivities of St. Morpello's Eve, just before the Festival of Moon Blossoms. Large tables were placed outside under gigantic colored tents embroidered with the insignias of the Li Halan and Decados royal families. Acrobats, Vorox wrestling and Icon Petal Dances followed, and the entire court wore masks. Festival was in the air, and mimes performed autumnal songs on small harps painted with carnival colors.

Rakai and Sidera were seated at the main table, dressed in the seasonal robes of spring and fall, with some of the Decados delegation.

At the main table Duke Maximino wore a replica of Emperor Alexius's coronation suit, even down to the black woof-seal lining on the boots. Upon closer inspection, however, the Li Halan insignia was seen on the sleeves. The statement was clear to all: Prince Flavius Li Halan should be Emperor.

Baroness Ninochka's large butterfly wings fluttered to invisible commands; she came, near naked, as Princess Desiderdre Li Halan, famous in family lore for bathing in the Garden of Seven Pains. Dark-pink color patterns shifted in her liquid wings, and she wore a perfume the scent of mingled summer nectar. The spur of her hind wings dripped fragrant liquid. *Regina Lepidoptera*, the duke named her.

All the court wore brilliant disguises: here and there Empyrean Angels mingled with clowns, and ghosts made small talk with sage Obun masks hiding accountants' assistants.

Rakai gripped his wife's hand, hard. He found himself gazing at the baroness and duke. She was pressing his right arm, laughing at some intimate jest between them, while minstrels performed on Octave lutes and Obun nashas the alluring "Maiden of the Snows." She knew something, something of what her Lord, Prince Hyram, found out there, maybe some sort of alliance with the Ancient Opaque Ones who hungered for the stars, Mrabb and S'zul, Ardghestoom and Tolak, the names falling from his memory.

Ah, but we are playing a very tricky game, Rakai thought. We are trying to draw them out in an intricate dance. It is the work of saints we do, in battle with the darkness, on a hidden chess board most dare not admit exists. The Darkness is real.

And in his mind Rakai saw himself, a knight drawing a sword of flame, standing between the abyss and the green lands beyond. But then he pulled back, and reflected. No. There is a third truth here. Life is unequal, and some are born powerless and others with power, and there are horrible things done in the name of power, for no other reason than preserving wealth and privilege. But the Darkness is real.

And why was the Vorox killed? Instantly Rakai realized the strong sense of scent the race possessed. The Vorox had stumbled onto something. Rakai wondered what?

Somebody screamed.

A commotion rang out. An aid to Baroness Ninochka suddenly seized her and pushed her down. Two masked skeletons, part of the assembled thong, opened machine gun fire at her position, stinging the air where she had sat seconds before.

The heavy oak table was pushed to the side, providing security. Glasses and plates crashed. Bullets sung into the wood surface. People scrambled for safety. A woman yelled in pain. The duke's men covered him with their bodies, and Rakai placed his body over his wife's.

Two hastily thrown grenades exploded above the baroness. Rakai heard a loud roar, and then a ringing in his ears. Glass fell on him like a hard rain. The baroness' bodyguard absorbed the explosion's impact, and bits of flesh and wood rained down on the floor. Their shields were up, but the bodyguard was bleeding and unconscious, the table on fire, and red wine from smashed bottles (Pen Quan '22) spilled over the tile floor.

In a flash, three of the duke's fox-masked retainers drew service revolvers and fired back, killing two of the costumed assailants instantly, sweeping them in an intense cross fire which injured four guests. The third costumed skeleton, positioned to the right of them, ran at the recovering baroness, baring a three-fingered push dagger. A ducal guard covered her with his body, but a heavy amphibious tail sent the assailant flying with a second to spare.

Too'kara the Oro'ym, wearing a sad peasant's mask, leapt up, and struck the man when he attempted to rise. He had been walking to the main table when the attack began, and reacted swiftly. The duke's guards were on the masked skeleton while the baroness was helped up.

She was stunned, and slightly bleeding from a fragment gash in her arm. More troops rushed in. Large Vorox warriors screamed commands, securing the area. The masked skeleton figure wriggled out from the guards, injecting two of them with a lethal poison on his knife blade. He fled into the night, chased by armed retainers.

Already men were inspecting the two dead assailants. The masks were removed, revealing two gardeners from the Palace staff.

The duke calmed everybody down with a gesture. "Some people will do anything for an invitation," he said, picking a strawberry off a morsel of cake that had survived the commotion. Music struck up, and eating and dancing continued, while quick consultations between Li Halan and Decados security details commenced.

In the melting mists of unreality following the incident, some people left, dazed and confused. Baroness Ninochka weakly smiled, and made her way to the duke's side. Far off, they could hear shots fired in the night, as security forces exchanged gunfire with the fleeing assailant.

"Sidera, I must go," he told his wife.

"Be careful," she said, and hugged him.

Rakai ran down to the guest cottages. Suddenly, he heard footsteps following. Tamothog stood behind him, with a drawn Voroxian sword. His old friend was smiling an eager and ready smile.

"I smell fear and excitement in you, Rakai," Tamothog said. "You are going to battle."

"You can't come."

"I must," the Vorox answered. "I know something is wrong. You are searching. You are still a hunter. Tamothog places himself in your service."

"Very well, but you will never tell anyone what transpires this night," Rakai said.

"As it was on the planet of snow and ice, Brother!" Tamothog replied, smiling, folding his four great arms in a gesture of pride.

Rakai's mind raced down swift avenues. There were no enemy radio transmitters on the duke's grounds. Strong scramblers would be set up to make the meeting safe from surveillance. But who was the Sleeper Agent who eluded him? Maximino's trusted priest? The cook, the healer —suddenly, another flash occurred to Rakai. The guild doctor! No doubt the duke had access to Amaltheans, but at times, a less-ethically motivated medical doctor, an Apothecary, would perform services no Amalthean would. Doctor Brodering lived out on the island, nearby if needed, but remote, on his small estate. He was a refugee from Malignatius, a recently lost Li Halan world. This allayed suspicion.

Rakai went to his cottage, and produced the black robe and hood of the Hidden Martyrs. The Vorox was sworn to secrecy, and Rakai had to trust his old friend. Emerging into the night in the guise a robed and hooded monk, he watched Tamothog face fall into confusion, and then recognition.

They made to leave the estate, racing in the darkness toward the gardens and the front door. Armed guards, dressed behind wolf and fox masks, were out in companies, yelling to each other. Great flood lights shown from invisible stations, scanning the grounds.

"He's in the Garden of a Thousand Pictograms!" someone shouted, and armed men scrambled into the five openings of the pentagon shaped garden.

The garden, Rakai saw from their vantage point, was shaped in ancient Ur characters, calling, he could make out, on some power to appear. Invitation, protection, a gathering of celestial winds, protection and control of force; he read enough to realize that the giant garden had been altered into a summoning area for the baroness.

This is where she would demonstrate her power.

"Let's go," Rakai said. He had his handgun and sword, and the Vorox sense of smell could flush out a foe. They dove in the south entrance, running along tall hedges, turning sharp corners and racing down spiraling paths.

Twice they heard Maximino's men, yelling from over hedges. "We found Chou! Slashed in the throat." Evidently the body was still warm, and the killer doing his work.

"Too many men," Tamothog said, sniffing the night air. "Other Vorox enter, searching."

"Where would you hide?" Rakai asked, realizing that if the man were to switch costumes he could get out alive.

"There are underground entrances, used by the gardeners. I would go there, and escape."

Tamothog lead him down dizzying paths, twice smashing through the great shrubs to shorten their distance. A flood light shown down on the gardens now, and the shouts of the guards grew distant. They heard, somewhere, nervous gunfire go off, and some swearing, but then silence.

The sounds of trickling water reached Rakai. There, before a dragon fountain, was the skeleton costume, shed. Tamothog picked it up, smothering it to his nostrils.

"He is near," he said. "Doctor Brodering, but Vragan is also after him!" The Vorox shot down a path at full speed.

Rakai chased after, and then heard screaming. The Vorox turned a corner, and crashed down on two armed men, while a third fumbled for a gun. With one swipe of his fierce claw one man fell, screaming and blinded, while he crushed the other to him, three arms breaking ribs in a deadly embrace. The third man, hidden behind an elaborate peacock mask, stood up and fired shots into the Vorox.

Then Rakai arrived, silently, black as the shadows. Unseen, he shot the gunman's shoulder, and the man screamed. His energy shield deflected most of the bullet's force, but not enough.

"Look out!" Tamothog yelled, and suddenly a huge bestial shape descended on Rakai. Thrown to the ground, he looked up, beholding another Vorox, knife teeth sharper then steel, readying to tear into him.

Swiftly Tamothog leapt onto his attacker, and Rakai missed death by an inch as he felt the passage of great jaws narrowly miss him. His heart skipped a beat, and the musky smell of Vorox fur overwhelmed him.

The two Vorox rolled into the shrubbery, attacking and biting with giant fury and hate. Red blood shot into the dew-drenched grass. Their howls echoed over the gardens, and far off armed men ran in their direction. Rakai made out Tamothog's sword rising and falling, and then animal growling of such ferocity that his blood froze.

The two Vorox crashed through some hedges, and were gone from sight, snarling and yelling. Rakai faced the bird-masked man, whose shoulder was bleeding. The man injected something into his own arm, and then faced Rakai. Breathing heavily, he dropped his mask.

"I hate your goddam planet!" Doctor Brodering screamed. "I hate your backwater world!" He stumbled, and then got up while Rakai slowly advanced, regaining composure and aiming his pistol.

The doctor was in his sixties, bald and powerfully built, obviously a vigorous man.

He fired, but Rakai leapt into the shadows, turning a corner. The bullet glanced off his shoulder, his energy shield protecting him. Brodering pursued him. Rakai leapt to the shrubs. The doctor passed him, breathing hard.

Then Rakai aimed, shooting him twice in the leg. Again, something got through the pursuer's energy shield. Brodering fell, screaming.

Rakai walked toward him. At the last moment, the doctor turned. Rakai's sword cut across his hand, and he dropped his gun. Rakai saw him pull a three-pronged knife from a leather case.

"You're sick," the man spat. "There's nothing noble or romantic about this. You have the edge. But I have lethal Seddipin coated on my dagger. One strike, and you're dead."

Rakai stood still, saying nothing. Clearly his presence unnerved the man.

"Talk, damn you!" Brodering yelled.

Rakai stepped swiftly aside. They wearily circled each other, until Rakai lunged with a swift attack and parry, cutting his assailant's arm. When Brodering backed up, his injured leg buckled, and he collapsed into the earth. For a few seconds, only the sound of fierce Vorox combat reached their ears.

Suddenly Rakai heard someone. One of the agent's aides, injured by Tamothog, limped up, gun in hand. Rakai swiftly turned, bracing his body, and struck hard with his elbow into the man's chest. The assailant fell back into the shrubbery, and Rakai dove his sword into his chest with such quick expertise that the man died instantly.

Doctor Brodering, however, used the occasion to frantically search the grass for his fallen gun. Rakai's training took over. Turning from the dying follower (hidden behind a Moon mask), the poet narrowed the gap between his dueling partner. His sword locked with Brodering's dagger. Using this for leverage, Rakai pressed in close and struck the man in the groin with his knee, pressing his weight on his locked sword while the man fell. Then, giving his enemy no time to recover, Rakai turned the ridge of his sword directly into his opponent's heart.

Brodering coughed up blood. Rakai stepped on his hand, releasing the poisoned dagger, and then pulled the sword from the dying man's body.

"You cut my left ventricle," Brodering spat. "My right one— good joke — it's reinforced, engineered, never could have cut it. Had to get my left side." He began to laugh, then convulsions shook him. He scrambled for a grenade in his belt, but Rakai's sword cut his hand and he dropped it. It lay, inches from them. Brodering's face relaxed, and he ceased to struggle.

"Long live the Emperor!" the man said, and then a rasping noise escaped his throat, and he lost consciousness, his head falling back onto the wet grass.

The sounds of Vorox fighting drew closer and suddenly, two bloodied beasts rolling in a death's embrace, crashed through the shrubs. Rakai recognized his friend, and ran up, emptying the revolver into the giant head of the maddened enemy. A horrible scream rent the night, and then Tamothog applied pressure on the other's neck, until a slow snapping sound and rattling breath ended the contest, forever.

Rakai helped his friend up. He looked at Tamothog, injured and bleeding, and wondered if his friend would exist for him only in memory, in faded holograms and poems, after this night.

Far off in the gardens, there was gunfire. Other assailants. Rakai heard men approaching. Misty recollections vanished, and the dull throbbing of duty, the laborious heartbeat of place and station, returned.

Adjusting his hood, Rakai was astonished to see the Baroness Ninochka, laser pistol in hand. Behind her stood Duke Maximino, with a mixed Li Halan-Decados security detail. A white cloth covered her wounded arm, and she still wore her butterfly costume. Flush skin tones reflected off solar lights from the security party.

"Halt," she ordered, when the black hooded figure strode into view.

The men began immediately inspecting the bodies. The baroness's eyes looked into the dark hood, now tantalizingly just beyond her arm's reach.

"There are two Vorox here," she said.

"One is loyal," he answered, indicating Tamothog, modifying his voice to escape detection. The party hesitated to advance before the dark figure, and kept behind the baroness. She herself was scared, and fought the urge to turn, guessing in some sense that this figure represented the incarnate negation of herself. Baroness Ninochka knew of the Hidden Martyrs. She never dreamed she would meet one.

"That could be a clever costume," Ninochka said, and he heard the terror in her voice. "What better way to fool these people, then come as one above all laws?"

"Yours could be a clever costume, also, if you showed restraint. Supplicate your experience with wisdom. People don't wear what they fear in their dreams. Bad form, and a loss of taste, result, signaling anarchy, and a country without laws. Last stage, final passage, an old character named Mò, can denote the later and decadent stage of a school of thought."

Ninochka stepped back, caught off-guard, reeling. An inexplicable itch developed on the small of her back, and she felt her forehead dampen with moisture. This was not going as planned. Her composure began to shatter.

The Hidden Martyr pulled back, and she gave no orders.

Suddenly, Brodering opened his eyes. He pressed his belt, summoning someone. In a second, he was surrounded by aimed weapons.

"My duke," he said.

Maximino slightly bowed. "This is bad form, doctor," he responded, surprised at the identity of the man before him. "But it is my fault, eh? Trusting a guildsman." He shook his head, as if doubting his taste in wine.

"Baroness Ninochka," Brodering laughed, propping himself up. "She and I are old associates, Duke Maximino. I use to synthesize the Severan opiate poppy for her Jakovian spies on Malignatius against your people, during the war. Addicted people sell anything for a fix."

"Doctor," she responded, clearly identifying him in the tone of an old colleague. Ninochka's body began to quiver, and she saw her plans unraveling like autumn leaves blown by a sudden wind. She would have to seize control, swiftly, or all was lost. The Hidden Martyr and Brodering shattered her presentation and confidence, twin pillars of uncertainty gnawing at her resolution. But the garden, laid out to her plans, was the summoning spot, Ur characters and ideograms forming the bridge between the Ghost Wind and the physical world. There was a chance!

"You're the monster who killed Jessica," Brodering responded. "I swore on her grave to kill you if had the chance. I work for the Eye now, baroness." He fell into a fit of coughing, followed by convulsions. Blood mixed with his saliva dripped down his chin. He was slowly, agonizingly, dying.

"Your fate will be far worse than her addiction," the baroness screamed. "Look, Duke Maximino, the gift from Prince Hyram Decados, who controls the Ghost Wind." Her voice, uncertain and shaky at first, found resolve. Before the men, she began to sing an ancient song, inflections in her voice producing seven pitches. The Baroness held up her hand, and there was a black ideogram inscribed on it, the miniature design of the garden, altered to her precise instructions.

"Kwei, Wu, Mao, Yi, Wu, Chou, Kwei," her voice intoned to Rakai's ears. He sensed the breaking of gates, the summoning of spores, and rushed to halt her.

A distant howling rose, a thousand ghost voices from impenetrable distances, crying from dead universes, beyond the dark between the stars. Everyone was touched by the cold shrieks, at first a cold crescendo down the spine, then a wailing and clamoring of rising screams, until men grabbed their ears and madness descended. A cold wind shot down the avenues of hedges, a predatory force, ripping earth and plant by the roots, tossing men with the force of a tornado.

It gathered over the baroness, spinning and howling, a waiting beast, barely contained.

Ninochka spoke again, her voice repeating "Pha," over and over, in seven pitches. The arcane word denoted vibrations, a sword's edge, blasting and scattering.

Twisting and turning above her, the wind took on luminosity, the color of rainbows bled dry, of skeletal stars burning over ice worlds, the dull reflection of a ghostly shape in a stagnant pool. A scent of cold philosophy swept the air, dying hopes and mathematical madness encoded in olfactory signals. Slowly the howling ghost wind took shape, both beautiful and abhorred, a radial being covered in eyes, a gibbering demon dancing to the barbed strings of a mad marionette.

A long eye-encrusted leg, scaly and insectoid, touched the ground before her. The phantasmal being rose, above the hedges, a shifting shape of hues and icy dignity; a tentacled residue of vast uncharted regions of the night. It vibrated in masculine and feminine pitches, attempting to dress itself for the physical world. At one point a human-oid face, angelic, hermaphrodite, shimmered into appearance, weeping blood, to be replaced by whipping talons dripping brackish liquid, scorch-ing the earth below. Simultaneously beautiful and horrific, it moved toward Brodering.

A man came running, a gardener, summoned by the doctor. He screamed, and shot at the baroness. A bullet grazed her head, and she fell. Everything froze.

The wind demon no longer obeyed her commands.

Duke Maximino stepped back, his hand on his sword. The wind spirit shot free, frantically tearing up sod and tossing men aside. The duke's bodyguards pushed him back, firing into its glowing and dim-ming luminosity.

Unchained, it began crushing men indiscriminately, shooting mangled limbs into the garden at high velocity, screeching with painful tones, weighing heavily, crushing hope. The gardener was struck by a thousand-eyed leg, and crushed by winds emanating from the radial body, in small sockets below the eyes, until his remains fell as a fine rain. One of the duke's guards crumpled out of existence like a leaf vacuumed inside out before disappearing, pressed on all sides by hurri-cane blasts.

Rakai reloaded his gun, and shot into it. Several others did the same, with no result. Then Tamothog hurled himself onto the shimmer-ing wind demon, tearing and clawing. The radial form fell back, break-ing hedge patterns, lashing at the Vorox, while Rakai ran to the baron-ess. Taking her hand, he studied the ideogram on her palm, then cut the pattern with his sword. Her hand bled, and she stirred for a second.

The baroness woke, screeching in pain.

The pattern of summoning was broken, and the ideogram garden symbol hopelessly smashed by the fighting. The winds rose, and Rakai was knocked down, blown toward Brodering. Men clutched on hedges, and above them the howling gale lost its shape, wailing the loss of physical form, the strange pale lights fading, the eyes blinking out of existence like dying stars. Beside it, Tamothog spiraled far above them, until released, flung into the earth below with bone-snapping impact.

A last wail, a dying voice from a thousand dead stars, and the representative of the Ghost Wind was sucked back into the night sky, beyond all lights, into the cold, cold winds of unheated regions.

Rakai ran to Tamothog.

Tamothog was mortally wounded, blood and entrails streaking down his damp coat.

Gently Rakai stroked the great warrior's head.

"Vragan was false," his giant friend rasped. "He has paid for breaking his oath to Duke and Brother. There, beyond the fountain, is the tunnel. Must have entered from there. The spirit, brother, it was mad, it did not want to be summoned. Rather like an animal taken from woods to be trained."

Tamothog smiled at the irony of his remark.

Rakai withdrew his hood so only his friend could see. Tears swam in his eyes. A feeling of infinite lightness and vertigo briefly swept over him. Death was in the air, an abstract personification suddenly made intimate.

Tamothog spoke. "Yes, my time to die, yours for responsibilities and family. I have a daughter, Lupaar. See that she can see the star worlds."

"I will."

"She is on Vorox. Tell her her father was a great hunter, and loyal, and a friend to poets everywhere, especially small Li Halan poets who asked too many questions on Vorox songs. Now I go, Rakai, to the woods of Vrontha, to the great hunt of heroes. Listen? I can hear the drums, calling us... "

A smile crept across the warrior's face. Then a last breath of life escaped through carnivorous teeth, and the garden became still. Involuntarily, blood gushed from the mouth and nostrils, and urine was released in great pools.

Where the Vorox had fought the spirit, a shrub pictogram depicting the Voice of Lightning was shattered, the graphic depiction of the reverberation of thunder splintered into unknowable mystery. Chaos had entered the garden.

Rakai wept, gently stroking the giant's hair, until between sobs he ritually chanted an old Vorox song, learned on Malignatius, "Vada Mekko,

Nadata, Vada Mekko." The song of parting.

The others approached, and he hurriedly placed the dark hood on before swiftly disappearing into the shadows, leaving the party to carry the bodies out.

The Duke was helped up from the hedge he had been flung into. The baroness couldn't move. An aide wiped her brow, and the baroness felt suddenly dizzy. She had been grazed on her head by the bullet, and the host she carried was gone now, leaving her feeling weakened and old. Seeing this fanatic monk clad figure struck her deep in her chest, and she labored to return her breathing to normal. Her mouth was dry, and she worshipped the mental image of cool water.

They look too much like executioners, she decided.

Then she cried. It was gone, Prince Hyram's gift, and she had failed. She had lost control of the wind spirit, momentarily, and lost everything. The gift was gone, the weapon of alliance, her demonstration to Duke Maximino shattered by a humble gardener's bullet.

She looked over at Brodering, who smiled a weak smile before losing consciousness again.

The chaotic pictograms of the garden began to form into a cognizant shape, the characters denoting trust, a man standing at his word, writing the word, an epistle, modified from the old Urth Zhong Guó character, xìn. It shifted around the Vorox bodies, nourished on their blood.

Rakai slipped out of the garden, unseen. No one followed the black clad man. In the night he heard flitters overhead, and men running, chasing shadows and rumors.

* * *

All was not fully explained until after he dropped his report off. Two days later he received a response, from the urn, Vorox script on a paper bag:

> Fortunate Saint,
> You performed brilliantly. Without you Brodering's escape was certain and the spirit from beyond the borders unstoppable. Dr. Brodering died of your wounds the following morning, only briefly regaining consciousness. He informed those present that years ago, his first wife, Jessica, became addicted to

the manufactured Decados drug, selchakah, by Baroness Ninochka's hand, on Malignatius. The Guild Doctor synthesized the drug, and his own wife was addicted to ensure his loyalty to the Jakovian Agency. Jessica died of effects resulting from her addiction.

Attempting to rebuild his life, Brodering came here, after Malignatius was lost to the Decados. During the Emperor Wars, the Imperial Eye, recruited him, knowing his ties to Duke Maximino. Using the very drug that destroyed his first wife, he built a network among the duke's staff of selchakah addicts, who sold information for injections. Brodering created a lethal derivative of the drug, which he used to inject a wounded Vragan, thus turning the Vorox into an addict. Traces were found in the Vorox's veins.

Brodering's handlers and superiors were the Milios. When they disappeared, he became the senior Imperial Eye representative on Icon. What destroyed Brodering was his hatred of House Decados. Disobeying Imperial Eye protocol, he informed his underlings that orders called for the assassination of Baroness Ninochka. His hour of revenge had struck, and the baroness practically delivered into his hands.

Baroness Ninochka has received a new assignment, tending crumbling estates on the cataclysmic world, Pandemonium. If the information on what transpired here gets out, expect her sudden death from an unusual illness, the usual Decados method of dispatching embarrassments. No doubt the Decados will say she was infected, alone, by the Ghost Wind, and was a sad, isolated case of the dangers in exploring the uncharted regions. Security cameras caught some of the chaos in the Garden of a Thousand Pictograms.

The Decados were hoping that Duke Maximino would ally with them, although for what long-term goal remains unknown. The baroness was to offer the power of the Ghost Wind to Maximino, even infect him with its spores — back to her old games of addiction. You and Brodering forced her hand before she was ready. We will keep a close watch on Duke Maximino. While loyal to his brother, he is prone to helping the house by sudden enthusiasms, not shared with others. We are consider-

ing, as recompense for the sudden disappearance of the Milios,
sharing the information with the Imperial Eye.

Discontinue the old drop, and place any messages beneath
the granite rock in the Garden of Twelve Autumns.

Rakai finished the visit to Icon in the company of his wife, walking
among the blossoming trees. Her drowsy look, and grip on his hand,
spontaneous and joyful, allowed him to reenter life.

Sidera remarked on the liveliness of Maximino's Court, where the
strict adherence to ritualistic behavior was diluted, and the Mandate of
Heaven seemed less a concern. The poet nodded. He did notice one
thing, which added to the illusion of Icon. Entertainment, shown on
the magic lantern transmissions: It was the peasants, more Orthodox
than anywhere else in the Known Worlds, who cried and cursed and
cheered at the show "Nobles Also Weep." Rakai had known enough of
propaganda in his life, but it was on Icon that he saw it for what it was,
perpetuating images it wanted to be true across a different reality.

He thought of this again, the beautiful illusion like the creation of
perfect calligraphy. Rakai started to sketch an old Ur pictogram for
beauty, but lengthened a line, and added three cross strokes, fencing off
the symbol which read, more or less, "Beauty removed by Dreams from
the World."

Outside the space transport, the lights of a thousand thousand
stars glowed, and Rakai thought that the dichotomy of imagination
and reality could be overcome by rising above them, seeing imagination
as reality, as higher dimensions see unity in the seeming strife of the
lower ones.

The stars shown before him, giving Rakai the illusion of perma-
nence in the ever-changing, entropic universe. Their clusters became
patterns of signs and myth in his imagination, portents of the Pancreator's
indescribable mercies.

Yet there was a void here too, empty holes in the tapestry of night,
where no light shown. The void sings by the lack of design, by the
absence of luminosity. Far off in space, where the light of the stars
grows dim, a cold wind blows.

A Song to End All Songs

Daniel Greenberg

A part of the Unit has strayed, and cannot hear the Start-is-the-End Song. Long ago it sheared off and no longer coheres to the Unit. Now it lies broken into a jagged multitude of unconnected beings. One of these multitudes is now trying to return to the Unit. So it has come back to the cradle of the universe, the planet Severus. This multitude calls itself Decados.

The soft, pliable Decados beings came to us wailing and weeping from their every orifice and pore. Their pores must always weep, for their vessels lack jointed exoskeletons. Their orifices must always wail, because they cannot raise their voice in the Start-is-the-End Song.

The Start-is-the-End Song tells us all that the Decados lost. They lost their exoskeletons, and now must face their predators swaddled in no other protection than a motile sac of spongy gel. They lost their Song, and now must commune only in mournful croaks and cackles, in plaintive imitation of the Start-is-the-End Song. Most pitiable of all, they have lost their place in the Unit, and now their multitude sees itself as many loose and confused fragments. They cannot listen together. They cannot act as one. They cannot be part of the Unit.

They call us Ascorbites, because they do not see that we are the Unit. They do not see that the Unit is all there is. They cannot perceive the Unit, even when the Unit is in full array before their sense receptors.

Were they whole, they would also be the Unit. Were they whole, they would be swaddled safely within exoskeletons. Were they whole, they would join us in the Start-is-the-End Song. But they suffered an unknown injury in some earlier state, and they were peeled like a beetle from its shell. We strive to instruct them, but they do not learn.

This element of the Unit has learned well. This element of the Unit is called Ven-keel, and is newly hatched from Tan'zhom state into full adulthood. In the Tan'zhom state, Ven-keel heard the Start-is-the-End song, and learned all there is to know.

All the lost multitudes like the Decados do not know all there is to know, and so they continue to try to learn new things. Yet they never enter the quiet of the chrysalis and listen. So they behave erratically, and preoccupy themselves with trivial and empty pursuits.

* * *

Well, I bought a flitter. Primer gray with a few dents and some laser scoring on the pilot's side. Eight thousand 'birds at Deacon Jerry's Charitable Used Salvage for the Poor and Hungry Thrift Shop. Deacon Jerry said I've never had a Gannok in here before. I said, at these prices, I'm not surprised. But if you want to know the truth, that's actually a great price for a flitter. My bootleg Shantor skin racing gloves cost more. OK, not really more, but close.

OK, it's more a hopper than a flitter. But since it's from the stolen goods side of Deacon Jerry's business instead of the dehydrated peas side, it's actually in pretty good shape for the price. Now that's what I call charity. All Deacon Jerry wanted was that I get it offworld as soon as possible and leave without a receipt or warrantee. Which was fine with me, since I want to get to Severus as soon as possible. And who needs a warrantee when you can memorize repair manuals by flipping thorough them?

I stuck around Criticorum long enough to fix up the hopper, though. Which gave Deacon Jerry apoplexy. I warn you, you damn, stinky ape, he yelled. Get that damn hopper off this damn planet now. Not a man of many adjectives, the good Deacon. I just snickered at him, and told him if he wanted to get rid of me and my hot hopper, he'd have to misappropriate me up a few extra absorption struts.

So I blew out the fuel tanks, upgraded the boosters, beefed up the acceleration absorbers in the pilot's seat, and completely rebuilt the timers to burn a rich fuel mixture of my own devising. It runs a lot hotter, but flies a whole lot faster. Much faster than the specs, and with vertebrae-cracking acceleration. Pretty much perfect for grave robbing, desecration, and loot hauling. I mean archeology.

I'm discovering hot new skills like dodging Air Yachts, careening around buildings, finding unguarded fuel depots, chewing the fat with curious rocket jockeys and Charioteers, buying esoteric tools, and leaking my stinky skin oil like crazy 'til I'm sticking to the pilot's seat. Sheer joy.

These human engineers love to brag about what they do, and if you listen, they'll give away more design secrets for free than they would sell you at any price. Of course, it helps if you're a three-foot critter that looks to the humans like a beloved entertainment species from their home planet. So lucky for me we Gannoks evolved to a shape that resembles Urth monkeys and not Urth banana slugs or something like that. The loudmouths don't realize that monkey see, monkey learn.

So now I know enough to maintain, improve, and fly the thing. Another year or so, and I'll be skilled enough to pilot an Explorer. Then I'll drop a few hundred thousand on an Imperial Lekaf. Learning to fly it will be the easy part. The hard part will be whipping up enough 'birds. So looks like I finally have to make Deacon Jerry happy, and jump to Severus, world of mud and bugs. And priceless loot.

* * *

The Decados are agitated. Their actions have become erratic. The Song tells us this is a precursor to a new incursion. And so it is. Many Decados went out from the preserve into which we have carefully herded them. They swaddled their pliable, fleshy parts in armor. This is to imitate the exoskeleton for which their bodies yearn.

We silently followed the Decados. We moved swiftly along the tree-tops. Many times they stopped. Many times they carved away the filaments of the forest to sift the dirt for more rocks. Many times they collected the stones they found.

But they came near to the Broken Place, and we fell upon them. We chopped away their false carapaces, and feasted on their flesh. We tore open their vessels, and planted our pupae. We took up the stones they collected, and carried them back to the preserve, where we gave them to those Decados who heeded our telling of the Song by staying within their preserve.

But the Decados will leave again. The Song tells us they will leave again. They can do nothing else, as long as they do not hear the Song. They will leave again, and come to the Broken Place again. And we will fall upon them again.

Mourning for their lost exoskeletons, they will always wear false carapaces of metal. Mourning for their part in the Start-is-the-End song they will always croak false songs. And mourning for the Unit, they will always return to Severus, cradle of the Universe.

* * *

So I landed on Severus. The place is beautiful. If you like oppressive, sweltering, sticky jungles full of massive, lumbering jungle lizards who are always hungry; murderous, hyperthyroid crickets who are just smart enough to be dumb; and cranky, miserable Decados tricked into working here. I think I'm the first sentient being to come here knowing what the place is really like.

So I'm bunking down in New Pasha. It's a squalid, sprawling mining town devoid of all charm. Which is to say that it's just every other Decados settlement on Severus. The officials are very suspicious of me and spy on me a lot. I told them I'm a geologist, and showed them my permission papers from Duchess Nastasia of Malignatius. I entertained at her fifth wedding, and she gave me a cracking good set of forged noble seals. I told them I'm a geologist. As long as I tell them I'm a geologist out to do surveys, they'll think I'm secretly a miner out to pilfer their jewels, and won't suspect I'm really an archeologist out to plunder their artifacts.

The rest of the locals are a surly lot who were all pretty much tricked into coming here, and only stay because they have no better options. Their lives are made tolerable by a clutch of decadent pursuits that distract them from their bleak, unpleasant, and often short lives in the mines or in the jungles. They're all very entertained that I'm stupid enough to come here of my own volition. And I'm very entertained by them. We spend a lot of time just laughing at each other.

My hopper's custom impact dampers got badly chewed up in transit, even though I told the Charioteer that would happen if she used the unmodified bays in her ship. I wheedled a big damaged goods fee from her employers, and then fixed the damage with a few of Deacon Jerry's spare absorption struts. So I used her cash to treat a large gang of locals to an evening of boozing and pipes and unsavory pursuits that they won't soon forget. A lifetime of good works can't earn the kind of loyalty that a night of carousing money buys. So now a few barfuls of miners love me, and told me about some places where they've found rich veins of gems but can't get in due to Ascorbites. I may have to scoop up a few to defray expenses. Gems, not Ascorbites. The miners repeatedly warn me about the Ascorbites, since the bugs don't seem to mind taking huge casualties to kill a few expeditionary miners.

The miners tell me a lot, because I'm the most entertaining thing they've seen in a long time, and the only Gannok they've ever seen. Or smelled. My delightful musk is our only impediment to our grand old time. These heavily fortified buildings hold tight to my funk with the death grip of an Urth Orthodox priest clutching the collection plate. Fortunately, some of them have so ruined their noses with pipes that they barely notice my smell. And can my delightful aroma really be more noxious to them than the gagging reek of their stale pipe smoke after it's chemically bonded with their unlaundered work suits for five straight shifts?

So we spend our nights giggling in mutual amusement. And by day, I blast the hopper over the riverbed, skimming upstream into the Pancreator-forsaken jungle, searching for the Ur ruins.

* * *

The Song tells us that when newcomers return to the cradle, they seek a return to the Unit. They seek a return, but do not know they seek a return. They must be forced to hear the Song. And when they do not hear the song, they may become food.

A newcomer arrived. We watched his huge, flying carapace tear a hole in the sky over the river. We dashed through the trees to follow, but his false exoskeleton was far too fleet, and too far above us. We communed, and found that the newcomer spent his time looking at glittering stones upriver. He spent his time looking at glittering stones, but did not stop at any place long enough to collect any.

But he seems very different from the others. He looks around more than the Decados. He listens more than the Decados. But he leaks more than the Decados.

If he looks, perhaps he will see the Unit. If he listens, perhaps he will hear the Song. We must know if he can hear the Song before we lay our eggs in his flesh.

* * *

So today I got thrown out of New Pasha. It's no big deal. I've been thrown out of better places, like my home planet Bannockburn. But that's a long story. I was safely back in New Pasha, and was heading to the Prince Igor saloon after a long day of artifact hunting. I mean prospecting. I mean geologizing. I was whipping northbound on the Boulevard of Paradisiacal Gardens in my trusty hopper, which I just got slathered in a new coat of blue metallic lacquer to protect it's oxidation spots from the eternal Severus drizzle, when this strung out Decados ore processing foreman on a sleek, antique hoverbike plows into me.

Now the trick to driving a big rig like a hopper amidst a swarm of little flitters is to defer to them whenever possible. Like a gentle giant frolicking through a field of porcelain dolls, you have to be ever vigilant for the telltale tinkle of crushed powder underfoot. You'd think this is obvious, but it's one of several reasons I won't be going back to Madoc any time soon, even though I still yearn for fresh bozak fish.

So the foreman careers off my front starboard flank. And wouldn't you know he spider-webs the blue metallic lacquer in three places before it had time to finish setting, which means I have to have the lacquer on the whole panel completely stripped and reapplied instead of just buffed clean like the way you can with fully set lacquer.

He flips ass over elbow and plops into a mud pit just off the main road, just missing the paved street and certain death by about three feet. The hoverbike did not miss the pavement, and cratered. The mud saved the foreman from a terminal case of road rash, and, more importantly, saved me from having to use up the last of my noble seals to beat the manslaughter rap.

So the local peacekeeper red lights my hopper, and I'm in real trouble until I make the ill-tempered official crack up over my incisive impression of the twitching hover bike rider and the comical way his mangled arm keeps flapping up while we all wait for an autodoc to airlift him. The peacekeeper busts a gut at my dead-on impersonation of Canon Buchanan and that thing he does with his upper lip when he's declaiming about other people's sex lives. Decados always love that. So he finally he lets me go with a warning and a promise to entertain at this big party he's throwing for his kid's coming of age. Like I'm cheap entertainment for the overindulged spawn of some vehicular traffic pedal pumper. Fortunately he doesn't force me to spend two hours running a complete post-impact diagnostic screen before taking off again.

So I'm grumbling over this new obligation as I ease the hopper back into the Boulevard of Paradisiacal Gardens. It's getting dark as I turn a gentle left on Silen and note that the readouts show some minor damage to the stabilizers. I speed up to get more lift and then pound on the control panel and armrests for a while. The damage means I'll have to blow two, three days fixing the stabilizers before I can head out of New Pasha again. Stupid foreman. Well, I thought with a smile, finally coming to my senses, the extra time will give me a chance to find out what kind of junk jewelry the peacekeeper's wife has collected. And that's when I splattered the pedestrians.

OK, I didn't really splatter them.

There was this flock of Decados matrons socializing in a busy cross-walk ahead, chattering about the latest courtly gossip and oblivious to the ground vehicular traffic around them. Which only makes sense, because there was no ground vehicular traffic on Silen at the time. Just a lone metallic blue hopper whisking West overhead, speeding up and rapidly losing altitude.

As I saw the ground (and the matrons) rapidly approaching, I pulled back on the collective as sweet and graceful as an Ur-Ukar slipping the shiv between your third and fourth back ribs. Only nothing happened. I was still headed straight for the matrons. They continued casually strolling into the killing zone, oblivious to the smelly, hairy angel of death bearing down on them with six tons of metallic blue death.

What I didn't know was that the hoverbike accident had accordioned the port torsion bar on my elevation stabilizer. I was losing all lift except the default hover elevation, which puts the wings at a height of, in precise technical measurements, the neck wattle level of a Decados matron.

Thinking fast, I decided to panic. I swerved to port and gently dipped the left wing. Right into the pavement. A shower of sparks lit up the twilight on my port side and glinted brightly in the corona of every fat raindrop that hung suspended in the evening air between me and the matrons. The wing groaned in complaint over my callous disregard for its proper angle, and I could hear the hideous sound of metal shear. The hopper pivoted slightly on the unexpected axis of its port wing, and the right wing whipped up past the matrons, nearly clipping their wigs as it swung me toward the silo on the left side of the road. They stared in terror as a sweaty little monkey expertly piloted the almost-lethal hopper to a whining, squealing halt just down the street.

The funniest part is that the peacekeeper who let me off with a warning the first time got busted down from flying the cushy city pa-trol to walking the frontline jungle patrol. Looks like he won't be able to afford a big party for his kid, after all. Unless the New Pasha peace-keepers have a generous death and dismemberment package. So on the bright side, I won't have to humiliate myself entertaining his kid's friends.

Which is just as well, since I'm not allowed to set foot in New Pasha again. Or any town on Severus.

The worst part is that they exiled me even though I used up all but one of my Malignatius seals. No, the real worst part is that now the Charioteer can charge a hazard fee to pick me up, which is more than I got out of her for my damaged impact dampers. No, actually the real worst part is that they kicked me out before I could fix my stabilizers. I don't have the lift to stay safely above the treetops. Until the jump ship comes back to pick me up in about two weeks, it'll be just me, the jungle, and the Ascorbites. I can hardly wait. I wonder if they like impressions?

* * *

The newcomer has brought his false carapace outside the preserve again. This time he travels close to the ground, and glides slowly around the trees. We can now follow him, and we watch him carefully. He approached the Broken Place, and we communed. The Song made clear our actions. The newcomer was now our food.

* * *

OK, I have to admit I was completely in the wrong to fly off after the bike crash without running the diagnostic screen. But that didn't stop me from yowling like an Avestite waking up in a brothel. I didn't change their minds about expelling me, but I did manage to make their day more ominous. Evict me, I yowled, and doom and destruction will rain down on New Pasha in the form of a plague of Ascorbites! They tossed me out on my ass, and I wondered how long it would take for 'Scabite doom and destruction to rain down on ME.

The answer was — three days.

When they tossed me out, I raced through the jungle in stark terror until I reached the nearest empty plain. I parked there and took some shots of Decados vodka to calm down, figuring that I could see any 'Scabites coming from far enough away to scoot away. But then I got bored.

The Reeves say that sentient beings are motivated by only two things. Greed, and fear. They may want to add boredom to that. Anyway, for two days I chewed my rations, tossed back vodka, and thought about the loot that was just sitting there all unclaimed, until finally my fear completely choked, dismembered, and hid the body of my fear. So the next sunrise I scooted back into the jungle.

* * *

We watched from the trees as the newcomer defiled the Broken Place. We communed with the Start-is-the-End Song, and our attack became clear. But I heard in the Song something I had not heard before. So I asked elder H'Chur'ff if the newcomer could be at the Broken Place in search of the Song. We do not know this kind of newcomer, I said. He is too small and oily and covered with filaments to be Decados. The Decados are not seeking the Song, but this one may be, and that may have brought him to the Broken Place.

Elder H'Chur'ff told me I was only very newly hatched. Ven-keel is too close to Tan'zhom stage, he revealed to me, and Ven-keel still believes there are things to be learned. We who are older know that there are no new things to learn. So we will not learn that the newcomer seeks the Song. If he did, that would already be in the Song, and we would know it.

I could think of nothing to say to that, so we fell upon the newcomer's false carapace and pounded our way into it.

* * *

So I found the Philosopher's Stone today. Nothing like mortal peril to concentrate the will and get you motivated for greatness. I'll have to remember that if I ever run a scam as a highly paid consultant to rich merchants.

I had caught glimpses of the 'Scabites all day. They were watching me, but didn't bother me. I would have to act quickly.

I was prospecting up by a breathtaking waterfall, when I saw the deep drop in the undergrowth. Readings showed uneven soil patterns. The coordinates were not quite the same as on the map I found in the Ur ruins on Bannockburn, but then the river could have changed its course over the millennia.

I started probing it, and my readings peaked. It was my ruined Ur outpost. There wasn't much left, but something down there still had its own energy source! There definitely were artifacts here. I launched my digger, and sent it to work.

And that's when the plague of locusts hit.

I had just gotten back into the hopper to remotely monitor the digger when the proximity alarms went off. If the bugs had jumped me one minute earlier, I would have still been outside, setting up the digger. And I would have been bug juice.

The autodefenses activated before I knew what was going on, and the sound of cracking lobster backs diverted my attention from my newfound wealth. Two Ascorbites blew to bits before I could think to take over manual control, and three more took lesser wounds and dropped to the ground. They rest were all over my hopper, bashing the lovely new metallic blue lacquer, which had finally set, and had a lustrous sheen that you could see yourself in, reflected deeper and deeper the further you look. It wasn't the cheap stuff, but the custom Hawkwood import that glints differently in every different kind of lighting. The blue reflections of my laser blasts were spectacular blossoms of turquoise fire over the nosecone, as I cut a swath through the bugs.

They broke through the dome over my head, and a claw raked the acceleration-absorbing seat to the right of my head. I pushed my head as far back into the seat as possible, and hit the boosters without going through the acceleration cycle. My neck cracked anyway. But the 'Scabite's arm slithered right out of the cockpit and he flew off the back. I swerved around twenty foot wide trees and prayed my concentration would remain focused until they were all thrown clear. Every greasy hair on my body bristled at a ninety-degree angle, and my heart pounded like a splinter rifle on full auto. Miraculously, I didn't hit a single tree. I finally shook all the Ascorbites loose. All but the one that was clinging to the underside of the hopper.

* * *

The Song declared that our attack party would die that day. Elder H'Chur'ff landed above the head of the newcomer, and broke through the false carapace to scoop out his succulent brain. A flash of dazzling light struck my thorax, and I fell. The anguish in my thorax was so loud it seemed to shut out the Start-is-the-End Song. My legs were weak, and bleak fears and doubts filled all the parts of me where once had been only the Song. Still, I knew my course. I had to do the last thing I was told to do. So I crawled to the false carapace. I lifted myself up, and gripped one of the carapace's legs. I clawed at its underbelly, and it flew away quickly. I watched the others fall from the top of the false carapace, but I held on. The leg of the false carapace dug into my wounded thorax, sending lances of pain through me, but the pain was nothing to the pain of the emptiness where once had been the Song. I was as lost a fragment as the newcomer. Surely death would be better. I am nothing.

* * *

I'm now the richest little monkey in the universe. The Philosopher's Stone is about the size of a bocce ball, and shaped like a dodecahedron. It's very heavy, and veined like dark red marble, but with a pliable skin that bunches and wrinkles to the touch like a rotting ujea fruit, but then straightens out again to look like polished marble. It's creepy to hold.

Unlike other Ur artifacts, this one has a clear activation switch. Some of those other artifacts have, like psychic switches or utterly alien controls. But this one has a simple knob. The only problem is, I have no idea what the Philosopher's Stone does. If it even does anything at all after sitting in the pit all those eons. The rest of the crashed ship was pretty thoroughly decayed, but this thing looks good as new. It would be fun to put it outside the walls of that Pancreator-forsaken mining city and activate it from orbit. Just to see what would happen. But instead I think I'll just sell it for a king's ransom. Then I can afford to buy a Plague Bomb for New Pasha. Then again, if I could figure out what it does I could sell it for an emperor's ransom.

Yeah. An emperor's ransom. I could enjoy that, I mused as I flew back to the crash site, splashing wounded Ascorbites with my sparkling lancets of light from my forward lasers. I could do what I've always wanted to do — take a break from tearing around the Known Worlds and spend my evenings lazing around in pastoral settings, contentedly lying on my back, watching spectacular sunsets. That would be better than anything.

As I landed at the crash site and cautiously climbed out of my hopper to retrieve the digger, I noticed the squirmy feeling of greed replacing my fear. Forget the damn sunset. I could buy a little moon somewhere and retire into a comfortable armed camp. I hauled up the digger, which had sifted through the charred junk in the crash site and reeled in the Philosopher's Stone. An armed camp, with every kind of diversion available, and lots of imported Gannoks, who would be so sorry they ever voted to kick me off Bannockburn. I put the stone in my vest pouch along with some sample scraps from the crash site, and hauled the digger back to the hopper. Yeah, an armed camp, where I can become comfortably old and bloated in the tender care of toadies and sycophants.

I was shoving the digger back into its bay when an Ascorbite leaped off a lower strut and plowed into me. We hit the ground and he savagely plunged a claw into my right arm. I reached for my laser pistol and realized that my right arm had decided not to work. I reached for my left laser pistol, and realized that I don't carry a left laser pistol. I reached for anything else, and realized that getting your intestines filled with alien eggs is one of the top ten worst suckiest ways to die. I could understand dying like this if I was broke little monkey, but I have a pocket full of treasure. The rich are not supposed to suffer. The Reeves told me so.

* * *

Did the Song flee to punish me for questioning the word of Elder H'Chur'ff? I do not know. Will the Song return if I kill the newcomer? I can not know. The Song will not tell me. I slid from the leg of the false carapace, and staggered, hunched over, beneath its great metal belly. But the Song sang not. The newcomer approached the false carapace, and I tore into his pulpy body. But the Song sang not. He fell, and I beat his little form. But the Song sang not.

The Newcomer reached into his pocket for the gem he took from the Broken Place. He clutched a knob on it, and his eyes disappeared into his head. I leaped off him. He was hearing the Song.

* * *

So the main thing about the Philosopher's Stone is that it pretty much floods your conscious mind with everything going on around you until your conscious mind is overwhelmed and you run out of conscious mind to hold it but it still keeps growing and flooding in anyway until you can see your conscious mind is left far behind you but it keeps on growing and flooding in anyway even though...

So I was pretty much blotto, and at the mercy of the bug. Who didn't bother to kill me. Instead, he jumped off me. I noticed, along with noticing everything else in the universe, that the bug had taken a nasty thorax wound that pulverized part of his Ascorbite communication mechanism. He can no longer send vibrational signals that make up the Ascorbites' very limited mass mind. How interesting. Of course, everything else in the universe was pretty interesting, too.

The bug's life must be utter hell. They get strange impulses over their vibrational sense receptors. Without them he's not plugged into his hive. He's exiled. Better to die than live a life he can't comprehend. I thought that, while he was off me I would extinguish him, for his own good, but I couldn't figure out where I left my body.

"You hear Song," he rasped, in that unpleasant mockery of speech the Ascorbites use when they have to speak to non-Ascorbites.

"You could call it that, I suppose." I replied. Or tried to. I was busy examining the cell structures of the leaves of a succulent plant in a window box in New Pasha, and couldn't seem to find my mouth.

He fell to his knees. I'd have thought he was worshipping my god-like consciousness if I wasn't completely aware that his tissues were drained of a lot of the cocktail sauce the Ascorbites use for blood.

I tried to get up. But I was too interested in the star formations around Severus to notice where I left my legs. Don't let the Eskatonic Order fool you. Omnipresence takes some getting used to.

So both of us just lay there like idiots. One who was greater than a god and one who was less than a bug. But neither of us could move.

And that's when the rest of the Ascorbites landed on us.

* * *

Had I heard the Song, I would have known long ago that the upriver raiding party was approaching. I would have known that they would rescue me, and destroy the helpless newcomer. They flailed their mandibles toward me, but the Song sang not. Did they pity me? Did they despise me? I could not know.

They sniffed at the body of the newcomer. They could sense that he was different. Then they lifted their staves to kill him. How could they not sense that he heard the Song?

I forced myself up. I crawled to them. I used the crude and difficult language of the Decados to tell them. He is one of us, I told them. He hears the Song.

They bludgeoned me with their staves, and I did not know why. The Song would not tell me. At length, the raiding leader spoke to me in the language of the Decados. You are gone from the Song, he said.

You are a stranger. You are gone from here. He raised the tip of his spear above my eye, and plunged it down.

Directly above my eye, his spear splintered into a thousand shards, which flew in all directions except down in my head. He leaped back. The newcomer stood on his feet. His voice flooded me, much louder than the Song ever was. It thundered inside me, and shook my every muscle as it reverberated. It flooded the others as well.

This wounded Ascorbite is not a stranger, he told them. You may not kill him. You have to take him back. He may be blind to your Start-is-the-End Song, but he has deeper wisdom because of it. Listen to him.

But they did not. They fled into the forest. The newcomer turned to me. Sorry, big fella, he told me, making his thunderous voice more gentle. They are afraid of you and won't take you back. They blame you for my being able to shout louder than the Song. I'm afraid they'll want to kill you on sight. Tough break, pal.

* * *

Don't let anyone tell you that enlightenment feels good. I felt horribly stretched over and worn out and used up as I came down from having the local star cluster forcibly shoved into my frontal lobes. When I let the universe slide out of my head and gratefully returned to my very limited physical senses, my body felt about as strong as a plate of warmed-over noodles. The world seemed dim and small after all that. I was limp and numb except for the lacerations on my right arm, which began to sear like Vrasht bugs were gobbling it up. If the 'Scabites had called my bluff and stuck around, I'd be baby formula now for some larva now.

Despite his own extensive wounds, the Ascorbite picked up my mangled carcass and dragged us both into the hopper. Which was dash decent of him, considering that a few minutes ago we were trying to rip each other's guts out. It was also dash imperative of him, since I was too brain fried to move. We lay there, bleeding all over the freshly scrubbed cockpit, and just appreciating being alive, in between cursing out being alive.

I couldn't muster the strength to talk, so we just lay there as the intermittent drizzle soaked us and puddled under us. I drifted in and out of consciousness watching multi-colored birds fly lazy circles overhead. The bug was so still that I though he might have died. But he occasionally twitched and made a hooting sound.

Toward late afternoon the rain stopped and a faint rainbow lit up the Severus sky. The soft light from it woke me up, and it looked sweeter than all the cosmic events I had been forced to experience while the Philosopher's Stone had control of my head. With the rain stopped, we could hear the bleeping of bugs and the gushing, churning sound of the nearby waterfall as it plunged into the river. We watched the sun set over the forest canopy, turning the whole sky a brilliant crimson as four-inch glowing bugs flashed their lights in an eons-old invitation to love.

As the warm fragrance of honeysuckle floated through the shattered cockpit, I noticed an odd sensation pass through my body. Rigor mortis? No. Something even more alien. Something so strange it took me completely by surprise. I was relaxed.

By nightfall, the really huge Severus predators began to lumber by, looking for a tasty morsel that was already wounded and ready to die. Bright stars poked through the tree canopy above, winking in the twilight.

"We must leave," the Ascorbite rasped.

"Who died and made you Emperor?" I demanded.

"I understand not. It is because we have not died yet that we must leave," he keenly observed. "Were we dead at present, our leaving would not—".

"Yeah, yeah, yeah," I grumbled, grimacing as I pulled myself up in the seat. My anguish wasn't from physical pain since my wounds were completely healed, but from the anguish of having to leave this little slice of paradise.

I eased the hopper into a slow crawl, and gently swerved away from the inquisitive nose of what looked like a twenty-foot armor plated hamster.

The Ascorbite looked over at me. He was a busted up mess. For some reason, the Pancreator decided that all other species would have to live with the consequences of their wounds for a long time. That's probably why they all take everything so seriously. Since my formerly mangled right arm was fine except for a little tenderness, I wondered how much it would cost me to find a sawbones who could patch up the Ascorbite. I pulled out the surgery kit and handed it to him.

"Here. Find something to plug those holes in your chest plate.

You're leaking on the upholstery."

He just looked at me.

"You no longer hear the Song," he said.

"Not now. Maybe later. It takes a lot out of me. And protecting your pea-brain from your buddy's spear totally wiped me out."

"I no longer hear the Song," he said ruefully, turning back to look out the cockpit window.

"Aw, cheer up," I said. "Hey, if you're a good little cricket, I may just let you take a toot on the magic Philosopher's Stone. That's got more song than you can handle!"

"Yes," he said. "More Song."

We drove in silence for awhile, watching the forest come alive with night.

So now I have this faithful Ascorbite companion. With some of the things I find myself saying, it'll be good to have someone to watch my back.

Surprisingly, Ven-keel is really not bad company. He believes absolutely everything I say. But he's not afraid to tell me when he thinks I'm wrong. Like he talked me out of raining death on New Pasha after I scammed our way in and got us patched up. But that's OK. Now that I've got the Stone, we've got bigger fish to fry. Like that private moon.

* * *

I no longer hear the Song. But now I know the Song is not all there is. Perhaps now I can find out what else there truly is.

The Eyes That Judge, The Hands That Heal

Richard Lee Byers

After lunch, Bishop Bloddic's square, fleshy face was often even ruddier than it had been before, while his breath smelled of vixenberry wine. This was one of those afternoons. With his drooping eyelids, the stout, black-robed ecclesiastic looked as if he'd rather nap than grant a subordinate an interview. Still, he hadn't canceled the appointment, one must at least thank the Pancreator for that. "Father Martinius," he said.

"Matthias, Your Eminence," the other cleric said diffidently.

"Matthias, of course, forgive me." Bloddic waved a plump, beringed hand at the chair in front of his imposing desk. "Sit down and tell me why you wanted to see me."

Inwardly, Matthias winced. He'd explained it all — well, not *all*, of course, but enough — in the petition he'd written, but Bloddic evidently hadn't bothered to read it. Matthias had never been very good at communicating face to face with his superiors, but now there was nothing for it but to start at the beginning.

"Uh, you may remember, Your Eminence, that you generously granted me one day a week away from my duties in the records office. To research the life of St. Saxo the Healer, who grew to manhood right here on Criticorum, and write the story of his youth."

Bloddic nodded. "I dimly recall that. You've been at it nearly a year, haven't you? You must be just about finished."

The younger man swallowed. "In one sense. I've learned all I can here, but my findings have inspired me. I'd like to retrace Saxo's wanderings among the stars, discover all there is to know about him — you'd be appalled at how much time has obscured — and write a definitive hagiography. I'm sure that the work will buttress the faith of anyone who reads it."

The bishop blinked. "Are you serious?"

"Yes." Matthias hesitated. He hadn't wanted to volunteer any more, but he could tell that if he didn't, Bloddic was going to dismiss his request out of hand. "In addition to simple information, I hope to find Saxo's final resting place, the site of which is presently unknown. That would enable us to bring his bones home to lie in state in the cathedral. Very possibly to work miracles, like the cloak of St. Hombor on Shaprut, the helm of St. Mantius on Tethys, or the skull of St. Kharmian on Aragon. Think how glorious that would be! Pilgrims would flock to view the relics, and — forgive me if I'm being crass, but you yourself always say that the Church must mind its finances if it's to minister properly to its parishioners — fill our coffers with offerings in the process."

Bloddic smiled indulgently. "That would be grand. *If* you could actually locate the blessed healer's remains. But really, what are the chances after all these centuries?"

"There's at least *some* chance, Your Eminence. You'd be surprised at what I've learned already." As soon as the words were out of his mouth, he wanted to take them back.

But Bloddic didn't ask for details. He just said, "No doubt. So why not be satisfied with those discoveries? Go ahead and write the paper you originally intended. I'm sure someone will publish it in one scholarly journal or another."

"With all due respect, I'd hate to suspend my research now, when there's so much more I might attempt. Even if I never find the relics or any more information of consequence, Questing is one of the major virtues, isn't it?"

Bloddic eyed him sardonically. "You feel ready to emulate Paulus the Traveler, do you?" It was obvious that he regarded Matthias as a prissy, scrawny mouse of a man, the last person who had any business embarking on an adventure across the Known Worlds. "I wonder why, whenever a fellow decides to dedicate himself heart and soul to one of the virtues, it's always one of the *glamorous* ones like Questing or Justice, and never Humility or Discipline. I'm sorry, Father, but you're needed here, performing your regular duties, and even if you weren't, it's a question of money."

"I don't expect to travel in luxury, Your Eminence. All I need is a letter of introduction from you that will allow me to catch a ride on any Church transport that's headed in a useful direction, beg a piece of bread at any seminary or abbey I find along the way, and persuade curators to open their libraries to me."

"And if you employed such, sooner or later one of your benefactors would send the diocese a bill."

"But — "

"You've already heard my answer, and it's no. I look forward to reading your treatise."

* * *

By midnight, the great cathedral complex was dark and silent. The residents had celebrated the final mass of the day, and now nearly everyone had retired. As, his armpits clammy with sweat, Matthias advanced down the corridor, he fought the impulse to hunch his shoulders and *skulk*. The pale marble statues in their niches seemed to frown at him reprovingly.

He reached the office of Bloddic's secretary without encountering any roaming sentries or other nocturnal wanderers. He glanced around a final time, making absolutely sure no prying eyes were watching, then tried to slip one of his pilfered keys into the keyhole. His hand shook, tap-tap-tapping the instrument against the lock before he finally managed to insert it. In the stillness, the clinking seemed horribly loud.

But no one came to investigate, and once he was inside, he found everything he needed sitting out in plain view on the secretary's untidy desk. One of Bloddic's lesser seals, along with a stack of his stationery. If Matthias hadn't known better, he might almost have suspected that his fellow functionary knew all about his plans and had decided to help him.

He took the top sheet of illuminated parchment and dipped one of the secretary's carefully sharpened quills in the inkwell. Like everyone else in the records office, he'd learned to forge Bloddic's handwriting. It was far less trouble to append the great man's signature oneself than to send back a document that arrived without it. He lifted the pen, then faltered, quivering in the grip of a fresh spasm of anxiety.

He'd first heard the legends of St. Saxo at his mother's knee, and instantly come to idolize the holy man whose wise eyes could discern the balance of good and evil in every soul and whose puissant hands could cleanse a planet of plague or exorcise a demon. He supposed that he'd entered the Church in emulation of him, and when he'd set out to unearth the facts of his youth, his sole purpose had been to glorify him.

But that was before he'd learned of the gruesome accident that had befallen Saxo in his eighteenth year, when he was only an unskilled laborer toiling in the featherstone mines. The accident and its consequences. That was before he hit on the idea.

At first it had seemed such an outrageous notion that he'd laughed and tried to put it out of his mind. Yet in the months that followed, it stubbornly refused to fade away. Instead, it grew ever more plausible and persuasive, until it finally led him here.

Here, where he felt as if he were about to step off a precipice. Did he truly mean to betray the trust his superiors had placed in him? Forsake the only life he'd ever known?

Yes, he thought suddenly, scowling, furious at his own timidity, yes, by the Holy Flame, he did. Because he was a priest who'd never felt the presence of God or saved a soul, and if he balked now, that was all he'd *ever* be.

He wrote the necessary words and signed them with Bloddic's name, complete with the flourish the bishop employed when he was feeling expansive. That accomplished, he melted some red wax with a spidery-looking little mechanism that some Charioteer had likely imported from off-world, then affixed the seal to his handiwork. With any luck, given his inconsequential role in the cathedral hierarchy, penning and filing documents that no one ever consulted again, he'd be safely off-world himself before anyone missed him.

* * *

The foliage was the color of rust, and if Matthias stared at it for a time, he could see it moving ever so slightly, as if combing some sort of sustenance from the air. The black and yellow birds — if that was the appropriate name for them — had simian heads and a chattering cry to match. Something was tingeing the atmosphere with a spicy aroma the like of which the priest had never smelled before. Even the twilight sky was different — pale, with a greenish cast, and *two* moons floating in the east.

Matthias had known that Aylon would be an entirely new world, but he hadn't realized what that truly meant. When he'd stepped off the shuttle onto the town common, a barrage of exotic impressions instantly overwhelmed him. He felt faint, and his stomach churned. He desperately wanted to close his eyes and shut everything out.

But gradually, and to his astonishment, his malaise gave way to wonder. Perhaps it was something akin to the pleasure an innocent baby felt, when everything that caught the eye was a mystery and a marvel. At any rate, Matthias could gladly have spent the evening just drifting around the field, drinking in every sensation that came his way.

But idle gawking wouldn't bring him any closer to the object of his search. Scowling, telling himself that the unfamiliar plants were merely plants, the animals, animals, and the townsfolk, townsfolk, he struggled to crush out his wanton curiosity. Then, his manner sober as befitted a seeker on a holy quest, he set out to find the city archives.

* * *

The chronicle was profusely illustrated. The figures were stiff and uncouth, and the artist hadn't even attempted anything resembling perspective. But the subject matter — St. Saxo taming the river dragon, or rebuking the Usurper of Pordago, his golden eyes and alabaster hands aglow with holy light — inspired reverence even so.

Unfortunately, the text, an archaic version of the thick local dialect, rendered in minute characters possessing a bewildering array of long, looping serifs, was brutally difficult to read. At last even Matthias felt compelled to rest his aching eyes.

He turned toward the tower's Byzantine window, which generally afforded nothing more than a view of Istakhr's yellowish sky. Aylon had proved to be a false lead, but clues led him to this world. Today, however, several pillars of dark smoke scarred the firmament. Indeed, now that he'd seen them, he realized he could smell them as well, a nasty, burnt-meat stench. He wondered what was going on.

A gangling, freckled adolescent boy, clad in the powder-blue cassock that was the uniform of a novice hereabouts, appeared in the doorway, a tray bearing Matthias's midday meal — a tumbler of crimson fruit juice, a crusty roll, and a bowl of steaming, fragrant vegetable soup — cradled in his hands. The youth had been waiting on the visitor for weeks, and Matthias had gradually taken notice of him in a perfunctory sort of way. Now he observed the dark circles that had appeared under the novice's eyes, and the grim set of his mouth.

"Is something amiss?" Matthias asked. He gestured toward the window. "All that smoke..."

For an instant the boy peered at him as if he were a simpleton, then composed his features into a more respectful expression. "The duchy's in the grip of an epidemic, Father. We call it the clawing sickness, because of the way the afflicted tear at themselves, or anyone who tries to stop them. The smoke is from the pyres. We burn the dead to keep the disease from spreading, though it doesn't seem to be doing any good." He hesitated. "The sickness reached the capital nearly a week ago. You must have heard someone talking about it."

Feeling vaguely ashamed, Matthias shook his head. "No. I spend so much of my time alone up here... Everyone has been very hospitable to me. I'm sorry about your troubles."

The novice frowned. "Father, please forgive me if I'm speaking out of turn. But if you're *truly* sorry, if you want to help, well, you'd be more than welcome to pitch in."

Matthias sighed. "You have no idea how much I wish I could. But I'm not a physician nor even a trained nurse."

"There are plenty of other tasks that need doing. Feed the sick. Clean them. Prevent them from hurting themselves. Pray with them, hear their confessions, and give them last rites. Haul the bodies to the fire. Everyone else is helping, from us novices right up to the abbot himself."

"As I said, I wish I could. But my bishop sent me here to perform *this* task." He waved his hand at the stacks of codices and scrolls scattered about the room. "It's a sacred trust. I'm sure your abbot understands."

"Yes, Father," replied the novice in a flat, uninflected tone. "If you say so. Please excuse me." He set down the tray, turned, and strode away.

For a moment Matthias wanted to run after him and say that he'd help after all. But he held back because he knew that he'd told the boy the truth. He had nothing to contribute. He wouldn't even be able to comfort the dying, any more than he'd ever known what to say to any of his parishioners during the awkward, frustrating days when he'd striven to be a *real* priest, before his superiors took pity on him and reassigned him to the records office.

Surely the Pancreator wanted him to keep faith with his quest so that he could one day do some *real* good. Frowning, he returned to his studies.

* * *

The subterranean fortress-city was full of images of St. Saxo, from the crude cartoon daubed on the sign of the Cleansing Hands, the barony's most notorious tavern-cum-brothel, to the towering basalt statue in Sangreal Plaza, beneath whose pitying gaze the young aristocrats gathered every evening to practice their fencing, or, often enough, to duel in earnest.

Matthias's devotion to the legendary healer had never wavered, but during the three years he'd spent on Malignatius entombed here underground, he'd begun to hate the sight of the icons all the same. Because they seemed to be mocking him. Gibing that he'd lost the trail and would never pick it up again.

But he'd never permitted them to drive him to despair, and now they had no more power to trouble him. Because, after flattering and cajoling his way into a senile old knight's home to inspect a collection of moldering commemorative paintings, he'd finally determined that, local tradition notwithstanding, Saxo wasn't buried on this world after all. He'd arguably worked his greatest miracles here, but then he'd moved on. Matthias even had a good idea of where.

Grinning like a fool, he barged through the door of the boarding house, where, cramped for dormitory space, the local diocese had procured him lodgings. After the first six months they'd set him to work copying manuscripts to earn his keep as well, but he forgave them for squandering his time. He could forgive anybody anything, now that he was finally in motion again.

He bounded up the stairs and into his tiny room, lit, like the rest of the establishment, by masses of spongy phosphorescent fungus flourishing in small, spherical vivaria. He yanked open the big drawer set in the wall, snatched his shabby carpet bag from beneath his cot, and began to stuff his meager possessions inside.

As soon as he buckled the satchel shut, he was off again, plunging recklessly back down the steps. The shuttle ascended to the spaceport floating in geosynchronous orbit above the city every night at nine o'clock. If he hurried, he could make it. He was halfway to the door when someone gasped.

Startled, he turned. Her green eyes wide, a smutch of black mushroom flour on her cheek and an apron tied around her ample waist, Goodwife Hlint, his landlady, stood gaping in the doorway to the kitchen. "What are you doing?" she asked at last.

He beamed at her. "It's finally time for me to move on."

"You mean, right now?" the widow quavered. "Just like that?"

"Yes. So, if you'll excuse me — " Belatedly, he registered her stricken expression.

He supposed he knew why she was dismayed. She was a gentle, sentimental soul. That was probably the reason she'd always taken such good care of him, and done her clumsy, uncomprehending best to lift his spirits whenever he felt discouraged. At any rate, she deserved a courteous leave-taking, and so, although he was all but twitching with impatience to be gone, he forced himself to tarry a moment longer.

"I'm sorry," he said. "I didn't mean to be rude, running off without a word of good-bye."

"It's all right," she replied, like a child denying that her scrapes and bruises stung. "It's just that all my other boarders come and go before I've even had a chance to get to know them. But you've stayed so long that I was starting to think you'd *always* be here."

Perplexed, he cocked his head. "But I always said I'd be departing one day."

"I *know* that," she said, a tinge of irritation in her voice. He couldn't tell if she was vexed with him or herself. "I — never mind." She forced a smile. "Will you stay for one more meal? Supper's nearly ready. It's sourcrab in wine sauce, and those chocolate tarts you like."

"I can't," he said. "I mustn't miss the transport. Thank you for everything." He awkwardly took her hand for an instant, then turned and headed for the street, his pace quickening with every stride.

As the door closed behind him, he heard a choked, broken sound, but he was in too much of a hurry to think about it until he was seated aboard the shuttle, watching the dark, frozen surface of the planet fall away beneath him. Then he wondered if Goodwife Hlint had sobbed.

* * *

The fat, slovenly man with the greasy black curls studied Matthias's frayed, faded forgery, mouthing the words as he ran his finger along the lines of script. Even from across the dusty desk, the traveler could smell the sour, unwashed stink of him. Like everyone else in this untamed frontier province, the big man wore a side arm, in this case a bone-handled hunting knife, while a gnarled cane which looked as if it could double nicely as a backup weapon leaned against the gray stone wall behind him. Matthias very much doubted that the margrave had appointed the fellow librarian because he possessed any aptitude or enthusiasm for the work. Rather, the position was a sinecure for an injured retainer whose lameness precluded more strenuous labor.

The fat man finally looked up. "*What* is it that you want?"

"Just what the bishop's letter says," Matthias replied patiently. "I'm researching the life of St. Saxo. My studies indicate that after he performed the deeds for which we revere him, he retired to this very continent. To live out his last years anonymously, in solitary contemplation. I want to consult your archives to see if anyone has left us any account of the holy man's hermitage."

The librarian snorted. "Sounds stupid to me."

Matthias did his best to mask a pang of irritation. "You may be right, but it's still a legitimate request. You see my credentials." He waved his hand at the letter.

"Yeah, a dirty rag of a note twenty years old."

"Sometimes a quest takes a long time."

The librarian smirked. "A 'quest,' is it? Well, aren't you the grand and glorious knight errant, in your threadbare coat and worn-out cardboard shoes."

"Forgive me. I wasn't trying to give myself airs. Of course, I'm only a simple priest, humbly begging your help to complete the errand my bishop gave me."

"After all this time, are you sure that this Bloddic of yours is even still alive? Even if he is, his planet is way the hell on the other side of the Empire. I doubt that my master has ever even heard of him, let alone owes him any favors."

"Still, isn't your lord a faithful son of the Church?"

The librarian chuckled. "I don't know how it is where you come from, but here on Cadavus, the grandees of House Decados have been known to butt heads with the Church, and the margrave has done more butting than most."

Matthias took a deep breath. "Be that as it may, it isn't as if my studies will do any harm, or even put anyone to any inconvenience."

"Oh, I don't know if we can be sure of that. These old books and papers can fall apart at a touch. It might be irresponsible of me to let you read them, unless you can convince me that it's very, *very* important to you. So I can rest easy, secure in the knowledge that you'll handle them with the proper care and respect."

Matthias sighed. "In other words, you want a bribe. Tell me how much. I'll go earn the money and come back another day." An educated man could always find work, writing out letters, deeds, wills, betrothal contracts, and other documents for the illiterate.

But the librarian shook his head. "I don't want money. There's not much to spend it on in this grubby little garrison town. To tell you the truth, my problem is that I have trouble finding the proper sort of companionship." He screwed up his lumpish face in a wink. "But I'm told that heavy men are considered comely in some parts of the galaxy. Maybe it's that way on your planet."

Matthias gaped at the other man. "You can't be serious."

The librarian smirked. "Yep."

"But I'm not that way! I'm not drawn to other men, and even if I were, I'm a priest! My vows..."

"Oh, I don't mind about any of that. But if you do, if it's too much to ask, then walk away. What the hell. You'll only be pissing away the last twenty years of your life."

"This... this is unconscionable! What if I report your malfeasance to the margrave?"

"Try if you like. Nobody cares what happens down here in this filthy cellar, just like nobody cares when a local boy takes advantage of some penniless stranger. Hell, priest or no, a shabby little tramp like you couldn't even get in to see the margrave, and even if you did, it would just be your word against mine. So what's it going to be, Father Quester? Will you minister to a poor soul in need of comfort, or spurn me the way the proud merchant spurned St. Maya?"

Matthias thought wildly of beating the curator into submission, but knew that the notion was absurd. Lame or not, the other man was bigger, younger, armed, and no doubt an experienced brawler. Nor was there any hope of slipping into the archives night after night until his researches were finished, not when the castle was well patrolled for fear of an incursion by the local indigenes.

If only there were another library or comparable repository of knowledge on the continent, somewhere else Matthias could go to conduct his investigations! But there wasn't. In this uncivilized place, with its bloody, chaotic history, he was fortunate to find any records at all.

And foul creature though he was, the librarian was right. Matthias had traveled too far and too long to abandon his mission now, even to escape this degradation. He tried to speak his acquiescence, but couldn't force the words out. At last he managed to give a jerky nod.

While it was happening, while he was cringing and shuddering under the librarian's gloating gaze and brutish pawing, he tried to lose himself in thoughts of St. Saxo, whose eyes and hands had had their own overwhelming power, but to exalt rather than repel. He prayed to the saint and the Pancreator that his sacrifice would not be in vain.

Nor was it. Two days later, poring over an architect's diary, he finally discovered the site of his idol's grave.

* * *

The cybersurgeon had set up shop in a nondescript little storefront facing an alley, with no sign outside to lure clientele. Such a lack of ostentation was probably prudent for a man practicing a trade that some people regarded as unholy. But the guildsman himself was a walking advertisement for his art, with a studded silvery appliance grafted to the right half of his hairless scalp, a pointed brazen ear, and a round black ocular mounted in the center of his forehead. Whirring and clicking, the lens telescoped in and out as he bent over the table to examine the relics.

Matthias looked on, holding his breath, his pulse beating in his neck. When he'd broken open the soggy, rotten remains of Saxo's coffin, he'd found his heart's desire. From the sockets of the crumbling skull stared a pair of golden eyes, and at the ends of the yellowed radii and ulnae lay a set of snow-white hands. The prosthetic devices the young saint-to-be had received after the mining accident maimed him.

If a chalice, a cloak, a fountain, or a scrap of bone could work miracles simply because they'd once been associated with a holy man, then imagine the power that ought to reside in Saxo's very organs, the sagacious eyes and gentle but mighty hands extolled in a hundred legends, which lay intact before him! If a pious fellow had them fitted to his own body, might he not become something very like a saint himself?

The exultation for which Matthias had waited so long lasted perhaps a minute, wilting abruptly when he remembered that, for all he knew, the organs might *not* be intact. They looked all right to him, but he was scarcely knowledgeable about such things. It was entirely possible that time and the damp earth had corrupted their inner mechanisms.

Only a technician could tell him, or do what was necessary if the prostheses would still work. Matthias briefly considered turning to the Church for aid. But he was only a lowly priest who'd deserted his post, and even considered simply as an ordinary relic, his discovery was valuable. It was all too likely that some ambitious oblate or magister would confiscate it for himself.

Thus, Matthias had no choice but to go back to work until he'd earned enough to pay a cybersurgeon's hefty fee. It had taken him a year and a half, during which he'd lived in constant fear that some thief would steal the prostheses. And now at last he was about to discover if his striving and fretting had been to any purpose.

The ocular contracting to lie almost flat against his brow, the guildsman straightened up. "They're still functional," he said in a crisp baritone voice. "They're old, maybe even Second Republic. Built to last, not like the junk we make nowadays. I'll give you twelve hundred firebirds for the lot. To be candid, it's less than they're worth, but I doubt that you'll do better on this rock."

"I don't want to sell them. I want them attached to me. Immediately, if possible. I've brought enough to pay."

The cybersurgeon peered at Matthias. Humming and chattering, the black ocular extended itself again. "You don't seem to be infirm," the doctor said after a time. "You do understand that these devices are basic prostheses, don't you? They won't give you any superhuman capabilities, just make your grip a trifle stronger and sharpen your middle-aged vision a hair." He smiled wryly. "There are those who would say that's scant compensation for becoming an abomination."

"I have my reasons," said Matthias, proffering his money. "Will you help me or not?"

The cybersurgeon accepted the Reeves scrip, examined it for signs of forgery, and slipped it in his pocket. "Would you prefer a local or a general? I recommend the latter. It wouldn't be all that pleasant staying awake, knowing that I was carving pieces of you away, especially when you saw the scalpel coming down at your eyes."

"Can you do it without any anesthetic at all?" Matthias asked. He certainly hadn't planned to propose such a thing, but as soon as he heard the words come out of his mouth, he knew that it was the right choice. The operation would be the beginning of his new life. He should experience it as fully as a mother and infant experienced the trauma of birth.

The cybersurgeon stared at him as if he were mad. "I *could* just paralyze you and leave your sensorium alone. But my god, what are you, a masochist? Even if you are, I guarantee you, the experience will be considerably more extreme than any whipping or — "

"I understand. It doesn't matter."

The cybersurgeon grimaced. "Very well. But afterwards, remember that I warned you. Take off your shirt, and I'll prepare the instruments."

The pain *was* excruciating. Matthias fought his natural instinct to flinch away from it, even if only within the confines of his own mind. Rather, he tried to savor every moment, and finally, at the heart of the agony, he found something else. A power that swept him up and up into ecstasy, and then away into darkness.

* * *

When Matthias woke, the cybersurgeon was bending over him. "You finally passed out," the doctor said. "Your body has more sense than you do. How do you feel? Any discomfort?"

"No," Matthias said.

"There shouldn't be any more." He eyed his patient sourly. "Unless you're going to insist that I extract the anesthetic chips."

"No. This is fine." Matthias hesitated. "Then... the procedure's over? I really have them?"

"Look for yourself. You can move now. In fact, you can get up whenever you like."

Eager yet frightened, Matthias lifted his hands in front of his face. His own sallow, aging skin with its sprinkling of hairs and blemishes gave way to the smooth whiteness of the prostheses just above the wrists. He willed the fingers to wiggle, and they did. He clasped the hands together and felt them lock. The doctor looked on with the bored, indulgent air of one who had witnessed such tentative experiments countless times before.

Matthias strained to sense the holy power supposedly sleeping in the artificial extremities. He couldn't. The hands just felt like hands. He sternly commanded himself to have faith and persevere, yet after a minute he began to tremble at the suspicion that all the struggle and hardship of the last twenty years had been for nothing.

"Something wrong?" the cybersurgeon asked, his ocular ticking as it extended. Ignoring him, Matthias scrambled off the operating table and over to a mirror suspended on the wall.

Luminous golden eyes, the whites absolutely clear, peered from his pinched, haggard face. He leaned close to the glass, staring intently, trying to discern something beyond the simple strangeness of them. He felt a whimper building in his chest.

Then, sudden and overwhelming as a lightning strike, he *saw*. Yet his attention didn't focus on the artificial eyes. It locked on the truth etched in the wrinkled, sagging flesh surrounding them.

He saw meekness, dedication, and a desire to do good, but those virtues were scarcely more than a shell. A mask for hypocrisy, coward-ice, greed, and self-absorption. He was gazing at a man who'd disdained every blessing and shirked every task the Pancreator had set along his path. Who truly *had* wasted his life, whether the prostheses had the power to work miracles or no.

His grief and self-loathing made him sob and drove him to his knees. As if of their own volition, his new hands rose and pressed against his temples. Fire blazed through his head, burning him clean. For a moment the process was as terrifying as it was painful, and then the anguish yielded to a perfect stillness.

"Are you all right?" said a baritone voice. "Tell me where it hurts."

The kneeling man looked around. A fellow in a green, bloodstained gown, a silvery helmet-like appliance grafted to his scalp and an ocular protruding from his forehead, was crouching over him. The kneeling man had no idea who this stranger was, but he could tell that the fellow was genuinely alarmed on his behalf. Touched, he jumped up and hugged his well-wisher.

"Nothing hurts," he said. "I feel wonderful. But God bless you for your concern."

The bloody man awkwardly freed himself from his embrace, stepped back, and looked him over, the ocular sliding in and out. "Well, as I told you before, everything *seems* fine," he said a bit dubiously. "I guess you simply felt peculiar for a moment? As if you might not be the same person anymore?"

The man who'd just risen had no idea what his companion was talking about, but he sensed that it wasn't important anyway, so he simply smiled and shrugged.

"That happens once in a while," the man in the bloody gown continued. "If you're feeling up to it, we do have one more matter to discuss. For a small additional fee, I can freeze and store what I removed. In case you decide you aren't happy with what I put on."

"No need," said the other man, still not truly comprehending. "I'm very happy." A shaft of warm yellow light suddenly fell through the grimy window. He realized that the sun must have just come out from behind a cloud, and the thought thrilled him. "I'd like to go outside now, but I hope we'll meet again. Good-bye." He started for the door.

"What about your shirt and satchel?" asked the man with the eyepiece.

The other man almost turned back around, but then two little boys and their pet collie ran past the window, looking so joyful and full of life that the sight tugged him irresistibly on. "You can keep them," he said.

He wandered through narrow, cobbled streets, delighting in the music of people's voices, the intricately braided trunks and branches of the azure trees and shrubs, and even the acrid smell of the bleating scarlet animals the drovers were taking to market. Only gradually did it occur to him that he didn't know the name of this town, or his own name for that matter, and even then the realization seemed utterly unimportant. After a time he noticed a wheezing old fellow who appeared to be having difficulty unloading barrels from a cart, and headed over to offer him his help.

Dark Places

James A. Moore

"There really are demons, Joshua. I know that now."

Those were the words I found on the paper Arden Meloush pinned to his chest, just before he killed himself. There are many types of darkness, just as surely as the suns are fading. I know, because I recently encountered the worst of it.

There is a place on Byzantium Secundus that few people like to speak of, a place that does what it can to heal the darkness of the mind and, in some cases, fill the void of the soul. True, the Church is supposed to handle matters of the soul, but there are times when even the most dedicated priests must admit defeat. In these cases, the choice is between death and the Oubliette. Most people don't quite know which is worse. In death, at least, there is the hope of the Empyrean if you've done well. With the Mind Physicks of the Oubliette, the end result tends towards Gehenne more often than not.

The tower of the Oubliette on Byzantium Secundus is in one of the finer parts of the capital city. Unlike many offices for this group of specialists, most of the customers sent here to have their minds healed come from wealthy families. Sometimes, the stress involved in the political arena is too great. Other times, the right amount of money can purchase any secret you want from the mind of one brought in, and can insure that the information remains confidential.

The Oubliette is seen as a necessary evil. Ever since the suns began to fade the number of people with "fragile minds" has grown. The dwindling light is seen as a portent of evil, a sign that we have sinned too much. It is not for me to say if the doomsayers are wrong in their assumptions. Most only believe the situation will get worse, and I'm beginning to agree with the masses.

It's fair to say that most of the Mind Physicks are less-than-ethical in their actions. Far too many are still trying to understand the workings of the psyche, and are glad to gain their knowledge in any way they can. But there are exceptions, albeit only a few, who truly wish to heal those who have surrendered their sanity.

Arden Meloush was one of those rarities. His record for actually bringing his patients back to a semblance of sanity was far greater than the average. He used few chemicals to get his desired effects; instead, he used his mind and his words to find the secrets hidden in the darkest recesses of his patients' minds, to find the thoughts that hid themselves from the light of reason.

I met Arden years ago, when we were both journeymen with the Charioteers. I continued on with the guild, but as for my friend, he felt the need to explore the darker places, areas that made the void between the stars seem almost clear in comparison. Despite our differences in employment, and my need to travel almost constantly, we managed to stay in contact and became good friends over the years. Like me, Arden believed in the Pancreator in a vague way, as an entity that must surely exist, but not necessarily one that cares about the lives of mere mortals.

Meloush was a true healer. At least, until he met Nathaniel Hawkwood. Hawkwood was an important client, to say the least. As a second cousin of the Emperor, his care was not only lucrative, it was likely a matter of life and death for the Mind Physick who took on his case. Arden Meloush was the only one even willing to deal with the man.

But I suppose a little background information is necessary. Nathaniel Hawkwood was not a favored member of his family. He was, in fact, considered an embarrassment by many in his noble house. Where most royals preferred to work within the house, taking whatever tasks were assigned them, Nathaniel chose to pretend his family did not exist. He was still young, and his rebellion was acceptable within reason. After all, there were few nobles who hadn't felt the need to leave the nest for a time — even Emperor Alexius is reputed to have been something of a rebel in his day.

But Nathaniel took his freedom from the house to a level few had in recent years. He disappeared for a while, and the family put out offers of reward without really worrying. Nathaniel was known for such vanishing acts, but he seldom got into much trouble while he was away. His tendency to make up false names and avoid the noble courts covered up most public embarrassments.

Then he joined the Muster. No one knew he'd signed on with the Slavers guild, not even the Slavers, if their claims of ignorance are true. He had money and connections to the more illicit trades, people who could have forged false identity papers for him. There's no reason to believe the Muster would have risked the wrath of the Emperor for one more member, especially not for a member with no marketable skills aside from a fast sword hand and a good aim with a blaster.

From what little I've been able to discover, the young noble was ambitious and ruthless. In other words, he was perfect for the Slavers. It takes a certain lack of ethics to be a Slaver. Nathaniel apparently had little trouble with the notion of stealing or buying one person to sell to another. He was also rather well known for sampling the wares on long journeys. Not precisely the sort of man who confessed his sins to the Church, I suspect.

So I suppose it was almost inevitable he would end up with the Oubliette, but I don't think the circumstances were exactly what anyone could have predicted.

As I stated previously, I am a star pilot for the Charioteers. Not a prestigious job, but one I've always loved. There are mysteries waiting to be discovered beyond the Known Worlds. Some are likely best left alone, to be sure, but where there is discovery, there is always risk. And I have always longed to discover new things, to see wonders that few have ever seen. Unlike many of the merchants within our guild, I feel no need to dress outlandishly, though I'll confess to a few odd pieces of clothing I've picked up along the way.

The *Whereabout* was on her way back from a journey to that most despicable of places, the planet Stigmata, where we had delivered more weapons to the Muster soldiers unfortunate enough to fight the Symbiots. We took a few lucky souls back with us, soldiers able to be leaving the wretched place, destined for a chance at recovery from all they'd seen. Or to put that as eloquently as Captain Astor-Smythe did: "We've got a load of broken brains going back to Byzantium Secundus, and then we got ten days of freedom." Ten days on the Throne World, and all of them spent doing as we pleased.

Astor-Smythe is a lewd, vulgar man with too many bad habits to list. He is responsible for many things, including showing me the joys of Sathra — that moment of eternity when the ship is traveling between jumpgates in a transdimensional space we will likely never understand — and stopping me from getting addicted to the same sensation. "Best to save it for special celebrations, Joshua. Too much of a grand thing is unhealthy for the mind." He is also my direct superior and one of the best pilots you could ever hope for. Between the two of us, we have the jumpkeys to nearly every single known jumpgate. We make a great deal of money, and we're not afraid to use it.

So we were relaxed, and we were content. The jumpgate was in sight of the *Whereabout* and we would soon be out of this hell system and on our way to women, fresh food and a dozen glasses of fine wine.

Have you ever seen a jumpgate? I don't mean an illustration, or even a magic lantern's moving image. I mean the real thing. I have seen them hundreds of times, most of the ones we know of, and still they take my breath away. These massive rings, these monolithic sculptures floating in the darkness, normally at the very edge of a star system, are simply too large to easily comprehend. That anyone, *any thing*, could have built so massive a device still boggles my mind. The images carved onto the jumpgates, the faces both angelic and demonic, the odd runes that even to this day no one has deciphered, are a wonder in and of themselves, especially when you consider just how large the visages are. A hundred times over the size of any living human, and flawless despite their antiquity.

The *Whereabout* is a substantial ship, but nearly a hundred more of the same size could pass through one of the jumpgates along with her and still there would be room for more. Astor-Smythe once told me he guessed it would take a century of effort using the best mining equipment to carve one of the devices from a sizable moon... assuming you could find a moon large enough. Even then, it wouldn't be anything but a sculpture, not like the true thing. To think that someone built these treasures and then simply abandoned them is always something of a mystery to me. I have never understood what could have gone through the minds of the Anunnaki that would make them leave these wonders for others to find. But I'm grateful to them.

Just before we began the jump sequence, Astor-Smythe eased back on the propulsion and turned the ship slightly off course. We drifted away from the gate and moved toward the great emptiness beyond it.

"What are you doing?" I asked him, a bemused grin on my face. He was known for pulling stunts just as strange as this, for no particular reason. Perhaps because he had experienced Sathra many more times than I had, or perhaps because he was simply stopping to appreciate the beauty of the stars, faded and dimmed or not.

The captain looked back at me, and the brooding set of his thick brows over the long, hawkish nose let me know that this was no jest. "Look to starboard, past the brightest star, and tell me what you see."

I stared hard, looking past the light of the star and saw nothing. I was about to make a comment to that effect when a hint of motion caught my eye. Everything in the heavens is constantly in motion. No star remains still, nor do the planets around them. But there is very little in the great vastness of the void that moves fast enough for the naked eye to see. Moreover, this object moved against the gentle pull of the orbiting planets behind us, in the opposite direction. Most people, myself included, would have never noticed it. Astor-Smythe is not most people.

Before he could make the command, I did exactly what I knew he would want me to. I went to the *Whereabout's* think machine and commenced trying to discover what the object might be. If the ship's sensors could detect anything of worth, we would most certainly take a little extra time. The Scravers Guild might be the best at finding odd treasures, but we weren't foolish enough to let one slip by if there was a chance.

It took only a few moments to discover that what was floating in the distance was Urthish in origin. But the true surprise was its age: a lifepod from the time of the Second Republic. Even if it were empty, the technology aboard that vessel was worth a fortune. What a find!

I know what you're thinking, and you're right to think it. Go off the beaten path on a quest, in the territories near Stigmata? Madness! Even foregoing the risks that the Symbiots might have planted another trap, the Emperor, the Church and the guilds were all in agreement that the area was simply too dangerous. They had patrol ships in the area at all times, waiting for the chance to destroy anything drifting from forbidden territories. The dangers of infection are simply too great for anyone sane to consider, and for those foolish enough to go against their own common sense, the Imperial Fleet was waiting to eliminate the opportunities.

But Astor-Smythe was enthralled, mesmerized by the idea of investigating our discovery, and so was I. It never really crossed my mind — or his, I suspect — to worry about the legalities and the risks. As we pulled up alongside the small craft, I put on my vacuum suit and exited the ship in record time. Before I left, several of our "guests" for the return trip asked what the delay was. The captain made up excuses, said that the engines weren't functioning properly, and that I had to investigate. The arguments were continuing to mount when I finally stepped into the void.

Moving through the vacuum of space is often risky, but it is also something I love. The feel of the suit against my body, the free floating dance with the edge of eternity... words can never describe that sensation, anymore than they can adequately explain Sathra. I managed to connect towlines to our treasure — we couldn't risk firing grapple guns at such a prize — and got back onto the *Whereabout* without event.

After towing the pod into the cargo bay, and then replenishing the atmosphere, Astor-Smythe joined me in a quick examination of our find. He paused only once, to explain to one of our five passengers that complaints about the delay would only result in a faster meeting with the Pancreator. The man took the hint and went back to his quarters.

Perhaps matters would have occurred differently on a ship larger than the *Whereabout*, but we only had a two-man crew — Astor-Smith and me. Most of the vessel's space was used for cargo or carrying passengers. We didn't need anyone but ourselves to manage the freighter. I've found myself wondering again and again if the entire matter might have been avoided if only we'd had one rational person on the crew. I don't mean to say that I'm irrational by nature, but to have overlooked the rules without a second thought must mean that I was not behaving normally when we found the lifepod and, as I've said before, Astor-Smythe was not the most conservative of souls.

And so, for want of an extra crewman, our lives were changed forever.

The name on the side of the small vessel was pitted and scarred from its time in the void. It didn't take long to open the hatch. Inside the ancient relic we found three things: an ancient think machine, a gem the likes of which I had never seen before, and Nathaniel Hawkwood. The think machine made no noise. The odd crystal glittered blackly from facets unlike any I had ever seen. As I gazed at it, Nathaniel Hawkwood rose from the interior of his near-coffin with a scream of absolute terror, and then fell unconscious.

He was dehydrated and near starvation. We did what we could to tend to him, sealed the holding bay, and placed our unexpected guest in a room near the bridge. Astor-Smythe had me pilot us home while he tended to the needs of a man he'd never met.

Throughout the journey to Byzantium Secundus, we barely managed to get any words from our new arrival, but he was hardly silent. He screamed sometimes until we were certain his throat would explode from the pressure. Other times, he simply rocked back and forth on his cot, moaning or crying softly. Throughout the journey, Astor-Smythe doctored him; I think he recognized the missing member of House Hawkwood, despite the Muster insignia printed on his clothes.

At least Hawkwood ate, though that seemed all he was capable of doing for himself. Astor-Smythe had to clean him regularly, as he would soil himself without ever noticing. By the time we were nearing Byzantium Secundus, I had successfully communicated with representatives of the Hawkwoods. It was not easy to manage: There are always threats against the Emperor, and the ongoing feuds between the noble houses are well known to almost all of the star pilots. While I imagine that many of the tales I've heard about what the Decados are willing to do and how the al-Malik manage to carry off some of their odd stunts are purest fiction, if even half of what I've heard is true it's a wonder the empire has held together beyond the first fortnight.

The urgency of my requests was taken seriously, and we were given an escort of ships to protect our precious, if demented, cargo. Astor-Smythe allowed the Hawkwoods to claim their lost son, and accepted their generous reward for finding him, as well as the larger amount they paid us for silence. He did not, however, give them the lifepod. That he stored in place of our own lifepod. The Hawkwoods, disdainfully looking at the standard lifepod they were told was the means of their scion's salvation, gladly left it to us. Astor-Smith split both of these unexpected bonuses with me, as was his usual style. He is the captain of the *Whereabout*, but he is also a very fair man.

That should have been the last of the matter as far as I was concerned. It was not.

Three days after I started my short vacation, I met up with my old friend, Arden Meloush. Arden had changed little, save that his hair was thinner than before, he had more of a bald spot on the top of his head, and there was more gray in his mustache. In other words, he was not aging gracefully. Just the same, his smile was as broad as ever, and our mutual affection for the finer things in life had not altered in the least.

We met at his home, not far from the Oubliette tower where he worked. After his lovely wife, Alynna, had served up a meal the likes of which I would have killed for when in space, we sat on the balcony of his home, looking over the lower parts of the Imperial City, and enjoying the mild chill of the evening as the rain pattered down. Alynna sat nearby, reading from the scriptures. If there was ever any one thing I envied Arden for, it was the beauty and kind nature of his wife. Had he not been one of my best friends, I would likely have pursued her. Instead I contented myself with the whores I could find who bore her a passing resemblance.

We had caught up on the last few months, and both of us were enjoying the pleasant company, when he brought up the subject of his latest patient.

"I can't mention names, of course, but I've found a patient who might well be of interest to you." His deep voice was soft, not quite a whisper, but close. "The man claims he found a new jumproad, from Stigmata."

"Near Stigmata? What was he doing out that way?" I kept my cool, though even the prospect of a new jumproad was enough to make my heart flutter. New territories to be explored, new worlds to see for the first time. Such notions were like treasures to me.

"Well, he was working with the Muster. I suppose he was dropping supplies to the soldiers, or some such nonsense. Frankly, Joshua, I've never wanted to know too much about the wretched affairs of the Muster. The less you know, the better you can sleep. At any rate, he and his ship apparently found another jumpkey code, which in turn led them to a new, unexplored system, if his rantings are even remotely true."

"By the Pancreator! A Lost World off Stigmata? Do you have any idea why he's even alive? Fooling around near Stigmata is outlawed. By all rights, he and his crew should have been blasted into debris."

"Well, from what he said, he was picked up in a lifepod, and the fact that he's a noble might have something to do with it." Arden smiled, a rather bitter grimace, as if he'd just tasted something foul. "The young man is well connected in all the right places. The Emperor himself granted the man his freedom. I shouldn't be telling you any of this, Joshua. If you spread it around, my life will be very short indeed."

"Then why are you telling me, Arden? You and I have been friends for a long time, but is it wise to spread that sort of thing around?" I spoke then because I felt the need to say something, while my mind roiled with the risks Captain Astor-Smythe and I had taken, completely unawares. Some time later I listened to the records of my communications with the Hawkwoods, and no where in those recordings do I mention where we found Nathaniel. A good thing, too. Had I been that foolish, we'd have been vaporized by a dozen warships just on the off chance we'd been infected by Symbiots. They'd have been well within their rights.

Arden was speaking again. "I've only told you and Alynna. Both of you are people I can trust, and I only mention it to you because of your... passions for the unknown. You must promise never to tell where you learned of this."

"Naturally, Arden. You've nothing to fear there. I just wish I had more specific details about this new system, or even about the codes used to find it. A find like that is once in a lifetime."

Meloush sat in silence for several moments, his brows knitted together and his eyes staring out past the city below and towards the palace. He reached into his jacket and produced a pipe, which he slowly and methodically packed with the foulest blend of tobacco I've ever come across.

I was already lamenting the loss of my potential find when his words came to me past a plume of yellowish smoke. "You can have more details if you wish, Joshua. The boy is my patient. It's only been three days, but I've already begun to make progress."

"But won't you get yourself into trouble that way? Bringing in a stranger to listen to the ravings of a nobleman?"

"You are not a stranger. You are a Charioteer star pilot, and therefore could be of use to me in understanding my client's degraded mental faculties." I looked sharply at my old friend, wondering what he was thinking even as hope spread through my chest. With eyes half-lidded, and an unusually calm expression on his face, he lowered his left eyelid in a wink. "There are ways around almost any problem, Joshua. You should know that by now."

And so, after having enjoyed three days of relative peace and comfort, I made plans to join Meloush at his place of employment, eager to gain forbidden knowledge about a jumproute that I could never officially use. The stars beckoned to me and I had every intention of listening, regardless of the consequences.

The very next morning Meloush and I met outside of the Oubliette compound. Seen from a distance the building was elegant in its style, if more than a touch archaic. Up close, the building was still lovely, but had a rather disturbing atmosphere. I could almost feel the fear and pain suffered by the patients before I ever heard them.

When we were inside, Arden tried several times to assure me that the screams I heard were all a necessary part of the healing process. Perhaps he could have done a better job of it if he hadn't looked so unsettled himself. The halls of the building were labyrinthine, and seemed to follow no rhyme or reason. Even the doors along the various hallways made no sense. Some were larger than others, and many of them were made of wood while others were fashioned from steel. Through the numerous lower levels we walked, moving past doors which held back men who had lost themselves to their own personal demons and, perhaps, to the darkness between the stars. There were also strange markings on the walls, though I have no idea if these were notes placed by the healers of the Oubliette, or the demented writings of the patients. I found them discomforting.

On one occasion, we passed an open entranceway to one of the rooms, and I could see a man inside lying wrapped in a cocoon of fabric, his body restrained, while two men prodded him with large electrified rods. I was assured that this was a standard treatment, and while I believe Arden meant that, it seemed that the two Mind-Physicks meting out the shocks were enjoying themselves far too much. The poor man screamed with each shock, and I could see that there was something very wrong with his eyes, with their shape and their color, though I could not explain to you exactly what made them stand out.

At every door we passed, I heard the sounds of damnation, screams erupting from throats long since bloodied, the blasphemous words of souls lost to the Pancreator, and the whimpers of people who could no longer face the light of the day without cringing in fear. The noise only lessened as we rose through the levels of the sprawling madhouse and reached the areas reserved for paying clientele.

I'll confess I'd always thought the need for the Oubliette was grossly exaggerated, but having passed through the halls, I was grateful not only for the establishment, but for the locked cells the wretches were kept in. So I was rather surprised when the sounds faded to a tolerable level, and when the stench of human waste passed away to be replaced by perfumes. The stark, barren hallways with stains of dubious nature were gone, and in their place lush carpets spread, and paintings of all natures

covered the walls. One almost wondered if the nobility somehow managed to go insane with more dignity. There were, it seemed, several
advantages to wealth once one entered the Oubliette. Truth be told,
wealth seems to help in most cases.

At the far end of that last corridor, Arden Meloush reintroduced
me to Nathaniel Hawkwood. I almost didn't recognize him. The man
had been bathed and dressed in fine clothes, and had eaten more than
rations from a starship. His hair had been trimmed down from the
matted lengths it had achieved when he was in the ranks of the Muster.
All of these things were different, but they weren't what made recognizing him difficult. The true difference was that he was conscious, coher-
ent, and not screaming or crying.

Nathaniel Hawkwood looked human again, and almost sane. The
only part of him that hadn't changed was his eyes. They were dark,
handsome eyes, but looking into them was rather like staring into the
eyes of a well-crafted doll. Even when he looked directly at you and
spoke eloquently, his eyes betrayed nothing of what lay hidden behind
their glassy depths.

Arden, ever the proper gentleman, introduced us formally to each
other. If Hawkwood recognized me, he made no mention of it. I was
grateful for that. While I have always trusted Arden Meloush, I didn't
want anyone knowing the laws I'd broken while saving Nathaniel's life.
After several minutes of pleasantries, Arden got down to business.

"Nathaniel, I'd like you to tell Joshua what led up to your rescue
from a lifepod so far from civilized areas."

As soon as the words were out of Meloush's mouth, Nathaniel
Hawkwood twitched, as if he'd been unexpectedly slapped. His full lips
drew in on themselves, becoming a bitter slash, and his face seemed to
age by a dozen years. The only thing about him that didn't seem to
change noticeably were his eyes. Those eyes stared back, first at Arden
and then, very slowly, they came to rest on me. For just a moment, I
thought I saw recognition lurking in their depths, then that faint light
dwindled and I stared into a deep brown void again.

What animation had been in Hawkwood's voice was gone when he
spoke again. His mellow, aristocratic tones seemed hollow, the palest
imitation of what they should have been. When he talked, it was almost
like listening to a recording, as if every word had been rehearsed long in
advance.

"Captain Armides was in charge of our expedition. We'd just sold a batch of slaves to the Decados on Severus, and we were supposed to be heading to Istakhr. But there was a small matter of a discovery to take care of first. You see, the captain had found something while on the planet, a discovery that would have driven the Decados after us like the Inquisition after a heathen if they'd known about it. Severus is home to the Ascorbites, and there's always a bit of money to be made trading things with them. Some of their primitive art sells for a great deal, especially among nobles. They may be blood-sucking bugs, but they are talented artisans.

"I don't know what he traded with them, or how he managed to get such a prize from them, but Armides came back to the ship with a new jumpkey."

I imagine I must have half leaped from my seat when he said that, because for just a moment his face twitched into a smile, and he nodded at me.

"I rather thought that would catch your attention, Joshua. A new jumpkey, and one that was supposed to work on the Severus jumpgate. It didn't.

"By the time we reached Istakhr, the captain began to think that maybe he'd been cheated. The key failed to open any of the gates on our journey. Our next shipment, however, was bound for that nightmare world, Stigmata. We supposedly had slaves to carry, more meat for the front lines, or so we told everyone. We were actually bringing new weapons, new inventions to be tested against the Symbiots. We would have to lie, because the Church doesn't like new technology. If they saw the sort of firepower we'd be carrying, we risked being burned as heretics.

"The Church forgives many sins when you are up against the Symbiots. They allow technology that would never be permitted elsewhere, because the damnable monsters are too dangerous. Nobody wants to see them take Stigmata the way they claimed Absolution and Daishan. But that doesn't mean the priests like to see new technology. Everything we transported was new, experimental, and very, very dangerous.

"We managed to deliver the goods without incident. I never saw the Symbiots, but I saw plenty of their victims. They were torn apart, burned, shredded and even melted by the attacks against them. Those were just the ones lucky enough to die. I've heard rumors about what happens to some of the survivors." He sighed, and shivered briefly. "We were going to use the new jumpkey and see where it took us, because maybe we'd find something the Muster could take advantage of, Second Republic technology long thought lost, or a world the Muster could claim for their own. Either way, the side trip promised to make us wealthy people if we pulled it off successfully.

"At the gate, we were questioned by an Inquisition patrol about our business in the Stigmata system, and were forced to wait while a group of Inquisitors came aboard and searched the ship. Had they caught us before our delivery, I don't think we'd have been allowed to leave.

"Captain Armides waited patiently while they searched, and even asked for a prayer for our safe journey. The inquisitors gladly gave their blessings and then left. Within ten minutes they'd reboarded their destroyer and moved out to make a survey of the area. That was when Armides tried the new key again. This time it worked. None of us knew if we should cheer or not, but we were all excited.

"Not knowing what waited for us on the other side of the jumpgate, the captain decided our best bet was a slow trip through the portal. That was a wise choice. Had he been going at anything close to the normal speeds, we would surely have been destroyed. Just past the edge of the jumpgate was a monstrous ship, the likes of which I have never seen. The captain was hard pressed to slow us down and avoid a collision.

"It only took a moment to realize the ship was Urthish in origin. Though my training in ancient Urthish isn't much, I recognized the words written on the side in letters five times as tall as a man: *Corporate Ship Yotaru*. It was intact. Our ship's think machine had no records of any such craft, though that part is hardly surprising. I cannot properly impress on you the size of the *Yotaru*, save to say it was as large as any Imperial dreadnought but far more ornate. It could not have been less than a kilometer from bow to stern, and if I had to hazard a guess, I'd say the hull was at least five meters thick."

My mind reeled at the very notion. A ship that size could hold hundreds of souls, and enough food stuffs to travel for years in comfort. More importantly, a ship that size would be priceless. Surely anyone would pay a generous ransom for a treasure like that, and more still if the technology aboard her came from the Second Republic, back before we forgot most of what we once knew about the laws of the universe and how to bend them to our will.

As if he were reading my mind, Hawkwood turned to face me and nodded slowly. "I can see it in your eyes, Joshua. The same thoughts that came to me and to all the others when we saw the *Yotaru*. Imagine the wealth one could earn from the sale of such a fine vessel. Imagine the power it must surely contain. That's all we thought about as we looked at her.

"It didn't take long for the crew to agree to an expedition, and that in itself was taken by some as a sign from the Pancreator. Have you ever tried getting twenty or so guildmembers to agree on anything? It's like performing surgery on a Vorox without knocking the beast unconscious first. I've seen guild meetings that were little better than riots enough times to know.

"We left five people on our ship, enough to handle any emergencies. The rest of us crossed over to the *Yotaru* as soon as we'd managed to anchor the two ships together. Finding the entrance portal to the relic was easy enough, but getting it open was a matter of almost an hour. The long years alone had left the vehicle without power, and debris has crusted itself to the entrance. But our engineers managed it soon enough, and we entered the great ship prepared to find almost anything.

"What we found was a detailed map on the wall. It showed a complete schematic for the entire ship, and even had a marker to show where we were in relation to everything else. The *Yotaru* was meant for staying in space a very long time. She had to be. The map covered every level of the ship, and there were ten levels! She wasn't a ship at all, but a small city. There were rooms for hundreds of people, and gardens built inside the *Yotaru* to provide food and oxygen, although the forests had not survived their years of abandonment. We hadn't merely found a massive cruiser; we'd found a madman's dream. The rooms were decorated with levels of wealth you can barely imagine. I was raised a Hawkwood, with wealth and luxuries many people will never know, but I was stunned by the excesses I saw in even the smaller cabins. I've been on luxury cruises, the sort designed to let you see the stars in comfort. This was much the same idea, but far, far larger in scale.

"You couldn't have kept the crew together with a blaster at each person's temple. There was too much to see, and even with over fifteen of us, we would be days exploring in an organized fashion. The group broke apart, heading to different areas where each suspected they'd find something worth investigating. I went with the captain and his first mate and two others to investigate the bridge of the giant ship. Getting there was a monumental effort in its own right. There was no power in the ship, and movement was easy enough, but the air was stale and not all of us had vacuum suits. I, of course, had one, having been born to wealth, and was thus prepared, as were those whose duty it was to repair our ship. With no power, the doors were a barrier to be overcome by brute force, made more of a challenge by the nearly perfect condition of the ship.

"These days, one expects to see hull rats on any vessel, either dead or alive. There was nothing. No hairs from the vermin resting in the tightest corners, where rags can't quite reach. No droppings. Not even a scent of their urine, from what the others told me. I decided to be cautious and keep my mask in place the entire time: I've heard tales of what happens to people when they breathe bad air, and I don't like taking chances. The captain mentioned the lack of vermin infestation, and I in turn noted that there was scarcely any dust to be found. Nor any bodies, for that matter. In the three levels we had to pass through to find the bridge of the *Yotaru*, there was no sign that anyone had ever been on the vessel. At least nothing we could see with the fusion torches we brought aboard.

"Looking back on these events, I have just realized something else. The ship had likely been floating in the void for centuries with nothing to fuel the atmosphere and no light to reflect from the metal walls. But for all of that, no one who went aboard her grew cold. You've certainly been outside a ship at some point, Joshua, to repair a door or only to check on why the sensors weren't up to par?" I nodded my agreement. Most pilots have been in the void at least once, if only for training purposes. "Have you ever been out in the vacuum of outerspace without feeling the cold as if it were a living thing? Yet no one so much as shivered, and the breath of my fellows did not rime the air."

Both Meloush and I were speechless. He had to be raving, that was all there was to it. Outerspace is cold, unless you are very near the closest sun, and these days even that is no guarantee. Still, if they'd boarded a powerless ship, most of them should have been freezing within minutes, especially those foolish enough to go without a proper suit.

He paused for a moment, considering the ramifications of what he'd said, and then he continued as if he'd done no more than mention the weather. Arden pulled free his pipe and filled it with tobacco, his hands a bit jittery. All the time I stared into Hawkwood's dark eyes and wondered what he might be seeing.

"We eventually made it to the bridge. It took time, and we were all a bit weary when we finally arrived, but our goal was now within reach and that gave us a certain extra energy. The control center of the *Yotaru* was as big as the front garden I can see out my window. A dozen or more seats and small tables were situated along the walls of the stark room, stations from which different tasks could be performed, I suppose. I've been on transports smaller than that bridge. Again, the scope is so hard to imagine, I have trouble explaining it well enough to make it clear to you.

"The captain was excited, understandably, by the condition of the entire area. Each device was pristine, each instrument seemingly unharmed by the time spent uninhabited. As a group we walked from one station to the next, looking over the instrument panels and marveling at the complexity of each device. Compared to what we had arrived in, the *Yotaru* must surely be a miracle of technology. The Church would have seen us burned as heretics for the words of praise we spoke.

"Then the first mate found what could only have been the captain's chair and sat upon it, his hands running over the controls and caressing them with a lover's touch. I don't think anyone was more surprised than he was when the lights of the control arms suddenly came on. I have seldom seen a man leap that high in my life, and as there was no gravity to stop his ascent, his skin split against the metal of the ceiling.

"We scarcely had time to make certain he was not badly injured before the lights from the captain's chair spread across the entire bridge. After hours in the near darkness we were all but blinded by the sudden illumination. And the light that poured forth! It was so white as to seem silvery, and so abundant that high noon on any planet seemed mild in comparison. I won't lie to you, it was an effort on the part of the captain to keep us calm. I was all for leaving that place as quickly as possible until he reminded us that our ancestors had likely flown to new worlds in ships just as large and just as powerful. Even then we stayed skittish as young colts. That light was unnatural, and it gave us the first chance to truly look around the bridge and understand the sheer size of our find.

"We were startled from our contemplations when gravity suddenly gave us the ability to stand — and to fall, which most of us promptly did. The feeling of weight was not as great as that here, on this planet, but it was substantial.

"Even as we reexamined the command center with avid curiosity, the floor beneath us began to vibrate subtly. From the bank of windows that looked out into the void, we could see the lights of the *Yotaru* begin shining across the length of the ship. I was filled with wonder and terror alike as I finally saw the full scope of her. Sleek lines of metal and light ran for a distance that made me gape like a brute on the way to the slaughterhouse. Running from one end of the ship to the other would have left a man exhausted.

"I must have stared through those great windows for half an hour, stunned by the knowledge that humans had once been able to create such marvels. I would have continued to stare if the first mate hadn't grown so excited by his find. Despite the gash on his head, he was all but dancing like a child at a party thrown to celebrate a birth-anniversary. He'd discovered a star map that seemed almost to grow from the very fabric of the ceiling.

By the Pancreator, what a map! All the routes of the Known Worlds are but a fraction of what waits out there, a tiny portion of the worlds where humans once dwelt. The Known Worlds are far smaller than what our kind once called home. Dozens of places were mapped out here, worlds we have not seen or traveled to in centuries were listed. And held in slot beside these worlds... jumpkeys."

Excitement? I could scarcely contain myself. Even if half of every word from Hawkwood's mouth was a lie, the potential rewards of that map were enough to make my head spin. Lost worlds, entire star systems that had been cut off from Human Space for centuries. With that map, I would surely go down in history, praised as one of the great explorers of our times. Astor-Smythe and I could well retire from simple transports, with enough wealth to put the noble houses to shame. To be the first to lay claim to those worlds would guarantee a lifetime of leisure. And the madman sitting before me had all but put them in my hands. That star map would make me wealthy beyond my wildest dreams, if I could but find that one unknown jumproad and procure the *Yotaru*.

My daydreams were broken when Nathaniel spoke again. "I know that look, Joshua. The expression you wear now is the very same as our first mate upon finding the star map." For the first time, I felt that I was actually the focus of Hawkwood's attention. Instead of staring through me, he actually looked at me. What I saw in those eyes was not madness, but rather an odd mixture of envy and pity that chilled me to the core. I've known the look before; it was rather the same look one gets when talking of the Sathra with other pilots who've experienced the addictive sensation and dearly wanted to do so again.

"Nonsense," I said. "I'm no fool. That map would be a treasure, true enough. But I don't have the jumpkey, and it could take years to even activate a random code in the jumpgate at Stigmata. Even trying would likely be trouble enough in that place, and not worth my life if I'm caught." I defended myself more as a reflex action than out of any sense of desperation. It was, after all, a madman who was telling the tale. I had nothing to fear.

"Nonsense? Perhaps. Perhaps not. I warn you, listen to the rest of my tale before you decide whether or not to make the journey." I nodded, and he began his story again.

"Sometimes I think time must move differently in space. Before I knew what was happening, we'd spent a week examining the interior of the *Yotaru*. With the air proving untainted, I removed my vacuum suit and joined the others who risked their lives, trusting the ancient hulk to sustain us. I can't begin to tell you what we did, save that I soon knew the complete layout of that massive vessel. We never tried to move her; we were too busy examining her for flaws and for evidence of her crew's fate. In all that time, we never found a single body, nor any sign that anyone had ever been aboard. We were unsettled by that knowledge. Each and every one of us made comments at one point to another, but there was always someone else to note the wealth we would likely make when we returned to the Known Worlds.

"Armides finally decided he'd seen enough. With barely a moment's notice we were to prepare for departure in the *Yotaru*. Our own ship was almost considered mere debris by that point. It was small and ineffective; the *Yotaru* was far more powerful, and she had weapons enough to defend us from any imaginable threat. She might have been a luxury ship, but her creators weren't foolish enough to trust in others to treat her that way. Most of the crew was excited by the notion. At last we would claim our prize and be on our way back to the Known Worlds with a powerful vessel and knowledge enough to make even the Church forgive us our transgressions. Worlds of wealth would be ours. Even my own family would have to accept that I had value when I returned, and

I cannot express how much that meant to me.

"Despite the quick commands of the captain, despite the crew's eagerness to be on our way, it still took almost a day to prepare for the journey. Everything of value on our ship was hauled over to the *Yotaru*. Though there was air and stores of food, we did not wish to take unnecessary chances. Who knew if the food was still good?

"We were cautious in our way, but hardly as wise as we should have been. Though it took Captain Armides and his first mate a great deal of time, they'd managed the basics of the controls to their own satisfaction. They even began to train me on some of the systems in the hopes of having another to take turns piloting the ship through the void. Still, I was in training, and no one other than the captain himself was going to start the *Yotaru* on her trip.

"I was away from the bridge when we began our voyage. Armides wanted the lifepods along the hull checked for integrity and stocked with supplies in case of an emergency. I was in charge of that task. As I walked along the hallways with my crew of assistants, I marveled again at the technology involved in making the ship, and I considered the risks to my soul. What if the Church was right? What if using the technology was, in fact, the equivalent of dealing with demons? I thought about these things and then dismissed them. Utter nonsense. I had used weapons all my life, traveled on ships for years, and nothing had ever come about to make me believe in demons. There was, I felt certain, a rational explanation for why the suns were fading and why the occasional peasant appeared to suffer from demonic infestation. Delirium in the case of the latter and a change in the texture of the void for the former, perhaps. In time we would know the answers. I am, after all, an educated man.

"I was speaking with the first mate over the squawker when it happened. My crew had just finished with the first section of lifepods and we ready for a break. I called to the bridge and asked what our status was. The mate was happy, I could tell by the sound of his voice: 'We're under way. Captain Armides has just turned her to face the jumpgate.'

"The words had barely come through the speaker when I heard the first scream. The noise was loud, and the poor wretch who uttered so unholy a sound must surely have lost no less than a limb. As the voice called out from only a few feet away, I thought one of my crew had captured an arm in one of the doors to the lifepods. The pods were well built, but hardly meant for toying with. Once they were shut, they were designed to hold out the vacuum of space, and that meant they sealed very tightly. I saw a slave lose a hand that way once, meddling with a lifepod and thinking of escape. Instead, the fool lost his life, because we hadn't the means to save him from so grievous a wound.

"I looked over my crew, only to find all six of them looking about just as excitedly. Seeing that none of them were injured, I spoke urgently to the first mate, trying to discover if he or the captain was injured. They were not. But even as he assured me, I heard the scream again, pouring through the speaker-box and filling the air with enough sound to make my teeth rattle in their sockets. As I covered my ears in an effort to escape the hideous wailing, I saw the others with me do the same. I also saw something else... something darker.

"It was only there for an instant, but I clearly saw the figure of a man writhing in pain. The problem was, I saw him through the hull beneath my feet. Not as if the steel had suddenly become transparent, but as a part of the hull itself. The figure moved, twisted and thrashed, and the metal of the floor moved with it. As I looked down, horrified by what I saw, one of the men with me reached out to touch the agonized form. Before his hand made contact, the poor wretch disappeared, leaving behind an unblemished floor.

"Hoping to find out if anything similar was happening elsewhere, I yelled into my squawker, but it seemed dead. I reached for the communicator on the wall. I never even touched the device. The flow of blood from the speaker stopped me. I spoke before of a slave who lost his hand. This was far worse. The crimson ichor didn't merely trickle as from a minor wound, it flowed forth with the strength of a river. I was knocked off my feet and carried by the tide of blood, as were the men who stood with me.

"Perhaps the mate tried to reach me, to see if anything was wrong. I will never know. A moment later, the speaker cried out with his voice, screaming shrilly and begging for mercy. The mate was a big man, one who kept his position aboard the ship as much by force as through experience. He had a voice like distant thunder, but in that moment his throat produced the same sounds one might hear from a mere child. I do not know just what occurred after that, but I heard a wet, tearing sound and then his voice stopped. I could still hear Captain Armides over the speaker, but he, too, sounded wrong. He was crying, whimpering and, a moment after that, another wet sound came and he was silent.

"The men with me looked about with wide eyes and bared teeth. I joined them, and was dimly aware that my crotch had grown damp. I'd wet myself. I, who have fought against far greater numbers in combat without ever feeling fear, who have seen the worst sights you can imagine at Stigmata, who have even done battle against the Symbiots, pissed myself like a newborn.

"I might have been embarrassed if I hadn't been so terrified. The ship began to vibrate. Not the hull, not the walls around me or the floor beneath me, but the entire ship. Where the feeling before had been the gentle vibration of the engines felt from a great distance, this was entirely different. It was unhealthy. There was no pattern of motion, no controlled rattle caused by the energies that powered the *Yotaru*. There was a great quaking, and a thousand smaller bumps and bangs, as if the very walls around me would shake themselves apart.

"One of the crew, a youngster on his very first voyage as I recall, tried to run from the hideous vibrations. He managed a dozen paces before the floor beneath him buckled and rose. The metal itself added its shriek to the cacophonous din as it warped and lifted and reshaped itself. For a moment a woman seemed to rise from the ground as if coming out of the waters of a still lake. Then she changed. As her torso breached the floor — an awkward phrase, as she was still a part of that very floor — she screamed in rage or just perhaps in pain. I watched in horror as her delicate hand reached for the fool's leg. I stood transfixed, as the 'flesh' seemed to melt away, leaving bone and sinew, all of it composed of the metal beneath his feet. Her face peeled back until there was little more than a skull, and all the while she rose from the ground until she stood next to the lad, holding him off the floor by one leg.

"She screamed then, and he joined her. With the easy strength of a mother lifting her infant, she turned him around until he faced her, and she roared with an unholy rage. The creature opened its mouth and a wave of change came over her, taking any semblance of humanity away and leaving only a skeletal figure that had none of the beauty I'd seen lift through the metal hull. A second later the creature's teeth clamped down on his wildly thrashing head and peeled his face away as if tearing the rind from a fruit.

"While the dark thing feasted on the poor fool's flesh, the ground around her began to buckle and seethe. The lights that had kept us cheerful for the last week began to flicker and fade, even as the hull began giving birth to other, stranger things.

"We ran. There was no reason to our flight, for surely any monstrosity that could hide between the layers of steel could follow us with ease, but we ran. The wall beside me formed a mouth twice the size of my body and vomited forth a cloud of blackness that buzzed and swarmed. Just after I ran past that regurgitating orifice, I heard another of my crew scream as the things coming from its depths covered him. One by one, all fell to horrors more twisted than the ones I'd already witnessed. Tentacles penetrated one poor soul and violated him in a hundred ways as they slowly tore him asunder. Another exploded into flames as she ran past me, parts of her body falling away like sandstone crumbling beneath a terrific weight. I did not see the other deaths, but I heard them.

"I ran blindly, hoping against hope that I would find salvation, and find it I did. I stormed into one of the lifepods, and without a moment's hesitation I struck the button that would jettison that island of sanity away from the foul madness of the *Yotaru*.

"Seconds later the door was sealed and the engines had pushed me far from the ship we'd all hoped would bring us great fortune. Whenever the rotation of the lifepod permitted, I looked at the massive spacecraft. Aside from the spot where my haven had rested against the hull, it remained unmarred. It had also grown, I'm convinced of it.

"Had I but examined all of the escape vehicles before the madness began, my story might have been different. But the lifepod I'd chosen was malfunctioning. There were no controls for the thrusters that sent me careening away. They were ruined beyond my ability to repair."

Hawkwood laughed then, a bitter, hopeless sound that chilled me to my marrow. His eyes were darker than ever, and in their corners I saw tears as yet unshed fighting for freedom. He did not succumb.

I couldn't help myself. I was enthralled by his story, drawn in despite the wild claims. "How is it that you managed to get through the jumpgate without a jumpdrive? How did you manage to escape?"

Hawkwood listened to my questions and shrugged his shoulders. "I do not know. I know only that I was found sometime later, adrift, and brought back here by souls caring and foolish enough to bother with the likes of me." He looked directly at me as he spoke, and I knew I was right in my earlier assumption. He had recognized me, despite his state when Astor-Smythe and I found him.

"How long were you lost in the void, Nathaniel?" The words startled me. I was so lost in Hawkwood's tale that I had forgotten Arden's presence.

"That is perhaps the most impossible part of my tale," he answered, his voice low and lost. "If the calendar is accurate, and if I have not truly lost my mind, I was adrift for 87 days."

"Impossible! You could not have survived for that long, especially in a lifepod." I couldn't help but protest. The best anyone can hope for from a lifepod is a week's air and supplies. More than that simply cannot fit in one of the tiny capsules. "You'd have starved or frozen long before then."

Hawkwood stared at me through half-lidded eyes, his face blank. "I know. I should be dead by now. I shouldn't even be in the Known Worlds. Why I am alive is a mystery to me." Having said his piece, Hawkwood turned away from us and curled himself into a ball on his bed. Moments later, he was asleep, or pretending slumber with remarkable skill.

Arden looked at me and gestured for me to follow him to his offices, which were, thankfully, merely across the hallway, on the same floor and not in the bowels of the Oubliette. "So, Joshua. What do you make of his tale? Can you now understand why the man is here, safe from the outside world?"

"Aye, that I can. He has lost his grip on reality." He poured us both a stiff drink. A few moments passed in silence, and then I asked Meloush the question that I needed answered so desperately. "How could even a part of his story be true? Have you checked the records for any evidence of his claims?"

"I don't have access to Muster records, Joshua. Nor do I believe they would allow me a chance to look at them even if I did." He looked at me pointedly, and smiled a thin little grimace. "You, on the other hand, are a Charioteer. I suspect you could possibly find the information I need to assess the truth of his claims."

I wagered that I could, given a bit of time, and after finishing my drink, I left. I never planned on investigating, but the story Nathaniel Hawkwood told would not leave me in peace. It was only a matter of passing around a few firebirds and knowing who to speak to for me to find the information. A Muster ship, the *Jarod Amad*, a freighter bound for Bannockburn, was recorded as lost after dropping her cargo on Stigmata. She'd been reported missing over one hundred days ago. Her captain was a man named Andres Armides. Hawkwood's claims of being in outerspace for 87 days could well be true. But if so, what sustained him during that time? How had he lived, and how could he have come back through the jumpgate in a lifepod?

I spent two days learning the information and then recovering from the knowledge. I also took the time to speak to Astor-Smythe, telling him the tale and asking if he'd discovered anything from his examination of the lifepod. He told me in a very tired voice that he would let me know more by the next day, and that what he'd discovered up to that point made no sense.

That night, I had dreams the like of which I've only with a fever. I dreamt of Astor-Smythe reaching out for the black gem we'd discovered and screaming in pain when he finally touched its oddly faceted surface. I dreamt of Hawkwood's journey through the void in a lifepod that had long since failed him, clutching that same gem to his body and gibbering madly. I dreamt of Arden speaking softly as he approached Hawkwood's shivering form, a syringe held behind his back and glistening with sinister poisons for the mind. I awoke screaming the next morning.

On my seventh day of a ten day shore leave, I visited Arden Meloush at his home. Alynna, ever the gracious hostess, prepared another plate at the dinner table. Arden and I spoke on the same balcony as before, and though the scenery was as stunning as it had previously been, I found the chill in the air took the pleasure away. The chill in the air, and the chill in my very soul.

After I'd told him of my findings, Arden spoke of what he'd learned since. "He confessed to a bit more since last we spoke, Joshua. He tells me that there were other things with him on his long journey back. That those things chose to let him live and even activated the jumpgate for him when there was no hope of escaping the damned star where the *Yotaru* rested."

"Do you believe him, Arden? Do you think what he claims is possible?"

"I know he believes it. And I don't doubt he found the *Yotaru*. I did some very careful research, and I know that a ship by that name was lost a long time ago. But I don't believe in demons. The Pancreator I can accept as real, because we had to come from somewhere, but demons are another matter. No, I think he might have murdered his crewmates himself, out of fear that the technology they found could get them all killed." He shook his head and grimaced. "The Church is very particular about what anyone knows. They aren't fond of anyone bringing back technology that they can't control, and they've done a wonderful job of making sure the ignorant peasants know how 'evil' technology is."

That statement alone could have brought the punishment of the Inquisition onto Meloush, and it was a sign of how strong our friendship was that he dared make such a comment to me. Still, he knew I didn't follow the dictates of the Church any more than he did, that I didn't believe in demons either, and that helped.

"Tomorrow I shall try something new with Nathaniel," he commented. "I have certain drugs that can induce a sleeplike state. With those drugs I shall endeavor to find the truth behind his delusions. His family has hopes for his cure, and I cannot accomplish that without knowing the complete truth."

I asked to be allowed to join him, but he declined. "There are some things I'd rather you not know about my profession, Joshua." He shrugged rather sheepishly. "What I do is not always... pleasant, and I would rather not have you look at me differently when this is all over. Please don't ask this of me."

Despite my desires to force the matter, I agreed. I would know the end result, which was the important part. Alynna informed us that the meal was ready. As always, the food was excellent, and I found myself wishing that I had met my best friend's wife before he had.

Two days later, I heard the news that Nathaniel Hawkwood was dead. Though the family tried to keep the matter quiet, I knew where the man had been and who had attended to him. I left immediately for the Oubliette, barely taking the time to grab my weapons should the need arise to help my friend make a hasty departure. The Hawkwoods are nobles, and their word is law. There was the possibility of a price on Arden's head, and I planned to make sure that no one collected that price. He was my friend, and despite our numerous differences, I cared for him.

I paid good money for the fastest transport I could manage. Every fiber in my being demanded speed, and my sense of urgency only grew the closer we got to that grim tower. Within minutes of arriving, I had bullied my way past the few guards and made my way past the maddening screams of tormented souls to the relative silence of the top floor. I passed Nathaniel Hawkwood's room on my way to my friend's office; though the door was only slightly open, I could see the crimson stains and smell the drying blood that covered every visible surface.

I arrived too late for Arden Meloush. His body was hanging from the rafters of his office, suspended by a sheet he'd torn into strips and tied together. The makeshift rope ran from the pinnacle of the ceiling down to his neck, and there was easily a meter between his feet and the floor. Two others of his profession were already there when I pushed into the room. They stood together, staring at his slowly rotating corpse with an avid fascination. I've little doubt they were considering examining his brain in the hopes of finding some sort of abnormality.

"What happened here? What happened to Hawkwood? To Arden?"

One of them simply giggled at me, a short man with too little hair and too much perfume. He was drooling. The other stared for a moment, as if unaware that I was capable of speech. Then he replied, his gray eyes looking all around and his blood-covered hands still trembling.

"Arden Meloush gave Hawkwood an injection. It was a simple injection of plant extracts from Severus. I've used them before, almost everyone has..." He faded out for a moment, his thin lips trembling and his nose quivering like that of an animal sniffing for predators. When I stepped toward him, he cringed and continued. "It wasn't supposed to happen like that! He gave Hawkwood the Severan Mind Juice and instead of sleeping, the man started to scream! He flailed around as if he'd been impaled on a lance, and then he exploded!" The man's voice continued to rise in octaves until he was shrieking like a child in agony. He grabbed me, shaking me as if to make his point more clear. He was smaller than me, but his strength was terrifying. "Something came *out* of him!" The man looked at the blood on his own hands, blood he'd now covered me with, and back away, horrified. "Do you understand me? Some *thing* came *out* of him!"

They ran like frightened children when I screamed obscenities towards them and cut Arden's body free.

I said my last good-byes to one of my oldest friends and closed his eyes before I noticed his last written message to me.

"There really are demons, Joshua. I know that now."

Nine little words that sent shivers up my spine, written in Arden's tight penmanship, and written in blood. I took the note with me when I left.

I was uncertain what I would do. Rather than take a transport again, I walked along the streets, looking, I imagine, as dumbstruck as the Mind Physicks I left behind with Arden's body. I kept running the story over in my mind, and I could easily see why Arden would have killed himself. For one thing, he was always a logical man, and if something really did come out of Nathaniel Hawkwood's body, he would have a great deal of trouble accepting the change in his perceptions of the universe. For another, he was already as good as dead. Hawkwood had been in his care, had died after receiving an injection from him. Suicide might be preferable to what they would do to him. The questions would go on for hours, questions about why he had killed Nathaniel, and who had paid him to commit the crime. There would never be peace for him again.

A few hours later, I shared the news of Arden's death with Alynna and held her while she cried. I promised to look out for her, and to help her, just as I knew Arden would have wanted. I stayed three extra days on Byzantium Secundus, arranging for Arden's funeral and for fresh supplies to be delivered to the *Whereabout*. I have wished for Alynna for years, but I cannot have her now, not ever. Not in that way. She is all I have left of Arden.

When the time finally came, I went back to Astor-Smythe, prepared to tell him everything in detail. I was too late. He was dead when I arrived. I found him curled into a fetal position in the holding bay of the *Whereabout*. His long dark hair had gone white, and his eyes, glassy with death, stared madly at the lifepod from the *Yotaru*. Whatever had killed him was nowhere to be seen, but I suspect if I'd been willing to look long enough into his dead eyes, I would have seen its reflection cast back at me.

I found a small cylinder clutched in his right hand, held there by a death grip. Though it took time, I managed to pry it free. And there I had the answer to my questions about Hawkwood's story. All the answers I needed. The cylinder was a jumpkey, one different from any I or

Astor-Smythe have ever owned. Of the strange black gem and the ancient think machine I found no trace.

Somewhere beyond the edge of the Known Worlds, in an area that is flatly outlawed by the empire, there is a ship drifting in the darkest part of the void. The ship is dangerous, to be sure, but she holds a treasure that is well worth the risk.

The *Yotaru* holds a star map and jumpkeys that detail the locations of worlds long forgotten. I joined the Charioteers to find treasures just like that map. I'm not as foolish as Captain Armides, nor as easily frightened as Arden Meloush. I have a ship, and she is a treasure. All I need is the map and the keys; the darkness can claim the rest of the *Yotaru* and her dubious treasures.

And so I leave this place. I have taken on extra crew, men and women I feel I can trust. This envelope is to remain sealed, and passed on to Alynna Meloush in the event that I do not return within the next two years. I've paid good money to the Reeves to ensure that all I own becomes hers if I fail to appear before the appointed time. The Reeves will be tempted to read this letter and perhaps to plunder my meager possessions, but they will not do so. Like me, they are professionals.

I am not a religious man and I seldom bother with prayers, but I think that has changed now. I will make my peace with the Pancreator and hope for the best. Unlike the priests of the Church, I am not afraid of knowledge. I am afraid of ignorance.

I am not afraid of the dark places in the universe, nor the ones that dwell within the minds of sentient beings. I am merely afraid of what that darkness might hide behind that darkness.

Worldsong

James Estes

This was not at all how I'd envisioned my return to Pentateuch.

In my mind, I saw it: I would be in my usual seat on the bridge of the *Prophet's Dream*, at the otherwise unmanned communications station, with a clear, unobscured view of my homeworld through the main oval viewport. The small bright orb would grow in our sight as we approached — slowly. Pentateuch has its own speed, and haste is a thing of scorn, so I would be sure that we were not rushing to Pentateuch but rather savoring the journey.

I would soon be able to identify various continents and seas: Shekinah, Malador, the Helspont. Then we would break the atmosphere, the *Prophet's Dream*'s stabilizers compensating for turbulence and friction. Piercing the cloud cover, we would ultimately glide across Shekinah, awaiting a landing confirmation from the spaceport, all the while marveling at the cascade of oranges and reds and yellows from the rising sun — I always envisioned the arrival in early morning — and the canopy of green forests beneath. Then confirmation would come, and we would glide silently toward Heliopolis, and with but the slightest shudder the ship's landing gears would descend. Finally we would land, the gears absorbing the impact so it felt as feathers touching on velvet.

And then I would show my companions my homeworld. Roaaaonooooa, the Shantor Windspeaker, would roam the plains, running free and spirited; Siyyad al-Malik and Lissa Anstrom would scour the marketplace for crafts of unmatched quality, while sour Loannen vo Mardenni would meet with my fellow Eskatonics and challenge their philosophical inquiry to his satisfaction. Some time later (perhaps a week, perhaps a month) we would depart my home and continue our pilgrimage across the Known Worlds.

But now most of my companions are dead, the *Prophet's Dream* abandoned, the pilgrimage crushed — and I sit in a windowless cargo hold, aboard a makeshift bench of lashed together crates and boxes. I am not casually returning home in triumph, as a respite from adventuring; I am running home a coward, fleeing the pain of my past. I appreciate irony, even irony at my own expense, but the irony here was too strong, too bitter.

But at least I was returning home, I told myself. And even if this unworthy claptrap vessel — seemingly held together by twine and force of will alone — was destroyed during re-entry, and the ship became my funeral bier, I would at least die content knowing that I had returned home. (This, at least, was what I told myself to quell my churning stomach.)

Indeed, perhaps my journey home was best this way. It was the best I could do, as it were. My other option was to remain at Spacestation Cumulus another month and await the Eskatonic-sponsored ship which would eventually dock there, and transport me and any other waiting Eskatonic to Pentateuch in some modicum of austere comfort and safety for a minimal cost.

But I couldn't wait; I knew I had to return home. I could locate no other ship with plans to visit Pentateuch in the immediate future, nor could I afford the cost of private charter. So instead I did the best I could, paying the pittance that afforded me seating in the cargo bay of the *Silent Lady* — the most poorly-chosen name I could imagine for this noisy lumbering barge. But transport was transport, and the sooner I could return to Pentateuch and find peace, the better.

Perhaps, I hoped, Pentateuch would provide me the restful sleep that fate has denied me these past few months: maybe I will sleep uninterrupted, without the visions of Siyyad's crushed skull, of Roa's maddened whinny, and the demise of our pilgrimage. Pentateuch, to me, was safe haven, and so I endured this uncomfortable transport to sooner arrive. Perhaps, I even wondered, this unpleasant voyage was penance for my own loss of faith.

And then we landed, hardly the cat's-paw gentle landing promised by the ship's captain, but not the gut-wrenching catastrophe I feared. The captain entered the cargo bay just as I untied the last of the ropes that served as my safety harness, to announce the already-evident "we've landed" and follow it with an insincere "I hope your trip was comfortable." Perhaps he had come to personally check on my safety, but more than likely he was here to check the cargo — an intention made evident by the way he didn't seem to wait for a response as he began surveying the cargo hold for any broken or fallen drayage.

I thanked the captain for his services, gathered my own belongings (one shoulder satchel and a heavier, worn canvas duffel) and descended the landing ramp. Still in my priestly mantle (though I felt more the

liar for wearing it), I made my way to the port authority, where I arranged transport, and caught a ride on a cargo-laden skimmer — this
time perched atop a barrel like some hesychast hermit — that traversed
the short distance between the spaceport and Heliopolis. I saw the spires
of the Cathedral of Saints Paulus and Horace, rising from the city
center and drawing us like a beacon, the sun glinting and sparkling off
the uppermost windows. Within a matter of minutes we'd covered the
distance to the Aleph Quarter, where the skimmer stopped at a guild
warehouse; and there I took my leave.

I had not yet decided whether I would return to the Naos and seek
lodging, or whether to seek complete solitude and anonymity and take
housing in one of the many hostels and inns that could be found
throughout the city. But standing there on Pentateuch, seeing the cathedral silhouette in Pentateuch's crimson dusk, I knew that the Naos
called to me — or I yearned for it. Even if I silently doubted the teachings of the Prophet and my own religious order, I still felt drawn to the
succor of that which raised me and brought me to adulthood. Enjoying
the first moment of peace I'd felt since Nowhere, I decided then to
return to the Naos and seek the lodging due a wandering Eskatonic. I
had left the Naos naive, and full of faith, but I had returned experienced and full of doubt. But I had also learned of the value of secrets,
and my doubt would remain a secret for now.

* * *

My first night, the dream returned. I had not had the dream for
several days, and I thought perhaps I had eluded it; but lying on my cot
in the Naos cell I had just occupied, the dream returned in full force. It
brought me back to Nowhere, where our pilgrimage ended in blood and
tears.

I awoke, a scream almost clawing its way out of my throat, bathed
in sweat. I would not long be able to hide my dreams from my fellow
Eskatonics, I knew. There were some who can look at you and know
what ails your soul — and I suspected who these individuals were, and
knew I could try to avoid them. But even the most dense novice can be
awakened in the middle of the night by a screaming hysterical dreamer
— and this is precisely what I feared I would be if my dreams (or nightmares, such as they were) took the better of me and returned me to that
night on Nowhere.

Once more I questioned how long this would last, and would I ever find peace; and discerning no answer from the darkness of the room, I wept — silently, burying my sobs in my pillow.

* * *

For the first week I slowly reaccustomed myself to life at the Naos, speaking with as few people as possible. There was something about my demeanor that led many younger priests to avoid me instinctively, if not intentionally. By day I meditated in the Naos gardens; at night I took to studying the Omega Gospels and the Digamma Apocrypha, especially the consoling Fragrant Hymns of Leandor (long my favorite of sacred texts). But these were just hollow acts; I read the sacred texts in search of faith but found only pen and ink, the sacred books nothing but empty vessels on a sea of doubt.

Ultimately I sought out my confessor, the aging Sister Theophila, and in her cell, I spoke of my distress. I began with my adventures soon after leaving Pentateuch, and ended with the tragic night at Nowhere. By the time I was through, the daylight sounds of activity outside her window had slowly dulled to the quiet of night.

She thought over my predicament — which I had unveiled to her in full, omitting nothing — her eyes closed in thought so long, her breathing so regular and rhythmic I feared perhaps she'd fallen asleep. I sat still, uncomfortably aware of how every sound I made seemed so exaggerated by the silence.

A silence she finally broke. "You had a terrible time — I understand this. You sought the Pancreator among the stars, and what you ultimately found instead was emptiness and sadness." I concurred with her assessment, and waited for more; her advice when I was a Novitiate was always welcome.

"And so now you seek peace — and faith? I can give you neither, lad. I can only pray for you, and hope that one day you find both the peace and the faith you seek." She looked out her window at Nuz, Pentateuch's moon large and white like chalk. "I've told you nothing you didn't already know, or couldn't have heard from the dullest peasant. But I hope that in providing you a chance to tell your tale, you'll make sense of it."

I stared at her, dully. Had I come here just to talk, or in search of answers? But beyond the numbness, I felt it again — that glimmering of peace, and I knew that her audience was therapy enough for now.

She stood up and began waving me away. "Now go! I'm an old woman now, and the Pancreator knows I need my beauty rest!" She offered me a light peck on the check as she saw me to her door. Before I turned to go, she extended her hand, and put her palm atop my head. I bowed my head in supplication, as she prayed, *Shadows fall, but the light of faith shall not be dimmed. Walk in the steps of the Prophet* — a common Eskatonic prayer for those in need or those about to begin a journey. I thanked her for her time, and returned to my own cell.

I did feel a bit lighter — this was the first I'd told my story to anyone since Nowhere — but I wondered how long this would last. Her sympathy and kindness would bring me some measure of comfort, but they would not bring me faith, nor would they ease my sleep. Knowing this, I prepared for another night of restless slumber.

That night, though, I slept uninterrupted.

* * *

Almost a month passed. My nights were still mostly restless, but only a few were broken by dreams of Nowhere, and a few actually passed uninterrupted. One dream differed significantly, though — I was again on Nowhere, reliving the horrors of that night, but a fierce wind blew, and in the distance I heard a woman singing. I had no explanation for that dream.

I broadened my activities so that I was frequently out of the Naos, exploring the byways of Heliopolis, reacquainting myself with her streets and plazas. I watched the local artists in Eurus Plaza — poets and paint-ers and musicians, each with their story to tell. And I visited Aleph Plaza, strolling among the merchants of curios and oddities and other exotic bric-a-brac that were now almost commonplace to me.

But I remembered having been a young tertiary, recently arrived on Pentateuch. Though I claim this planet as my homeworld, I was born on Istakhr. A young noble from a family of ancient lineage but no money, my questions and interests caught the attention of a traveling Eskatonic — one who feared the Orthodoxy would do more to squelch my faith than to nurture it; and on his authority I was sent to Pentateuch as a tertiary, to study the ways of the Eskatonics.

En route to Pentateuch — a trip which my sponsor also paid for — I had begun to hear tales of this planet: its vast fields, of sage and poppies and tall kalinthi grasses; its peasantry, a hard-working people for whom poverty was not synonymous with squalor; its travelers, an odd and eclectic bunch of scholars and poets and mystics; and the Ghost Wind.

The Ghost Wind — the Scirocco, the Psi-storm — that strange and inexplicable storm which swept the surface, sometimes bringing out-landish events in its wake: disappearing cities, psychic powers, visions of heaven and hell. Would I see this Ghost Wind? Would I be swept up in its power, its magic, its majesty? I equally feared and longed for the Scirocco, which was itself just part of the greater, mysterious Weltgeist, the pattern of enigmas that ruled Pentateuch.

And living on Pentateuch, I did see the Scirocco. Anyone who lives on Pentateuch has some contact with the Ghost Wind — but my experi-ence, like the experience of most — was ultimately uneventful. Traveling to the Shulel rainforest, with a group of other vacationing novitiates, our chartered air yacht was enveloped by a fierce electrical storm which appeared out of nowhere. We all knew instantly what it was, as strange bolts of energy filled the sky and encircled our ship, buffeting our vehicle and forcing us to land lest we crashed. But that was it — no visions, no psychic manifestations. There was one of our midst, a young lady named Lorenn who was reluctant to discuss the experience after-ward; before the trip we were rather close friends, but afterward she grew more distant, and she would soon leave the Naos and the Eskatonic Order, and set out for the stars. I heard tales afterwards that she began to demonstrate psychic abilities, and was on the run from the Church — "Freedom before Penitence!" was her defiant cry before she disappeared from sight.

But I never again experienced the Weltgeist, and in truth I had little desire to. It was hardly the romantic encounter I had envisioned, and my own studies in the Digamma Apocrypha sated my imagination and my yearning for the mystical. My studies brought me faith and strength. Having returned to Pentateuch, I slowly felt my strength returning, but still my faith was as elusive as the Ghost Wind.

* * *

Another week passed. Again I had the dream, and this time I could see the woman singing, her dark form silhouetted by moonlight, her long hair blowing fiercely in the wind. I could not understand her words, and the tune was unfamiliar to me. I could not sleep afterwards, so I read the Hagiography of Saint Orion, who in his old age grappled with the very same issues I did, and these readings led me to re-examine my situation.

Was my return to Pentateuch the healing balm I'd expected, or was I simply avoiding my pain? True, I had had a horrible experience on Nowhere, but I lived to tell about it. Was my slow recovery and gathering of strength the effect of having returned to my homeworld, or simply a matter of time? And would hiding on this agrarian, bohemian world afford me the opportunity to meet my doubt and overcome it, or was I simply hiding and hoping for my dark demons to go away on their own? These were questions I could not answer immediately — but like others of my Order, I allowed metaphysical speculation to numb me to the present: the greater the notions I had to grapple with, the less I actually had to feel.

Finally I sought a mid-morning break in pursuit of freshly roasted joloba beans, with their exquisite bouquet and aroma like lavender and clove and dhee. One could occasionally find them imported from Pentateuch in other agoras across space — but there they were often old and stale and rarely worth their exorbitant cost. Here on Pentateuch, they were plentiful, and I decided to succumb to my cravings.

The crowd seemed particularly boisterous today, I thought, as I roamed among the stalls of the Plaza's agora. The crowd around the joloba-seller's stall was too thick, so I contented myself with a cup of steaming kalinthigrass tea and headed toward the stall of Johann Carver, a noted bibliothecary with whom I had done business before. I was surprised to find a gaggle of Orthodox priests perusing some of his wares. Aware of what types of "questionable" literature they might find, I caused a bit of a theological ruckus (the type we Eskatonic priests are universally notorious for) and they drifted away in disgust.

"You owe me one," I whispered with a wink to Johann. I had some books already in mind — books I had found previously in my travels, but were trapped aboard the confiscated *Prophet's Dream*, and which I suspected I'd never see again.

"There's no denying it, Brother Lathan," Johann said, gripping my hand. "I don't really have anything that would get me in trouble, but I'm sure they'd moan and gripe about something here, and otherwise ruin my day." He smiled amiably, a wide grin broadening his wrinkled face.

"I'd heard tales you'd returned to Pentateuch, but this town is full of rumors." We chatted a few moments, and seeing the Orthodox priests now out of sight, Johann said, "Let's go inside and talk." He gestured for a clerk to come take his place at the stall's main table, and led me behind the table.

We entered a large tent, one that was far more durable and expensive than it looked. Within the tent were two chairs and a small table for conducting private business, as well as a few trunks with more books — those too expensive or rare to leave at a public table.

We took our seats at the table, and engaged in some small talk — I inquired about his family, and he inquired about my health; finally we moved away from casual chit-chat as Johann inquired, "What can I find for you, Lathan? Just what could a famous traveler not already have that a humble bookseller like myself could provide?"

A shadow must have crossed my face, and he fell silent.

"I once did have a rather nice personal library, but it must now be... replaced..." The pause was less for drama than due to a sudden dry throat, and I cursed myself for my visible emotional frailty. "I'm not even sure where to begin, and to be honest I don't really know if I even want to replace them. I'm in a transition right now, so I guess I'm open to anything."

Johann thought for a few moments, then stood up and reached into one of the crates behind his chair, rummaging — carefully — through the crate's contents, finally removing something. It was a book-shaped box. He sat again and rested the box on his lap, his hands placed atop it.

"Being a bookseller in Heliopolis, I am accustomed to eccentric customers," Johann began. I smiled and nodded, but allowed him to continue — it was his way to tell a story with each item he offered, and his stories were always engaging (if not entirely credulous.)

"A month ago, one night before closing, a young woman came to me, asking if I would accept a book.

"I figured she was trying to sell me a book. It is not unusual of course, but I doubted she would have something of interest to me. She was a pretty lass, to be sure, but she looked like she came in straight off the Plains of Jorel, maybe from a ranching or farming family. Dressed in plain clothes, pretty in their own way, she smelled of draga-sweat, and soil, and colirr-flowers: on anyone else an unattractive odor, but on her a rich, musky scent. But anyway — I figured her mother had probably died and the lass, probably illiterate, thought her mother's almanac or other such book to be a rare volume of fine poetry or the like.

"Still, I humored her. She seemed pleasant, and in a way reminded me of my mother, as I imagined she would be like when she was young. So I said that I might buy a book, and asked to see it. I figured I might give her a pittance from my pocket, a fortune to hers.

"She gave me this box." Johann gave me the box to inspect — made of wood, perhaps stained mellior-wood, of exquisite craftsmanship. It was tied with a simple cord.

"I also admired the workmanship, and carefully opened the box. Go ahead, open it yourself. You'll note that there are no visible hinges in there, by the way."

It was as he promised: the box broke open on invisible hinges, revealing a leather-bound volume within, one that looked brand new. I removed the book, and opened it. The contents were handwritten, in Old Urthish. The very first page read, in a fine script, *Walking in the Prophet's Steps: the Memoirs of Kere Baullot*. The date read 4526.

Johann continued, "I had never heard of this work, and I figured it to be a handwritten copy of a printed volume I did not know. But I admired the workmanship, and thought it might be interesting to someone else. I was prepared to offer a price when she held up her hand, and said 'It is not for sale. I ask you to take the book. You'll know when to give it away.' With that, she left, and disappeared into the crowd."

He paused here, probably for dramatic effect. (Booksellers are all alike.)

"Lathan, do you know who Kere Baullot was?"

I nodded an affirmative, and though I guessed he already knew the answer, I said, "He was a poet suspected of plotting against the Orthodox when they controlled this world. One of the Marabout, he publicly claimed to be a priest of the Eskaton and follower of Saint Deimos, though such was forbidden at the time. The Church accused him of paganism and terrorism, and sent agents to find him, but he went underground, leading the resistance against the Orthodox. He was last seen en route to Mount Tabor. It is unknown whether his ship crashed or whether he was taken by the Orthodox or simply disappeared."

Now Johann nodded, "Yes, I know this now. But then I had never heard of him. I did research, and learned who he was. In the course of my research I continued my assumption, that this book was a handwritten copy of a previous book. But in my research I came across some of his original poems, preserved in your Naos library.

"I read these poems. I didn't understand them. But that doesn't matter. What matters is that they were in the exact same handwriting as the volume you now hold."

I had seen and experienced enough in my travels that I learned to disguise my surprise. Besides, I couldn't be that surprised — this was Pentateuch, the planet of enigmas.

"So I tried to read these memoirs. The grammar is too dense for me to penetrate. But I knew that I held something special in my hand. I considered selling it, until I remembered my visitor's parting words. She wanted me to give it away. So I packed it away, and made myself forget about it, knowing that eventually I would remember it.

"Lathan, that book is yours. I give it to you. Read it, and maybe you'll get more out of it than this old bookseller. Maybe you can verify its contents, or its authenticity, or maybe it will just be a good read."

He stood up. "We've never talked religion, Brother Lathan."

He was right. We hadn't. Maybe that was why I liked him.

"But I believe. And in my heart I believe, just as I believe in the words of the Prophet, that this book was meant for you."

There was little else I could do. I protested at first, but he wouldn't have it; and then I gratefully accepted the book, and hurried back to the Naos, contemplating on the morning's strange turn of events and regretting that I'd missed out on the joloba beans.

I then retreated to my cell and began reading Kere Baullot's memoirs.

* * *

Three days later — spent almost entirely in my cell, with only the briefest breaks for food — I was still reading the memoirs.

Johann was correct. The grammar was dense. And I wasn't entirely sure of their authenticity; it would have taken much more work than I had put into it, and I would have had to track down some paleographers (either other Eskatonics or trustworthy members of the Booksellers Guild) to verify their authenticity.

But in my heart, I believed them to be true. I believed that this perfectly preserved book, looking no more than a few years old, was five centuries old, that it contained the lost writings of Kere Baullot, a poet-mystic-resistance fighter from the days of Pentateuch's occupation. These memoirs contained some of his well-known poems, as well as some I'd never seen before; they detailed snippets of information on his early life on Manitou and his first contacts with Duras Barbelo's *Stellar Apocryphon*; and they discussed his emigration to Pentateuch, and his becoming a Marabout — one of the planetary guardians of Pentateuch, the mystical wanderers who care for the world and her inhabitants, the rangers who find their calling as a result of the Ghost Wind.

I read late into the night, or, more precisely, early in the morning — without any timekeeping devices in my cell, I suspected that dawn was but an hour away. With only a handful of pages left to the book, but my eyes too tired to read any further, I closed my eyes and finally considered the question that begged to be answered.

Did these memoirs end up in my hands just as the conclusion of a series of unusual but otherwise meaningless occurrences — passed from an ignorant farm-girl to a well-meaning bookseller to a confused priest?

Or was there a meaning to their delivery to me? Was I to believe that fate, that destiny — that the Pancreator, even, though I loathed to think of it — had intended for me to receive these memoirs. (My stomach tightened at the thought.) And if this is the case: then why?

I could barely articulate the question to myself before my head slowly dipped onto the desk and I slept, resting my head on this ancient-yet-new volume. And in my sleep, I dreamt once more.

I was again on sand-swept Nowhere. The smell of blood filled my nostrils, and blood was splattered on my clothing: human blood, Obun blood, Shantor blood. But beneath the blood was another odor, something rich, and sensual, and one I didn't recall detecting before. And, in this dream, a fierce wind blew sand into a frenzy, filling my nose, my lungs, and choking me. And beyond the screaming, the wailing, was that voice again, singing that unfamiliar tune. But this time the words were clear:

> *To my right, the abyss;*
> *To my left, blood and fire:*
> *Behind me the past, before me the future,*   ·
> *I walk in mystery.*
> *Yet my footfalls are strong,*
> *For I walk with the Prophet.*

I was no longer on Nowhere, for in the distance, rising heavenward was Mount Tabor, and hanging in the sky above it was bright Nuz, familiar Nuz. The windswept wastes of Nowhere were now the windswept sands of the Megiddo Desert. But still, as that night on Nowhere, beautiful Roa advanced toward me, threatening to trample me as he had Siyyad's skull —

And I awoke, in my cell again. I lifted my head to see dawn welcoming a new day to Creation. The memoirs were still on the desk, the book cracked open. Struggling to clear the cloud of confusion from my mind, I reached down and randomly flipped through the last, still-unread pages.

I froze. There, but a few pages from where I had stopped reading, began a poem in Kere's unusual Old Urthish metrical style, beginning with the words "To my right, the abyss; To my left, blood and fire..."

* * *

Three days later I was aboard a commercial cargo-hopper which originated in Pentateuch; its first destination (and my point of departure) was Aztlan, in Megiddo.

Once more I sat in the cargo hold, tethered to a makeshift seat, reflecting on recent events. Kere Baullot's memoirs ended during his journey to Megiddo — approximately the time and place of his disappearance. Between my strangely shifting dreams (visions?) and the memoirs, I knew that the next stage in my journey would be to visit the Megiddo Desert: perhaps there I would find my final healing and recover my faith, and I could once more set out for the stars, renewed and reinvigorated. Or, my cynical side offered, I would just have a little desert vacation.

At my feet were my belongings — only one bag this time, the essentials I would need to travel about Pentateuch. The others I left with Sister Theophila, after having informed her of my discovery and my intent to travel. For this portion of the journey I chose to abandon my Eskatonic garb in favor of a nondescript traveler's clothing. My only weapons were a machete and slug-gun, the former carried more as a survival tool and the latter mostly for show.

The hopper set down in Aztlan, and left without me. I stayed on in the town, a walled city built atop rock, a haven of stability in the ever-shifting sands of the Megiddo Desert — a city which was a ghost town during my last tenure on Pentateuch. Although centuries old, first built during the Second Republic, it was abandoned without explanation for most of its history. Only in recent years had a colony of Ur-Obun traveled here from their homeworld of Velisamil.

I saw that the Obun of Aztlan were culturally distinct from most other Velisamilun, however. Instead of the intricate garb of their brethren, these Obun wore simple white robes and cloaks, like pilgrims or monks. I had further heard in my travels that the Obun of Aztlan did not conduct themselves like "normal Obun": they barely participated in the Umo'rin, the ruling Obun Federation, and they did not adhere to the Ven Lohji sect of the church, following instead an Obun Eskatonic.

I mustered a few words of Lojmaa, which I'd learned from Loannen, and tried to engage a few of the townspeople in idle chatter. Though they responded, these Obun seemed more guarded and distant than most others I'd encountered. In all, though, they were neither conversational nor rude, and I was able to conduct my business with them, purchasing a hardy draga-beast and desert rations. One Obun offered to hire himself out to me as a guide, to Mount Tabor, but I turned down the offer. I desired solitude and independence.

That night I ventured beyond Aztlan, heading westward toward Mount Tabor — not really knowing whether I would reach it or veer off at some last-moment whim. I rode the draga-beast, my provisions and supplies packed over its back, a sand-filter strapped to my cowl. For three days I traveled by night and rested by day — at times over shifting sands, other times over barren rock. The reptilian draga-beast was surefooted and reliable, if not swift. I had brought provisions for weeks in the desert, and knew I could return to Aztlan for more if necessary. In a worst-case scenario, I also knew I could kill and eat my mount, but that was not a flavorful prospect; dragameat is nutritious but tasteless.

I met a few other travelers, some Obun and some human, no doubt on their own pilgrimages to Mount Tabor, and stopped to talk with them briefly. I noticed that they treated me with some deference, as though I were a guide — the blind leading the blind, I figured, though I was glad to be of whatever help I could. Every day, I slept soundly (all things considered), my rest uninterrupted by dreams or visions.

During my fourth night's travel, the Ghost Wind struck.

It came, as it does, out of nowhere: a fierce wind raising the desert sands in a frenzy; tendrils of eldritch energy snaking through the air, uniting heaven and earth in a pattern of arcane lightning. My hackles raised; the draga-beast panicked, and threw me to the ground; one foot was still caught in its stirrup, and as it tried to flee the surrounding storm, it dragged me. Pain exploded in my skull, and before the blackness engulfed me the last I heard was the beast's excited and terrified squeals. My foot slipped from the stirrup as I slipped into unconsciousness.

I awoke, still buffeted by sand and wind, still hearing the animal's excited squeals over the howling winds. But then I knew that I wasn't hearing a draga-beast, but a Shantor. My eyes snapped open.

I was on Nowhere, and it was that night. I was with my companions, taken by surprise with Roa's sudden treachery.

Siyyad al-Malik was the first to fall, beneath the weight of Roa's hooves; the back of his skull was completely crushed, and he lay face down in a pool of blood-muddied sand. Siyyad was more than the noble sponsor of this expedition; he was my friend and my companion. My heart began to race.

Loannen vo Mardenni was next: as he reached for his sidearm, Roa's war-spear tore into the Obun's sternum, then through his back, splintering within his graceful body. Loannen slumped to the ground, the Shantor's lance skewering him, and Loannen's cry of pain ended in a gurgle and a moan. Loannen was a bit sour and sometimes secretive, but he was a good Engineer and a trustworthy companion.

Then Roa turned on me: I was the next closest, having run to Loannen's side. My Eskatonic mantle, which I wore so proudly, was obscured by the dark lifeblood of my companions. I was unarmed, and unprepared, and could scarcely offer a prayer of repentance in the seconds as Roa reared threateningly on his back hooves, and prepared to trample me. Roa, the Shantor warrior — I still remember my excitement when I first met him, and the long conversations we held late into the night. Only that night, I looked at him with terror.

I didn't hear the first blast, perhaps I heard the second; but I definitely heard the third blast, as Lissa's sidearm tore into Roa's flank, breast, and skull — and Roa's blood also splattered my clothing, before he toppled over. My mantle, a sign of peace and wisdom, was stained with the blood of three species.

Weeping, I removed my blood-stained mantle, a mottled testament to the failure of our pilgrimage and my own faith, and packed it away.

As I hid it away, so did I put aside my belief and my faith. I still wore other a priestly mantle, as required by my religious vocation; but it was a false banner, and as I traveled I knew what dark, sad secret was tucked away in my belongings. For months I struggled to understand that night and Roa's sudden treachery.

Was the Shantor's attack long in planning — or did some madness seize him? That a Shantor and an al-Malik would travel together was surprising, and some skeptics predicted that Roa would turn against Siyyad, whose family lorded over the Shantor for years. But we all knew better; we four were family, a family of different species united by love and bonded by adventure.

And here I was, re-living the entire event. When would it stop? With Lissa's anguished and tear-filled departure into the wastes of Nowhere, a lamenting wanderer? My departing Nowhere, seeking my own under-standing to the events of that night?

No — the winds swept up around me again, obfuscating my view, and I caught in the heavy breeze the scent of draga, of melliorwood, of kalinthi and colorr, of all the smells that reminded me of Pentateuch. My pulse raced with anticipation.

I stood on a plateau, high above desert wastes. Before me, bathed in moonlight, was a statuesque, unmoving equine form. To many, one Shantor looks as another, but I knew better. I recognized Roa from his height, from his markings, from the way he carried his mane, and from the simple war-harness he wore. Roa was no cynical Darkwalker: he was a warrior proud and true, from a long line of Shantor warriors.

This ghostly vision of Roa stared nobly ahead. At his feet was his spear, broken and bloodied.

The wind rose again, temporarily, then quelled. I stood face to face with the spectre of my friend, my enemy.

"You question me," came the translated voice from Roa's *dolomei*, the computer-translator at his throat. Was it a question, or a statement?

"Why?" The question burst from my throat, uncontrolled. "We were a family — " My throat broke, and before I could continue, I collapsed at my knees, doubled over, wracked by weeping. I came seeking peace and I found only a deeper pain. *Let this spectre trample me, as Roa desired in life. Take me now, and end my pain.*

Was that what this was about? Did some sorcery conspire to give Roa the opportunity to complete his Godforsaken treachery?

"A traitor with us," Roa said, seemingly oblivious to my pain. "My will a castle, under siege. My actions, not mine."

What? For a brief moment I wondered, as I had many other times, how Roa's wind-speak would truly sound if I understood it, knowing that no *dolomei* could ever convey the grace of a Shantor's tongue. Then I turned back to the situation at hand. I pulled myself together, I rose.

"You attacked Sayyid," I responded, between tears. "Was it because he was an al-Malik?"

"No," snorted Roa. "Sayyid my friend. Like you, as brothers were we. But Loannen — false."

Loannen false?

And the wind encircled us once more — returning me to Nowhere.

Only now, it was different: I knew, without question, that I was in the memories of Roa's shade. And this time, I saw the truth, and I saw it through the eyes of the Shantor.

I saw myself sitting, reading, as I had that night, and I felt Roa's respect for me, and his love. *God*, I pleaded, *why are you making me feel this?* And I saw Siyyad, through Roa's eyes, approaching the Shantor to speak. Behind them, Loannen, our Obun Engineer companion. And I felt Roa's horror as he was no longer in control of his own body, but felt Loannen's mind reaching out and controlling the Shantor like a horse-puppet: as he rose up before an astonished Siyyad, and brought his hooves crashing down on his beloved friend's head. And through Roa's eyes, I saw the look of satisfaction that momentarily crossed the Obun's face. Then I saw myself stand, mouth agape, oblivious to Loannen.

Somehow, Loannen's mental grasp of Roa's actions slipped. I felt Roa's rage as he seized his own spear in his mouth and drove it through Loannen's breast before he could cause more harm. And then, I — Roa — raised up on my hind legs, and I could see myself standing before him, terrified. I trumpeted my rage and turned to the Eskatonic priest, ready to announce what had happened.

Then, Lissa stepping forward, her sidearm raised. Her noble lover had fallen, and she only understood what was visible, not what was true.

I died with Roa, as he dropped to the sands of Nowhere, felled by Lissa's gun.

The winds rose again, and then they left me. And I was back on the desert of Megiddo, with my draga-beast in the distance, skittering nervously.

The moon shone brightly overhead, and I felt Roa's shade, unseen, but watching, and I knew it had been released — released from my hatred, and my pain. I heard, riding the swiftly fading winds, the song of my dreams: Pentateuch's song, for I know now that it was she who stood in my dreams, singing, to bring me here. Pentateuch's own world spirit, known by many names, had come to me, bringing me the truth.

I reached within my pack, and found bundled within it, my original mantle: the one I had hidden from sight and mind, so I would not see its blood-stained banner. I unrolled it, and it shone, clean and new before me. The blood was gone, and with it, my pain, my confusion, and my hatred toward Roa. I slipped this mantle over my clothing, and whispered a prayer to the Pancreator.

Finally, I understood. The pain, the confusion which had become my companions over the past few months and had burrowed deep into my heart and stomach finally left me, and I felt free: I breathed deeply, inhaling the scents of Pentateuch as I'd never sensed them before. My faith was restored, and even more — it was greater, for it was faith married to understanding.

The draga beast slowly returned to me, and we rode together. I was no longer headed toward Mount Tabor; and neither did I care to return to Aztlan. In truth, I no longer cared where I was, for as long as I was on Pentateuch, I was home. I had an entire world before me, a world which I understood, and loved. I had reclaimed what I lost, but I no longer desired to return to the stars. There were others whose destiny led them there, as mine once had. But now, my destiny was here, on Pentateuch. She had touched my heart and my soul.

If the Pancreator was justice, Pentateuch was his mercy: and the Ghost Wind was the breath of God. Pentateuch was more than just a planet; she was a mother, a guiding spirit, a friend, a boon companion. In my time of need, she brought me answers. Though I did not understand Loannen's motives, I did not care to. Strangely, perhaps, I never trusted him, but Roa I loved and trusted; and the pain I felt at Roa's seeming betrayal was cleansed, washed away with my tears and the Ghost Wind — the Ghost Wind which brought me visions of the past. From the Windrunner's shade I saw how things truly were. He gave me the truth, and in return, I gave him justice.

And in both, we each found peace.

Lights of Cadiz

Andrew Greenberg

As he surveyed the revelers dancing, drinking and gossiping at Sylvania Decados' birthday ball, Emilio van Gelder remembered a Second Republic magic lantern version of a grand masquerade. Flawless men, women and others mixed easily in a glowing hall, bright with color and the shine of perfection. They engaged in witty conversation while arguing issues of critical import. Maybe such events occurred regularly on Byzantium Secundus, the Emperor's throne world, but here on Cadiz parties like Sylvania Decados' were the rule.

Childhood diseases (and some more recent) marked the skin of many far-from-flawless guests. Their clothes, though elegant and tasteful, showed the signs of repeat wearings and the stains of previous affairs. The electric lights in the main hall flickered at odd intervals, and smoky torches lit less critical rooms. Scented candles failed to completely mask the hall's many odors, generated through generations of use. Servants scurried to and fro keeping the candles lit, refilling drinks and seeing to other needs, but their constant toadying reminded Emilio too much of the planet's many poor. Even when entering the ball Emilio had had to maneuver past some of Cadiz's many beggars before Decados guards drove them off.

Now he breathed deeply, brushed away imaginary threads from his faded silk doublet and prepared to throw himself into the party. Despite its many imperfections, Baroness' Sylvania's party attracted the best of what Cadiz had to offer. The planet's eminent nobles and richest merchants mixed freely, accompanied by occasional religious leaders and off-world dignitaries. While conversation did not have the sparkle Emilio remembered in the Second Republic holograms, he could tune out the braying of the less worthy figures and concentrate on that of the more intelligent attendees.

While not himself a powerful noble, Emilio benefited greatly from his family's close ties with the ruling House Decados. House Van Gelder affiliated itself with the Decados almost 500 years ago, and the two have worked closely together ever since. A tingle ran down Emilio's spine as he remembered why he first began attending Cadiz's many functions.

His parents, ashamed at their own forced subservience to House Decados, had withdrawn from the planet's social whirl. Afraid of what important information they might miss and anxious to use the parties to increase his own prestige, Emilio began intercepting their invitations and going in their stead, determined to resurrect his family's past glory. His smile faded as he thought about how poorly he had fulfilled his earlier ambitions.

Soiree merged with soiree in his memory. None stood out, and while he had met most of the planet's leading figures, he primarily associated with other, less-influential young nobles. Their main objectives seemed to be attending as many parties as possible, bedding as many of their ilk as they could, and managing to live off someone else's largesse as much as possible.

Emilio licked his lips as he again reminded himself to keep an eye out for any nobles in a position to help his family, and he began his rounds through the ball. Despite his best intentions, he instead soon found himself in a cluster of young nobles critiquing the last party they had attended and planning tonight's conquests. Instead of witty repartee, he found the most inconsequential of phrases falling from his lips as he talked.

Suddenly weary of his own conversation, Emilio turned away from his fellow nobles, looking for a polite way to make his escape. He glanced at the main doors and then took a harder look. Silhouetted against the huge fake wood doors stood a figure straight out of his ancient magic lantern show. Long black hair flowed down her honey-pale shoulders. Though her gown appeared surprisingly modest for a Decados party, it had a glow of delicacy about it lacking in other outfits, and it shone with its freshness.

At least one of Emilio's fellow carousers took note of his new fixation and whispered in his ear. "I'm also amazed Sylvania managed to get her to attend. I hear our Baroness actually considered going to church on the off chance of inviting her." Seeing Emilio's look of confusion, she continued. "That's Celestra Li Halan, daughter of Baron Kaosiung Li Halan."

Emilio's eyes widened with astonishment. The Li Halan made a great show of their piety, and Baron Kaosiung, as the house's leading representative on Cadiz, took this to even greater extremes. While some Li Halan would appear at these parties, ostensibly representing their house, no one expected the Baron or his family. While Emilio knew of his great wealth, he never suspected that those vast estates housed a daughter.

Now aware of her identity, he also noted her uncertainty at proceeding beyond the entryway. Breaking off from his informer, he made his way to where the Li Halan stood. "Lady Celestra, I haven't had the pleasure of seeing you since we met at Nigold Cathedral. Sir Emilio Van Gelder," he said, bowing low.

She glanced up at him and laughed nervously. "It's been years since I've been to Nigold. Did you always wear your hair like that?"

Emilio smiled, his charade having survived its first test, and one of his dark hands stroked the dreadlocks of his hair. "No, my lady. I'm afraid my parents would never have permitted such an appearance before I gained my own title. This is a recent addition. Long hair is quite against tradition." It also made things more dangerous for Van Gelder following a traditional path, for enemies could easily grab it, and it made disguises harder to apply.

Celestra smiled a little at this and seemed to relax. "Our parents find the most irrelevant things to be of importance. If my parents had not been off planet, I would never have made it here. My own brother tried to forbid my attending this very party tonight. I practically had to sneak out of my own home." She smiled carefully. "At least two of Lanzhou's guards followed me here. He sees enemies everywhere."

Now it was Emilio's turn to laugh. "Really, your brother should have had no fears. On all Cadiz there can be no place safer than Baroness' Sylvania's."

"According to my brother, there is no place more dangerous for my soul." Emilio knew better than to confirm or deny that assertion, and instead offered Lady Celestra his hand. For the next two hours he shepherded her through the party, introducing her to the more interesting guests, dancing with her an appropriate number of times, and ensuring that her wine glass stayed constantly full.

He felt her slowly relaxing as the party continued, but he felt his own anxiety increasing. He knew most of the guests at the party, and realized that his monopoly of her attentions could only last so long before a more influential attendee decided to step in. As they danced he could feel more and more eyes turning on them, taking in her lithe figure, long black hair and emerald eyes. Self-conscious anxiety began

to gnaw at him, and he felt the heat rising to his brown cheeks. Therefore he was actually relieved to hear her begin worrying that she needed
to leave.

"Well then Lady Celestra, shall I return you to those escorts your
brother provided?" he asked.

At this she turned to him with a determined look in her eyes. "I
know what they say about House Van Gelder. Can't you make those
guards go away?"

Her request surprised Emilio and made him rethink the innocence
he had attributed to her. Long ago his house had found itself on the
brink of extinction. In order to survive, it had turned to practices both
foul and vicious. Thus the Van Gelder had a well-deserved reputation as
assassins and regicides, having turned themselves into weapons of the
deadliest kind. Ancient rumors spoke of assassins using grotesque chemicals against their targets, blowing up hundreds to kill one, and even
manipulating their children's own genes to create perfect killing machines. While Emilio's parents had rejected this part of their heritage,
Emilio had found the reputation both helpful and a hindrance. That it
would attract this young Li Halan did not shock him. More than one
youthful noble found it exhilarating to associate with a possible mur-
derer.

"Wait for me by the door," he told her, and made his way toward
the kitchen. Like his parents, Emilio had also decided to forsake the
way of the dagger, but his childhood training had prepared him for
such practices all the same. A brief survey of the streets outside the
mansion revealed Lady Celestra's two shadows as well as a third she
never saw. A few mantises spent on two of Sylvania's servants bought
Emilio a cloak and promises of aid. With the cloak in hand he met
Celestra at the doors.

"When I wave, take my hand and run," he told her. Taking care that
she could not be seen from the street, he motioned for a servant to open
the doors and then walked out. He glanced around and stretched. At
the prearranged signal, dozens of beggars descended on the startled Li
Halan guards, overwhelming them with demands for money. At the
same time Emilio beckoned for Lady Celestra, threw the old cloak over
her and the two hurried away through Cadiz's twisting streets.

Several blocks later they stopped, laughing and gasping for breath.
"I can't believe you beat the cream of the Li Halan guard with mere

beggars. Oh, to see my brother's face when they tell him!" She threw her arms around him and his own circled her in a strong embrace. She did not pull away as his lips met hers, and a tiny spark passed between them. They stayed locked in their embrace for more than a minute before Celestra shyly pulled back.

"I'm glad you didn't hurt them," she said quietly. "It was stupid of me to ask for that."

Gently taking her hand, Emilio drew her back to him. "I'm sorry to say that I could not fulfill that wish. I've rejected that part of my past," he said as if covering some ancient wound. In fact, Emilio had never involved himself in any of his house's less seemly endeavors, but he knew admitting such would lessen the exotic aura he strove to cultivate. He held her for a moment before looking up and down the road. "Shall we find another party?" he asked.

Celestra shook her head in refusal. "Do you know where my family's home is?" she asked. "I've long dreamed of bringing home someone they didn't know — or approve of. This is the longest I've ever been alone without my family, chaperones or guards. Would you escort me home?"

The Li Halan mansion was not far from the party. All the planet's leading families maintained city estates close to one another, and the couple reached the mansion within minutes. The tall, elegant building stood quiet in the night, and Celestra guessed that the guards remained unaware of her departure from the party. Using her keys to enter the building and Emilio's ancient training to avoid encountering anyone, the two made their way to Celestra's top floor chambers, finally creeping in through the balcony doors. They again burst out laughing.

Laughter led to another embrace, and soon the couple found themselves on Celestra's down mattress, below the bed's silk canopy. Emilio's experienced hands carefully removed her green gown and let it fall to the floor. Despite the room's warmth she shivered, and Emilio again took her in his arms. He covered her face and shoulders with kisses as he removed his own doublet and shirt, and then lowered his face to her chest.

Emilio's preparation as an assassin began long before his birth. Generations ago his ancestors decided that years of training were not enough to create a master assassin. Instead they set about supplementing their natural talents, choosing a select few house members to have enhanced children. Some of these children had poison ducts in their mouths and hands. Others could see and hear far beyond the normal human range.

Somewhere in Emilio's genealogy lay an ancestor who could kill with electric shocks and use his tongue like a third arm. Emilio had inherited these traits. Unwilling to kill, he had still learned to utilize these abilities. His tongue, now playing over Celestra's breasts and stomach, could extend far from his lips, and his hands, now running over her hips and thighs, could release small, almost imperceptible electric tingles.

Emilio had taken great care to keep his abilities concealed, using them only when he felt his partners would not notice. Celestra's combination of inexperience and alcohol left him sure she would not realize his changes, and he used them fully. Her golden skin shook with each caress he made, and her dark nipples hardened as his tongue wrapped around them. When he lowered his head between her strong, lithe legs, her back arched at the first pressure from his tongue, and he felt her hands pull at his dreadlocks with a fierce intensity.

As his tongue played across her inner thighs and between the lips of her mound, he became fully aware of her innocence. As he brought her to her first release, he gently used his fingers to break her maidenhead. Then he rose up, kissed her on her gasping throat, and carefully thrust into her.

The rest of the night faded into pleasure as he let himself go. He felt her passion grow through the night as if making love to him broke every shackle her family had used to trap her. His own desire grew as she became more and more exuberant. He used his tongue on her repeatedly, every time leaving her more and more excited. When they finally ceased, it was from exhaustion, not spent desire. They fell asleep in a tangle of limbs, hair, sweat and sheets.

They awakened when the bedroom door slammed open, and Emilio felt himself yanked from the bed. "Filthy mutant!" he heard someone scream before he went crashing to the floor. He barely had time to face his attacker before the man was on him again, pounding away with a flurry of fists and curses.

Then the fists paused as he heard Celestra shouting, "Lanzhou, no!" He saw her hands grab his attacker and Emilio managed to throw the man off. Desperately scrambling to his feet, he got his first good

look at his attacker. Despite the look of fury splayed across his countenance, his resemblance to Celestra amazed Emilio, and the sudden realization that this must be her brother left him unprepared for a renewed
assault.

"He sent you, didn't he?" the man yelled. "You won't sully us. No
one will believe you."

Before Emilio could respond, Lanzhou Li Halan charged him with
a yell of "Damned freak!" and the two crashed through the balcony
doors. Only the iron railing kept them from both plummeting to the
distant earth. The first light of morning reached them as Emilio strove
to break Lanzhou's grip. Instead he found himself slammed against the
balcony wall.

Twice more Emilio felt his head and back driven into the wall. "No
one knows about us," Lanzhou whispered as he drove Emilio back
again and again, a his visage twisted with a mad hate. "He can't prove it.
You won't be his proof!"

Despite the battering, Emilio managed to wrap his leg around
Lanzhou's. He crossed his right arm over his body, grabbed his attacker's,
and yanked. Lanzhou flew backward, hit the railing and spun over.
Emilio, horrified, leapt forward and just barely grabbed him before the
Li Halan lost his tenuous grasp on the railing. Even as Lanzhou dangled
in air, desperately holding Emilio's hand, hate danced in his eyes. "I'll
bury you in the sewers!" he yelled.

Emilio felt an involuntary tingle run down his spine. Sparks flew
from his hand. With a pained gasp Lanzhou let go, the surprise of the
shock causing him to release his hold. Emilio could do nothing but
watch in horror as the Li Halan plummeted to the ground far below.
Only when she screamed did he realize Celestra stood behind him. As
he turned she fled from the balcony and through the doors of her
chamber. Emilio collapsed as guards poured into the room and dragged
him off to the mansion's ancient dungeon.

Emilio had no idea how much time passed before the guards finally returned to his cell, bringing his clothes with them. He dressed
under their watchful eye and then they led him off through the mansion. They finally stopped at one unassuming door, opened it, and
motioned him through.

Celestra, ashen skinned but composed, sat at a table covered with
electronic think machines and other technological relics. An old woman

stood next to her, glaring fiercely at Emilio and desperately clutching a jumpgate cross. "My brother had my room monitored," Celestra said without looking up. "Apparently this is not the first time he decided to watch me."

She turned to the woman standing by her. "Reverend one, would you leave us for a moment?" The old woman's eyes filled with horror, but she managed to stifle her protests and walk angrily out of the room. As the door closed, Celestra collapsed on the table. Emilio ran to her, only to have her stiffen at his first touch. Without saying a word she pressed a button in front of her, and Emilio saw the image of himself and her appear on a screen. It showed them as they were last night, as if an eye had hovered directly over them. Emilio saw the ardor they had shared and heard the whispered words of love that had passed their lips. He also saw sparks light up the darkness, occasionally illuminating the unnaturally long tongue flicking across Celestra's writhing body.

For the first time he felt shame at what he was, but this passed as Celestra took his hand in hers. She pressed another button and other images appeared. These were also of Celestra, but not from last night. Images of her bathing, dressing and relaxing passed over the screen. "I have no idea how long he has been watching me," she whispered. Sorrow again flooded her eyes, and Emilio knelt down to wrap his arms around her. To his amazement, tears of his own poured down his cheeks while Celestra regained her composure.

"Did you mean to kill my brother?" she asked.

"Never, Celestra, never." He laid his head in her lap as he said this and felt her fingers stroke his hair.

"I believe you," she announced quietly, "and as my family's only representative on this planet, I pardon you." She involuntarily glanced around the room before continuing. "There is more that you do not know. Our family confessor has only now told me."

Celestra again looked down. "We are alike, you and I. You did not kill my brother today." Now she looked him fully in the eyes. "He was me." She ignored Emilio's look of confusion and continued.

"My parents took over the Li Halan estates on Cadiz for one reason – to avail themselves of its Decados birthing facilities. They could have no children of their own. My brother was bred in a test tube and I was formed from a flake of his skin. His birth was unnatural and I am his clone.

"Someone suspects. Our cousin, Do Anh Li Halan, has been asking questions. He is an Avestite." Emilio shuddered at the mention of that fanatical sect. Should it discover his nature, even his noble title would not save him from the Inquisition's flames. His whole family would likely burn.

"I do not know how much of my brother's anger was because you made love to me and how much was because of the danger you represent. Our cousin would use this as evidence of our crimes. Maybe Lanzhou also saw too much of us in you and feared what might happen if our lines mixed. In any case, Do Anh is arriving soon. You must be gone before he arrives."

Emilio could only nod, and Celestra continued. "Even this world may no longer be safe for you. Leave Cadiz. Leave me.

"I will do years of penance, but someday I want to be with you again. Find a place where our sins can wash away." She hugged him one last time before again begging him to leave, and he followed her command.

Once outside the mansion's walls he summoned a flitter and directed it first to him to his family's house and then to the spaceport. With what money he had he booked himself passage to Malignatius and began the long journey away from his home.

Just Plain Folks

Sam Inabinet

Jed Grimson, sheriff of West Mikkelshire, stood exactly two meters tall, by one meter wide, by one half of one meter deep at the chest, and when he clapped his hand to the back of his neck and rubbed it back and forth, as he often did, it made a sound not unlike two stones being ground together.

"Hurrisy?" he muttered. "Ah ain't never heard tell of no hurriticks 'round these here parts..." The rumble of consternation deep in his breast sounded like an antique combustion motor. "Y'sure ye ain't come ta the wrong village, pawdray?"

Padre Procrustes of the Temple Avesti eyed the sheriff warily.

"The entire continent of Grikkor is being scoured, Sheriff Grimson. We will leave no stone unturned in our pursuit of evil, West Mikkelshire included." Then, in a less confrontatory tone, he added, "The baron speaks highly of you, however, so I suspect that I shall find nothing untoward here."

"Ah do mah best, pawdray. Ah mean, gettin' the townfolk ta mass regular, an' all. Nearest church'd be Saint Athanasia's at Mikkeli-on-the-Knoll, which ah guess ye noticed is quite a haul from here. A day's travel either which way by brute-cart. Won't do ta empty the entire town out fer two days outa ev'ry week, so we all take worship-day in shifts. Half the folk head on up there one week, t'other half go next week. Ev'rybody gits ta go take mass at least twice a month. 'Tain't much, but it's the best we kin manage with whut we got."

"I would think the baron might allow you some more efficient transport, considering the revenue this province's crop brings to the barony. Does it not anger you to think that he might not be giving West Mikkelshire its due rewards?"

"Folks 'round here's content ta work the land like they always have, and the Pancreeter pervides more'n enough ta go 'round an' then some. Ah think ye'll find that we's all just plain folks here. We all trust the baron ta do whut's best fer ev'rybody. An' if'n he kin turn a li'l profit on whut we don't need, then bless 'im, too. He's a good, kind man.

Ain't nobody else that'd trust the likes of me with a post like this'n, once the Wars was done with."

Seeing the heart-felt sincerity that shone from beneath the sheriff's brick-like brow, Procrustes had to bite his tongue to restrain a bitterly cynical laugh. In truth, the Baron of Mikkelshire was robbing these simple folk blind, squandering his "li'l profit" on illicit pleasures in the resort isles of Grikkor's tropical northern coast.

On the other hand, he could understand the sheriff's feelings. The Grimsons were monsters, abominations, man-made war machines that nobody wanted to acknowledge or have around. Born in the vats of guild laboratories, paid for with noble coin over the objections of the Universal Church, manufactured to serve on the front lines in the last desperate years of the Emperor Wars, they tended not to fare as well after the Wars as this sheriff had. Having fulfilled their purpose, most Grimsons were blasted into oblivion by the selfsame nobles they had fought for; others were shipped back to the labs of the Supreme Order of Engineers, there to suffer fates too horrible to consider. Those few that survived were either kept as little more than slaves or lived as reviled outcasts until they managed to find work as shock troops with that guild of mercenary ruffians, the Muster.

"As you say, sheriff. And it bespeaks volumes of your character, that you pursue the duties of your post with such diligence, and in accord with faith. I feel that you may understand, better than most, the exhortation of the Prophet, namely, that we should strive to transcend our base origins, to become something greater than the role that chance and, er, accidents of birth, have laid upon us."

"Ah cain't claim ta unnerstand much of nuthin, pawdray, but ah do 'preciate yer kind words."

Together they trudged down the hill toward the sheriff's home. Procrustes was struck by the fact that, after their brief exchange, he felt within himself some guarded measure of respect for this blasphemy against nature that lumbered beside him. Many of those born to more fortunate stations in life could learn a great deal from this — this... (this *man*? Certainly not.) — from this *creature's* honest devotion.

* * *

West Mikkelshire, a sleepy farming village nestled in the foothills of Leminkainen's Grikkor mountain range, hardly looked like the lair of heretics, but the priest knew from experience that appearances could deceive. Only months ago, a headstrong Eskatonic deacon wandered into the polar regions south of the mountains on some unnamed mission, was captured by an Antinomian warlock and eviscerated in an orgiastic ceremony of demon-worship. The warlock's patron, an ambitious baron acting in collusion with the barbarians of the Vuldrok starnations, was apprehended but the warlock himself remained at large. The Earl of Grikkor realized he had a problem on his hands and convinced Bishop Norden to call in the Avestite sect, renowned for their zeal in finding and prosecuting enemies of the faith.

And so Padre Procrustes found himself entering a village of squalid hovels clustered around a handful of stone buildings. There was a general store, where produce and livestock were bartered for surplus equipment from surrounding provinces. There was a smithy, where bent plowshares were straightened and lowing brutes were shod. There was a tavern and inn, where farmers went to blow greasy froth from leathern jacks of viscous grog after a hard day in the fields. And there was the sheriff's office, which doubled as a courthouse and prison. Here, Procrustes noted, the jail cell door had rusted open and the cell itself had been used to store surplus sacks of millirice. Is it any wonder, he thought, that the jail sees no use, when the town peacekeeper can juggle pack-brutes one-handed and has the complexion of weathered maxicrete?

That evening, the padre supped with the Grimsons, suffering the company of the sheriff's good wife and son, and enjoying a liberal sampling of crude but hearty West Mikkelshire cuisine. The Grimson home was a single-story log cabin which Jed had built himself since no other residence in the village could accomodate his massive frame. Here in his slightly oversized rough-hewn domain, the sheriff devoured over half of a table-setting which would have fed a dozen normal-sized folk, then leaned back contentedly against the sturdy cabin wall and began picking his enormous teeth with the blunted end of a leatherworker's awl.

Tad Grimson appeared to be a strapping, if somewhat obese, lad of some ten or twelve years old. His tiny dark eyes and broad upturned nose were set in a ruddy round face surmounted by an almost angelic cap of blond curls. Painfully shy, his eyes remained fixed on the priest as though he had never before seen a man of the cloth in person. At his father's surprisingly gentle prompting, however, he mumbled a halting recitation of the Children's Gospel and even followed it with some passages from the Little Catechism, both of which he seemed to know by heart. Procrustes was stupefied to learn that the boy was a mere five years of age, having evidently inherited much of his father's size.

Mrs. Grimson, whose first name the Avestite was never to learn, nearly matched the dimensions of her husband. Though not much taller than the priest, she carried well over a hundred and fifty kilograms of combined muscle and blubber on her wide raw-boned frame. Thick-limbed and powerful, even by comparison to most serf-wives, she handled the massive earthenware crocks of stewed vegetables and hardwood platters of roast ribs as though they were dainty confections on fine porcelain. Jed Grimson must have searched far and wide for someone to take to wife, Procrustes thought, because only a woman like this one could withstand —

With a shudder, the priest left the thought unfinished. Later that evening, in the privacy of his own quarters, he tied a few extra knots in the end of his leather flail and very nearly succeeded in scourging the image that thought had inspired from his mind's eye.

* * *

The padre's room at the West Mikkelshire Inn was small and spare, furnished only with a plain writing table and stool, upon which rested a chipped ceramic pitcher and basin, and a cot with straw bedding under a shabby homespun quilt. Larger, more well-appointed quarters had been reserved for the priest, but the spartan sensibilities instilled by the Temple Avesti led Procrustes to demand the lesser room. This endeared him to the tavernkeeper, a Mr. Big Lu, who had already been paid by the bishop's office to reserve the larger, more expensive room.

When Procrustes entered the tavern-room shortly after dawn, Big Lu stood behind the bar, face split by a broad affable grin, thumbing the clean end of a dishrag into a well-polished shotglass, exactly as he had when the priest last saw him the previous evening. Big Lu had not been named for his height; standing on a platform of old crates behind the bar, he barely met the priest's gaze at eye level. Rolls of loose fat bunched up around his neck, jiggled from his bare forearms, spilled over the top of his trousers and around his wide apron. Every visible part of his body was mottled with freckles of at least three distinct hues and a tuft of reddish hair sprouted from the crown of his head. Procrustes

nodded at the man's boisterous greeting and indicated the table where
he wished to take his breakfast.

As the tavernkeeper waddled back to the kitchen, something caught
the Avestite's eye. On the wall behind the bar hung a long mirror, Big
Lu's attempt to "bring a touch o' class to th' joint." It looked to have
once been a noble lady's dressing-glass, stripped of its ornate frame and
discarded or sold cheaply once its surface had become tarnished. One
cracked corner, probably damaged in transport, sat in its new frame at
a slightly downturned angle, affording Procrustes a view of the bottles
and jugs in the shelves beneath the bar. Lying within easy reach across
an upper shelf was the business end of a halberd.

It was of the "Lochaber" type favored by most Hawkwood
footsoldiers, sporting a convex axe-blade to the front, a sharpened spike
sticking straight up from the top, and a wide hook curving out the
back. The shaft had been snapped off about a meter from the top, just
where the langets ended, and had been wrapped with leather. From the
look of the thing, it appeared to have been employed in a variety of
uses. The sharp end of the hook had been hammered back, and Procrustes
guessed that Big Lu might have occassionally used it to restrain a drunken
farmer who turned belligerent. The thick crust on the spike suggested
its utility in unclogging drains, or some similar purpose. The axe-blade
had been recently sharpened, he could see, and the reddish-brown stains
clinging to its side struck the Avestite as rather sinister.

When the tavernkeeper returned with his breakfast, Procrustes asked,
"Tell me, Goodman Lu, do you get many travelers passing through West
Mikkelshire?"

"Why, precious few, bless ye, father!" the fat man laughed. "Th'
baron's man, 'e comes out ev'ry 'arvest t' check up on th' year's crop,
an' men from other villages come t' trade an' such, but that's 'bout it.
Mikkelshire ain't no crossroads barony no-'ow, an' most folk in th'
county is a-scared away by th' stories anywise."

"Stories?" Procrustes had been briefed on this by a canon at Saint
Athanasia's, but feigned ignorance to draw the man out.

"Oh, y'know, th' usual dam' foolishness! Travelin' man stops fer th'
night, ain't never aheard from again. My gran'pappy said them stories
was old back in 'is day. Mighta been some kinda incident back in
Vladimir's time, was th' way 'e reckoned it. Folks roundabouts keep
tellin' it, 'cause... well, I shouldn't really say..."

The disappearance was, in fact, a matter of public record. A guilds-man passing through West Mikkelshire later turned up dead, a peasant had been hanged for the crime, the authorities pronounced themselves satisfied, and nothing else of the sort had occurred in the barony during the five centuries that followed. But the sparse court records that Procrustes had studied at Mikkeli-on-the-Knoll seemed to hint of similar events in the region dating back to the Fall. And the Avestite's trained senses told him that Big Lu was holding back something. "Why shouldn't you say?" he asked.

"Well, I don't wanna seem unkind. It's just, well, y'know 'ow folk can be..."

The Avestite's eyes darted right, then left. It was well before noon, and the tavern was deserted. "No, Goodman Lu, I don't believe that I do. How can they be?"

The man stared at Procrustes with the quiet terror of a trapped animal, beads of sweat appearing on his forehead. "It's just that, y'know, they're... jealous. Jealous of our lands, our crops. Ain't no place else on Grikkor can produce like we do 'ere. An' ev'rybody's just, y'know... jealous." Shoulders now clenched, Lu twisted his dishrag until it was knotted rock-hard between his fists. Procrustes returned his gaze, uncertain of just what to say. Then the fat man shook with a stifled sob. "Oh God, that's pride, ain't it? I — I'm guilty of th' Sin of Pride!"

Procrustes laid a hand on Big Lu's fists. "The Sin of Pride, perhaps, or simply an uncomfortable insight into human nature. I suggest you take it up with your regular confessor at Saint Athanasia's. In the meanwhile, relax. I certainly can't enjoy this excellent breakfast seeing you in such distress."

"Sorry, father, an' bless ye! I'll be on th' carts next worship-day, I swear!" Big Lu hustled away, wiping his face with his apron, a broad-cut affair forming a full skirt around his expansive waist. Back in the kitchen, he splashed cold water on his face. The priest's eyes followed his exit, lingering on the broken corner of mirror with its ill-concealed halberd-head.

Most likely used to butcher hogs, Procrustes thought, *but I had best keep it in mind. House Hawkwood doubtless cares little for the loss of a cheap, mass-produced weapon, but a charge of battlefield looting could be a useful addition if more serious transgressions come to light.*

* * *

Padre Procrustes spent the day watching the villagers labor in the fields, preparing the ground for that year's planting. He noted the odd clothing styles some of them affected, which were to be found nowhere else on Leminkainen; heavy voluminous tunics, more suitable for winter wear than this moist, hot spring day, and thick turbans worn veiled, a fashion more common among nobles on the al-Malik worlds. Crude decorative stitching adorned most of the cuffs and collars, and the padre realized with a start that most of the laborers were wearing what amounted to their worship-day finery. The soil and sweat that was quickly covering them must have been the first stains their good clothing had ever suffered (unless there was a high-grade Republican laundry engine stashed away somewhere in the village.)

Work in one field halted when a potato was discovered, its sprouts erupting through the rocky terrain at the field's southern perimeter. The Kartor brothers, identical twins who served as the villages head brute-drivers, led a wagon out to the spot, where shovels and pick-axes were deployed to pry the thing free from its nest of stones and thick roots. But it proved itself to be too firmly situated in the hard ground; men with hatchets and saws were called, who toiled awkwardly as their tools snagged in their clean robes. Finally they succeeded in breaking the winter spud apart and loading it onto the cart in five uneven sections

The produce of West Mikkelshire was exported to the richest courts in the Empire, and had long been the stuff of fable. Carrots as long as broadswords; spinach-leaves the size of a lady's cloak; pumpkin-melons so large that, once one had been hollowed, a peasant family of six could sleep inside in relative comfort. This last image was to be found in favorite children's tales from all over the Known Worlds. The padre recalled his first sight of a West Mikkelshire pumpkin-melon shell, many years ago in the grubby backstreets of Sanpietro on Pyre.

He had risked the ire of his father to sneak out with some friends and attend a performance of the Jumbledy-Pog Tinies, a troupe of amateur thespians whose extemporaneous "morality plays" (more play than morality, really) were becoming a matter of notoriety among the youth of Sanpietro. The title characters, the Tinies themselves, were happy-go-lucky freewheeling folk portrayed by a mixed group of children and dwarfs, whose unlikely but uproarious adventures among the garish cardwood and plyboard set-pieces invariably ended with a celebration of mutual affection in the cozy pumpkin-melon rind they called home.

Procrustes grinned tightly at the memory and rubbed the back of his thigh absently; the punishment exacted by his father for that little escapade still aggravated him when he visited humid planets. Lazily sweeping his eye across the idyllic pastoral scene before him, he tried to recall what eventually became of the Tinies. That had been shortly before his father had attained a position of prominence in the Sanpietro Cathedral, which he used to campaign for more stringent monitoring of the content of morality plays. One seldom heard the Jumbledy-Pog Tinies mentioned after that.

Years later, by then a zealous young pilgrim stalking the poverty-stricken alleys of his home town, Procrustes tracked a larcenous selchakah-addict back to his lair, which turned out to be none other than that selfsame pumpkin-melon husk, partially collapsed by dry rot and dessicated by Pyre's desert climate, half-buried under a refuse heap. A member of Procrustes' squad even remarked that the drug-addled thief might, once enough grime had been scrubbed from his face, bear some facial resemblance to one of the old Jumbledy-Pog cast. No further comment was ever made on the matter, though, since none of the young pilgrims cared to admit that they had ever wasted any of their early years enjoying such frivolous trash as the Jumbledy-Pog Tinies.

"Uh gut me a thee-horry 'bout thum thangs..."

The Avestite was startled from his reverie by a low mealy-mouthed voice from just over his shoulder. He spun and squinted up into a narrow chinless face, thick-lipped with dull gray heavy-lidded eyes and comically huge ears that stuck straight out from the sides of the head like the semicircular handles of a jug frothing over with dirty white hair. The face worked its lips across its buck teeth, then, with a sharp bob of its skinny neck, cleared its throat to speak again.

"Yuh wunnuh hear ut?"

"I, ah... what?" the padre stammered.

"Muh thee-horry."

"Your... er..."

"Huh-bout thuh crups!" The face's arm waved dismissively out at the fields.

"Oh — the crops! Yes, yes. Quite splendid!" Procrustes turned toward the fields momentarily, taking the opportunity to step back, so to have a better look at this person. The frame supporting that singular face was tall and lanky, its round shoulders, narrow chest and disproportionately short thick legs lending it a very bottom-heavy appearance. He (or possibly she — or, most likely, it) eschewed the current fashion of West Mikkelshire, clad instead in homespun bib overalls, ill-fitting brogans and a thin cotton undertunic sporting a faded print of some troubador's mock crest. The padre stifled a giggle when he realized that, with the addition of a pendulous bulbous nose and a straw hat, the serf presently accosting him would look exactly like those early depictions of the village idiot, a recurring character in The Little Catechism of Constantius and Constultius.

"But, tain't right, is ut? Thangs uh-growin' all giganticull like that! Dun't ut seem a might unnaturull tuh yuh? Dunt yuh think thuh Pancreeyuh-tor wud see ut as uh mockuh-ry of His plan? 'E dun give us thuh bounty of thuh urth, but d'yuh think he had THAT in mind?" The serf flung his arm at the departing brute-cart, which lurched and bumped along the rutted dirt road, the unsecured potato sections rolling about so vigorously that they threatened to tip the sturdy wagon over. "Folk in this villuj, they gottuh work ten times as hard at thuh tillun', thuh plantun' an' thuh reapun' just tuh put uh meal on thur own tay-bulls, much less bring in uh harvust big uh-nuff tuh keep thuh barun happy! Whur's thuh justus in ut, Uh ask yuh?"

The man was getting emotional, on the verge of hysterics; his breath came in erratic gasps and a vein throbbed on his flushed temple. Procrustes spoke quickly, trying to calm him. "The situation here is not so uncommon as you might think, my good man. When our forefathers first emigrated from Holy Terra, cradle of our race, and cast their seed upon the soil of distant worlds, they found that some plants grew in odd ways to adapt themselves to alien climes. There are many places throughout the Known Worlds where certain crops may grow to sizes that would seem outlandish elsewhere. That such overgrown fruits are fit to eat has been proven by the repeated tests of priest and guildsman for centuries agone, and every noble's taster from here to Vau-space can assert their delicacy. When the Lord sets such a feast before us, it is not meet that we should complain that it be more than we can eat at one sitting!"

"Huh!" The syllable was spat at him in contempt. "Yuh're uh fuggin' hippuh-crut, just like alluh yur kind!" Before Procrustes could draw a breath to reproach the serf for his insolence, the tirade had begun in earnest. "Yuh preach an' yuh preach, but d'yuh evur PRACTUSS whut yuh're preachun'? Yuh tell us tuh shun alluh thut high tech an' such, but yuh dun't say nuthin' 'bout ut when yuh're thuh ones reapun' thuh benifuts! Yuh'd cummit thuh same sins yuh're always warnun' us 'bout!"

The padre had recovered some of his composure, and leveled his fiercest gaze at the serf. "What sins would those be, then?" he demanded through gritted teeth.

"Dun't act like yuh dun't know! Ever'buddy un Lemunkainun knows whut went un 'round here! Tain't no 'aliun climes' thut caused this kinda growth, else it'ud be thuh same all ovur thuh planut! Thangs wuz done tuh thuh soil here! Dark evul thangs! Thangs whut ain't planned un by no Pan-creeyuh-tor, but whut wuz thuh work o' man in hus pride!"

The Avestite folded his arms and scowled impatiently. "Speak plainly man! Just what are you trying to tell me?"

"Ain't yuh figgured ut out yet?" The serf leaned in close to the priest's face. "Our soil here's been TAINTUD! Taintud, by thuh godluss sciuntusts of thuh SUCKUNT RUH-PUBLUCK!" These last words were delivered with such vehemence that Procrustes' face was showered with a spray of saliva.

Suddenly the serf's knees nearly buckled as a massive hand dropped decisively upon his shoulder.

"Ain't ye got work t' be doin', bwah?" Sheriff Grimson muttered in a low even tone. So startled was the serf that his eyes seemed to pop almost free of their sockets. He turned and mumbled a sheepish assent to the sheriff, then took off around a bend of hill with an ungainly, loping gait.

But before he left, he had given the padre a sideways look and hissed under his breath, "Yuh just thank 'bout ut, priest!"

* * *

And think about it Procrustes did, much later that afternoon over an iced sweet-thistle tea in Big Lu's tavern. The overweaning hubris of the Second Republic, which drove its scientists to tamper with the natural order of things in defiance of the Prophet's admonitions, was common knowledge throughout the Known Worlds, the stuff of tales told late at night around dying fires. While many of the horrors spawned during that "age of marvels" had been uncovered and destroyed, still more lurked in the unlit corners of the Empire, as any Avestite pilgrim could attest.

But should West Mikkelshire be counted as such? It was true that this part of Leminkainen had been one of the last refuges for the more radical Republican geneticists in the days of the Fall. In fact, the continent's name, Grikkor, was a corruption of Agricorp Interstellar, the most infamous offender in that field, so the incredible properties of the soil of West Mikkelshire could very well be the result of some mad experiment. There were, however, other aspects to consider.

Not all of the high technology that survived the Fall was necessarily evil; starships, certain think machines and the great terraforming engines that kept the Known Worlds habitable for humanity were maintained for the common good. Even the Temple Avesti had conceded that the nobility could bear the burden of such awesome power, provided that they heed the wisdom of the Universal Church when deploying it, of course. Whatever their origin, the West Mikkelshire crops had been crucial in saving Leminkainen from the famine that struck this region of space after the Fall; were it not for the produce from this village, Leminkainen might have ended up as one of the barbarian starnations of the Vuldrok, rabid plunderers beaten back beyond the Leminkainen jumpgate by Vladimir himself.

"Sounds like ya had a run-in with ol' Pudmo there!" Big Lu explained when Procrustes spoke of his encounter with the awkward serf. "S'posta be out at th' grazin' lands, keepin' a eye out fer wolves an' such, but ol' Pudmo, 'e's got a problem keepin' 'is mind on anything. Guess ye noticed, 'e ain't th' most sociable-like soul ye could ask fer, neither. Kinda th' town gossip, ye might say, an' 'e takes it inta 'is 'ead ta tell folk just what they don't wanna 'ear, an' keep tellin' 'em 'til they go 'way or just pop 'im one in th' vittle-hole! But, well, 'e's 'armless 'nough, once ye get useta 'is ways, so folks 'ere-bouts puts up with 'im. Tell ye right now, 'e can spot a wolf stalkin' th' 'erds twenny klicks away, long as 'e keeps 'is mind on th' job!"

It was about an hour or so before dusk, and the tavern was filling with exhausted farmers, drinking, talking over the day's work, and trading inane jokes that they all seemed to know by heart anyway. Some villagers took up musical instruments in a cleared corner and began plunking away at familiar favorites; "Greenstompers," "Spotted Brute" or the haunting and melancholy "Ballad of Knuckledown Lonesome." It was a scene common enough for any peasant village anywhere in the Known Worlds, but there were certain things about it unique to this particular village that Procrustes could not help but notice.

For one thing, Big Lu's tavern was not a last refuge for field laborers to simply inebriate themselves and vent their collective spleen before trudging home to nagging spouses and bawling brats, as was the norm among most of the peasantry. It was, of all things, a family place, where wives and husbands too frail for the heavy work of farming filtered in to act as Big Lu's serving staff while their children frolicked, danced and chased one another beneath the tables and around the legs of their parents.

This custom of having families together at tavern was not completely unheard of, but was rare enough to pluck at the Avestite's sensibilities. It was often associated with moral decay, as children were unduly exposed to the uninhibited side of adult life, but when Procrustes looked around him he saw nothing of the sort.

A few card games were in progress, without any sign of gambling involved; closer inspection revealed that the games themselves were slightly more complex variations of those played by children throughout the Empire — Fisherman's Haul, Spinster's Choice, Will-o-whist, Slapdoodle and the like. The only inebriant in the house was Lu's thick spiced grog, which was never offered to the children and in which the children took no particular interest. There was no evidence of prostitution, infidelities or even casual flirtations. The almost preternatural wholesomeness of the scene left the hardened pilgrim feeling somewhat at a loss for even minor sins to focus upon.

For another thing, the farmers of West Mikkelshire did not bother to doff their "work clothes" once their work was finished for the day. Those who wore the full heavy robes continued to wear them even while relaxing in the casual environs of Big Lu's, tripping on their own hems, overturning chairs and clumsily sweeping drinks and food from the tables. Such accidents were held to be of little account, met with gentle humor and good-natured assistance from servers and fellow patrons alike. Those who affected the veiled turbans did not remove their veils, even to eat or drink. The padre noted their awkwardness in trying to lift delicately balanced fork-fulls of food up behind the fabric to their mouths, or in trying to drain drinking-jacks without revealing the lower halves of their faces.

Besides the almost comical gracelessness of the scene, the combination of sweaty, unwashed, heavy-set bodies, covered in heavy fabrics soiled with a full day's labor and crowded into a close, low-ceilinged room, resulted in a cumulative odor that was spectacularly pungent, even for a room full of serfs.

Why would they ruin their worship-day best like this? the Avestite wondered. Perhaps this is intended for my benefit? That must be it — they want to put on a good showing for the visiting priest. I should have the sheriff tell them that they shouldn't bother. Let them save their church-going clothes for church.

* * *

After three days of pleasant but ultimately fruitless observation, Padre Procrustes found himself going a little stir crazy. He had at least another day or so before returning to Mikkeli-on-the-Knoll where the Avestite caravan would collect him, and he had found no evidence whatsoever of antinomy, paganism, heresy of any sort, or even the numerous petty sins that were to be expected in an outlying village such as this.

Polite overtures to the Kartors, the Millors, and other prominent families of West Mikkelshire gained him their hospitality and enabled him to conduct casual interrogations regarding the village's affairs, routine matters which quickly had him bored to tears. He listened for hints of a Vuldrok accent in all those to whom he spoke, knowing that among Leminkainen's serfdom were many of the barbarian raiders' descendants, to whom the fleeing warlock might have turned for aid.

Most of the people — especially those who insisted on wearing their unwieldy, now-ragged robes — had little to do with him. This was to be expected; pilgrims of the Temple Avesti were preceded by a fearsome reputation, and were seldom welcomed except in locales where they had consistently proven themselves to be champions of the common folk.

Rare it is that an Avestite finds himself in a land wholly devoid of sin, but by this time that was exactly how West Mikkelshire appeared to Procrustes. So much so, in fact, that he had begun to lose faith in his own finely honed instincts, his unerring ability to ferret out the perpetrators of even the most seemingly inconsequential evils. There was some justification for taking pride in his ability; he had battled an escaped monstrosity from the Genetech cartel on Malignatius, tracked down shape-shifting Symbiot infiltrators on Shaprut, and provided backup for the demon-hunting Kalinthi. So perhaps he could be forgiven for the vague, formless suspicions that hung over him like a dark cloud.

Can it be that I'm getting too old for this job? he thought. Have I become one of those caricatured pilgrims from the decadent magic lantern shows, a rabid pyromaniac so anxious to cleanse the world with purifying flame that I begin to see evil where there is none? O Saint Pietrarcholus! What would my father say to such thoughts? No. There is something amiss in West Mikkelshire, I know it! This village is keeping some dark secret from me, and by the blessed Prophet and all the Saints, I shall find out what it is!

Such thoughts chased each other back and forth in his skull as he absently trod an aimless meandering path around the outskirts of the village. Three days of watching the planting, conducting pointless interrogations that invariably degenerated into vapid small-talk, and poring over endless town records written in awkward childish hands had atrophied his zeal. He found himself negotiating an urge to unpack his flamer and asbestite robe and conduct a surprise midnight search of West Mikkelshire, kicking in doors, overturning bins and shattering every container large enough to hide a human being.

But this town was not so remote and unpoliced that such actions would go unquestioned; every Avestite searching for the warlock on Grikkor would have to answer to Bishop Norden for any action taken against the locals, especially if they came up empty-handed. And then there was the daunting prospect of facing down Sheriff Grimson, who already looked as though he had run through a dozen flamegun blasts unscathed.

Lost in thought, the priest had been following the curve of a small creek. Through the turmoil in his mind, he gradually became aware of a tuneless humming from somewhere just ahead. Rounding a bend in the creek, he found himself overlooking a broad patch of silty mud formed by the curve of the bank. Near the center, partially obscured by reeds, crouched young Tad Grimson, the sheriff's son, diligently working in the mud at some task Procrustes could not see. His bare back and shoulders were smeared with mud, and his canvas short-trousers, secured by a length of thick twine, were quite soaked. Nearby, the lad's discarded tunic lay heaped upon a dry boulder, along with a makeshift fishing pole.

The boy's golden locks were plastered to the sides of his head with mud and sweat, and Procrustes could clearly see, for the first time, his ears, which protruded slightly and came almost to points at the tops. When the Avestite edged sideways a bit to get a better view of what the boy was doing, Tad's humming paused for a second and one of his ears twitched, almost swiveling in the priest's direction. Then he resumed his song and his work.

Reaching deep into the mud, he pulled up a handful of more solid earth, almost like clay. This he packed between his big hands, rolling and pressing until he had a thick disk with a slightly rounded top. Then he scooped up some of the more watery silt from the top of the mud and carefully dribbled this in two crossed lines on the top of his disk. Holding the finished piece up to the sunlight, he nodded to himself and placed it aside on a patch of dry ground, in a row with a half-dozen similar creations.

Mud-cakes, the padre chuckled to himself. Or, as some of my cruder playmates used to call them, brute-biscuits. No matter where you go in the Known Worlds, certain things never change, I suppose. I have even seen noble toddlers instinctively take to the mud when their nanny's attention lapsed long enough. Used to make them myself, long ago, on those rare occassions when we actually had enough rain on Pyre to form mud.

Tad selected one of his earlier cakes, which had sat in the sun long enough for the top to have hardened into a dry pale crust. He brought it to his face and, to the priest's shock, bit off a healthy mouthful. Suddenly the sweet innocence with which the Avestite beheld the scene was replaced by disgust, and possibly a hint of something darker. Procrustes reminded himself of who — of what — the lad's father was. He saw the creature wallowing in the mud before him in a new light; the pug nose, the pointed ears, the heavy, oversized body, all suggested something that was distinctly less than human. Procrustes was struck by the thought that, were he to loosen the twine belt and pull down the back of the lad's trousers, he would see a tiny corkscrew tail growing from the base of the spine.

Tad turned, smiled and said through clay-smeared lips, "Good day to ye, pawdray! Howdy, Pa!"

Procrustes turned. A few meters behind him stood Sheriff Grimson, motionless, massive arms folded across his broad chest, an unreadable expression upon his stony face.

How could he have come upon us so, Procrustes wondered, without the slightest sound to mark his approach? But of course! The Grimsons were manufactured for combat; besides the massive strength, the armored skin, they must have been granted some innate stealth and unnatural speed to offset their bulk. Most impressive. And not a little unnerving.

Jed Grimson asked his son, "Ye git done alla them chores that yer Ma set ye, Tad?"

"Sure, Pa. She tol' me Ah could go ta play when Ah was done..."

"Good lad." The sheriff's eyes met Procrustes' and he jerked his huge head back and to the side. He turned and trudged back toward the village; Procrustes followed, glancing back in time to see Tad Grimson take another big bite out of his mud-cake.

When they had left the creek out of sight beyond a fold of hillock, the padre asked, "Do you think it wise to allow your son to eat mud like that?"

"Ain't done him no harm yet," the sheriff replied. "An' it's a dam' sight better'n whut he useta eat when he'd wandered off on his own." He stopped and turned to face the priest, so suddenly that Procrustes nearly broke his nose on the sheriff's breast-bone. "Look here, pawdray. Ah know mah boy ain't right. Up here, Ah mean." He thumped a heavy finger against his temple. "His Ma an' me knew we wuz takin' a risk havin' a young'un, whut with me bein' whut Ah am, an' all. But we wuz in love, an' reckoned we'd love whutever child the Pancreeter give us just the same. An' all told, Ah gotta say we wuz blessed. Ah've heard tell of other Grimsons, whut tried ta have a family, in secret, y'know, an' whut kinda monsters sprung from their loins... God's been truly kind ta us, an' there ain't a day goes by that Ah don't praise His name the moment Ah wake up."

Procrustes remained silent, staring up into that inscrutable cliff of a face. Jed Grimson turned his eyes toward the thatched roofs of West Mikkelshire, just visible over the next hill.

"Ah've been given the chance ta make a honest name fer mahself, an' that Ah've done as best Ah can. An' there's a place fer me here, which is more'n most of mah kind can say. An' mah boy, well... Weak in the head or not, he's mah boy, an' for so long as he draws breath there'll be a place fer him here too."

Padre Procrustes could think of nothing to add, so he said nothing. Together the two men walked back to the village, each silent in their own pious contemplations.

* * *

As twilight approached, the Avestite paced his room restlessly. From the floor below, the sounds of an evening at Big Lu's tavern drifted up; music, laughter, jovial shouts, the stomp of lively peasant dancing, the clatter of wooden plates and leathern jacks. Through the small glassless window he could see the last of the field laborers heading toward the tavern entrance.

Suspicion had congealed into a dark heavy lump in the Padre's breast, distracting him from his prayers. Never mind that these serfs enjoyed a higher standard of living than all others of their station; that could be attributed to the unique nature of their produce. Never mind the unusual variety of regional dialects concentrated in this one village; the baron kept very tight control over the population, severely limiting its comings and goings — this was no colony of escaped peasants from other worlds. It was the preternatural normality of West Mikkelshire that was so stifling, and it had forced an unspoken vow in the priest's heart. He would scratch that surface, crack the shell of normalcy that encased this village and discover whatever it was that was being hidden from him. Despite Jed Grimson's endearing, almost painful, forthrightness, Procrustes had traveled enough of the Known Worlds to be certain that there was no such species as "just plain folk." Everyone had something to hide, from decadent nobles and filthy-rich guildsmen to the lowliest serf; even the most upstanding members of the Universal Church of the Celestial Sun had skeletons in their closets, as the Temple Avesti well knew.

Brooding upon this fact, the priest hefted his money-pouch, spare change he had brought to cover tolls, tips, bribes and any other expenses his mission might incur. A handful of crests and wings, perhaps a half-dozen full firebirds; somewhere in that mix was an old Vlad's-head, a coin centuries old that bore the profile of Vladimir Alecto, the First Emperor. Not the rarest of items to be sure, but certain to fetch a few 'birds from some rich youth just starting his first coin collection.

In all, the contents of the pouch hardly comprised a fortune, by any means. Except in the eyes of a serf.

Padre Procrustes stood, and took a moment to practice slumping his shoulders and letting his legs go rubbery beneath him. He unlaced his collar, pulling it around to hang at an awkward angle. He tucked one side of his cassock into his sash where it dangled in an undignified manner, as though he had just finished urinating and had forgotten to untuck it afterwards. (A few small droplet-stains on the robe underneath would complete that illusion, but he decided against it.) He dabbed a bit of rubbing alcohol on his lips and beard, then, pouch in hand, he lurched into the hallway and started down the stairs with a somewhat theatrical stagger.

In the main room, a seasonal event was taking place. A few times each year, Big Lu had explained, the populace of West Mikkelshire arranged to purchase an entire keg, and then Jed Grimson would try to swallow as much as he could before taking a breath. Small side bets, usually negotiated in the barter of special services or crafted goods, were placed by some of the townfolk. (Although, in truth, this bit of gambling was entirely optional, a mere sidelight to the spectacle of the sheriff's performance.)

The local band slammed their way through "Hickory-Neck Chase," whipping the dancing folk into a stomping, hooting frenzy. Procrustes rarely took notice of folk music, but found himself impressed with the band's skill, crude and untutored though they may be. Up front, a squat, barrel-chested vocalist with a comically long neck made use of an octave range that would shame most cathedral-choir soloists. One gaunt spindly youth sat curled around the neck of a bass ukelute, his long spidery fingers almost blurring as they danced across the frets. The drummer, hidden behind the rest, would have needed an extra pair of hands to keep up the frenetic polyrhythms that got faster with each chorus.

When the "Chase" reached its explosive finale, the dancing couples cleared the center of the room and a barrel was rolled in and set upright. Big Lu popped the bung, tasted the contents with an expert air and pronounced them fit for consumption. Then a drum roll started as the sheriff stepped forward.

Grimson hoisted the keg to his lipless maw and slowly tilted it up amid a mounting cheer from the villagers, his thick arms so steady that not a drop of the foul grog could be seen trickling down his square chin. Then he set the half-emptied barrel back on the floor, turned, strode with deliberation to the tavern's entrance, and released a resounding belch that rolled out across the fields, echoed off the surrounding hills and set distant wolves to howling.

Watching the huge creature grate the back of his broad hand across his mouth, Procrustes wondered just how much effect alcohol had upon a Grimson's physiology. It probably varied between different breeds, he thought, seeing that the sheriff remained steady and apparently uninebriated by the enormous amount of drink he had just imbibed. (Despite this, a trustworthy farmer had been selected earlier in the week to act as deputy for that evening and the next day, during which time Jed Grimson was officially considered to be "off duty.")

Meanwhile, amid the laughter and cheers following that incredible belch, a measuring-stick was lowered into the keg and a name was read from the notch closest to the wetmark. This season's winner was little Anney Loomer, a cherubic waif of no more than seven or eight years whose family had sponsored her "wager" with several yards of their own homespun linen. A raucous whoop-and-huzzah was raised in her honor, and the other bettors settled with her parents, extending warm and hearty congratulations. Tad Grimson placed a crown woven from buttercups, mayagolds and wild star-lace upon Anney's head, then his father lifted her gently and set her on the bar. There Lu treated her to a sundae of churned sweetcream and fruit wedges topped with a light sprinkle of his own precious and closely guarded brewing-sugar.

The Avestite watched the young girl pretending to feed a wedge of cherry to her constant companion, a button-eyed cornhusk doll large enough to wear Anney's own cast-off clothes. And he said to himself, my timing could not have been better. This is probably as close as West Mikkelshire ever gets to drunken debauchery.

Stomping up to the bar, Procrustes bellowed, "Good people! As some of you may be aware, my stay in your fine village will be at an end upon the morrow. You have all made me feel as welcome here as any man of my calling has ever been made to feel, treating me to the bounty of your fields as well as that of your hearts. Never has any pilgrim passed through a land of such fine, gracious and upstanding folk as yourselves, and I feel it only fitting, in the eyes of the Pancreator and his Prophet Zebulon and all the Saints recognized by the Universal

Church, that I should repay your kindness with some small measure of my own!"

He had them now; nearly all of the conversation in the room had stopped and most eyes were turned toward him. When a dour, hard-nosed representative of the Temple Avesti suddenly appeared in a state of obvious intoxication, bawling about charity and kindliness, even the most untraveled peasant knew that something was up. To prove them right, Procrustes held up his pouch of coin and dropped it heavily upon the bar.

Dead silence reigned in the room. Every face stared wide-eyed and slack-jawed, aping the expression of Anney Loomer's cornhusk doll. There was more hard currency in that pouch than in the entire village put together.

"But think not that this is mere charity. I am not a rich man, who can throw money around without thought or care. What you would have of me, the best amongst you must win through your own guile and craft..." He tried to utter this last phrase with what he hoped was a provocative and devilish leer, but play-acting a part like this one had never been his strong point, and he had not done any undercover work since the Emperor Wars had ended.

To be certain that he would not be misunderstood, he snatched up his pouch and lurched to a nearby table where a card game had been in progress moments before. Dropping the pouch in front of an unoccupied seat and sweeping up the cards, he fanned the deck with a passable flourish and managed a single-handed cut without scattering the cards across the room. He sat down heavily and scanned the sea of incredulous faces. "So who among you is game?"

Most of the men at the table edged away uncertainly, but one remained, leaning back in his chair with his arms folded and one eyebrow cocked skeptically. This was Myklos, the potter, if Procrustes remembered aright, who asked, "How shall we bet 'gainst ye, when we've no money of our own?"

"Well, let us see how thinly Goodman Lu can slice that dried honeyroot vine hanging by his pantry. Let each slice equal one quarter-firebird; you can place your bets in vine-chips. Each man keeps whatever real coin he might win from me, of course, as is only right. Now—" Procrustes leaned forward "— if after a dozen hands any man at the table holds greater winnings than mine, I shall cede my entire purse, to be distributed amongst you folk or put to such use as the village elders see fit."

"And if ye win?" Myklos demanded. "Will ye take yer winnings in vine-chips?"

"If I win..." The priest smiled. "I believe Goodman Lu has one radish left in his cellar, one which he has not yet begun to shave slices from yet, one with the skin still intact, that would stay fresh during a long space voyage. Let that radish be my payment if I win. You see," he added conspiratorially, "my father is close to the Bishop of Pyre, and I happen to know that the bishop has a special fondness for the radishes of West Mikkelshire."

"What do I get out o' this, then?" Big Lu cried. In answer, the Avestite dug a crest out of the pouch and tossed it to the tavernkeeper.

"Why, the honor of serving us, my good man!" Procrustes knew that the crest, or half-firebird, was more than enough to buy several rounds of grog for a handful of thirsty men, possibly even covering some of the cost of the radish in question.

Myklos sat immobile, and most of the villagers simply glared, incredulous and maybe a little scornful. Nobody in the room seemed interested in taking the bait, causing Procrustes to worry that he had perhaps overplayed his part. "Will none of you take up this challenge?" he entreated, his eyes darting from one face to another, seeking a glimmer of Pride or Greed that he could play upon.

Then a voice emerged from the crowd: "Uh'll play yuh, priest."

It was old Pudmo, stepping forward and raising his hand in what seemed to be an uncharacteristic gesture. This galvanized the room, as people leaned together and began to mutter to each other. Hooking a chair around with his foot in invitation, Procrustes mentally thanked the village idiot. It seemed that none of the villagers wanted to be shown up by the least respectable member of their community. Three more men came forward, and then Myklos unfolded his arms, placed his hands on the table and sat upright in his chair.

"Right," he said. "Ye can deal me in."

Big Lu cracked open the seal on a brand new deck of cards, then wrestled the honeyroot vine across his chopping-block and began slicing it into thin even sections. Procrustes sat with his back to a windowless expanse of wall, facing the bar where he could see half of his reflection in one end of Lu's long mirror. Pudmo sat to his right, with

Myklos directly opposite. To the Padre's left were Franck, eldest son of the village's milling family, and Rollo, the burly apprentice of the local blacksmith, whose rugged good looks were marred by a large goiter-like growth on the side of his neck, kept partially concealed with a home-spun scarf. Between Myklos and Pudmo sat an old tanner whose name Procrustes could not understand due to a pronounced speech defect, and whose face was always hidden under his veiled turban. It was agreed that the game of the evening would be Spinster's Choice; a child's game known to all, it was nevertheless complex enough to allow for the char-acter-assessments, contests of will and outright bluffing required to keep small-stakes gambling lively.

Most of the tavern's patrons kept a respectable distance as they hovered around the table, whispering to one another. Elsewhere in the main room, conversations resumed and children danced as the band plunked away at some light unobtrusive tunes.

The first few hands were played tentatively, the dowery-wagers kept small, as the priest and his opponents tried to size each other up as players. By the close of the third hand, Procrustes decided it was time to raise the stakes a little. He bet twice as much as before, and attempted to feign suppressed excitement over his mediocre hand. The others fell for his bluff, and groaned when they realized they had been taken.

Have to be careful of that, he cautioned himself. I don't want them to think that I'm just here to shark them out of some free produce.

But the damage appeared to have been done. It was all he could do to lose enough of his smaller coins to keep them interested. Franck and Rollo placed timid, one-chip bets, and Myklos seemed to have resigned himself to the same. Procrustes lowered his eyes and considered the courting-pair he held.

Then he snapped his head back up when he heard Myklos push a handful of chips to the center of the table. The potter met his eyes, a hint of a smile at one corner of his mouth. Then the tanner equalled the wager, his old eyes unreadable as they peered over his heavy veil. And Pudmo did likewise, concealing his motives with a slack, almost bovine, countenance.

Wary now, Procrustes called. None of the hands at the table were particularly exciting, and Franck seemed genuinely astounded that his low three's-a-crowd won him the entire dowery. The three heavy bettors — Myklos, Pudmo and the tanner — shook their heads, but with some humor. After all, as long as one of the villagers won, they all benefited.

Then the Padre noticed that Sheriff Grimson was looming over the table, heavy fists planted on his hips, scowling down at each of the players in turn. He stayed there for the next couple of hands, finally turning his attention away when nothing untoward occurred.

Procrustes pushed his Vlad's-head into the dowery, pretending not to notice what it was. Franck and Rollo did notice, however, and immediately raised their bets with ill-stifled excitement. If the other three saw what had been placed before them, they gave no indication, but raised as well.

The priest was pleased that his gambit had worked, and even more pleased when he gained the dowery back with two pairs in a double-date. The eager greed he felt from either side of the table was familiar, almost palpable; his trap was now properly baited, the flies humming about the spider's lair. Time to start playing this game for real, he told himself.

The next hand was dealt in an atmosphere of tense determination. No extraneous words were spoken as all concentrated intently on their hands. Whole volumes were transmitted in the guarded glances that shot back and forth between the serfs. The surrounding crowd, however, had not seen the antique coin on the table, and their attention began to stray. Whispered exchanges grew into low conversations, and within a short while it was once more business as usual at Big Lu's.

While arranging the cards in his hand, the Avestite was distracted by a strange sound. It was that growling, low-tech petrol engine rumble that emanated from Jed Grimson's chest when he was troubled. The sheriff was standing some distance away, looking at the table with a dour expression furrowing his stony face. Procrustes could not make out just who Grimson was staring at, and the other players were too focussed upon their cards to be aware of the sheriff's attention bearing down on them.

Still pretending ignorance of the Vlad's-head from his purse, the Avestite worked his next few hands with an almost sadistic cat-and-mouse charade in mind. With a bad hand he would bluff wildly, sacrificing crests and wings but keeping the more valuable coin close to him. But with a good hand he would hesitantly push it forward, then win it back with ease. This drove his opponents into a silent frenzy; if one of them could win that old coin, he would not bet with it again, and thus become the richest man in West Mikkelshire. The game would essentially be finished, regardless of the overall outcome.

When Procrustes pushed the Vlad's-head into the dowery once more, a new sound emerged from Jed Grimson.

"Pudmo!" he barked, not loudly but with vehemence.

"Whu-hut?" Pudmo drawled, blankly looking up from his cards. "Uh ain't done nuthun'..."

Procrustes glanced at the village idiot. Slack-jawed and wall-eyed with animal insipidity, Pudmo reminded the priest of how his childhood friends would try to look innocent when some transgression was in danger of being disclosed. I'm getting close, the Avestite thought. It won't be long now.

"Ah reckon this here game's done gone on long 'nough," the sheriff grumbled. "We all 'preciate yer kind gesture, pawdray, but all this here 'citement's keepin' th' young'uns up past their bed-time. 'Bout time ta cash 'em in, boys."

This pronouncement triggered a chorus of dissent, not only from the players but much of the surrounding crowd as well. Some of the more prominent villagers huddled around Grimson, whispering up at him with fervent entreaties. Obviously unused to hearing disagreement from his neighbors, he apparently took his role as public servant seriously enough to bow to the will of the majority.

"Awright, awright," he relented. "But ev'ryone plays on the level, y'unnerstand? Fair an' square." He wagged a thick finger at Pudmo. "Ye just watch it, y'hear?"

"Oh, Uh wull, shuriff. Uh wull!" Pudmo assured him. (Was that a smirk that tightened the corner of his mouth? Time to find out, the Avestite decided.)

With a full suitor's flush, Procrustes regained the Vlad's-head easily. The pile of vine-chips before him was almost embarassing. To assuage his conscience he bet the last of his full firebirds on a low courting-pair, and lost to Rollo's dancing quartet.

Procrustes' next hand could not have been more perfectly assigned had it been dealt by Saint Pietrarcholus himself: all court cards, just one short of a bridal pageant. Struggling to conceal his excitement, he flicked his Vlad's-head into the dowery with a show of forlorn resignation, and tried to affect a hopeless air when it came his turn to discard.

With a haphazard, almost drunken movement, he pulled the top card off of the trousseau-deck, dragged it across the table, over the table's edge and sent it spinning to the floor, where it landed the better part of a meter from his chair. Franck, Rollo and all the folk nearby politely averted their gaze from the fallen card. Sighing heavily, Procrustes bent down to grab it, keeping his right hand on the table with the cards fanned out and held upright.

Leaning as far out to the left as he could without toppling from his seat, he pretended to grope drunkenly at the floor. From this awkward vantage, he could just make out the gaming table in the side of Big Lu's bar-mirror. There were Franck and Rollo in profile, and just over the back of Myklos' shoulder the priest could see his own hand holding his cards at the table's edge. Pudmo and the other player were just out of sight beyond the mirror's frame. Procrustes strained a few more centimeters to the left, trying to get that angle so he could see what, if anything, Pudmo was doing.

Then he saw it.

Floating in space a little above and behind his card-hand was a wet glistening orb no larger than a half-firebird. No, not exactly floating; a strand of sinewy tissue connected to the back of the thing and extended off of the mirror's edge. Upon the face of that pale fleshy globe was a dull gray iris, which dilated as it swiveled to scan the cards in Procrustes' hand.

Then the thing jerked out of view as a high-pitched shriek stabbed at the priest's right eardrum and he slipped off the edge of his chair, landing heavily on the floor.

The shriek drew out into a shrill cry of pain, through which could be heard the clatter of an overturned chair, the thud of another body into the floorboards of the tavern, the flailing of arms and legs. The remaining players half-leapt from their seats, then froze in position. A collective gasp arose from everyone in the room. Procrustes swiftly regained his feet, his feigned drunkenness forgotten.

In the dim corner beyond the table, Pudmo kicked spastically, nearly hidden from sight beneath the broad armor-plated curve of Jed Grimson's back as the sheriff crouched over him, apparently holding him down with one hand.

"Aaaoowwgh! Quit ut, Jed! Yuh're hurtun' me! Stop ut!" Pudmo squealed and clawed ineffectually at the Grimson's thick hide.

"Ah tol' ye ta play fair!" the sheriff growled back at him. "Din't Ah tell ye, bwah? Din't Ah?"

"Sheriff Grimson!" Procrustes barked, deploying a tone of voice that had once caused a hard-bitten Hazat man-at-arms to crush his own toe with his rifle-butt. "Unhand him at once, before you do him an injury!"

So angry was the sheriff that he did not heed the priest until his deputy stepped forward and stammered, "Uh, Jed, ain't ya s'posta be, uh, off-duty, like?"

Only then did the sheriff stand and back slowly away from the corner. The priest pushed past him to tend to the whimpering Pudmo, who lay curled up with his head in his hands. Procrustes checked his limbs and torso, finding no bruises or fractures. He gently pulled Pudmo's hands down, then choked on the bile rising in his throat when he realized just what it was he had seen in the mirror.

It was indeed Pudmo's own left eye, connected to its socket by a long supple stalk which seemed to be able to flex and twist in any direction. But now it dangled limply, violet welts spreading from where the sheriff's hard fingers had closed around it. Pudmo cradled it gingerly in trembling fingers, slowly and carefully retracting the damaged stalk back into the socket. The Avestite staggered backward, queasy, struggling to control the sudden churning of his stomach and spinning of his head.

In all of his travels through the Known Worlds, Padre Procrustes had never confronted anything to prepare him for this face-to-face encounter with the Changed. The grisly handiwork of bodiless abstract demons was one sort of horror; the metamorphic monstrosities of the alien Symbiots another. But they were each so utterly unhuman, so antithetical to the very concept of humanity, that one could learn to steel oneself against the nausea they inspired. This, however, was different.

The Changed had been human once; that is to say, their ancestors had been human, back in the early days of the Second Republic. But, as the accomplishments of Republican science became more and more miraculous, the pride of Republican scientists grew into hubris, and the Prophet's admonishments against unrestrained technologies were forgotten. They had unlocked the secrets of the genetic code, and plunged into wild erratic experimentation, like children at play, without regard to the consequences of their actions. They sought to "improve" upon the human form, ignoring the care and wisdom with which the Pancreator had designed it.

Most of the victims of these experiments were destroyed during the Fall; the Temple Avesti had been instrumental in seeing to that. But some had escaped this fate, either with augmentations that helped them appear normal, or by living on the run, in the shadows of urban back alleys and in remote, lonely places. For the past thousand years they had lived and bred in hiding, passing their vile traits on to their off-spring. One of them might occassionally gain the patronage of a deca-dent noble or outlaw guildsman (for how else had the genetic technol-ogy used to create the Grimsons been recovered?), but most met their end on the pitchforks of fear-maddened peasants, or kissed by the cleans-ing flame of a diligent Avestite pilgrim.

Pudmo looked up at the priest, viscous tears pouring down the left side of his face. "Uh guess this here's whun Uh get burnt at thuh stake, huh?"

I may share that stake with you, Procrustes thought grimly. Every-body in this room just saw me rush to this foul creature's aid, even ordering the sheriff back in doing so. I have seen what hysteria can do to the low-born, and I shall no doubt be destroyed in the panic which is about to sweep this town.

Never one to shy away from his fate, Procrustes straightened and turned to face the room. The band had stopped playing, and in a deaf-ening silence the folk of West Mikkelshire stood immobile, their faces unreadable as they stared back at the priest. The stillness was broken only by young Tad, who rushed to his father's side, whining, "Ah'm a-skeered, Pa!"

The sheriff encircled his son with a protective arm, but his eyes never left the priest's face. Through clenched teeth, he asked, "Whut now, pawdray?"

Something was very wrong here. Where was the sickened loathing, the blind animal panic? No serf had ever reacted so coolly upon seeing one of these leftover Republican horrors. Much less an entire village, upon finding that they had harbored such a thing in their midst. Could it be that they had simply not seen what Pudmo was? Perhaps the card table was in the way, blocking their line of sight. The Avestite glanced over at the other players. Their eyes were not on the cowering mutant in the corner, but on Procrustes himself. Haltingly, he forced his mouth to answer the sheriff's question.

"This will... have to be reported... of course..."

A surreptitious movement caught his eye. It had come from where the two Kartor brothers were leaning with their elbows on the bar, thumbs hooked in their belts. The nonchalance of their double pose was ludicrous, considering how tense the situation was. But Procrustes had no doubt as to what he had glimpsed — it was something he had learned to spot in the intrigue-ridden courts of the Decados, Hazat and al-Malik; knowing what it was had saved his life time and time again in back streets, filthy alleys and remote brigand-haunted roads on Cadavus, Pandemonium, Nowhere, even on Byzantium Secundus itself. It was the furtive crossing of the arm from one side of the belly to the other, the drawing of a concealed weapon beneath the cloth of a tunic, robe or cloak. One of the Kartors was drawing from the left, the other from the right.

And yet each brother kept both his elbows on the bar, both hands in plain view in front of him.

Then Procrustes caught sight of the broken corner of the bar mirror. The hidden halberd-head was pulled from its place, hefted by a muscular prehensile tentacle covered with tri-colored freckles and a light fuzz of pale reddish hairs. At the other end of the bar, Big Lu ground rag into shotglass with excruciating slowness, his jaw set hard, his brows furrowed low over his eyes. Elsewhere in the room, there were other secretive motions, the rustle of limbs under heavy robes, the wet rasping of unseen orifices, the faint sucking sound of a dagger-like shape clearing a fleshy sheath.

O Saint Pietrarcholus, am I not the greatest fool ever born? Procrustes wondered, feeling his head reel and his knees begin to tremble under his cassock. *Have I not heard my own father speak to the Inquisitorial Synod of the "Circle of Change," a conspiracy of the genetically altered plotting the downfall of humankind? I thought him a paranoid old fool then, and here I have stumbled into the very heart of that whereof he spoke! If ever I make it out of this accursed village alive...*

Sheriff Grimson cut in on the Avestite's thoughts, grumbling, "Just whut is it ye'll be reportin', then, pawdray?" His hand was on his son's head now, his massive square fingertips gently smoothing the boy's flaxen curls. The priest was reminded of his own father's hands, aged clutching bird-claws, always grasping, plucking, jabbing, chopping dismissively, pointing in accusation, wagging in admonishment...

And Procrustes asked himself, when did my father ever touch me with such tenderness?

"I shall report the truth, Sheriff Grimson, just as I always have." With the throng poised to spring upon him and tear him to pieces, he held his hand up firmly and spoke quickly. "I shall tell the baron what an excellent choice he made in appointing you sheriff of West Mikkelshire. I shall tell him how, even on your night off, your vigilance was such that you were able to catch a card-cheat, er, red-handed, as it were. That's probably only a trifling matter as far as baronial law is concerned, so I imagine it will be left to you to administer punishment as you see fit. And I will be sure to point out that it was the only criminal activity of any sort that I witnessed during my entire stay here."

The collective sigh of relief that filled the room nearly bowled the weakened priest over. But Jed Grimson was not yet satisfied. "An' what'll ye be tellin' yer friends in th' Church, pawdray?"

"Exactly what the Inquisitorial Synod, at the behest of the Earl of Grikkor, sent me to find out. My mission in West Mikkelshire was to uncover any signs of heresy. After stringent and thorough investigations, I must say that not only is there no hint of heresy here, but that I found the populace of West Mikkelshire to be the most honest, God-fearing, and, above all, faithful folk that I have ever come across in the Known Worlds. Well, except for Pudmo, but you'll see to him, won't you?

"Furthermore, I shall recommend that the Synod have the baron set aside a suitable portion of the profits from West Mikkelshire's crop for the construction of a church within the village, and to pay for one of your own people to attend a divinity school, so to occupy said church upon its completion. 'Tis the very least you good folk deserve."

A thrill ran through the crowd. Many were fearful that this would bring unwanted attention to their secluded enclave, but they were overruled by the majority who agreed that a church was just what the village needed. Some disagreements broke out as to who would be the best candidate for ordination. Amid the excited chatter, the sheriff said to his son, "Tad, y'help yer Ma clear out th' jail-cell, an' make sure that lock still works. Pudmo, yer comin' with me, bwah."

"Wait uh minnut!" Pudmo cried as Jed grabbed him under one arm and heaved him roughly to his feet. The card-cheat turned his good eye imploringly on his fellow villagers. "Who's gunnuh watch thuh hurds fur wulves while Uh'm locked up, huh? Who's gunnuh do that, Uh ask yuh?"

There was a pause, then someone said, "Why hell, Pudmo, cain't ye do that from th' jail?"

Procrustes' knees finally gave out and he collapsed on his chair, laughing just as hard as anyone in the room. Even Jed released an explosive chortle.

"Awright, folks," he said. "Fun's fun, but we still got the plantin' an' all ta do t'morrow. Let's pack it in fer the night!" There was a chorus of assent as people began to file out of the tavern and Big Lu gathered jacks and platters.

Franck and Rollo got up to leave, but Myklos said, "Hold it. We ain't finished here." Leaning forward, he swept Pudmo's winnings to the center of the table, burying the nigh-forgotten Vlad's-head. "I'm calling this hand," he intoned solemnly.

Everyone sighed wearily, but agreed. Rollo flipped his cards over, showing a high courting-pair. Franck's hand was little better, with a middle three's-a-crowd. Procrustes bent down to pick up his dropped discard, but Lu stopped him.

"There's no need fer that, father. Ye can have th' radish, an' with my compliments, bless ye!"

"I thank you, Goodman Lu, but I owe my opponents at least this much," the Avestite rejoined, and laid out his cards. The one from the floor was a deuce of bouquets — so much for that bridal pageant, and the antique Vlad's-head as well.

Myklos leered, savoring the moment as he turned over his cards, one by one, to show a suitor's flush. "Ha!" he cried in triumph as he reached for the dowery.

But then the tanner spread his hand. All court cards, pages, squires and a knight: groom's-march, which beat a suitor's flush.

"Dammit!" Myklos shouted, pounding the table with his fist. Then he straightened, looking up at Procrustes with wide eyes and pursed lips. "Uh, sorry 'bout that. Please excuse me, padre."

The priest smiled indulgently and made the sign of the jumpgate cross. "*Ego te absolvo,*" he said.

Transfiguration
Jackie Cassada

"I had nothing to do with my sister's disappearance!" Lady Carolandra Justinian glared at her mother. "If you hadn't made her believe that the family honor — such as it is — depended upon her marriage to Evan Hawkwood, maybe his reported death wouldn't have mattered so much to her. After all, she hardly knew him."

Wordlessly, Lady Antorianna finished folding away her younger daughter Juliette's unworn wedding gown. The news of Evan Hawkwood's failure to return from an encounter with marauders over the planet Cadiz had crushed her dreams of linking her family to the imperial line. Turning her back on her rebellious older child, Antorianna allowed Carolandra the opportunity to slip out of Juliette's room without prolonging a fruitless conversation. Only after she heard the door close, signaling that she was alone with her vanished daughter's possessions, did Antorianna retrieve the handwritten note she had found carefully tucked away in the folds of the wedding dress. *She meant for me to find this, but not until I could face the sight of our family's shattered dreams.*

> Loyalty unto Death not only stands as our house's motto, it also marks the ancient form of our family's betrothal oath. My pledge to Evan Hawkwood has not altered simply because of his alleged demise. I intend to live up to both tenets of the Justinian code.
> Forgive me,
> Juliette Justinian (Hawkwood)

In her own chambers on the Justinian estate, Lady Carolandra tried to ignore her feelings of concern for her younger sister's fate. In truth, she had not lied to her mother. She had not influenced Juliette's decision to take control of her own fortune in any way. All she had done, when Juliette had visited her late last night, was give her a location and remain silent until Lady Antorianna discovered the note this afternoon.

Privately, Carolandra had rejoiced at the wedding's failure to take place. Her opposition to House Justinian's habit of marrying off its best and brightest daughters into other lines doomed the house to continued obscurity. She had nothing personal against Evan Hawkwood; in fact, his reputation spoke well for his character. He would have probably made a good match for Juliette, who, until now, seemed concerned only with acting the dutiful daughter.

Carolandra shook her head. *I never thought she'd have the nerve to strike out on her own.* She felt a sudden twinge of worry at the thought of her naive and inexperienced little sister traveling into space on a desperate and probably doomed rescue mission. *At least, if she dies trying, it will be more than generations of Justinian broodmares have done.*

* * *

"What makes you think my cousin — at least, I think he's my cousin — still lives?" Baroness Morgein Hawkwood considered the young woman standing awkwardly before her in the close cabin of the *Star of Ravenna*.

Juliette Justinian squared her shoulders and met the older woman's gaze without flinching.

"A Decados communiqué two days ago reported that Evan Hawkwood's personal ship went down somewhere near the Hironem reservation on Cadiz. There were no survivors. The Decados family offered its profound sympathy to Evan's family. They, in turn, notified us so that we could cancel the preparations for our — my and Evan's — wedding." Juliette's voice trembled slightly at the end of her speech.

Morgein nodded. "I received word about the accident from my own sources," she admitted. Her expression softened. "I'm sorry," she said. "This must be hard on you —"

"Mother thinks I should put it behind me and get on with my life," Juliette said softly, "and by that she means another marriage to a house that can advance the standing of House Justinian."

"I'm familiar with the practice," Morgein said. "Apparently you see things differently than your mother does."

Juliette nodded. "First, I don't believe that Evan's ship 'crashed' over Cadiz. My fiancé was due back at Delphi and had no reason to make a casual trip through Cadiz air space unless he intended to land there. If that were the case, then there would have had to be some compelling reason for Evan to travel so far out of his way." She took a deep breath. *I might as well just say it.* "I think someone lured Evan into landing on Cadiz in order to spring some sort of trap."

"Someone like a member of House Decados?" Morgein prompted.

"Just after Dame Lilian's message to my family, Konstantin Decados sent this gift to me by private messenger." Juliette reached into her shoulder pack and produced a carved orriswood box. Opening the box, she held it out for Morgein to view its contents, a long-stemmed marifleur, dried and treated with a preservative.

Morgein raised an eyebrow. "Do you know the significance of the marifleur?" she asked.

"I believe, according to the customs of House Decados, that this flower signifies an intention to initiate a courtship," she said.

Morgein shrugged. "The Decados were never a family for prolonged periods of mourning, so I'm told."

Juliette felt her cheeks grow red as she remembered the rumors linking Morgein with at least one Decados consort. *Maybe I was wrong in coming to her.*

Seeing her consternation, Morgein laughed softly. "I see you've heard stories about me," she said. "Don't worry, whatever my personal tastes, I remain a Hawkwood. It suits me to have a widespread circle of acquaintances of all kinds," she added.

Juliette nodded, recovering control over herself. "I certainly didn't come here to comment on your associations," she said.

"No, you didn't," Morgein said. "Just why did you come to me?"

"I want your help in finding Evan," Juliette replied. "I don't believe that he's dead and I don't believe that Konstantin Decados' offer to court me is coincidental. This gift came with a note of condolence from Konstantin Decados," she added. "He and Evan were sworn enemies. They'd met on the field of honor several times and Evan always drew first blood. I think Konstantin would have preferred a duel to the death had he thought he stood a chance of winning."

"The fact that Konstantin wants to capitalize on your sudden availability doesn't necessarily mean that he is linked with Evan's accident—"

"It was no accident!" Juliette blurted. "I felt —" She stopped herself before she said more than she wanted to. She busied herself with closing the box and returning it to her shoulder pouch.

Morgein rose from her seat and clasped Juliette firmly by the shoulders. "Look at me!" she ordered, her dark eyes focused on the younger woman's face. "What did you feel?"

"Nothing," Juliette said. "I felt no indication of Evan Hawkwood's death."

"You are a psychic," Morgein said flatly. "Am I right?"

Juliette nodded. Morgein released her grip on Juliette's shoulders and returned to her seat. "Sit down," she said, her voice abrupt but not unkind. "I've been rude to keep you standing about like some petitioner," she added, motioning to the other seat bolted into the cabin wall.

"But I am a petitioner," Juliette said. "And, yes, I'm also a psychic."

"Did Evan know this about you?" Morgein asked.

"Yes," Juliette replied. "The first time I met him was at our betrothal party two years ago. I expected that he would be a typical Hawkwood, brave and proper and —"

"Boring as brute droppings," Morgein finished. Juliette smiled in spite of herself.

"I didn't expect to find his company so enjoyable," she said. "There was an instant rapport between us. Mother encouraged the two of us to take a stroll in the gardens and get acquainted. He was very easy to talk to and before I knew it, I had told him about some of my — studies."

"You mean your psychic studies?" Morgein asked.

Juliette nodded. "It just sort of slipped out. I was afraid at first that he would withdraw his suit once I'd told him about my gift — or curse — but instead, he wanted to know more about it. He was the one who suggested a Bond between us."

"And that's how you know he's still alive?"

"I'd know if the connection was broken," Juliette replied. "I would feel something shatter inside —"

"I know," Morgein whispered. Juliette waited for her host to say more, but Morgein remained silent for a few minutes, her eyes fixed upon a small gold ring on her little finger. Finally, she looked up, her face betraying none of her thoughts.

"This alters my assessment of the situation," Morgein said. "Even with your abilities, we may not succeed in what you want to do."

"I have to try, anyway," Juliette insisted. "If you won't help me, I'll find someone who will, but you were my first choice."

Morgein smiled. "In spite of my reputation for associating with Hawkwood's enemies and flouting tradition?"

"Those aren't the only rumors," Juliette said quietly.

"What else have you heard?" Morgein's voice contained just a hint of something sinister.

"I've heard that your lifestyle serves a greater cause," Juliette replied, choosing her words with care, "and that you are a true daughter of your house."

"Nicely phrased," Morgein said, leaving Juliette with the feeling that she had just passed some sort of test. "You will owe me a considerable debt if I help you," the baroness continued.

"I know," Juliette answered.

The tension in the cabin suddenly dissipated and Morgein stood up, signaling the end of the interview. "Ask one of my crew to show you to the guest cabin, where you can stow your things," she said. "We'll lift off in an hour or so. On the way to Cadiz, you can tell me all you know — or have heard — about Konstantin Decados, and I'll start calling in a few favors."

* * *

"Your body already shows signs of a full-fledged selchakah addiction," Konstantin Decados remarked conversationally as he refreshed the dermapatch positioned just over Evan Hawkwood's carotid artery. "I don't suppose the last few hours — or have they been days? — were very pleasant for you."

Evan Hawkwood tried to focus his eyes through lids too heavy to open completely. Halfheartedly, he tested the restraints that secured him to the med-cot. His muscles, weakened from what seemed like an interminable period of uncontrollable withdrawal spasms, barely responded to his commands.

Konstantin noticed the almost imperceptible movements of his captive's arms and ankles and shook his head, a pitying smile touching the edges of his mouth.

"I'm surprised you still have the heart to try to free yourself," he said. The Decados noble watched as a few more heartbeats carried the drug through Evan's body, bringing blissful release to tortured muscles and nerves. Involuntarily, Evan Hawkwood sighed with relief.

"That's better, now, isn't it?" Konstantin asked, not expecting an answer.

Evan struggled through thick waves of fog that clouded his brain and thickened his tongue, trying to form a single word.

"Why?" he asked, the question bringing with it a small sense of accomplishment.

"Why?" Konstantin repeated, his voice soft with mockery. "Because I intend to use you. Once your body has established a sufficient dependency on selchakah, I shall release you so that you may return home with whatever lie you choose to tell your family to conceal the shame of your capture and addiction. It would never do for a scion of your house to admit that you lost a contingent of loyal soldiers and succumbed to the lure of a proscribed drug. And I, of course, will deny any complicity in your fall from grace and honor." The Decados noble paused for moment and watched the play of emotions cross Evan's face, now flushed with the heat of the drug as it coursed through his veins.

"I will be only too happy to help you concoct a suitable story, one that won't leave too many questions unanswered— something involving a ship malfunction and weeks of directionless wandering before you managed to stumble upon a Decados patrol who brought you to safety. Of course, by that time, your death — and that of your men — would have already been reported. I'm sure we can work out the details to suit both of us."

Evan heard his captor's words coming from a great distance and tried to respond to them with the outrage and anger that he knew he should be feeling. Instead, a wave of hot, liquid pleasure washed through him, sweeping away all his righteous intent except for a frantic shake of his head and a barely mumbled "N-no —"

Konstantin laughed. "We have been through this before," he said. "Soon enough, my proposal will sound more reasonable. Especially when you are once again starving for the comfort and ecstasy only selchakah can give you. Think about it until I return."

Patting his captive's restrained arm companionably, Konstantin rose and left the tiny, antiseptic room in the cellar of his private residence in one of Cadiz's tenement-cities. Nearly abandoned by the house's finer members, the planet now served mainly as a hive for illegal activities and, occasionally, as a refuge for young Decados nobles eager to indulge themselves without even minimal restraint from their more cautious elders.

Soon I will have my own pet Hawkwood spy, eager to spill his family's secrets — and perhaps a few Imperial ones as well — for a taste of selchakah. And if he chooses instead to admit his addiction and seek release from it, his shame within his house can only hurt him. This is one duel I cannot lose.

* * *

Seated in the parlor of the Decados lord's villa in the hills overlooking the city of Taraquino, once a center of commerce on Cadiz, Juliette Justinian watched her host with undisguised fascination. Baron Istvan Decados, in appearance and mannerisms, challenged her own long-held stereotypes of his house's legendary decadence. Tall and muscular, with short-clipped dark hair and lively, deep green eyes, Lord Istvan dressed in a simple black uniform adorned with the mantis-crest of his house. The starkness of his clothing complemented the tasteful, almost spare furnishings of his reception chamber. Somehow, Juliette had expected her host's surroundings to be more — sumptuous. Beside her, Morgein Hawkwood seemed relaxed, almost at home, in Istvan's company. *Perhaps the rumors are true about the two of them.*

Istvan had listened carefully as Juliette — at Morgein's prompting — related her suspicions about the fate of Evan Hawkwood and its connection to Konstantin Decados, carefully omitting any reference to her bond with the Hawkwood knight.

"My nephew, unfortunately, has never been known for his subtlety," Istvan Decados remarked in between sips of Severan wine, brought from his personal cellars to please the palates of his two guests. "And I may surmise from your unexpected, though not unwelcome, visit that you wish for some intervention on my part in this matter — if, indeed, it proves to be founded in fact."

Juliette glanced toward Morgein, as if expecting the older woman to answer. Morgein inclined her head toward Juliette and raised her own wine-glass to her lips.

It's up to me, then. Juliette nodded her head, not trusting her voice for the moment. The motion gave her an instant to compose her speech. "I would be pleased if you could make inquiries into the matter," she said, hoping that even so few words had not committed her to some impossible debt.

Istvan Decados raised his eyebrows and smiled, not at Juliette, but at Morgein. "I understand she has been under your tutelage for only a short time, my dear," he said, "and already she shows great diplomatic promise." He returned his attention to Juliette. "I congratulate you on your exquisite tact," he said, "particularly after so bald an accusation as the one you have presented to me."

Juliette felt her face redden and hid her momentary embarrassment behind a generous sip of wine. Morgein held out her own glass for Istvan to refill, and Juliette used the diversion to focus her concentration on her host.

Istvan settled himself once more and turned to Juliette, who now regarded him steadily, a look of intent and sober attention on her face.

"I shall look into the matter at once," Istvan said, "as a favor to both of you." He stressed the word "both" just enough to elicit a wry smile from Morgein.

"I expected no less," the baroness replied at the same time as Juliette murmured a soft word of thanks. After a few more pleasantries, the two women rose to take their leave.

"There is one other small thing," Juliette said, withdrawing a small orriswood box from an inner pocket of her traveling cloak and placing it in her host's hand. "Please redirect this to its owner with my regrets."

* * *

"There was no sign of falsehood in his agreement to help," Juliette informed Morgein once the two women were safely off planet. Morgein nodded, intent on watching the interplay between her navigator and pilot as they plotted the course to the nearest jumpgate. After approving the coordinates and leaving her navigator to enter the information into the ship's think-machine, Morgein turned her full attention to Juliette.

"I didn't expect Istvan to lie to us," she said.

"Then why did you give me the signal to use my talent to read his intent?" Juliette asked. "I might have been caught—"

"Precisely," Morgein said. "You might have been discovered using sorcery upon a member of one of the Noble Houses, yet you took the risk anyway — and succeeded in getting away with it. That shows some courage and commitment, don't you think?" The Hawkwood baroness smiled warmly. "Besides, I wanted another glassful of wine. It was an excellent — and rare vintage."

* * *

Delayed by more than four months, the wedding between Juliette

Justinian and Evan Hawkwood nevertheless drew a fair number of luminaries from both houses — as well as a pair of unexpected guests. Accompanying Baroness Morgein Hawkwood, Baron Istvan Decados conducted himself with the poise and gallantry of his position as Evan Hawkwood's timely rescuer. The story of Evan's close brush with death, the presumed loss of his men in the crash and his slow recovery in the care of Lord Istvan circulated among the wedding guests until it seemed a factual accounting, even to those intimately aware of the truth.

Istvan apologized profusely to Lady Antorianna and to Evan's parents for the miscommunication that led to the Hawkwood knight's reported death. "I should have known better than to delegate such a delicate message to an underling," he had said. "In truth, I was unsure whether or not my patient would survive his injuries and so instructed my nephew to convey a message that did not raise false hopes. I fear he misinterpreted my instructions."

During the reception and ball that followed the ceremony, Juliette accepted a private wedding gift from Lord Istvan — a thin golden necklace with a multi-faceted Malignatian diamond. "It might please you to know that it was, so I'm told, mined from the planet's frozen interior by the hands of one known to both of us," the baron informed Juliette as he placed the necklace in her hands. "My nephew shows a great deal of promise in his new position as assistant mining director for our diamond concerns on Malignatius. Of course, he is learning the industry from the ground up, you might say."

Morgein Hawkwood took her cousin Evan aside to congratulate him on his rescue and recovery and to offer her ship as a conveyance for the couple's nuptial holiday.

"I suggest an extended journey through the stars as the perfect way for the two of you to get to know one another," she said.

"And to allow me enough time to fully rid myself of certain unhealthy influences?" Evan responded with only a hint of bitterness.

"That, too," Morgein acknowledged.

After his rescue by Istvan Decados and his subsequent delivery aboard the *Star of Ravenna,* Morgein and Juliette had their hands full trying to remove Evan's guilt at surviving at the expense of his men and to restore his sense of lost honor. Even now, Morgein was unsure whether she and Juliette had succeeded. Only time would tell.

* * *

"He's sleeping," Juliette said as she joined Morgein in the captain's cabin of the *Star of Ravenna*.

Morgein nodded. "He'll spend a lot of time doing just that until the last of the selchakah addiction has left him, and even then—"

"He'll never be the same, will he?" Juliette's voice betrayed nothing other than a calm acceptance of circumstances.

"Probably not," Morgein replied. "But sooner or later he'll come to terms with his guilt and his failure to live up to his private image of Hawkwood honor. With any luck at all, he'll learn to find new definitions for integrity and courage."

"Like you did?" Juliette asked.

Morgein grimaced. "I always had my own understanding of what was important," she said. "As, I suspect, do you."

Juliette smiled her agreement. "I have a lot to thank you for," she said. "How can I repay you for all you have done for me — and for my husband?"

"I think you have some idea," Morgein said, "or you wouldn't be asking me a question like that."

"You tested my commitment at the home of Istvan Decados," Juliette said. "Was that just to see what I was made of, or did you have some other purpose in asking me to put myself at risk?"

Morgein leveled her gaze at the younger woman — now her cousin-by-marriage — and studied her for a few minutes without speaking. All in all, she liked what she saw.

"Your husband has gained more than he expected in marrying you," she said, finally. "For the immediate future, you will have to serve as his anchor while he struggles to recover from his ordeal. That will take up a good deal of your time and resources. Afterwards, however, you may find yourself at loose ends."

"Are you offering to teach me some of your alleged skills?" Juliette asked.

"Perhaps," Morgein said, "if the prospect suits you."

"I'll certainly consider it seriously," Juliette responded. "Especially since the evidence of your successful methods lies asleep in the next cabin. I didn't think so much could be accomplished with so little apparent effort."

Morgein laughed. "Most people still believe that open confrontations solve everything. It explains why duels are still so popular among most of the Noble Houses. As far as I'm concerned, however, in some battles there are no clear-cut heroes, just skilled and dedicated pullers of strings. And I sense that your hands are perfect for string-pulling."

Juliette nodded. "That leads me to another matter," she said. "Evan says that his men were probably taken by a group of Muster mercenaries. He thinks some of them may still be alive — though he hasn't any idea where they would be by now." She paused and let the words hang between them. *If I had a glass of wine, I'd drink it now.*

Morgein hesitated for a heartbeat before she stretched an arm out to clap Juliette conspiratorially on the back.

"I guess maybe you don't need to wait until Evan recovers," she said. "I may have a Muster connection or two somewhere."

"Thank you," Juliette said.

Morgein shook her head. "The proper response is, 'I owe you one.'"

Juliette Justinian Hawkwood rose to return to the cabin she and Evan shared aboard the *Star of Ravenna.* "I'll remember that next time," she said as she bade her host goodnight.

"I'm certain you will," Morgein replied.

Bazaar Companions
W. Keith Winkler

The starcruiser *Calypso* shot through the jumpgate with the slightest tremor, and entered the Byzantium Secundus system. Imperial frigates and cruisers hailed her, turning powerful laser turrets and meson cannons on the ship, ready to obliterate any unwanted or hostile vessel. The Imperial City, the seat of power from which Emperor Alexius ruled the Known Worlds was the *Calypso's* destination, and Chief Darla Farseer had run this jump more times than she cared to imagine.

"Starcruiser *Calypso*, on course for Byzantium Secundus. Over," she broadcast, once she was clear of the jumpgate. She ran her fingers through her dark hair, and removed the jumpkey from the ship's console. All around her, the panel was a mass of flashing lights and scrolling numbers, lighting her face in a weird halcyon glow.

"Acknowledged *Calypso*," came the static-laced reply from her ship's squawker, "this is Imperial Navy frigate *Mercy*, identify yourself, and your cargo. Over."

"Acknowledged," Darla quipped back, smirking at the arrogant tone of the Imperial Navy, "Charioteer Chief Darla Farseer piloting. Cargo consists of two passengers, and imports from Kish and Criticorum. Shall I transmit my manifest, *Mercy*? Over." Darla smirked, knowing the captain had no desire to see endless lists of dry goods. He was just trying to make her sweat a bit, and to remind her that in this system, everything was run by the book. She relaxed, confident that there would be no further complications. Chewing her lower lip thoughtfully, she waited for the confirmation, and contemplated some rest and relaxation.

"Negative, Chief Farseer," came the reply, "you are cleared to proceed. Check in with customs when you reach the planet. Over."

"Okay, *Mercy*. Over and out," she replied, then punched the engines to roar out and away from the jumpgate and its guardians. The week-long journey took her past Iblis, Magog and Aden, the outer planets of the system, to finally begin her descent towards the third planet from the system's fading sun.

Lady Marissa Li Halan sipped a glass of dry white wine while she made a list of the many individuals she was supposed to visit and flatter. She curled her lip in disgust at the necessary protocol, and then offered a quick prayer to the Pancreator to give her patience. She must do her duty first, as befit one of her station, then she could focus on personal interests. Having only come of age this past summer and finished her tutelage on her homeworld of Kish, she was eager to get out and see the worlds. Nineteen years of age, and the daughter of a baron, she stood to inherit land and fortune one day.

She sipped her wine, the last glass of the bottle, and slammed her notebook closed, a little more forcefully than intended. The sound echoed through the *Calypso's* small lounge, and caused the ship's other passenger to look up with a bemused expression on his dark, angular face.

"The rocks do not shape the river, milady," spoke Ahrim al-Malik. His voice was somnolent, and pleasing to the ear. "You wish to arrive at your destination before deciding to set out on a journey." He smiled at her, then went back to polishing a bright piece of jewelry, fashioned with Shaprut gold and numerous gemstones.

"I know, Lord Ahrim," she protested, "it is only that I have spent my entire life learning courtly protocols, Church litanies, and the proper forms of address for any given function. I suffered it all because I knew one day I would be free to travel and experience the worlds on my own! Now, my first trip off Kish, and I'm to go right back into what I know so well: the court."

"Is that so?" the elder noble asked, "why then do you call me 'Lord Ahrim'? I have not told you I am of the court..." His teeth seemed very white against his dark skin as he grinned at her. "I may be a beggar, or a soldier..."

She laughed, a musical sound that seemed precisely crafted for just such an occasion, and shook her head. "You are al-Malik, and my elder. I would err on the side of caution and call you by title. You are on this ship, one which my mother expressly hired to take me to the Imperial Court, yet you convinced Chief Farseer to accept your cargo of trade items. I expect you are a person of some rank or influence at the very least."

Ahrim merely bowed his head at her implied compliment, but said nothing to confirm or deny her suspicions. Instead he placed the first piece of jewelry down, and selected another piece. He soaked a soft cloth in a solution of mineral spirits and began to clean the tarnish off the intricate and delicate item. "What makes you certain you will find the answers you seek on Byzantium Secundus?" he inquired.

She sighed, blowing a strand of dark hair from her eyes, "I have some information that, should it prove true, will vault my name into circles all around the Imperial Court, and serve to set me on the path to glory!" Her eyes shone bright at the thought, and she smiled almost whimsically.

"Blackmail?" Ahrim asked, "from a Li Halan? That's unexpected..." Marissa was outraged, and moved to stand, her hand going for her rapier almost instinctively. Ahrim's eyebrow's shot up, his face broke into an amused grin, but he made no move to reach his scimitar. "Obviously" he clarified, "I misapprehend, or else you have a sudden desire to leave this life." His tone left little doubt that he could finish the duel, even if she began it. "Be still, child, and do not be eager to leave this life. Your exit, like mine, lies over the next mountain, and none of us know when we have reached the summit."

"The Li Halan do not engage in blackmail!" she replied coldly, and Ahrim smiled again, almost as if she had made a joke without knowing it. "I have information that leads to a stash of Second Republic tech. That's why I've brought along three trusted and capable men from my estate to aid me, and that too is why I need to reach the agora on Byzantium Secundus!" Her speech was impassioned, perhaps by the wine in her system, but it caused her to continue to glare balefully at the smiling al-Malik who had insulted her honor and slandered her house.

"Perhaps," suggested Ahrim, not even glancing at the noble Li Halan, "we may help each other. I am a collector and trader in rare antiquities, and you are obviously seeking something in the markets of Port Authority."

"What are you suggesting?" she asked shrewdly, taking her seat slowly. The Li Halan and al-Malik kept a healthy distance as houses. The Li Halan, with their devotion to the Universal Church, feared and distrusted the sly al-Malik, their mysterious ways and quasi-mystical practices.

"Merely that I may possess what you need, and a sale now would be less costly for you, because it would do away with the imposed taxes, tariffs and additional fees that I am going to incur on Byzantium

Secundus," he replied in his soothing voice. His eyes were warm and brown, and sought out her blue ones with an easy familiarity that she found disconcerting.

"I suppose there is no harm in asking," she mused to herself, then turned to address Ahrim in a clipped and business-like manner. "I am seeking an architect's map reader," she explained. Ahrim blinked, frowned, then turned to polishing his jewelry once again. Lady Marissa waited expectantly for some reply, but the older man merely sat, thoughtful and brooding. "Well, Lord Ahrim?!" she asked eagerly, "can you help me?"

He pulled on his dark beard, with only the barest hint of gray, and then clarified. "You are talking of a powered device, that when fitted with a map, illuminates it and allows for an incredible level of detail as well as allowing certain portions to be differentiated by different colored lights?"

"Precisely," she replied, her tone more serious as she realized he knew of the item she needed. "Have you ever seen one?"

"Why, of course," he replied nonchalantly, "I've seen many. The problem is that the maps that were used with these devices are rare items in and of themselves. They had nodes and circuits that had to match up with the device so they could be highlighted and illuminated. All such maps of any worth have long since been lost, or else lie in inaccessible repositories..." Ahrim fell silent as it suddenly dawned on him why Lady Marissa Li Halan would need a map reader. "Perhaps we could make a deal, milady."

"So, you do have a map reader in your collection, or are you all talk and gaudy jewelry?" she asked, flashing him a cold smile. He returned her grin, and then nodded.

"I have one, on board this very ship. I am willing to part with it, although they are not so common as I made them sound," he added.

"You lied, then," she clarified, "Typical."

"No, no," he said, holding up his hands to deter any conflicts, "I have seen several, but they are delicate. The one I possess is in excellent condition, and therefore represents a very high sale if I can find someone who needs it. It seems that you have need of it, which of course implies you have a map. You also spoke of a cache of Second Republic Tech, which is of more interest to me than an ancient map reader that I cannot sell. So, I'll give you the map reader in exchange for a cut of the cache."

"I'll be honest," she replied, stressing the word 'honest' as she stared at Ahrim, "I don't know that the map I possess actually leads to anything. But, I've done my research, and I'm convinced enough to give it a try."

"I am willing to take that gamble, Lady Marissa. I will give you the map reader, and if you are wrong, then I will consider it the price of adventurous speculation. But if you are correct as you think, then I will certainly demand a share of the find, as befits my sponsorship." Lady Marissa considered the words of Ahrim al-Malik. She knew his house was reputed to have close ties to the Merchant League, as evidenced by his ability to get aboard this chartered ship as it passed through Criticorum. Still, he seemed an amiable gentleman, and she could see no reason why their motives were anything but complementary.

"We'll be landing shortly, folks!" came Darla's cheerful voice over the ship's squawker, "so get your things together and prepare for sights and splendors unseen!" Ahrim extended his hand to Marissa, and raised one eyebrow in an unspoken invitation to deal. She smiled, excited at being in the Imperial City, away from home, and close to realizing her personal goals as well. Without hesitation, she took his hand, and the deal was done.

* * *

The explosion shook the Port Authority, startling citizens from all across the Known Worlds. Thick white smoke curled upwards toward the rafters of the enormous structure that contained a maze of stores, bars, restaurants, hotels, and other less obvious vendors. The size of a city, with more than a hundred thousand permanent inhabitants, this was the agora, the central point of economic exchange on Byzantium Secundus, and now the hum of commerce had been shattered.

As a crowd formed, a lone figure could be seen lying face down on the maxicrete. She wore clothes of excellent make, and a slim rapier was belted at her waist; she was undoubtedly noble. Her body lay crumpled, limbs all askew, with her hands and arms badly burned and still slightly smoking. Her entourage of three men lay nearby, barely moving and senseless, as blood poured from ears, eyes and nose. A whispered hush of speculation and concern swept through the crowd.

Looming over them was the blinking, humming monolithic form

of a fusion power station. The fusion cell was the basic unit of stored energy that powered all technological devices, from electric torches to blaster pistols. The noble woman and her party were apparently recharging their fusion cells when something went horribly wrong. Perceptive members of the crowd noted several smoking pieces of some technological device scattered about the area.

"Stand back, citizens!" called a clear, strong voice, as a handsome youth stepped from the crowd. His blond hair was closely cropped, and his beardless face was creased with worry and concern. He wore fine clothing of midnight blue hue, and a large cloak of white hung from his broad shoulders. He stared his challenge at the diverse and shifting crowd, as dozens of lights from shops and streetlamps reflected off his rapier and brooch, both bearing the Lion of Hawkwood.

As the Hawkwood noble attempted to clear away the crowd that was steadily encroaching on the still unmoving noble woman, a young acolyte of the Eskatonic Order rushed forward to kneel by her side. The crowd, sensing that order was quickly being restored to the scene, began to disperse. Only a few bored or curious onlookers remained. The young nobleman turned to kneel by the priest when a loud shout rang out.

"Halt!" called a heavy-set man in uniform, as he and three others ran towards the scene. "Halt in the name of the Authority!" Upon the arrival of the officials, many of the remaining onlookers slipped off into the marketplace. The Hawkwood drew himself up regally, proudly displaying the insignia of his house. The heavy-set man sent a warning glance to the other three uniformed men, and then continued in a more reserved tone.

"Good day to you, sir," he began, "I am Constable Justin Severns of the Authority, and these men are my deputies..." The young Hawkwood, and indeed he was but a youth, held up one finger, cutting off the constable.

"How is she, priest?" he asked the bewildered Eskatonic.

"Her Inner Flame has expired, left this vessel, and returned to the Pancreator's embrace," the priest replied sadly. He rolled the noble woman over, and all gasped at the charred ruin of her face, neck and chest. A heavy pendant of the jumpgate cross, as well as house markings on her clothing, identified the woman as a member of the Li Halan. With a quick and whispered prayer, the holy man began to comfort the three men who accompanied her.

The constable cleared his throat, annoyed at being cut off, and continued in a stronger tone. "I am Constable Severns, and these men are my duly appointed deputies. What has transpired here that leaves one noble dead with a Hawkwood and an Eskatonic standing over her corpse?"

The Hawkwood's face clouded with anger. "I am Sir Arthur Hawkwood, constable, and I resent your implied accusation. Moreover, your implication of the good priest, who even now comforts the wounded, speaks little of your character." The constable sighed, sensing the defensive anger of the youth, and held up his hands.

"Hold on there, Sir Arthur," he replied. "Men, investigate the scene and gather evidence while I interview these eye-witnesses." The deputies nodded and dispersed. "Now, Sir Arthur, perhaps you can tell me what transpired here? As well as the name of your priestly friend?"

"Constable Severns," Arthur replied in a frosty tone, "I am not acquainted with this cleric, but I suspect that he, like myself, was strolling this portion of Port Authority when a large and rather violent explosion occurred."

"Uh-huh," Severns nodded, making notes on a pad. "And you do not know this priest, nor the deceased?"

"No, constable, I do not," the Hawkwood answered.

"Sir," said one of the deputies, "we found these." They produced four small fragments of some kind of technological device. The casing was dark gray, and minute wires and circuitry were visible in the jagged edges and crevices. It looked very advanced by modern tech standards. The constable and Arthur looked at one another, and then glanced at the priest. The lanky Eskatonic was greeting the medical trauma team that had just arrived. He began helping load the three wounded men as well as the deceased Li Halan into their vehicle.

"Did anyone see anything?" asked the constable to his deputy.

"No sir," the deputy replied, "the few persons we could round up reported hearing a loud sound, seeing smoke, and then there was a crowd with this young Hawkwood and the Eskatonic standing near the body."

"Hmmm," the constable mused, and Arthur sighed in frustration.

"Am I to assume, constable, that I am a suspect?" he asked in a terse voice.

"If you like," the constable replied, "but I'm not officially placing you under arrest. I would however, request that you and the priest come down to the station with me and my men so we can get a full statement."

Just then the Eskatonic approached the two men. He seemed to sense some tension between them for he spoke in a tentative voice, almost as if he were interrupting.

"I'm Brother Golic Hiderion," he said, "I was on my way to recharge a fusion cell when the explosion occurred. I'm guessing her power cell blew up right in her face. Most unfortunate."

"Did you know her?" the constable asked bluntly. The priest blew a strand of sandy brown hair out of his eyes and shook his head.

"No, but I heard one of her injured companions call out for 'Lady Marissa'," he added. The constable nodded, and Arthur stuck his hand out to make the acquaintance of the holy man.

"I am Sir Arthur Hawkwood," the Hawkwood said, shaking Golic's hand, "and Constable Severns here has requested that we accompany him to his station and give a full account of what transpired. We seem to be the only eye-witnesses."

"I'll need to contact my Chapter House where I'm staying to let them know I will be late for the Twilight Reflections, but otherwise I can accompany you."

"No problem, Brother Golic," Severns said, "I'll send one of my deputies to deliver the message. Do you have anyone that you need to notify, Sir Arthur?"

"No," the young knight replied, "I go where I want, when I want."

"Ah, well then," the constable replied, making an effort to be more respectful to the nobleman, "if you will please both come with me." He issued some final instructions to his deputies, including Brother Golic's message, and then led the two 'witnesses' to a waiting skimmer. Within minutes, they were whisked through the streets of Port Authority, bound for the small constabulary.

None of them noticed the darkly clad stranger that lingered a few more minutes after their departure and then slunk off into the crowded bazaar.

* * *

Chief Jason Maurie awoke to the sound of someone knocking on his door. He rolled out of bed with a groan, and stretched. His arms spanned the entire width of the small garret he was given here in the Charioteers Guild Hall. The knocking came again, more insistent, and he cursed at the door, as his hands found the switch for the lights. The soft, steady light of glow lamps filled the room, and he jerked the door open. A young midshipman stood, shuffling impatiently from foot to foot.

"Whadda ya need, kid?" Jason asked.

"Sorry for waking you, sir," the youth replied, "but you have an urgent message from a personal friend..."

"What's her name?" asked the still-yawning pilot.

"Uh, no sir," the kid stammered, "actually it's from a Constable Justin Severns..." Jason started awake, and then snatched the sealed envelope from the kid's hand. He thanked him, before shutting the door and settling on the bed to read the note. He read it once, then again. He smiled to himself, and tucked it into the pocket of his worn flight suit. He had slept in it, again. He passed a comb through his hair, adjusted his rank pins, and buckled on his belt containing his pistol and jumpkeys. Scratching at his half grown beard, he sighed and shrugged. He had forgotten to shave again.

He left his room and passed through the corridors of the Guild Hall. Nodding to the familiar faces he passed, he tossed off casual salutes to higher rank guild members. He entered the main mess hall, which also doubled as the social center for Charioteers who were staying at the Guild Hall. Several of his fellow pilots were gathered together talking excitedly, and he quickly joined them.

"How yer keys hangin'?" he said by way of introduction.

"Not too bad, Razor," replied Serina, calling him by his call sign. Since time out of mind, all pilots had call signs that doubled as nicknames. Jason's stemmed from the fact he was perpetually unshaven. He smirked and ran his hands through his scraggly beard.

"Glad to hear it, Rig," he replied, tossing her call sign back at her. "Now what's the hot news?"

Immediately, Rig and her buddies began telling of the events from earlier that afternoon. An explosion in the Port Authority had left a young Li Halan noble dead. The Authority, as the guild in charge of the agora, was handling the investigation, but the Li Halan were already attempting to wrest jurisdiction from them. Jason smiled as the tale unfolded. He began to suspect why Constable Severns was so cryptic in his message, and why he wanted to call in a favor. Jason found the facts a little sketchy, and could imagine the rumors that were already flying. He said his farewells to his fellows, and headed out to see the chief of the motorpool about borrowing a skimmer for a few hours. It was always a bit of a hassle, but he usually got his way.

* * *

The Twilight Reflections were just ending as Brother Golic sighted the Chapter House of the Eskatonic Order in the Holy City of Byzantium Secundus. The Holy City was comprised of six concentric circles, or tiers, each higher than the first. The slight priest found the climb to the second tier, where his Order's house was located, always somewhat taxing. Constable Severns had kept he and the young Hawkwood some time, going over their stories, separately and together, and comparing them. He had begun to feel like a bit of a fugitive before the constable finally let them both go. He did caution them not to go off planet, and that he would be in touch with them soon. Brother Golic could sympathize with the man, for he was receiving a lot of pressure from the Li Halan, who wanted to perform their own investigation and uncover their own answers. He sighed, glad to be home, and was just about to climb the stairs to the main doors when a figure stepped from the shadows.

"Your pardon, brother," hailed the man. Brother Golic squinted, and paused as the figure stepped more fully into the lit street. He was tall, dressed in a rather rustic fashion consisting of riding leathers, a fine hide jacket trimmed in some strange animal fur, and bracers covering both forearms. His long auburn hair was braided with urroc feathers, and he wore a full beard and mustache. A large broadsword was slung casually on one hip, and a blaster pistol was holstered on the other.

"Yes, can I help you?" the slim priest asked hesitantly. The man nodded, and then cleared his throat.

"Well, yer pardon, sir, but I was in the agora today, when the explosion happened, and I wanted to give you something..."

"Perhaps you have me confused with the constable?" Brother Golic suggested.

"Well, beggin' your pardon, sir, but I don't really want to get mixed up with the constable," the rather rugged man explained, "you see, I noticed you and the Hawkwood fella talkin' to the authorities and figured that I'd give these to you." He held out a small leather pouch. Golic took it, and dumped out its contents in his hand.

Several fragments, similar to the ones he had seen in the constable's office, spilled out. Neither the constable or Sir Arthur could figure out what device Lady Marissa Li Halan had been utilizing when the fusion cell blew, for there were not enough pieces. Perhaps with these, they could reconstruct the device.

"I am Brother Golic Hiderion of the Eskatonic Order. How are you called?"

The man shifted nervously then shrugged, "Hand Alexander Trusnikron."

"Trusnikron is a noble house, although not one of the Five, but what is the title of Hand?" asked the bewildered priest.

"Sorry, Brother Golic," the noble replied with a grin. "It's the same thing as a knight. We just name 'em differently."

"Well then, Sir Alexander," the priest replied, deferring to the familiar honorific, "I will certainly see that these make their way to Constable Severns, and I will endeavor to leave your name out of it, since you seem to have reasons for not wanting to get involved."

"Bless you, Brother," Sir Alexander said, then walked away, melting into the shadows of immense cathedrals and quaint chapels.

"The Pancreator shelter you, my son," the priest called, and then wearily sought out his room.

* * *

"I am serious, Hector! That lowly guildsman practically arrested us! You would have drawn on him, I promise you, but then again, you are Hazat," Sir Arthur fumed to his friend.

"Most assuredly, had he tried to arrest Don Hector Eduardo de Hazat, he would have tasted my steel!" his friend replied, sipping his chilled wine and reaching for a piece of cheese.

They were in the estate of Arthur's cousin, Baron Eviathan Hawkwood. Arthur's cousin helped coordinate the Questing Knights of Emperor Alexius, and Don Hector was hoping to endear himself to the baron and enter those honorable ranks. The baron spent most every evening attending some social function or another, which left Arthur free to his own devices. He felt sure the he and Don Hector would enter the ranks of the Questing Knights, as soon as he was older. He would be eighteen in a few months, and Hector was already nineteen, but both men found themselves put off by the baron, for another year at least, and had become fast friends in the meantime.

"So you are supposed to just wait for some constable to summon you?" Don Hector asked, arching an eyebrow.

"Not exactly," Sir Arthur replied with a sigh. "The damn priest, Brother Golic, was so willing and helpful that it would have been discourteous for me to seem recalcitrant."

"And so you told him to call upon you if he should have need?" Don Hector asked with a grin.

"Yes," Sir Arthur responded, "and he assured me he would. I don't want to get mixed up in any investigation that involves a dead Li Halan!"

"Have you no sympathy? What was the girl's name? Was she pretty?" Hector asked.

"Lady Marissa Li Halan," Arthur replied, "and of course I sympathize! I couldn't tell much about her looks... why are you making that face?"

Don Hector's face was a mask of frozen anger, as if carved from slate. His hand dropped instinctively to his saber, but then he shook his head, and took a long drink of wine.

"I remember her," Hector said, "she arrived about three weeks ago from Escoral, on Kish. She had a chip on her shoulder and something to prove! She almost drew on my cousin, Don Diego, because she thought he eyed her lewdly! He did no such thing, but he was forced to apologize anyway. He is one of the most skilled swordsmen I know and she was but a girl. There would have been no honor or glory in his victory."

"Well she should not have been tampering with faulty tech," Arthur replied, "as best as I can tell, she inserted a fully charged fusion cell into some device and it blew up in her face! I thought the Li Halan were taught the Church's teachings against technology."

"That seems strange," Hector commented.

"What? Li Halan teachings? How so?" Arthur asked.

"No, not the teachings, the device. How many technological devices do you have that you don't know how to work?" the Hazat commented. "It seems like either the power generator was faulty and affected her fusion cell, or else she had never powered the device before, and it was defective. Like I said before, how many powered devices do you hang on to that might blow up in your face?"

"That's a good point," Sir Arthur mused, "why don't we ask around and see exactly how many friends or enemies Lady Marissa left behind?"

The Hazat held up his wine glass for a toast. "Sounds better than sitting around here waiting for your drunken cousin to come in with an entourage of pretentious knights. Lead on, Sir Arthur!" Arthur toasted him, and the two left to go speak to some of their peers.

* * *

Constable Severns sat in his small office, smoking a thick cigar from Pentateuch. They grew some of the finest tobacco, almost as good as Holy Terra. He looked over the report he had assembled for Count Alrich Li Halan, and it looked slim. It had been two days since the accident, and all he could really report was that Lady Marissa died when a technological device in her possession exploded. "In other words," Justin sighed, "you're girl blew herself up. Sorry. Now here's the bill for cleaning her off the floor of my bazaar." That would never do.

He mused over the evidence Brother Golic had dropped off yesterday. The constable had questioned him as to where he found it, and he answered with some story about an 'anonymous source'. Justin Severns had been in the Authority for twenty-seven years and he knew how to question someone when they didn't want to give the whole story. Brother Golic had squirmed like a whore in church, but Justin finally got the name out of him: Sir Alexander Trusnikron. That it was another noble, albeit of a minor house, made him feel a little better. He desperately wanted to avoid any guild-noble skirmishes, and the report he was going to file would not seem as one-sided if he could toss the names of a priest and two nobles into it somewhere.

He sighed and stood, stretching. In any event, the fusion generator had checked out. He had a contact in the Charioteers who had a contact in the Engineers, and Justin called in a favor that set a chain of events in motion. The bottom line was that a team of Engineers hustled over to the fusion generator within a few hours of the explosion, and regardless of whether it was malfunctioning or in proper working order, Justin had been assured of a clean bill of health. That's how favors worked among the Merchant League; everyone scratched everybody else's back, but sometimes they scratched too hard and drew blood.

He cleared some papers from his desk, and then took out a fresh sheet, preparing to start his report again. He was still waiting for his contact in the Charioteers, Chief Jason Maurie, to have his Engineer contacts look at the device fragments and determine what they were. It was pretty clear that it was some ancient device, and with any luck, they would be able to say that the Li Halan girl had ignored house and Church teachings and trafficked with heretical technology, incurring the wrath of the Pancreator, who judged her on the spot. Justin smirked; he sounded like the damn Avestites. He was under orders to do whatever was necessary to avoid conflicts between his guild and the nobility, and that was just what he was going to do. He had a meeting scheduled for tonight, and expected it would round out his report nicely.

* * *

Sir Arthur Hawkwood and Don Hector Eduardo of the Hazat rode the flitter from Baron Eviathan Hawkwood's estate. The constable had requested a brief meeting with Sir Arthur, and the young noble was bound by honor to oblige. He convinced Hector to come along, since the Hazat had some stories of the fiery-tempered Li Halan that the constable might find interesting.

The arrived at Port Authority, and then hired a skimmer to take them through the immense bazaar, past hotels, restaurants and taverns that offered cool drinks and a game of cards. Soon the squat, ugly building that was the constabulary came into view. They paid their driver and entered the small office. Constable Severns' deputy announced them at once, and they were admitted to a large conference room where Arthur noticed Brother Golic and some unfamiliar faces.

"Ah! Sir Arthur! Welcome!" Constable Severns greeted him in entirely too cheerful a tone. "And welcome to you, Don Hector, was it?"

"Yes, that is correct, constable," Don Hector replied evenly, his dark eyes meeting the gaze of everyone in the room. The Hazat noble wore a tight fitting dueling suit of black, with a large, stylish cloak of burgundy. His saber hung prominently on his hip, and he projected a most militant demeanor.

"May I present the others present?" Constable Severns replied. "To my left is Chief Jason Maurie of the Charioteers, a friend and fellow League member. Next to him, Brother Golic Hiderion, whom you know, Sir Arthur. On this side of the table, our rustic friend, Sir Alexander

Trusnikron, and the remaining seat is for you, Sir Arthur. I shall have my deputy bring in another chair for you, Don Hector."

"Well met, sirs," Sir Arthur replied, indicating Chief Maurie and Brother Golic, "and to you, beast-rider!" The Trusnikron noble inclined his head, acknowledging the greeting. His house was renowned throughout the Known Worlds as the best animal handlers, cavalry or beast tamers in existence. Both the Hawkwood and Hazat had used Trusnikron cavalry in past skirmishes, and their skill and honor was unquestioned.

Don Hector merely inclined his head to those present, but remained silent. The deputy returned with another chair, and the Hazat noble sat, his arms crossed and his dark eyes wary.

"I assume we are all here as witnesses to the unfortunate death of Lady Marissa Li Halan," Sir Arthur said, "and not as suspects?" There was a delicate cough from Brother Golic and the Trusnikron looked disturbed for a brief moment.

"Everything will be clear in time," Constable Severns assured the young noble, "now please sit down." They all sat, and soon were served cool drinks. As everyone settled in, the constable cleared his throat and began.

"As you know, two days ago, Lady Marissa Li Halan died when the powered device she was using exploded. The incident falls under the jurisdiction of the Authority, and as you are aware, I am in the process of investigating this incident," the constable paused to let that sink in.

"The problem," he continued, "is that the Li Halan have lost one of their young, and one who was seemingly destined for some rank and privilege. They are not going to be pleased with a simple guild report that indicates she blew herself up! And so, I have decided that you will be my investigatory team."

There were startled oaths, and murmurs of outrage. The nobles all looked vexed at being conscripted into what amounted to a charade. Sir Arthur was about to speak, but Chief Maurie cut in first.

"So what you're saying is that you don't want it to be the Authority versus the Li Halan thing, so you get a couple other nobles involved, some other guilds and the Church and it looks like a comprehensive and objective investigation?"

"Precisely," Constable Severns replied, "even though we could pretty much sit down right now and write up the report for the Li Halan. This way I fulfill my goal of not making any waves, and unfortunately, since this entire investigation is under my authority, I'm choosing to involve you all."

"How exactly do we all fit in?" Sir Arthur replied, his tone a little frosty. "And what stops me from just telling the Li Halan that you're full of wind?"

"Well, kid," Constable Severns replied with a grin, "You and the priest were the only ones left standing around when the smoke cleared, so that makes you witnesses right now, or suspects if you decide to be pig-headed. Either way I could turn your names over to the Li Halan and then you could step and fetch to their investigation — one which will take a lot longer than the day or two of your time that I'm asking. Now you chose to bring your Hazat friend along, and well, that just looks like an accomplice waiting in the wings to me... but, then there's our Trusnikron friend who was at the scene, found evidence, but wanted to avoid us so he gave it to the priest. Well, that right there is collusion between Sir Alexander and Brother Golic, as well as the fact that we could dig into Sir Alexander's past and find out why he doesn't want to meet me and my deputies. So far we haven't. Now, we both know that all of this could be done away with and exposed as false, but you'd be dealing with the Li Halan at that point and I hear they are a very, very conservative and by the book house. It may well take weeks or even months of your time to get disentangled from their inquest."

"And the Charioteer?" Sir Alexander asked, glaring balefully at the constable.

"Well, he's a friend of mine, and as a guild member, it's in his best interest to help me, or else risk contributing to a guild-nobility schism. The last thing we need now is a scandal that turns the guilds against the houses, all over the death of a Li Halan girl who more or less blew herself up!"

"What about the three men who were with her?" asked Brother Golic.

"Ah, well they are recovering nicely in the hospital, but know relatively little. Their liege was about to embark on some personal quest, and they were along to aid her in whatever way they could. They knew little of the details because she had not told them yet. They were just preparing to get a briefing over a meal, after they charged their fusion cells..."

"So, we play along with this charade so that your report looks objective," Don Hector uttered suddenly, "what do we get in return?" The others all looked shocked for a moment, then suddenly very calculating.

"Well, my Hazat friend," Constable Severns replied, "you will have my gratitude, which is impressive by itself, but coupled with my rank and guild, would prove beneficial to any of my friends who may find themselves in trouble on Byzantium Secundus, especially in Port Authority."

They all shot looks at one another; distrust, annoyance, even excitement from Brother Golic, who was smitten by the intrigue. But ultimately, Chief Maurie summed it up and concluded the meeting.

"We don't really have a choice, most of the work is done, and basically all we have to do is be seen together for a day or so. I think I can handle drinking with you bums for a while... besides, I'm waiting on my Engineer buddies to get back to me on what kind of device she was toting. So whadda ya say?"

"May Saint Paulus guide us in this quest! I'm in!" Brother Golic replied.

"Don't reckon I got much choice, now do I?" asked Sir Alexander. "I'm in for a bit."

"I'll do it," Sir Arthur said slowly, "I'm not sure I like it, but I don't want a fight between the nobles and the guilds either..."

"Nor do I," added Don Hector, "you can count on the saber of Don Hector Eduardo de Hazat."

"Excellent!" Constable Severns exclaimed. "Why don't you all figure out when you're next going to meet. Discuss a few things, and then after a day or so, come back to me and we'll assemble our information and I'll file a report!" He gave them all a long, slow wink. One by one they nodded, sighed, or grunted, then got up to leave. The constable walked them to the door.

Once outside the Constabulary, the Charioteer lit up a smoke. He inhaled deeply, then blew a cloud into the air. Sir Arthur, Sir Alexander, and Don Hector all stood together to one side, and the Eskatonic merely stood, deep in thought.

"It seems to me," the slender priest said, "that we should try to uncover as much as possible about the young woman and the circumstances surrounding her death."

"I agree, Brother Golic," Sir Arthur replied, "Don Hector and myself feel there is something odd about the device that exploded. We plan on speaking to our houses, as well some noble peers to learn what we can of Lady Marissa. Chief Maurie, you said you will know more soon?"

"Yeah, I should know something by tomorrow evening. What don't you like about the device?" the Charioteer asked, scratching at his beard.

"How many of you have a powered device that could possibly explode?" Don Hector asked rhetorically. "Since the fusion generator checked out, that means the device was faulty, and if the device would explode when powered, then she had never powered it before. I just get the feeling that there's more here than meets the eye. It's not as simple as Constable Severns wants to make it..."

"What are you suggesting, Don Hector?" Chief Maurie asked, his tone serious and his eyes wide. "Surely not an outright attack on a member of the Li Halan!"

"I don't know, Jason," Don Hector said seriously, "I just know it doesn't feel right."

"Well," added Brother Golic, "there are some rites I could perform that would allow me to feel if there are any residual forces, or patterns of fate lingering in the area where her Inner Flame was extinguished so violently."

The others looked at the scrawny priest, as he swiped at his mop of unkempt hair, and muddled through various theories. Sir Alexander shook his head and shrugged.

"I've got some contacts in the Scravers," he said, "I reckon I can drop her name in those circles and see if anything comes up to nibble at it."

"You know, it occurs to me," Don Hector mused, "that if we presented the results of our investigation directly to the Li Halan, then we prevent any problems with the Authority, and possibly earn the gratitude of the Li Halan. Seems like a win-win situation for everyone involved. What do you all think?"

"I think that is the way to go," Sir Arthur concluded, "are we agreed?"

"We're agreed then," Jason announced. "Now where shall we meet and when?" They bickered and discussed, but finally agreed to meet the following evening at the Final Jump, a rather low-key establishment known to Jason and popular with Charioteers. There they could talk amongst themselves without attracting too much attention. As they went their separate ways into the bustling agora, none of them noticed the lone bystander who watched a moment longer, then slunk off into the crowds.

* * *

Port Authority never closed. Only the crowd's ebb and flow gave any indication of day and night. As the afternoon stretched into evening, the patrons retreated into smoky taverns or glamorous restaurants to have a meal, a drink, and catch up on the day's gossip. The hot item for those privy to higher circles of society was the death of Lady Marissa Li Halan. An extensive investigation initiated by Count Alrich Li Halan had individuals from all levels of society scurrying to piece together the details of the young knight's death.

The Final Jump was one such smoky tavern and Sir Arthur Hawkwood sat waiting patiently for his companions. With luck, they would be the ones to put the picture together and report to Count Alrich and the rest of the Li Halan about exactly what had transpired. He sipped bitter beer from a pewter mug, as all around him, the din of conversation formed a constant numbing backdrop that served to shroud individual conversations in privacy. The waitress walked by his table and he ordered another beer. She nodded wearily, and yawned as she worked her way through the smoky room towards the bar. Somewhere, a fan kicked on as the room's ventilation system began to remove the smoke from the air.

The door opened, and a few heads turned. Arthur, dressed in more casual attire than yesterday, raised his hand to gain the attention of Brother Golic. The Eskatonic nodded and began to make his way towards the large table the Hawkwood had claimed. The young noble guessed that Brother Golic must fast regularly, as his form was so emaciated he resembled an animated scarecrow from one of his father's many fields on Ravenna.

"Brother Golic, have a seat," Arthur greeted the young priest, "what would you like to drink?" Brother Golic swiped his mop of hair from his dark blue eyes, and shook his head.

"I'm fine, Sir Arthur," he replied, "I've just dined with my Brothers at the Chapter House of our Order, and we heard a most excellent sermon on the Ethereal Agents of the Empyrean..." Sir Arthur tuned the priest out as he began to discuss 'Circles and Hierarchies of Metaphysical Entities'.

The arrival of Sir Alexander and Don Hector saved the young noble from any further lecture. The Trusnikron knight wore the same attire as yesterday, and Arthur wondered if the rustic noble slept in his clothing. The Hazat still sported the burgundy cloak that complemented his fine garments of gray and dark green. As they took seats, greetings were exchanged, and it was obvious that everyone had some tidbit of gossip or information they wanted to share. The waitress returned with Arthur's beer, and took orders for wine, fruit and cheese from the other nobles. Her demeanor had brightened considerably at having a table of nobles, and she even made a point to smile and answer, "yes, milord" to every order or request.

"Where is that blasted Charioteer!" Don Hector spat, as he craned his neck to watch the door. "It is already past time for our meeting!"

"Patience, Hector," Alexander replied, as his eyes roamed about the room for signs of trouble or a pretty face. In Alexander's experience, one usually followed the other. Jason appeared in the door about that time, still unshaven, and wearing the same wrinkled uniform from yesterday. He carried a satchel, and his face split into a grin when he saw everyone assembled.

"Hello all," he said cheerfully, "sorry I'm late. I had to pick up some drawings." He patted the satchel he held. The waitress approached, and her smile faded a bit at seeing Jason.

"Hello Veronica," he greeted her as she approached with a tray of drinks, "how about a thick Chirrah steak and a cold beer?" She smirked at the disheveled pilot and scowled, wrinkling her nose.

"You could use a change of clothes, Jason, and are you planning on paying your tab anytime soon? It's getting to be quite a novel..." Jason made a face, and waved her away as he took a seat. She put the tray on the table, and retreated back to the bar.

"Well," Don Hector asked, leaning forward, "what have you discovered?" All eyes were on the satchel Jason possessed. He shook his head and smiled.

"Nothing I want to go into just yet, Don Hector," he replied with a wry grin, "what did you discover from your family?"

"Well," the impatient Hazat sighed, "Lady Marissa Li Halan was a bit of a hot-head, considering her house. She seemed to favor glory and adventure, and offended easily. One of my cousins met her at court when she arrived and she almost drew on him because she thought he eyed her lewdly!" Alexander smirked, and Arthur nodded confirming the tale. "But," Hector continued, "as far as I could tell, she had not actively made any enemies."

"I can add a bit," Arthur cut in, "Marissa had been on Byzantium Secundus for a little over three weeks, visiting the court and paying visits to the various noble houses. She was young, having only recently completed her tutelage in Escoral on her homeworld of Kish. Her father is a ranking baron, and she was destined for an excellent marriage, and a ripe fortune. However, some of my family members said she had a rebellious attitude..."

"Which goes along with what I said," Don Hector reiterated, "So what? She was a young Li Halan out to make a name for herself. That's no reason to kill her..."

"Which," Brother Golic cut in, "I'd like to remind you that this could all be a tragic accident! Just because the seat of Imperial power rests on this planet does not mean everything has to be a conspiracy!"

"True, Brother Golic," Sir Alexander murmured, "but it never hurts to cover all the angles."

"Well," Jason sighed, "I'll go ahead and share what I found out. I talked to the Engineers about the fusion generator, and it checked out fine. No problems whatsoever."

"Did you figure out what that techno-gadget was?" asked Arthur, sipping his beer, and nibbling some cheese.

"Yeah," Jason added, "the pieces of the device we recovered proved to be part of something called a map reader. It was used by architects of the Diaspora or early Second Republic Era to read incredibly detailed maps drawn on thin, semi transparent silicon sheets. The lines were actually lines of circuitry that could be lighted in different colors to show different areas on the map. Or alternately, different maps could be stored on one page, with a different color pertaining to each map." The Charioteer paused to take a sip of his beer, which had just arrived along with his meal. He winked at Veronica and then turned back to his companions.

"Where would one get maps such as these," asked Brother Golic, "and why would a young noble woman possess such an item?"

"That's the thing," Jason replied with some confusion, "I cannot think of why she would need such a device. Most of the maps that could be used are in storage, the property of Engineers, or else would have no value in today's time. "I've got some drawings the Engineers worked up for me that show what the device would have looked like, and they also loaned me one of the maps that would have been fitted to the device." He opened the satchel and removed several drawings as well as a thin flexible sheet with metal contact studs around the edges and traceries of circuits running through it. They all studied the technical drawings, depicting the device from all angles, and then handled the map. They all came to the same conclusion.

"We found no map pieces," Don Hector stated, "and the fragments of the device we found would only account for about half of the item."

"That's what I was thinking," Jason added, "so where did the rest of the map reader go, and what happened to the map that was in it?"

"Maybe she didn't know what she had," suggested the priest, "and was merely experimenting with the device and it exploded?" His tone carried a subtle hint of righteous disapproval.

"What about you, Sir Alexander," asked Arthur, "what did your Scraver contacts tell you?" The gruff noble smiled his characteristic easy-going grin, and shook his head, causing braids and feathers to stir.

"Not too damn much," he spat, "the ones I spoke to were more interested in scavengin' the body for firebirds and her fancy sword than anythin' else. I'm certain there were Scravers around during the whole mess, so they may know more than they're tellin'..."

Jason was just about to speak when the table next to theirs erupted into heated conversation. Arthur's regal features were vexed, and Brother Golic turned to intercede. It seemed that Veronica had spilled a tray of drinks, and the men, all rough-looking traders, were not accepting her apology. As Golic rose to say some peaceful words, one of the men stood and backhanded the waitress, sending her spinning to the floor with a shriek. The nobles were on their feet in an instant, honor demanding action of them.

Don Hector Eduardo's face was a mask of rage, as he charged forward to grasp the man who dared strike a woman. He spat a string of curses, "Churl! Villain! Dark-spawned cur!" as he closed. Sir Arthur stood and drew steel, calling out a challenge to the offending table in a clear voice that could be heard above the commotion. Chaos was rapidly descending on the scene as patrons tried to clear away from the combat while the rest of the staff and the owner tried to restore order and eject the offending parties. In the midst of it all, a wiry, nondescript man calmly positioned himself near the nobles' table, his eyes fixed firmly on the drawings still scattered across its surface.

Jason and Sir Alexander moved around to help Veronica stand and get her out of harm's way. The other ruffians at the offending table grappled with the nobles, overturning tables and chairs as they cursed and fought. Arthur's sword had been knocked from his hand, but the young Hawkwood was not untrained. Don Hector seemed nearly unstoppable, shrugging off blows and moving with such speed that onlookers wondered why he even bothered to wear a rapier. Brother Golic was part of the crowd, urging Hector and Arthur to punish the brutish men who would strike down a simple serving woman. Jason and Alexander found the waitress stunned, unable even to stand. Thus, everyone was engaged or otherwise occupied when the wiry, dark-haired man sped from the crowd, slid across their table, scooping up the diagrams, map, satchel, as well as cutlery, plates and mugs, and dashed from the Final Jump.

There was a moment of stunned silence from the crowd, then Brother Golic called out, "Thief!" and with a surprising display of speed and agility, hiked up his robe and sprinted after the man. Hector and Arthur were oblivious, and both landed mighty blows to put their attackers down for the last time. As they began to congratulate one another on a well-won fight, the Charioteer and Trusnikron noble jumped up and sped for the door, only to encounter a group of tipsy patrons entering. The resulting collision almost began another fight, but Don Hector and Sir Arthur had grasped the situation, and pushed the other two out the door, amidst curses and yells.

Back inside the Final Jump, Veronica shook her head and rubbed her jaw. She glanced at the man who had struck her, himself showing a mass of bruises, and they exchanged a wink and a nod. They also exchanged winks with the group of drunk patrons who had entered just in time to collide with Jason and Alexander. All around them, patrons returned to their chairs, and the 'offending gentlemen' were escorted out the back door of the establishment and told never to return.

In the street, the party assembled to find Brother Golic walking dejectedly back towards them. His hair was damp with sweat, and his face covered with dust. One of his eyes was rapidly swelling shut, and he had a slight limp.

"What happened Brother Golic?" asked Hector, his face still flushed with the excitement of combat.

"He got away," sighed the priest dejectedly, "I caught him as he was heading towards a skimmer, but he was more skilled in the combat arts than myself. He staggered me, and while I was recovering my wits, he hopped in the air car and made his escape."

"We were set up," spat Jason. "Somebody knew we were meeting here, and what we were investigating." The Charioteer Chief cursed and paced around with an agitated gait, then calmed. "I suppose we were none to secretive yesterday in front of the Constabulary. We more or less made our plans in public, and any observer could have overheard us discussing things and planning to meet here. Damn!"

"But that means someone would have had to have been watching us for several days," Sir Arthur concluded, "which means that the explosion wouldn't have been haphazard. If there were spies there who watched Brother Golic and myself talk to Constable Severns, then they had to be there in advance, since we obviously did not know we were going to be privy to an explosion or the death of Lady Marissa." Don Hector glanced around the assembled group, and added his own curses to Jason's.

"Damn!" the hot-blooded Hazat growled, "Who played us like fools?'

"The Scravers," added Alexander, "they're the only ones who could have had agents in place, and it explains why my contacts seem to know so little."

"Why would the Scravers want a Li Halan dead?" asked Brother Golic.

"They don't," replied Jason, "or else they never would have tailed us here and stolen our documents. They want to know about the map reader."

"It seems to me," Sir Alexander added, stroking his beard, "that this little Li Halan gal wouldn't have needed a map reader unless she had a map. She came to Byzantium Secundus with a map, obtained the reader here, and it blew her up!"

"So, let's figure out who sold her the map reader," Arthur concluded. "Maybe they came to the same conclusion. If she's looking for an ancient map reader, she must have an ancient map, and maybe someone thought that was worth enough to kill for."

"Just like in a magic lantern show," Don Hector mused, "A treasure map is on the loose that can only be read by an ancient map reader, and everyone's willing to kill to get their hands on it."

"Well," added Jason, "the possibilities are endless. I mean, it could be new jump roads, or even a map to ancient Ur ruins, or lead to a lost city on a lost world, or..."

"Yes, yes," Brother Golic, added, "it is exciting, but then again, maybe it leads to nothing that even exists anymore. Hmmm? We need to find out where that girl obtained that map reader, and maybe we will be able to make some conclusions. Until then, all else is idle speculation."

"One thing is certain," Jason said, with a serious look to his fellow companions, "this investigation just got complicated and took a rather serious turn. I've got to go report this to Justin and get us some more time, as well as explain to the Engineers how I lost the map they loaned me. Ugh! This is not going to be fun."

"Jason," Arthur asked, "perhaps you could find out what ship Lady Marissa arrived on, and who flew it. If she arrived with a map, and was out to make a name for herself, maybe she talked about it. If we can trace her steps, then we may be able to figure out who she contacted and that may lead us to the Scravers."

"Or somewhere else entirely," Hector suggested, "and I for one do not want to square off against the entire Scraver's Guild. It had to be them who set us up in the bar..."

They all stood at a loss for a moment on where to proceed, and it was Brother Golic who spoke up.

"I have a ritual I can perform that may give us some divine guidance, but I need to perform it at the Chapter House of my Order, where I won't be disturbed," the slim priest explained. "I was going to do some investigation anyway, as you may recall."

"What exactly does this ritual do?" asked Jason, raising an eyebrow skeptically.

"Well, it's rather complicated, but in essence, it allows me to determine if several events are in fact connected, or if they are just coincidence. If I can establish that the death of the Li Halan, the theft of our documents, and the presence of an ancient technological device are all connected, then I may be granted insight by the Pancreator as to where the next knot in the thread of fate may lie..."

"It's worth a try, I suppose," Sir Arthur concluded, "and should keep us from going on a wild snipe hunt."

"If it works," added the Charioteer.

"Let's meet back here in a while," Sir Alexander suggested to Jason, "I've been thinking that the set-up in the bar went too smoothly, and some of those patrons had to be in on it. Like that bunch as we was runnin' out the door."

"What about the serving woman," Hector suggested, "could the whole incident have been devised by the Scravers?"

"I'm friendly with Veronica," Jason added, "and I would know if she had ties to the Scravers."

"No you wouldn't," Alexander answered definitively, "not if she didn't want you to. But, maybe you drop by a little later on tonight, to see how she's doin'? Then ya work yer charm on her, take her home or someplace quiet like, where I'll be waitin'. Then I think we'll have a friendly chat with Veronica, and we'll know real quick-like if she's one or not.

"I don't want any part of that," Arthur stated, "that sounds like sinister work for a noble, Sir Alexander."

"Yeah, well, maybe I wasn't always noble, eh kid?" the rugged Trusnikron replied. "Don't worry, I'm not going to hurt anybody." His expression, however, made his words seem less than reliable.

"Well, I say we all meet tomorrow morning, at Solcis, the spaceport on Tamerlain? There is a small cafe there, and nobody would look twice at a group of interested parties meeting with a Charioteer Chief," Jason suggested. They all agreed, and then went their separate ways, each urging the others to be careful.

* * *

Solcis spaceport was the least active of all the ports on Byzantium Secundus. Set on the continent of Tamerlain, it attracted only minimal traffic. A short flitter jump from Veridian, the largest land mass making up the continent of Galatea, Tamerlain was a rugged, unstable continent, with a thriving magic lantern industry and large numbers of aliens. The cities were spread out, and run more or less independently of one another. All in all, it made a great place to get away from the prying eyes in the Imperial City and Port Authority.

Sir Alexander found it pleasant, with its expanses of untamed wilderness, and as his flitter touched down, he felt a bit of regret that he couldn't roam its environs. He entered the spaceport, and located the small cafe where the others were already assembled. He smirked when he saw how plainly everyone was attired; just a group of freemen meeting over drinks for some conversation. A woman unknown to Alexander accompanied Jason, and Alexander frowned when he saw her Charioteer rank pins, marking her a Chief as well. She was tall and lanky for a woman, with a worn and patched flight suit and an ancient slug thrower on one hip. Her long hair was tied back in a ponytail, and her eyes shone with mirth. Alexander thought she was pretty, in a reckless sort of way.

"Alexander," called Brother Golic, "we're over here!" The beast-rider smiled and hurried his pace.

"How's everyone doin'," he asked in his gruff drawl, "did I miss anything?"

"No," Arthur replied, "we were just making the acquaintance of Chief Darla Farseer. Chief Farseer, meet Alexander Trusnikron."

"Trusnikron?" she asked with a grin, "you guys are supposed to be good with animals right?"

"Best cavalry ever to take the field," boasted Hector, "and still worth a damn after you knock them off their mounts too!" He laughed at his own wit, and Alexander smiled at the compliment.

"We've been known to find our way around a stable from time to time, and every so often some Hawkwood or Hazat lets us armor up and head out on the battlefield," Alexander added.

"Well, have a seat, then," Jason offered, "and I'll order us up another round."

"What happened with the serving woman?" Hector asked, "Jason won't say anything." Alexander smirked, and shrugged.

"She said it was a set-up, and says she was paid to drop the drinks at the table. She's a damn Scraver I'd wager, but I'll be damned if I could get her to admit it!" Alexander explained, pausing to take his drink from the waitress, and sip it. "I asked around some Scraver circles again, and got a little more information this time."

The others looked expectantly at the rugged noble, and he sipped his drink again before continuing.

"The Scravers were tryin' to track down a map reader, and thought that we might have one. They've got a bigger mess of trouble to worry 'bout now, though. Seems that someone with some connections paid a pile of birds to the Scravers to steal a certain item, only something went wrong with the job, and now their customer's madder'n a wet urroc at midnight!"

"What became of your ritual, Brother Golic?" Jason asked, as Chief Darla sat and listened to the narrative attentively. If she was lost with the story, she gave no indication, and most assumed that Jason had filled her in.

"I was able to determine that the presence of the map reader and the set-up in the bar were linked, but the explosion and death of Lady Marissa Li Halan did not seem to fit into the picture. The Pancreator did not grant me any further wisdom..." the scrawny priest finished in a dejected tone.

"So, we need to come up with a solid theory, and then present it to Constable Severns so that he can make the proper arrests," Sir Arthur concluded. "What can you add, Chief Farseer?"

"Call me Darla," she replied with a wink, "and Jason's more or less filled me in on what's going on. I was shocked. I can't believe that Lady Marissa is dead!"

"Did you know her well?" Hector asked.

"We had met a few times," Darla clarified. "I often fly for the Li Halan, and several of the families on Kish request me. Lady Marissa's mother chartered the *Calypso* — that's my ship — to bring her daughter to court on Byzantium Secundus. And now... she's dead." The pilot lowered her head, her face ashen and her eyes bright with moisture.

"Were there any enemies that she left behind on Kish that you know of, or anyone she ticked off when she arrived?" Jason asked, patting his fellow pilot on the shoulder. "Don't worry, Darla, I'm sure the Li Halan on Kish don't blame you for Lady Marissa's death. I mean, you did your part and got her here safely."

"Yeah, I know," Darla replied with a sigh, "it's just that she was so full of life! She was just a kid, Jason. She even asked about joining the Charioteers." She took a deep breath then continued, "Uh... anyway, to get back to your question, Jason. Yeah, I stopped off at Criticorum on the way, to refuel and take care of some personal business. Anyway, this al-Malik noble asked for a ride, and even though the Li Halan had chartered my vessel, he was going to the same place, and had some interesting items he gave me in exchange for passage, so I took him along. Lord Ahrim al-Malik was his name, and I know that he and Lady Marissa spoke at length during the journey."

"What's this al-Malik do?" Alexander asked, "and since when are the Li Halan and the al-Malik all snugged up together? I thought they'd just as soon spit at each other as look at one another!" He laughed a coarse laugh at the thought.

"He's a trader in rare items," Darla answered, "art, jewelry, antiquities. You know, uses his noble status to crash at various estates around the Known Worlds and makes some money by selling or trading items from one end of the jumproads to the other. I like him."

"The type of man who would know an ancient map if he saw one," Brother Golic suggested, "and might even have possessed a map reader."

"Yeah, but why blow her up?" Don Hector asked, "I fail to see the motive. Orchestrating the death of a young Li Halan girl for a map she carries seems a bit much, even for an eccentric al-Malik!"

"Well, we know the explosion is not part of the whole mess," Jason clarified, "at least, according to our good Eskatonic over here." His tone suggested he had little faith in the theurgical rites of the Eskatonics, but he didn't outright deny Brother Golic's claims. "I have a theory, that I think would fit."

"By all means," urged Sir Arthur, "let's have it!"

Jason scratched his beard, and tapped his finger on the table while he formulated his thoughts. The others sat attentively, and leaned forward as the Charioteer Chief began to speak. "Okay, Lady Marissa, who is out to prove something to the Known Worlds, brags to her al-Malik shipmate that she's going to be more than just a baron's daughter. She maybe even brags about having an ancient map. The al-Malik offers her a map reader in his collection, cause he figures he's not going to ever get rid of it anyway, so he cuts her a deal. She takes the deal, and everything seems straight so far, right?"

The others nodded, but kept quiet as Jason continued.

"Only, then the al-Malik starts thinking that maybe the map is worth more than the price he charged, and so he figures its no big deal to have the young, inexperienced Li Halan get robbed while on Byzantium Secundus. So he contacts the Scravers and tells them to get the map and a certain technical device, but never tells them that they go together. Well, something goes wrong. Somehow, the map reader the al-Malik sold her is faulty, and blows up! Now, the Scravers move in and recover what they can in the short amount of time they have, which could be the map, and a handful of pieces."

"But the al-Malik noble would be distraught, because he now has blood on his hands, so the last thing he wants is to be connected to the incident. Of course, the only reason we know he's connected is because Chief Darla admits to picking him up on Criticorum. That's not common knowledge to anyone else but us; we're the only people who even know that Ahrim al-Malik and Lady Marissa Li Halan met!"

Sir Arthur added excitedly, "I like this Jason, I think you're on to something! Continue!"

"So," Jason smirked, "the Scravers know they have something, but they don't know what this map is, and they definitely don't know what the device was, so they wouldn't know to look for a map reader. But they see us get involved with Constable Severns, and tail us to figure out if we're going to finger them. Alexander approached his Scraver contacts, so they definitely knew something wasn't quite right, which is why they set us up. They wanted to know what we knew, and once they had the drawings and the map, they put two and two together and realized they were sitting on some dangerous property."

"Dangerous as all silver-belled hell," laughed Alexander, "cause I bet this big-wig player is the al-Malik noble bustin' the Scravers balls to get the map he paid them to steal. Damn! They don't want to give it up, cause they know what it is now, but they don't want to go to war neither! Damn! I bet their runnin' 'round tryin' to find some way to read and copy that map, before they turn it over to the al-Malik! Damn Scravers, always tryin' to play both ends against the middle!"

"Well, that's as good a theory as we've got," Jason concluded, "so what do we do about it?"

"Well, the tragedy here is that her death really does seem to be an accident," Brother Golic stated in a somber tone. "I don't think anyone knew that the map reader would explode when powered, and it serves as a reminder to us all of the sins and tribulations brought on by technology. This device from times past has brought a lot of misery and grief to a lot of people, and no one knows if it actually leads to anything important!" Everyone fell silent at Brother Golic's words, and conceded that he was correct. They were all young and adventurous, much as Lady Marissa had been, and if their theory was correct, she had died blameless, just an innocent victim in a freak accident.

"I guess we go to Constable Severns," Arthur replied, "and give him our theory, then we go to Count Alrich Li Halan and tell him the same thing. At that point, we have completed our investigation and it is out of our hands."

"There is only one very small problem," Darla added with a grin, "you have no proof!"

"That's for the Reeves to figure out, not us!" Jason protested "we've done our part, now let's see if we can't get something for our time and trouble."

"Right then," Sir Arthur stated as he stood, "let's go do this and then be done with it."

* * *

They found Constable Severns at his district office, feet up on his desk and an imported cigar clutched between his beefy fingers. He was not happy that the two day investigation had placed blame at the feet of an al-Malik noble and unscrupulous Scravers. The fact that there was less than substantial proof also irked him, and he wasted no time in making his feelings known.

"I can't report this to the Li Halan!" he protested, "I ask you to give me a nice, clean investigation, and you come back with conspiracies and accusations! Do I look like I have a death wish to you?"

"Constable," Sir Arthur said, "you may be comfortable with cover-ups and mislaid deceptions in the natural course of your job, but we nobles are cut from a finer cloth than that, and such guile and treachery is not our common currency."

Justin Severns stared flatly at the noble youth. "Nice rhetoric, boy, but don't give me that! I was cleaning up after nobles and their messes before you were born!"

"Then what do you suggest, Justin?" Jason asked with a smirk and a shrug.

"How about this," the constable suggested, as he paced around the small cramped office, "I will file an official report saying that no evidence could be found to label the unfortunate demise of Marissa Li Halan as anything other than an unfortunate accident. Then, I will include your independent and unsubstantiated theory as a plausible, but unproven, possibility for the events that occurred in the agora two days ago. That should satisfy the Li Halan, and if they want to go on a witch-hunt, then they can risk it!"

Don Hector grunted. "Doesn't sound like we got too much out of this after all."

"No, no, on the contrary," Constable Severns cautioned, "I'm very grateful for your help in this matter, I'm just a bit upset at the outcome. I think you will all find yourselves to be well received among the Authority, and if there is ever anything I can do for you, please do not hesitate to call upon me. Now, if you will excuse me, I have to file this report and send a copy off to the Li Halan Ambassador."

With expressions from disbelief to disgust, they filed from the constable's office, and gathered out on the street. Citizens from all over the Known Worlds passed them with only a cursory glance, on their way to trade, buy or sell their wares. A gaudy hotel across the street promised a free light show in every room, and a corner bar blared out popular dance tunes.

"Well, I am overwhelmed by his generosity," Don Hector's caustic comment echoed all their thoughts.

Darla, still present, shook her head and wagged a finger at the Hazat noble. "Don't be so sure you didn't get something after all. Having the favor of an Authority Constable is no small thing, especially if you plan on staying on Byzantium Secundus, and even more so if you have a knack for getting into trouble..." The passionate Hazat started to make a retort, then fell silent and merely glared at the smirking Charioteer.

"Are all Charioteers so smug?" asked Sir Arthur.

"No," she replied, "only the really good ones. Well, thanks boys, it's been fun, but I've got a ship to run! Catch you around portside, eh Razor?"

"Yeah, I'll see ya around Darla!" Jason called, and then turned back to his companions. "Really guys, what did you expect?"

"I don't know," Sir Alexander replied with a shrug, as his gaze lingered on Darla's retreating form, "I just feel like we're coming up empty handed." The slim priest shrugged his shoulders.

"The Pancreator wills all things. I am glad that the young Li Halan was not murdered, but I am sorry that her possession of such a device caused so much trouble. As a Li Halan, I thought she would have been taught the dangers of innovation and technology, but perhaps her death will serve as an example to others, and strengthen their flame within, urging them to a greater understanding of the Pancreator's will..."

"Yeah," Sir Arthur cut in, "we all pray for the Pancreator's guidance, Brother Golic. Right now, though, I have to get back to my duties.

I've been neglecting them for the last two days while running all over the agora with you lot!" He smiled, and then bid them all farewell. "Perhaps we shall meet again," he added in parting. Then he strode off into the swirling crowd.

"I, too, have enjoyed this chance to aid in an investigation in the cause of justice," Brother Golic began, his narrow features animated as he shook each hand in turn. "I think that perhaps I shall seek out other mysteries, and not just those in the Empyrean. A detective of both the world and the soul, I think, has a good ring to it! The Pancreator's blessing go with you!" The Eskatonic trundled off through the crowd, already envisioning great mysteries to be solved.

"Farewell to you beast-rider, and to you Charioteer," Don Hector Eduardo of the Hazat saluted both men. "Should you have need of me, call upon me at my family's estate. We shall go hunting, or perhaps the chief will fly us to Leagueheim for some extended revelry! Farewell all!" With a regal swirl of his burgundy cloak, the Hazat strode through the crowd, threatening to step over those that did not get out of his way fast enough.

That left only Sir Alexander and Chief Jason Maurie, and the two sauntered off to a nearby bar to have a drink before parting company. They chose a secluded booth, and waited for their server to bring them a round of cold beers. Then, they saluted one another on a job well done, clanging the heavy pewter mugs together and taking a sip of the dark, bitter beer.

"So, Chief Maurie," Sir Alexander grinned, "do you reckon they ever suspected?" The Charioteer shook his head, and scratched at his beard.

"Not even once, Sir Alexander" he replied, "I think we got enough legitimate factions involved with our investigation that they never even suspected our ruse..." He smirked once again, and shook his head at the clever conspiracy. "I guess being noble has it's advantages, eh Alexander, even if you're only a lowly Hand?"

"Absolutely, my boy. Absolutely," the rustic outlander replied, "but being a Consul in the Scravers didn't hurt a bit either!" The rugged noble-turned-Scraver produced a map, the very one formerly possessed by Marissa Li Halan, and stared at the delicate traceries. "Where do you suppose it leads, lad?"

"Don't know Alexander," the slender pilot replied as he ran his fingers through his dark hair, "but wherever it is, I can get us there... just as soon as we get to Leagueheim and obtain a damn map reader!" The two conspirators laughed and toasted, spending several enjoyable hours theorizing on what treasures may lie in store for them. Finally, they collected their things and left, Jason calling out a reminder to be at Solcis spaceport first thing in the morning.

Neither one of them noticed the shadowed form tail them from the bar and then scurry off into the crowded bazaar...

The Noble Essence

Alan Bryden

Vaclav II, scion of House Vasalayana, led the procession upon his white horse down the cobblestone streets, fireworks bursting above. The people were out in force, dancing and clapping behind the gendarme's pikes.

The heathens in the east of Vaclav's small kingdom had been defeated at last — fools who had forsaken fear of the Pancreator. The worshippers had resurrected primitive Vuldrok myths and believed that Leminkainan's three moons were some triumvirate of gods come from the Vuldrok homeworlds to herald the conquering of the Known Worlds.

But now, the fiefdom of Isalight was safe from the poison. Vaclav smiled and waved to the cheering crowd — but still, his heart lay heavy at the treachery he had condoned.

Vaclav was a proud warrior king, leading troops even now in his 68th year. Courage in battle, valor and bravery were the things he sought for himself, his fiefdom, and his noble House Vasalayana. Vaclav would have never allowed the treachery if not for the Hawkwoods.

Centuries ago, House Vasalayana had assisted House Hawkwood on Leminkainen during the barbarian invasion, and Vaclav's ancestors had been honored with an independent fiefdom. But ever since, the greedy Hawkwoods had schemed against their former ally. There had been respite during the Emperor Wars, but those had been over now for three years, and the Hawkwoods had returned, offering endebting assistance with the one hand, and fomenting revolt with the other.

The specter of Hawkwood perfidy tipped the balance. As always, the Hawkwoods covered their tracks well, and no solid proof had been found, but Vaclav knew their penchant for connivance. So Vaclav had authorized a plot. The rebel's high general had been clandestinely approached with gold. Gold for himself, he was told — or for his assassins. Vaclav chose not to know any further detail. No doubt, however, the general was reminded of his beautiful young daughter and twin infant sons.

The palace of House Vasalayana lay before Vaclav, shrouded in a thick, artificial mist. Its gates were thrown open, and suddenly dazzling beams of light shot from the palace windows. Electric light was expensive in Isalight, reserved only for spectacle such as this.

And spectacle it was. The arclights shifted back and forth, playing across the crowded courtyard-like landing lights of a spaceship, until they came together, to shine upon Vaclav, and the crowd burst forth anew into cheers.

Vaclav turned his charger about, to face the crowd. He looked at his entourage behind him, led by General Nadia Rushingstar. Her harsh features belied her bright, energetic eyes. She'd accepted the plan to subvert the enemy's general, though reluctantly. In battle, she'd given no indication, bravely charging into danger with the troops at her heels, themselves honored to engage the bloody fray.

Further back, Vaclav saw James Idoru. Beautiful, young, dashing James, in his black mackinaw and dapper waistcoat. His features were genteel and smooth, and his eyes shone in the brilliance with an almost boyish awe. It seemed incredible that behind that innocent face was the mind that had conceived the subtle machinations that brought the war to an end. Only a select few knew of the plan to subvert the enemy general, and only Vaclav and Rushingstar had known that the plan had emanated from James Idoru.

James looked from the dazzling lights to the king. The younger man's face seemed so open, full of delight at the show. The war could have dragged on for years, with thousands more lives lost without James' brilliance. Vaclav gazed at James Idoru's face, his eyes, his joyous smile. Then he reeled his horse and led the procession to the palace.

The banquet hall was filled with the most important generals and nobles in Isalight. The queen sat opposite Vaclav on the long table — she and Vaclav still maintained a polite relationship, but little more. On the right, midway down the table, sat the beastly Hawkwood ambassador, with his sharp nose and slitted eyes. Without solid proof of the Hawkwood's influence, Vaclav had been unable to eject him. The ambassador even had the effrontery to refer to Vaclav as "Prince" — not "King." It was true that Vaclav had sworn allegiance to Emperor Alexius, so in the Emperor's company, he was properly a Prince, but that allegiance was to the Imperial Throne — not to any mere house! Centuries before, House Hawkwood had sworn to recognize the head of House Vasalayana to be King of Isalight, and that relationship had never changed!

It was a petty matter, but no doubt the Hawkwoods calculated it to gall the king.

Even more insulting, General Rushingstar and the crown prince flanked the ambassador, speaking familiarly with him! The prince and many of the younger set had taken up "all things Hawkwood," even affecting the appalling Hawkwood dress and accents. Vaclav saw Rushingstar say something to the ambassador and they both laughed. It was a disgrace. Vaclav prayed to the Pancreator that his son would see reason before the crown passed to him.

To his left, James abruptly stood, tapping his glass for attention. "A toast!" He said. "A toast, lords and ladies!" He had arrived on Leminkainan just a year ago, and many of the nobles looked down on him as a newcomer. Still, they knew James had the king's ear, so they ceased their conversations.

"A toast to General Rushingstar! For her crushing bravery!" The wording seemed odd, and the table was quiet. Vaclav felt his heart grow heavy, but James continued. "For leading our brave troops into the vale of tears and destruction, on whose back was delivered our salvation!"

"Hear hear!" the nobles about the banquet cheered, celebrating the general's bravery. But Vaclav grew hot. The comment was double-edged. James had made it clear that he felt his bribery had broken the rebels, and that Rushingstar had incurred needless casualties with her brave charges.

"Your majesty," said Rushingstar raising her glass. She was smiling graciously, though Vaclav could see a dark look in her eyes. Vaclav forced himself to smile and nod back.

* * *

The fireplace in Vaclav's suite roared, and Vaclav felt the heat. He stood in front of it, his clothing loosed.

James touched his arm. "I missed your embrace, my lord."

"By the Pancreator!" Vaclav whirled on him. "How could you say such a brazen thing!"

James turned his face away, and withdrew his hand. "My lord... I..."

"Your baiting of Rushingstar was uncalled for! Any reaction from her, and that ambassador might have guessed..."

"It was her hobnobbing with that... That raptor! That woman is no better than a Hawkwood at times! How could I tame my tongue?" James straightened, but looked to the wall, not at Vaclav. "That woman knows much more than she says."

James stared away proudly. His face was strong and gentle, warm in the firelight. Yet sometimes Vaclav recalled how foreign the young man was. James Idoru was of House Decados, a house with few representatives on Leminkainen. The Hawkwoods controlled the space about Leminkainen, and they severely checked the number of Decados who came here. Vaclav had met very few Decados — and none like James.

Decados and Hawkwood distrusted each other instinctively. They had fought each other bitterly through the Emperor Wars, and the first Decados Vaclav had seen in person was at a peace summit three years ago. That creature had been a hideous sight — her head shaven, a swirl of cicatrix patterned on her bare back.

But not all Decados were of that sort. Just over a year ago, James Idoru had arrived at Vaclav's court. He was a young noble travelling the Known Worlds to learn of its wonders. His perfect manners, his boyish demeanor had engaged the king at once.

And his hands. Those lovely, delicate hands, fingers long and thin, their skin soft to caress...

"James..." Vaclav took the younger man's hand. "James, it is over, and you saved many lives. Just as I expected of you."

James' gaze lowered suddenly. "My leige, I am sorry. Can you forgive me?" He turned to Vaclav and implored with his eyes.

Vaclav put his arms around James, and drew his body close. They stared into each other's eyes for a moment, then kissed.

* * *

Despite the late night, Vaclav rose early, as always. Much paperwork had accumulated. His office faced east, and Vaclav glanced now and then through the frosty window as the sun rose, warming the stones of the courtyard outside. Yesterday, flocks of his subjects had crowded in front of the palace, but now there was only the usual morning traffic of the working people. Vaclav smiled at his sturdy folk.

In the distance, down the wide avenue, he saw a horseman galloping past the scattered wagons and foot traffic. A single figure against the sun, but getting closer quickly, heading directly toward the palace. In a few moments, Vaclav recognized the woman's coat — blue, of the eastern guard regiment.

Vaclav leapt to his feet. He was out of the room and onto the front steps of the palace in a moment, the messenger only just bringing her horse to a halt, its body heavy with sweat despite the chill.

"Your majesty," the messenger gasped. A servant came from behind the king, holding Vaclav's greatcoat for him, and other servants helped the messenger from her horse. "Your majesty," she knelt before him on the cold stones. "The heathens, your majesty! They are advancing on the capital."

* * *

The heathens had nearly twice the 3000 that Rushingstar mustered — but they lacked a forceful general. They lacked a soldier king at their head — and they lacked the blessing of the Pancreator. Instead of waiting for the heathen army to advance, Rushingstar ordered cavalry contingents to strike out even as they were mustered — harassing the advancing army while it was spread out on the march, forcing them to slow or scatter, while infantry was organized for defense of the city.

The engagement took place the next morning, six miles east of the capital. At dawn, the forces faced each other across a broken plain, each side by now almost identical in strength — except in strength of will, and of leadership. When the armies clashed, only one side was relentless enough to take the day.

* * *

The night after was alive with bonfires. Vaclav rode with a small, hand-picked escort through the capital, where the people warmed themselves beside their fires, drank their ales. The atmosphere was jovial enough, but not with the elation of last night. The heathens had been beaten off, but there was still much to do. And many men had been lost.

Vaclav approached a bonfire, and the people doffed their caps, and kneeled in admiration for their king.

"Good people, good people," he said, and dismounted. "You have honored me this day. Your fight for the Pancreator will be remembered."

From the darkness, a horse approached quickly. Vaclav's guard was alert at once, but it was a messenger — from James. Requesting Vaclav to attend to an important matter.

James was in a small cottage two miles from the capital, using it secretly for his intelligence work. Guards stiffly saluted the king when Vaclav arrived.

Inside, a fire crackled in the hearth. The place had a pleasant, homey, feel to it, but for the crowd of quiet men and women, darkly dressed, and without expression — James' intelligence staff.

And in one corner, sat a man, stripped to the waist, and tied to a chair. Beside him stood a squat metal box, clusters of sharp silver spines protruding from it — their points hovering just away from touching the man's legs and arms, chest and face.

Vaclav blanched at the sight. An ancient, evil machine, made thousands of years ago in the time of humankind's technological hubris. A Decados noble family had kept it for many years, but James had convinced Vaclav to purchase it, and for the time being, they could keep it running.

"Your majesty," said James, "We found this man among the prisoners. He was disguised as a peasant, but his Hawkwood features made us suspicious."

James turned to the man in the chair. Indeed, his high cheekbones, his thin jaw distinguished him. He could almost be brother to the ambassador.

"We have extracted much information from him already. But let me show you, your majesty." He turned and activated the machine. Its innards creaked loudly, with the sound of grinding metal. "What is your name?" James demanded. The man's mouth quivered, but he said nothing. His eyes stared emptily. James adjusted the machine, and the man's body shuddered, his jaw snapping open and shut, but his eyes still unblinking. The grinding grew more pronounced, and a faint scent of burning carbon emanated from the spines.

"State your name!" James demanded again, louder.

Finally, the prisoner spoke, his voice jerky and mechanical. "I am Erasius Henry Hawkwood, of the 5th Native Assistance Corps." His jaw chattered again, and blood trickled from his bitten lip. The machine was sending electricity straight through his brain, forcing the information directly into his motor control system, instead of allowing the man any choice in his words. The ancient laws of energy flow forbade him to speak lies. "I am under orders from Victoria Hawkwood to assist oppressed peoples..." His whole body jerked violently. His glassy eyes seemed to swell, almost bursting from their sockets. "Against despots and... And..."

"Do you report to Rushingstar? Tell me!"

The prisoner's voice was lost in a gurgle. Blood spurted from his mouth and nose.

"Dammit!" James slapped at the machine's controls, but all at once, the top of the man's head sank inwards like a balloon gone soft. It was too late.

Vaclav gagged and turned away. Was this necessary? Could the war not be fought with honor and valor instead of torture? Yet here was proof that the Hawkwoods were doing the same! Assisting *Vuldroks* even! Yes, it *was* justified to use that machine, however awful it was, at least against foreigners and traitors. But still, the sight of that man's head sinking so...

"Your majesty," James' voice behind him. "You should rest now."

"Why Rushingstar?" Vacalv turned to James and demanded. "Why did you ask him that?"

"Your majesty should rest," said James. "I was only asking questions."

The machine whined down and the body gave one last jerk, the smell of burned flesh seeping into Vaclav's nostrils.

Yes, he should rest. He would see things more clearly in the morning.

* * *

The sun rose while Vaclav sat at his desk, writing the expulsion order for the Hawkwood ambassador. No explanations would be necessary — the connivers could only guess at how much had been discovered.

James had stayed out very late, but Vaclav had felt pleasure when he'd awoken to find James asleep beside him. The young man's features were so beautiful. Vaclav was satisfied. Finally, he had proof. "Native Assistance Corps" indeed. Covert agitators was what they were.

From his window on the courtyard, Vaclav saw Huweg Maarten, captain of the city gendarmerie approaching in the early light. Vaclav liked the robust fellow, bluff and open, and they enjoyed friendly times, when there were spare moments. Still, it was too early to bode a casual visit.

Presently, Maarten was invited into the study. He was strangely quiet.

"Your majesty, I trust you are well."

"I am, thank you, Captain Maarten. Tell me what brings you here."

"Mr. Idoru, my lord."

Vaclav furrowed his brow. "Yes?"

"Sir, he struck a gendarme last night. Wounded him. In front of many witnesses."

It couldn't be true — James striking a gendarme? It was absurd!

"He was attempting to force his way into General Rushingstar's residence. Crying that she was a Hawkwood spy!"

Vaclav paused a moment. Rushingstar's courage had been beyond reproach. Still, he thought of her familiarity with the ambassador, as well as her growing taste for Hawkwood fashions and weapons.

"Perhaps," said Vaclav, keeping his voice steady, "He was investigating. In any case, his position with the intelligence unit gives him the authority to enter private residences as necessary."

"Of course, your majesty. And the gendarmes involved have been instructed in this. They erred severely, being caught up in the general acclaim for Rushingstar. I only come to ensure you are aware."

"Thank you, captain."

Maarten paused. "Your majesty, General Rushingstar is very popular, and... There were many witnesses. Mr. Idoru insulted my gendarme in front of a crowd, and the general as well. Her connections with the Hawkwoods are not secret, however, so I trust no ill will come of it." He bowed.

* * *

The eastern village of Samar was small, and less filthy than many villages. And quiet, now that the population had been transported. In the weeks since the battle, there had been nothing but mopping up the heavily wooded countryside, and James' extracted information had proved valuable. This campaign would be the final one, Vaclav vowed. Vaclav inspected the dry dirt streets, and had the least offensive hovel cleared out as his headquarters. In the evening, a message arrived requesting Rushingstar to return to the capital to appoint a staff for a contingent newly arrived from the northern forests; she left for the city, but Vaclav chose to remain in the town. James was busy in the capital, but this village was remote, and it would take many hours for Vaclav to return.

If Isalight had the wonderous aircars and starships wealtheir nations had, returning to the capital would have been simple, but several years before, Vaclav had grown angry with the avaricious Charioteer's Guild, and had had them expelled. It was best, too, that his people kept to the simple life. So Vaclav retired alone to the headquarters office — oak-paneled, with solid, tasteful furniture.

James had admitted to Vaclav that the prisoner had never implicated Rushingstar, and no evidence had even later been uncovered. He'd only been on a fact-finding mission to the general's residence, but had lost his temper. James was very regretful, and had even apologized to Rushingstar and to Maarten in front of the king.

It still disturbed Vaclav. James screeching obscenities and slashing a constable with a sword — it seemed so unlike the young, gentle bedmate he'd known so intimately. Yet the report was confirmed. Vaclav, too, understood the people's grumblings. He could see how they would feel that James was receiving easy treatment for striking an officer. And Rushingstar's popularity had been at a peak when James had loudly insulted her!

Vaclav idly looked through the drawers of the desk, at pencils and blotters, blank envelopes. Evidence of the Hawkwood treachery could hardly be openly displayed, yet the king wished he could do something to help the people understand. He turned the latch on a cabinet. Broadsheets with garish headlines lay stacked on the shelf — "KING INVEIGHS AGAINST HAWKWOODS," "HAWKWOOD AMBASSADOR BOOTED — KING MUM ON WHY."

Curse their ignorance! Why did he even let these printing presses stay in business with the vulgar trash they turn out? He leafed through until an amateurish drawing caught his eye of a leering fop scooping brains out of a screaming child and stuffing them into his mouth. "DECADOS CANNIBAL ORGY!!!" screamed the headline. "DEMON-WORSHIPPING DECADOS SACRIFICING CHILDREN!!! DETAILS INSIDE!!"

Vaclav gasped as if a blow had been struck to his face. He stood aghast, the blood filling his head in a rush. "Vermin!" he screeched. He hurled the stack of papers across the room. "Foulest vermin!" His laser was in his hand and he set it peppering the papers with flames. "Foul Hawkwood lies!" His bodyguard burst into the room.

"Burn this hellish town!" yelled Vaclav. "Burn it to the ground!"

It was all a ghastly plot. The Hawkwoods hated the Decados, <u>and</u> they wanted Isalight — so they spread these brutal, hateful lies. Vaclav railed at his cowardly advisors for not having informed him before of these rumors, but they "had not wished to trouble his majesty with such baseness." They had been scared to tell him, that was what.

After giving the order, Vaclav immediately headed back to the capital. He must speak to James about this.

The capital was dark when the king and his bodyguard arrived. Vaclav wished he could see the faces of his entourage. With the Hawkwoods spreading lies and James' unwise actions, could he truly trust his own guard? Especially in their enthusiasm for Rushingstar? A year before, such a thought couldn't have crossed his mind, but things had changed. It seemed the more he did to unify his nation, the less the people trusted him.

James was not at the palace. Perhaps Rushingstar would be aware of James' location — she was a general, but she kept herself aware.

Lights were on at Rushingstar's residence, and servants were about. The king dismounted and the head butler bowed.

"Your majesty, Mr. Idoru was here an hour ago, as you must know!"

"Make sense!" said Vaclav. "Tell me where they went!"

"He stated that he had royal enjoinment to arrest the general, your majesty! She objected, but he insisted, and they took her away!"

Vaclav had given no such order! But where was James? And why? Had he found proof of Rushingstar's guilt?

The sun had not yet begun to show when the king and his guard approached the cottage, but it would soon. The sky was overcast, and dim flickers behind the shuttered windows of the cottage were the only lights. They approached silently. They came across guards, but Vaclav quickly ordered them to be silent. *He* was the king, and *he* wished to arrive unannounced.

At the door, Vaclav heard that hideous sound, that grinding metal — the truth machine. He heard too, an unfamiliar, angry, high-pitched voice, but too muffled to apprehend.

"Wait here," Vaclav ordered his men, and opened the door.

The fireplace was roaring, lighting the room in red glow. A heavy curtain blocked half the room. Two guards rose at the king's entry, but he waved them down. The noises continued from behind the curtain. The angry voice rose to a horrible screech. Who was this poor victim?

Vaclav approached the curtain, but one of the guards stepped to him. "Your majesty, no one is to..."

Instantly, Vaclav's rapier was at the man's throat, and Vaclav hissed in a harsh whisper. "How dare you! What is happening behind there? Is Rushingstar there?"

The guard shrank back. "No, your majesty — Mr. Idoru brought a hooded prisoner here. He told us that we would be executed if we even looked..."

"Get out," hissed Vaclav. He raised his rapier, and the guards cringed.

"Yes, your majesty." They quietly left the room, closing the door behind them.

Vaclav approached the curtain, smelling that charred carbon smell, feeling the heat of the fire at his back. The screech from behind the curtain was so hideous it hardly seemed to be human, but now, above the clanking din, Vaclav could just make out words. "Talk!" it seemed to shriek. "Talk, you whore! I will violate you body and soul!" Vaclav thrust the curtain aside.

At first the sight made no sense — nothing but a horrible mass of naked flesh, its arms and legs flailing on a heavy table. Until Vaclav realized that it was two naked figures spasming as one. Underneath was Rushingstar, on top was James.

The ghastly voice was emanating from James' mouth, utterly at odds with anything Vaclav had heard before. Below him, Rushingstar's eyes bulged impossibly, unblinking, blood leaking from the sockets. The machine clanked and ground, its spines piercing her body, shooting sparks beneath her skin. Above her eyes, her head no longer existed — only a sunken hole.

Still, James railed like a madman, as blind as Rushingstar. "*Tell me* you're a traitor!" he screamed. "Say it! *Say it!*"

Vaclav's sword clattered to the ground. Suddenly James turned, eyes clouded with fury. He ceased his exertions and regarded Vaclav like an animal would his prey. Then his eyes softened.

"Your... Your majesty..." He clumsily dismounted from the table, and shaking, turned off the machine. It wound down with a whine. "Your majesty, she was a spy! She was planning to assassinate you! Your majesty, this is the only way to ensure your safety! We must do this to creatures like her or all of your kingdom will be lost!"

Vaclav backed away from what approached him. James was naked, so beautiful and graceful, no longer the animal on the table, but the wonderful, gentle young man he had been so close to...

"Truly, your majesty," James' face was so innocent again, open and earnest. "Our enemies will stop at nothing. The people must be controlled or anarchy will prevail! It is a small sacrifice for the good of the nation and for your proud bloodline..."

It took an effort of will for Vaclav to tear his gaze from those lovely, imploring eyes. "No, James, no..." he stammered. "It is over. I have allowed a monster into my home..." He turned his back. "You will receive your punishment." Vaclav straightened himself, as a king should, and walked toward the door.

He heard James behind him pick up the rapier, heard James' feet rush towards him, an attack so clumsy a ten-year-old Isalight child could have blocked it. But Vaclav was no longer a child, but an old man who's spirit had been crushed.

At the last moment, he whirled – not to stop the attack, but to invite it. The sword sank to the hilt into Vaclav's stomach, and Vaclav grabbed James' hand in an iron grip. James flailed against him, but the blows seemed to be elsewhere, somewhere unimportant. Vaclav fell to his knees, drawing his lover with him.

"James," he whispered. "Even now, I could never hurt you..." The king gazed into the beautiful, frightened eyes in front of him. "But soon, I will not be able to protect you."

Vaclav fell heavily, with the weight of his years, laying his head on his lover's bosom, barely hearing the clatter of soldiers' footsteps rushing into the room.

Hot Ambition

Edward Carmien

Father Paul let his fingers trail across the half-healed scar on his left arm. It was still bright and vivid, and the skin itched when he stretched it. He had nearly broken during the test of penitence that had marked his promotion from deacon to priest. Nearly, but not quite. Now he had the satisfaction of looking down at his inferiors, much as the itinerant bishop he had recently served had looked down at him.

His crew knelt, heads bowed. No one stirred before him. Paul knew he could leave them kneeling thus for an hour if he wished, but there were things to be done on his ship — his ship! the thought still swelled his breast with forbidden pride — so he would have to leave that notion for another day.

"Two weeks have passed since we entered this system. Within days we will seek landfall on Leagueheim, playground of evil. We will not be landing at the starport. Navigator, check your maps. Find for me a suitable landing site in a so-called 'abandoned zone.' As for communications, my previous order holds. Only the automatic beacon will announce our presence. Our mission here is more important than the League's traffic control. Am I understood?"

"Yes, Father Paul," the six intoned. Or was it but five? Indeed, she was going to try his patience again. Sister Agrila raised her head.

"Father Paul, a question," she said. Her hair was brown, and her features plain and severe, but her eyes opened into dark depths Paul avoided when he could.

"Yes, sister?" he said.

"Why do we avoid contact with the Church? Are we to think our mission involves them in some way?"

Think what you like, Paul thought to himself, so long as you do not think the truth. "That is not your concern," he said curtly. Though only a canon, she had been highly recommended when Paul was putting together his inquisitorial crew. Lately he had come to think someone had wished to be rid of her.

Perhaps later in her career she would take more notice of the requirements of penitence. For now, Father Paul wanted no Orthodox priest to hijack his crew or deflect his aim. Perhaps he needed to help his crew put their mission in the proper perspective.

"Leagueheim is a planet of darkness," he intoned. "Our mission will not be easy, nor is it clear to me even now how we will accomplish the work of the Light." It would not be wise, Paul knew, for them to learn he had no notion of what he would find below. Something they would find would suffice, however, and as with his handling of the unfortunate Pan Asia incident, his glory would increase.

The far-off thought of becoming a bishop made his scalp itch, and Paul smoothed his hair. Time to finish this, he knew. "Rest well, and check your equipment. We will not have much time to accomplish our goal once we land." We won't have much time before an Orthodox priest sticks his nose into my business, he thought to himself grimly.

To end the meeting he intoned a brief prayer, then blessed them, each and every one. Even Agrila.

* * *

Two hundred meters from the landing site, Sister Agrila turned to look at the ship. She hadn't seen it this way before. It didn't seem very large, though from the size of her quarters it was easy enough to guess it was a tiny ship, as ships went. Father Paul's own personal inquisition, she thought, then quelled the unjust idea by clutching her jumpgate cross and fingering the carved flame that rose from the center of the circle.

For this first sweep they had split up. On the far side of the ship she could see the other team in their brown cassocks making their way across the landscape of rubble and stunted weeds.

Off in the distance, tall spires lit the dark sky with brilliant sparks of light. Leagueheim was a study in contrasts, she decided. The rich technology, supporting the grand arcologies and the many aircars she could see high in the sky... matched against this desecrated, polluted ground.

"Don't lag, Sister!" Father Paul's shout came through the dead night air loud and clear, despite being muffled by his breathing mask. She turned obediently from the view and hurried to catch up. He still hadn't spoken about the particulars of his mission, but if the navigator had taken his choice of landing sites, how particular could it be?

Again she ran her thumb along the smooth edges of the flame.

After an hour's search they found a settlement. The people huddling in the shacks must have kept watch, for when they arrived a small crowd stood waiting. She watched as Father Paul made his way to a small rise. He raised his hands, and the people gathered about.

The Father, too, was a study in contrasts, she decided. Portly where most Avestites were rail thin, for example. He did not brook a word against, or a word questioning, his authority, but he blithely ignored local law. Again she chastened herself for such dark thoughts. "I must resist pride," she murmured under her breath, knowing her mask would muffle the words for any but herself.

"People of Leagueheim! I am Father Paul. You know this symbol, and you know this tool of light." With that he brandished his flamethrower, and the crowd quailed before it. "Do not ask why I am here. Instead ask questions of your own heart. If you find yourself wanting, better to speak now... than later." His voice dipped in emphasis, and Sister Agrila saw many in the crowd shudder. Then a scream broke into Father Paul's impromptu sermon.

Someone ran, flailing her hands about. In the murky twilight provided by far-off but brilliant arcology lights, Sister Agrila thought there was something strange about the figure's clothing.

Exclamations of horror came from the crowd. Father Paul fell silent. Sister Agrila sprang forward, moving quickly despite her heavy garments. When she closed with the fleeing child, Agrila saw hundreds of bugs nearly covered her. Her screams were cut off suddenly, though Agrila could still hear the child gurgle and choke. Fighting down her own bile, she raised her flamer and tripped the ignitor. The small azure flame added a bit of light to the scene, but not much.

Now the child writhed upon the ground. She felt helpless.

"Roast her," said a man standing next to her. Others gathered also. Some stamped upon the ground. A few were running for their huts, while one was spraying something out of a crudely made bucket equipped with a hose and pump.

"What?" she said. The child began to shake with spasms, and she could see some of the insects — were they cockroaches? — leave their victim.

"There's nothing you can do," said the man. "It's too late. Not from the choking, from the poison. Too many bites."

She was spared the horror of roasting an innocent. One of her comrades raised his flamer and burned the child, bugs and all. Above the searing sound of the flames, the insects popped one after the other, like grain puffs over an open fire. There came a sickening odor of roasting meat.

"Careful, now," said the man, who hadn't even flinched. "One or two ain't bad, but if'n they swarm..."

The crowd began to sidle back to the cluster of huts. Others appeared with home-made sprayers and squirted the ground. Sister Agrila ended up in the crowd when Father Paul started speaking again.

"So you are punished for your sins," he said. He swept an arm straight to the side. Off in the distance a huge holographic advertisement flashed and whirled garishly. "So do all those who turn away from the light learn of their error."

"Just a sinless child," murmured the man next to her. "The bugs don't care whether you sin." Sister Agrila was careful not to turn her head. Such words would mean punishment if she heard them... officially. Though she knew it to be a minor sin, she pushed them out of her memory.

"In our time here we will show you the right path. Tomorrow at dawn we will hold a mass. All who live in this settlement will attend." It wasn't a question. Shouldering his weapon, Father Paul surged off through the crowd, returning to the ship. She tarried just a moment.

"What are these bugs?" she asked the man who had spoken during the Father's speech. His words marked him as a man who had his letters. If anyone knew, she was certain, he would.

"They are the devil's own," he said. Grimy from head to foot, his fingernails were dirty and split. Puckers and red, swollen bumps covered his hands and forearms. She noticed that his trousers were tucked tightly into his boots, and the seam covered with tape. "Once they were just legend, a problem other blocks had. Now they're here. Little Liana is the fifth to die in two weeks. Soon we will have to leave, and get our handouts once again from *that*." He gestured much as Father Paul had at the lights and structures of the nearby arcologies.

She bent and found a half-roasted cockroach. It was large, but otherwise much like the sort found everywhere humanity called home.

"Sister Agrila!" Father Paul called.

Saying nothing more, she trotted after her fellows. Surely enough, there was evil here. But her heart was heavy with the dangerous thought that it wasn't the sort of evil Father Paul was looking for.

* * *

Two hours before dawn, Father Paul was awakened by one of the two novitiates on board. He was a good boy, Paul thought as he rose and oiled and combed his hair. After a quick breakfast he met the rest of his team in the airlock.

Despite a short night of sleep, all appeared to be in good order. As they marched back to the settlement, he reviewed how the morning would go. First, a sermon and mass that would illuminate their sorry souls. Then, the confessional. He would surely find some sin that needed expiating. With luck, he would hear of a technology proscribed by the Church, something he could righteously eradicate, though for that he need look no further than the prideful arcologies that reared themselves far above the humble earth.

It was good luck the insects had attacked as they had. Providence had sent them just at the right time, he mused. That they were the spawn of the pollution that had made this land nearly unlivable he didn't doubt.

At the collection of huts, he directed the erection of a portable altar. The sun, screened as it was by the towering structures all around them, did little to announce itself. The area was even poorer and more benighted than Paul had thought. As he cleared his mind to begin his sermon, he noted the stunted crops, a makeshift well, and the wary, terrified aspect of the locals.

All for the better. Raising his hands, he began.

* * *

The sermon, as all of Father Paul's sermons, was drawn from the Fervitudes. Sister Agrila wondered briefly if he had read the Omega Gospels at all. Back at the monastery she had become used to her illiterate fellow novitiates, canons, and deacons, but surely a priest must be able to read! Repentant, she fingered once again the flame at her throat. In her shoe, her scrupula was particularly painful, and she dug her heel into it viciously.

She deserved the pain, if not more, for doubting Father Paul and questioning his ability.

"Ouch," said the young boy next to her. It was the novitiate Father

Paul favored.

One didn't speak during a sermon, she knew, no matter what the discomfort. One didn't casually look about, either, so she kept her eyes on Father Paul as he gesticulated and intoned "There is a flame — Oh Holy Flame!"

"Ah! Ah!" said the boy. Heads began to turn.

Sister Agrila lacked the strength to remain focused as she should on Father Paul's sermon. Turning, she looked to see what was the matter.

"Aaaah!" said the boy. He was covered in cockroaches. She caught her breath and acted quickly. With one hand she thumbed her flamer to life. With the other she lifted the boy's hood over his head.

Then she covered him with fire. Once again the bugs popped one after another. Some wiggled and ran, carrying holy flames with them. Letting go of the trigger Agrila kicked the boy's legs out from under him and rolled him over with her foot.

Trying to keep the flame from his face, she burned the hundreds of cockroaches on his chest and legs. He screamed and tried to crawl away from the fire, but she grimly walked along. Then she relented.

"Take off your cassock!" she yelled. "Take it off!"

Dazed, all he could do was stare at her. Then he grimaced. "Ouch! Ah!" There were still cockroaches underneath his clothing. She reached down and slapped him.

"Do it!"

He began scrambling out of his clothes. She batted away the cockroaches as he revealed them. His waist was covered in red splotchy bites, as was his neck and hands. Once more the man she'd spoken to the night before appeared next to her.

"What about this poison?" she demanded without preamble.

"He'll soon die. Unless you've got a healer." He frowned, then, the dirt on his face making the expression grim and primitive. "But this is strange. They've never attacked anyone during the day before.

"Will the boy live?" shouted Paul from behind his altar. A few others had looked, but only the man and Sister Agrila had attended to the boy.

"Yes," she said.

"Then let us continue."

"He needs a healer!"

"Take him to the ship." Father Paul ran his eyes back across his ragged congregation. "As you can see, many of you must have much to confess. We shall begin now. Line up. Those waiting may kneel...and pray."

Dismissed from the mass, Sister Agrila got the boy on his feet. Already he was beginning to shiver, though the air was moist and warm on Leagueheim. The man reached out to help, and she let him.

Better, she thought, that he not confess anything to Father Paul. She regretted the near-blasphemy the moment she thought it, and redoubled her speed. The boy stumbled once or twice, then his head lolled back.

"How long?" she asked, already breathless.

"A few hours," said the man

Good. He would be saved.

* * *

Father Paul looked again at his fellow pilgrims of truth. The morning's confessions had been fruitful. There were the usual confessions of lust, of pride, of unwarranted anger. Two had asked how the light could allow innocents to die in such a painful, awful way. He had given them the usual response: their lack of faith had led to their demise. The cockroaches were merely the hand of darkness claiming those with shadows on their souls.

Even the novitiate was present. Their medic was no Amalthean, but his potions had saved the boy from the toxic bite of the insects.

"Fellow seekers," he began, "our morning's activities have been fruitful. As is always the case, those we preached to were eager to implicate each other in the confessional. While no one sinner's words can be trusted, I have found what we seek." And not a minute too soon, he thought to himself. The local authorities couldn't be far off. They would be investigating him soon. He intended to be off this planet before that happened, with a successful investigation under his belt.

Not many Avestites could claim to have scoured Leagueheim. The Orthodoxy keeps us on a tight leash here, he thought, resolving again to avoid their notice completely.

"Our target is a man named Odolon. He traffics in proscribed technology, is a Preceptor who rejects the Church's views about the uses of science and machinery, and is an unrepentant Republican who has urged the people of the village to 'elect' a leader from amongst themselves. What is the punishment suitable for such a man?"

"Fire!" came the automatic response from the six bowed before him. Or was it only five?

He sighed, slowly and heavily. "Sister Agrila, do you see a more holy path to the light?"

The woman raised her head to him, but said nothing for a moment. Father Paul waited. He wasn't kneeling on the hard deck. He could wait.

"This man... what technology is he said to buy and sell?"

"A pump, when it would be more seemly to raise water out of the earth with strong arms. Electric lights, to illuminate the darkness when fire, holy fire! would serve as well. It is also said this man possesses a transceiver capable of picking up the unfortunate words and pictures that ooze out of the ether in this dark hive of technology."

"Forgive me my thoughts on this matter, Father, but these sins... seem minor. Should we not reward these people for trying to reclaim this polluted waste? That they need lights to help keep away the cockroaches seems only natural. To use an automatic pump instead of a manual pump isn't unheard of even in places that are more properly in tune with the Prophet's teachings. Isn't there a greater evil here, Father? These unholy insects! These cockroaches which have killed so many in just a few weeks! Don't they bear investigating?"

Father Paul felt his face go red. He was happy she bowed again, even happier no one else could see him clench his fists. It was not proper, he knew, to feel such anger. It wasn't improper for a canon to voice such questions, but It Wasn't Done.

After a few seconds, Father Paul decided she would go far in life, with a tongue as sharp as that. This wasn't one who could be ordered about blindly. Much as he hadn't been, he remembered. But her ambition, it seemed to him, burned too hot. He could see to it her ambition would burn her to the quick.

"The cockroaches are not Symbiots, Sister, merely a product of this awful landscape. The people of Leagueheim have much to answer for, 'tis true. But perhaps we should seek out more about these... things. My pronouncements about the man Odolon remain the same, no matter what we discover about these insects."

Switching gears, he spoke again to the group. "For what is the punishment due Republicans?"

"Fire!" came the response.

"And fire it shall be, come the dawn! For all of us save Sister Agrila shall go to this man's hut. We shall uncover his technology, and what shall we do?"

"Burn it!"

"We shall uncover his unclean spirit, and what shall we do?"

"Burn it!"

"We shall lead him to the light... with what?"

"Fire! Fire! Fire!"

"Let us pray... both for the success of our mission and for the success of Sister Agrila's investigations into the matter of these cockroaches. We will return to space no later than mid-morning, Sister, so make your search swift and thorough!"

Bowing his head, Father Paul led them through a final prayer, then blessed them once again. It would be an insignificant morning, as far as the inquisition went, but the report would look better than the reality of the matter.

And if he was lucky, perhaps the cockroaches would find Sister Agrila to their taste...

* * *

She could see the novitiate looking at the tape around her ankles, waist, and wrists. It was deep into the night, and the airlock was shut.

"Allow me to pass," she said. The bottles of Aqua Ignata felt heavy on her hip.

"It is night," he said, surly because his companion who usually shared the watch was still recovering from the cockroach attack.

"That is no matter. Do you not remember Father Paul telling me to be speedy with my search? I must begin now if I am to finish by mid-morning. Do you wish me to wake him so he can repeat his orders?"

The novitiate shuddered. Father Paul, they had learned during their months of travel, was a man unwise to cross. Without another word he operated the airlock, and Sister Agrila stepped out into the night.

It was dark, or at least as dark as it could get. The air was so thick with smog she could see no lights in the sky save for air cars whizzing to and fro. Shouldering her flame-thrower, she trudged to the collection of huts.

Once, she stopped and listened as she turned in a slow circle. There had been a hissing, it seemed, but she dismissed it when she saw nothing nearby. At the huts, she paused.

Odolon was almost certainly the man who had helped her save the novitiate, though he had not introduced himself. If she learned for certain it was he, she could do nothing. Agrila was within her rights to question Father Paul when invited, but she could do nothing against him.

Short on time, she resorted to the quickest possible way of finding him. Kicking in the nearest door, she triggered her flamer. She didn't need to, as light spilled over the floor beneath each cot. All the beds were in the middle of the scant room, she noted.

"Where is the man who helped me with the boy today? Do not say his name!"

"T-t-two huts d-d-down," said a startled and fearful man. Part of her blanched while the rest reveled in the reaction. It isn't every night the inquisition kicks in your door! She left without another word and kicked her way in to the man's hut. He was alone, also guarded from the cockroaches by artificial light.

"What?" he said, startled but amazingly unafraid.

"You remind me of an uncle. Berto, his name was. Come with me, Berto. You are called on to assist the Church."

She did not miss the many crates in his hut, nor the fact his hut was the largest. Jealousy had likely made his neighbor's tongues wag, but that was not her concern.

"But my name is O — " he quieted when she shoved the small blue flame in his face.

"You are Berto. Say no more. Keep the name. Dress. We go to search out the source of the cockroaches."

"But — " she inched the flame closer yet to his chin. Was that the sound and smell of burning hair?

He flinched and did as he was told. Outside, they moved away from the huts until the rubble of long-dead industry surrounded them.

Odolon — Berto, she reminded herself — cleared his throat. "We've looked, you know. We're not stupid serfs. After the first attack, two of us died looking. These things can live in a crack in the ground no bigger than your hand, they..."

"Then we find that crack, and we burn it."

"But all it takes is one queen, and thousands more live to swarm within days. The exterminators have been using fire for centuries. And they wear armor. Soldier's armor. Even with that, they die."

"They lack faith," she said simply, and fixed him with her gaze. "Faith and fire are both required. And I suspect something more than cockroaches. Do they attack in the light? Never, you say. Who do they attack during the day? An Avestite novitiate."

"You think..." he began, looking about in the gloom.

"I know. Now stand fast and be silent."

Kneeling, she closed her eyes and clasped her fingers around her jumpgate cross. As always, her thumb caressed the flame.

She was no Eskatonic, to make casual miracles with prayer, nor was she an Amalthean healer with an uncanny ability to bring the ill to health. But her faith was strong. And if she prayed... if she prayed...

"And it shines," she began.

After a time her knees began to ache. Sweat beaded on her brow.

"And it warms," she continued, heedless of the discomfort. Now her back hurt, and she noted there was some vague hint of dawn in the air.

"And it spreads..." her arms hurt, and where she'd drawn the tape overtight on her left wrist, her pulse throbbed in time with her words.

"And it consumes..." her voice grew hoarse and dry, and her head hurt. Was it dawn? The sun's holy light could hardly penetrate the sodden sky.

Then Sister Agrila fell silent. And waited. In her blank, resting mind a light grew. From a pinpoint in darkness it grew to a raging fire that consumed her conscious mind. Somewhere she heard a voice yelling, another voice asking if she was well. She ignored both.

The fire burned her until she was nothing but a cinder, then it burned her some more. When she opened her eyes she felt she'd been burned to nothing, nothing at all. What remained was weightless as light.

Or so it seemed.

She was standing, she noted, with an arm pointing directly away from her. Berto stood next to her, eyes round with awe. Her arm felt stiff, and she saw the sun was in the sky. She didn't have much time left. Father Paul, thwarted from burning Odolon for all his sins, wouldn't wait long after sating his holy vengeance on Odolon's hut and belongings.

Sister Agrila began walking where her arm directed. She found that if she walked away from the path it pointed to, it swerved to point where she should go. Clambering over rocks and tilted slabs of maxicrete, Berto tried to explain what he'd seen.

"You prayed, then you were silent. Then you stood, pointed, and screamed. I asked if you were well, I..."

"Hush," she said.

After a short time they came to a short cliff, what had once perhaps been the basement of a large building now open to the sky. Her arm pointed down, and down she went, climbing clumsily and then falling the last two meters. Berto climbed down without difficulty.

A faint hissing sound came to their ears. "That's cockroaches," said Berto. "Are you sure you need me with you? What good am I doing?"

"What good are you doing? You're living, Berto. A man called Odolon was to burn this morning. Illegal technology. Republicanism. Father Paul sought a sinner. He found Odolon."

"But I'm — " he began, clearly alarmed.

"You're Berto. And when we're done here, you'll go somewhere and you will go on being Berto."

"You're helping me because of the boy."

She shrugged and went forward. The vast basement left them feeling as if they were at the bottom of a huge box. The ground was split and fractured, but not badly. Then a circular pit became apparent as they moved toward it. The hissing grew in volume.

"This isn't a good idea. Exterminators die doing this sort of thing."

"They aren't armed with faith," she said simply.

"I don't believe faith can save me if they swarm," he said, tight lipped.

"Then you won't be saved."

Down in the pit, deep in the shadow, boiled tens of thousands of cockroaches. The hissing noise was louder than the sound of a strong wind. Sister Agrila thumbed her flamer to life and pointed it downward.

Some minutes later, the plume of greasy black smoke had abated. She looked down the pit once again. Dozens of cockroaches still scuttled amidst the smoking remains of the roasted thousands. An ancient ladder led downward. Slinging her weapon, Sister Agrila began climbing down. Her arm was hers to use again, she noted.

Berto stood mute, unmoving.

"Come along!" she challenged.

"You do this often?" he asked.

"Before this, I ordered supplies for my monastery. But it is all the Pancreator's work."

He snorted, but he moved to the ladder.

Once at the bottom, it didn't take long for horror to show itself. From a short distance down a low tunnel came a greenish glow, barely visible against the weak light from Leagueheim's sky.

"Come," she said simply, and forged ahead. Two meters into the tunnel, cockroaches out of reach of the earlier flames swarmed.

Chanting a blessing, Sister Agrila uncapped a vial of Aqua Ignata and poured it in a circle about her.

"They're climbing my legs!" shouted Berto.

"I suggest you brush them off," she said calmly as she ignited her flamer. Black smoke had been pouring out of the barrel; the clean fire took that reek away in a moment. Around them a circle of flame leapt up, and cockroaches again died by the thousands. But it wasn't enough. They dropped from the ceiling onto her hood and began chewing through the tough fabric as if it were tissue paper. Berto fell to the floor, covered with dozens of biting insects.

Sister Agrila did not curse Father Paul for sending her out alone. She did not try to brush away the cockroaches. Even as she felt their bites and the hot sting of their toxic poison, she contemplated an old story.

"Father Pontius Cciardi, hear my plea for succor against the minions of shadow and darkness..." she began. The point of light she'd seen when she prayed before reappeared as a raging torrent of fire. Heat ran up her nostrils and made her feel giddy.

Berto screamed, not in pain but in fear. When she turned to him, he shrank away. The cockroaches would be done with him soon, she knew. Reaching toward him, she realized why he cringed in fear.

She was on fire. Though she crackled with flame, she felt sluggish and slow. It took her some seconds to brush the insects away from him. Taking another canister, she pushed him aside and crushed it. A pool of fire cleansed a portion of the tunnel. With her hands she cleared a space for him to stand. Gratefully he took it, then hopped and patted at himself, trying to douse the flames she'd started on his clothing.

Turning, she faced the true enemy. Green and bulbous, it clung to the wall like a leech. At its nether end were tubes, and in those tubes dozens, no, hundreds of white egg casings. It was the mother.

Whether Symbiot or native Leagueheim mutation, she could not say. With a prayer on her lips she embraced it. As she did so there was a concussion from her side. Aqua Ignata sprayed from her hip to the wall, floor, and ceiling near her, roasting yet more cockroaches. Then her flamer's fuel canister exploded.

But she took no harm from the fire, or from the explosions. The bulbous thing writhed and lashed at her with slimy tentacles that crisped the moment they touched her.

In but a few moments it was done. She pried the husk from the wall and returned to Berto. They would both require the attentions of the medic back at the ship. Berto, close to shock, kept repeating the same question.

"Why... me. Why... take me. Why... me?"

* * *

Father Paul looked down at the kneeling canon. She was half-dressed, itself an oddity. Only her fireproof garments remained. If he was to believe her story, and he didn't, she had been forced to burn her undergarments because of the cockroaches.

"Hmmph," he said. He'd kept her there for several minutes while he reviewed her story. "This Berto. You're sure his name isn't actually Odolon?"

"No, Father," she said. "I'm not sure. But he answered to Berto."

The truth, he figured, if an Eskatonic's truth, a truth all wrapped up in rhetoric and cunning logic. Father Paul pondered asking her to change her habit. But no, he considered further, it wouldn't look good if a canon in his charge defected, no matter how eccentric she was.

"And what happened to your weapon?"

"Caught in the fire, Father." It sat next to her, melted almost beyond recognition. He wasn't sure, but he didn't think even Aqua Ignata could do that to metal. Twist and crisp flesh, wood, and plastic? Certainly. Metal? Hardly.

"And this husk?"

"It was producing the cockroaches, Father. Surely there are others. Perhaps this sort of thing is known to members of the League. It is said there are exterminators who study this matter. Perhaps they could say?"

Wisely, she did not mention again the possibility the cockroaches had been made more aggressive by some Symbiot.

"Hmmmph," he said again. "I will include your report as a sidebar. Give the... remains to Berto. See that the medic deals with his bites and send him home. Caution him to hurry, as we are lifting for space quite soon. Understood?"

"Yes, Father." She raised her eyes to him, and once again he tried to avoid looking into them. In a blink he saw what appeared to be flames. Shaking his head, he looked again, but her eyes were as dark and mysterious as ever.

"And dress yourself, canon."

As she removed herself, Father Paul allowed himself a contented sigh. The man Odolon had fled in the night, obviously guessing the inquisition would return for him. But his goods were burned, and the people of the shacks reminded that Republican beliefs would not be tolerated... at least not tolerated by priests of the Celestial Sun.

Yes, he reflected. Quite a good report on his record. A scourging on Leagueheim, something unheard of for decades. Quite, he decided, a feather in his cap.

* * *

Odolon, or Berto as he'd begun to think of himself, sat in the dingy apartment in the bowels of one of the great arcologies to which he'd once sworn he'd never return. In return for his basic dole, he served as a lowly janitor.

He'd gone hungry today to buy a special book, a book with blank pages, a cheap pen, and a large bottle of ink.

Setting the book before him, Odolon thought for some time, then wrote:

At first I questioned why I had been saved by Sister Agrila. Then I questioned why she had taken me into a nest of cockroaches, where I was set upon by hundreds of the stinging creatures, creatures which can kill in much smaller numbers.

Then I witnessed a miracle, a miracle she later concealed from Father Paul, her superior, and I knew the answer to my questions. I was to be a witness. This is the true and actual story of what I witnessed on the morning of the seventh day of the third month of the year 4998.

Inquisitors led by the Avestite Father Paul visited our humble agricultural experiment, which struggled in the shadow of the great arcologies of Leagueheim...

Rainy Season

Christopher Howard

The Dukedom of Harmony, Byzantium Secundus
8:30 Central Tamerlain Time

It was early morning, the sky dark with swollen rain clouds and the low places still shrouded with mist, when Kira first saw the monster. Kira walked her accustomed route to work, along the New Novgorod canals toward the massive brown and gray Water-Crafter's building. A low arched-bridge spanned one of the canal's tributaries and even though she was running late she stopped in the middle of the bridge as she always did. It was ritual, a way of clearing her mind and preparing herself for the factory with its loud clanging machines, smoking furnaces and petty bickering — a final moment of solitude. This was the back entrance to work and few people came this way. Here she could pretend, if only for a moment, that she was alone. Here the incessant crush of six billion other souls on Byzantium Secundus could temporarily fade into the background.

Another worker obviously had the same idea and silently glided by on his bicycle behind her, ringing his bell in greeting before slowly winding his way up the hill toward the guild house. Obscured by fog, today the structure was little more than a brown and gray smudge. Kira watched the biker dwindle into the mist before turning her attention back to the river. The water was a rippled pattern of green and muddied gray, reflecting the rain bloated clouds above and the dense foliage along the river bank. Kira briefly studied her reflection in the slowly moving stream. Straight, jet black hair surrounded a pretty, dusky brown face. Her reflected twin's moist brown eyes peered back out of the water, challenging her to see past them. Although familiar, they were the eyes of a stranger and had been so for almost a year now. Amnesia had taken her memory and with it her identity.

Kira stared hard for a moment, trying to penetrate the surface of the water as if doing so would somehow reveal the secrets of her previous life. The sound of the water tumbling against its banks seemed to whisper "remember." Upon close inspection the water's green and gray reflection gave way to the slow moving black sludge beneath it. Almost

a thousand years of heavy industrial pollution hidden by a few inches
of water, but the river surrendered no other secrets. Kira turned toward
the guild building, allowing her eyes to drift lazily across the water's
surface and to the nearby bank. Lush with long grasses, bristlereed and
creepers, the line between river and shore was interrupted only by a thin
band of yellow mud. As her eyes returned to the path they suddenly
stopped on a flicker from the nearby foliage. The glimmer vanished
and then reappeared. Kira realized with a start that there were two large,
bestial brown eyes staring back at her. Suddenly a burst of leaves and
splintering bristlereed shattered the silence. A large, golden-brown furred
shape hurdled from its hiding place and almost instantly disappeared
into the fog. A long mournful bellow followed it and then faded almost
as abruptly.

Kira wrapped her quilted gray rain-coat around her and retreated
from the bridge, up the hill toward work. A chill ran down her spine
and settled with a quiver in her knees. She didn't need to be a lifelong
resident of Byzantium Secundus — indeed, had always assumed that she
was not — to know that terrors abounded in the Harmony lowlands.
Tales of murderous trolls who stole children from their beds and of far
worse creatures had more than a kernel of truth to them. "Get inside,"
she thought. "Just get inside." Right now she yearned to be in the
factory with its loud clanging machines, smoking furnaces and petty
bickering. She would be happy to see her co-workers: Queeg, Amilla or
even, she thought icily, Wang.

As the guild hall came into view Kira joined other employees who
were entering by another path. A skimmer had overturned a brute cart
near the gate. No one was hurt but a small crowd had gathered and this
slowed down entry to the plant. It didn't matter. Kira felt safer already
among the crowd and was beginning to rationalize her encounter at the
river. She looked at the ox-like animal drawing the cart and noticed that
with its great mass and brown fur it could easily have been a twin for
the poorly seen blur by the bridge. Feeling better, Kira clocked into
work 40 minutes late and changed clothes at her locker, trading her
raincoat and boots for a welder's face plate and a pair of rubber-soled
safety shoes.

Kira usually told people that she worked for the Water-Crafter's
Guild, but in fact she was a Muster freelancer. She may not remember
what she did before one year ago, but she obviously had some skill with

metal. On the strength of this she held a pretty steady job with the Muster, rank of associate first-class, and could afford at least a few simple luxuries. Her current job was semi-skilled assembly line work at best, welding together flood-breaks and other machinery for the water guild's ceaseless battle against the planet's ever-rising flood waters. Even with the entire planet drowning, there was money to be made.

Kira peered casually around the hall at the other 40 or so people performing the same work. The shop was mostly female and had been that way since mid-way through the war which had recently put Emperor Alexius Hawkwood on the Throne of Worlds. Most of the fighters from Harmony in the last war had been male and someone had to "man" the factories while they were away. There had been some grumbling about this when the soldiers returned to find their old jobs taken, but these were boom-times on Byzantium Secundus and work of this kind was easy to find. Kira smiled 'hello' to Amilla who shared the next bench. "Wang's been asking after you again," said Amilla, rolling her eyes. Kira looked as casually as she could in the direction of the elevated glass supervisor's booth, hoping to see its vertical blinds shut, but no such luck. Wang caught her eye as she looked in his direction and leered back at her, licking his lips in a gross mockery of flirtation. Kira sighed and looked back at Amilla. It was going to be a long morning and she was almost wishing she had been trampled by the runaway brute at the river.

14:00 CTT

By lunch time Wang hadn't made any more advances beyond a lascivious wink and Kira began to think she would escape the day unscathed. During lunch she met Queeg at their accustomed table. Queeg was not Muster, but a crew-chief in the Water-Crafter's Guild. An alcohol problem had seen him booted from first a high-paying job in the Charioteers and then from the Seventh Fleet in the surrounding Caspian Ocean. Queeg didn't seem to mind. Now he did underwater construction, flood control and some tug-piloting when he had the chance. Kira liked him, despite his occasional bouts of alcoholic depression. He was what some would call a bruiser. He stood over 6' 5" and was burly and strong. He had a scraggly beard, a broad smile and a prominent scar across his weathered face. Some pinned him as "slow," but Kira realized that he merely took his time. As they ate, Kira told him about both the "monster" and Wang's advances.

"I don't know," she said. "It was probably a brute, but I've never seen one move so fast. It moved more like a cat."

Queeg listened and then thought for a long moment before replying. "It probably was a brute," he decided. "It happens around here sometimes. A brute gets loose and wanders for days before some lucky serf catches it. They can move pretty fast too when the mood takes 'em. I found that out right enough two years ago when I was ferrying some of them across a river and one broke loose from its stall. That's how I got this," he grinned, indicating a long jagged scar across his forearm. Kira smiled back. This was about the sixth story she had heard about how he got that particular scar. Last time it was a giant jellyfish.

"As for Wang," he continued, "if he gives you any more trouble, just tell him you're hitched up with me and that I'm the jealous type."

"I will. Thanks," said Kira.

18:00 CTT

Later that afternoon the floor chief, a matronly woman whom Kira particularly disliked, disapprovingly told her that Wang needed to see her immediately. Kira sighed and exchanged glances with Amilla before walking up the short flight of stairs to Wang's office. The blinds were, she noticed, shut. "You needed to see me, chief?" Wang swiveled around in his pneumatic chair, eyeing her from behind his thick spectacles. His wide, pink sweaty face and orange beard always looked comical with his "Hazat" black hair which looked for all the world like a toupee, but wasn't.

"Associate, ah, Kira," he began. "How long have you been with us? Five months?" Kira nodded her affirmation. "In that time you have been late a total of sixteen times; I believe today makes seventeen. Do you have any explanation for this breech of professionalism?" Kira wanted to say that, "well, today for example, I was almost trampled by a runaway brute," but stopped short when she saw the serious look on his face. "No, chief. I will try to do better, sir."

"Do not get me wrong, Miss, ah, Kira. In the Muster we value punctuality and you obviously have a *small* measure of skill, but there are other qualities we prize even more highly," he said, getting up from his desk and standing uncomfortably near.

"Sir?" asked Kira. She already had an idea, but felt fated to let the pageant reach its conclusion.

"Loyalty for one thing, Kira. That and the ability to play along with the rest of the team," he whispered. His hand moved remarkably fast for a man of his girth and fluttered up her belly before landing firmly on her breast with a tight squeeze. Kira, prepared, backed away, swatting his arm to the side. "I may weld for you, chief, but that doesn't mean I have to put up with anything else. I've quit better jobs than this before!"

Wang recoiled at her outburst, but only a little. "Really? How long ago was that? You remember back only a year; remember? Before here you worked in that refinery for three months and before that a laundry. Those are pretty nowhere jobs for you to be putting on such airs and, call it an educated hunch, I doubt you were anything better before you lost your memory." Kira seethed and was about to tell Wang exactly where he could put his "educated hunch" when he cut in again. "Or did you really lose it?"

"What?" gasped Kira, not believing what she had just heard. Her amnesia was such a daily fact for her that she couldn't comprehend someone questioning its reality.

"Loss of memory is just a little too convenient a story to me," Wang lectured in a patronizing tone. "A war just ended and everything is up in the air — records lost, people confused. A person, a guilty person that is, who wanted to create a new life for herself could do it easily by playing amnesiac. A few days care with those credulous Amaltheans and you have a slip of paper and a whole new identity. Well, not quite; legally you still don't have a last name, do you?"

"This is ridiculous! I don't have to justify..."

"Oh? I saw how you reacted when those monks gave their morality play here last month. People with nothing to hide don't need to fear the Inquisition." Kira stood transfixed with a mixture of shock and fear. It was true. For an instant her memory surrendered a smoky image of brown robes, blankets of cleansing flame, sparks flying between machinery and her outstretched fingers, and the smell of burning plastic. Then, just as quickly, the image faded. Wang probably had no proof to back up his words, but then Temple Avesti inquisitors rarely required proof. She gritted her teeth. "Do I still have my job here or not?" she asked in a feeble parody of defiance.

"Are you crazy? I threaten you with the Inquisition and you still think I want you working here? Clean out your locker, you stupid brute-

cow! Get a job farming or working with the Courtesan's Guild, because
I'll see to it that you never work for the Muster again!" Resistance gone,
Kira felt like an automaton, like one of those robotic golems built by
the mad Engineer in the magic lantern shows. She turned mechanically
and left the office, ignoring the concerned looks from Amilla and some
of her other co-workers. Outside the shop she stopped for a minute, hot
tears rolling down her face. The automaton was gone and she felt small,
stupid and scared. It took her three tries to open her locker and she
fumbled with her belongings as she left. As she walked, dazed, out the
entrance she almost literally bumped into Queeg. He was coming back
from a job and wore the traditional black and orange rubber suit of a
guild diver. Instantly spotting her distress, he fell in by her side. "What
happened, girl?" He asked.

"Fired. Finished. Kaput."

It was raining hard as they left. Queeg followed her down the water
slicked streets, listening to her halting story. "That bastard Wang," he
boomed. "Just say the word, Kira. Me and my buddies, we'll... they'll
never find the body! Over the pier, have no fear!" A half smile broke
across Kira's face as she pictured Wang kicking and struggling with an
anchor tied around his neck in the nearby canal. "Thank you, Queeg.
Maybe we should have something to eat first."

They walked down a main road in the rain, which mercifully
dwindled to a drizzle. They passed through the industrial quarter which,
like almost every other part of Harmony, consisted of uniformly looming and austere maxicrete government buildings. These were built during Harmony's brief period of independence over 400 years ago, when
the national government tore down most of the continent's Second
Republic architecture. It was Harmony that gave Byzantium Secundus
the nickname "the concrete capitol."

Kira and Queeg approached Saint Sabato's, one of New Novgorod's
few remaining pre-Fall cathedrals. Built to the disciple Maya in the
dying days of the Second Republic, the seven-sided cathedral had survived revolution, bombardment and purge to take its fated place as one
of New Novgorod's few remaining tourist attractions. As they entered
the plaza it stopped raining, and for the first time in weeks the sun
actually peeked through the clouds. Kira had always liked the building;
its soft rainstone turrets and graceful flying buttresses seemed to shim-
mer and breath in the thin light of the setting sun. Kira and Queeg sat

by a fountain, eating some candied scylax root they purchased from a strolling vendor and watched as the square filled up with people enjoying the brief respite from the rain. Red and gold banners flapped in the breeze and for a moment Kira could almost forget that Harmony, like the rest of the planet, was slowly sinking below the waves.

"You know it's true, don't you? Don't let this brief period of sunshine deceive you! The waters rise, oh yes! The world sinks with the weight of your sins!"

It was a hesychast, a mendicant monk, of the sort who often preached in the cathedral square. Bushy eyebrows grew in a thicket around crazed eyes. The man was painfully thin, bearded and, with the exception of a tattered cloth around his loins, completely bereft of clothing. "Yes, your sins madam," he spat at Kira, daring her to challenge his pronouncements. Kira tried to open her mouth, but couldn't seem to speak. She felt dizzy and as if a great weight was pressing down on her. "And your sins too, sir," screamed the man at Queeg. "And yours and yours as well," he continued in the direction of some wealthy looking pilgrims, one of whom displayed a symbol from the planet Criticorum on his bag.

"Why thank you, sir," said the pilgrim. "May I take a picture?" The monk turned away from Kira and Queeg, continuing his oration for his new audience. "It's getting a little late," Kira said.

19:30 CTT

Queeg needed to change out of his diving suit so they headed up a side canal toward his home. A steady rain had begun to fall and people hurried to their destination with scarcely a glance at each other. Queeg lived at the unfortunate end of several sluggish canals and half the flotsam in the city seemed to gather in a toxic soup near his home. Kira crinkled her nose as she always did along here, but Queeg was used to it. "Takes about two months," he had told her. Besides, the area was not prime real-estate and Queeg enjoyed the privacy. He often had the entire front courtyard to himself. It was night and the courtyard was lit only by a tall single light post. As Queeg fumbled with his keys, Kira scanned the three converging canals with some small distaste. Garbage, dead fish and other unmentionable objects swirled in a slow morass, only thinly coated by the rain. She turned to enter when she saw something else in the artificial light — a patch of golden-brown fur just breaking the water.

Kira darted to the railing and looked again. There was no mistake. Below was the massive form she had seen that morning, struggling weakly through the filthy water. "Queeg! Quickly, over here!" Queeg joined her at the rail. "Aye, I see it, girl."

"What is it?" she wondered aloud. Whatever it was, it was bleeding badly. Kira shuddered to think what kind of toxins were entering its body through the open wounds. As if in answer to her question, the furry mass made a desperate thrashing motion, trying to clamber onto shore. It failed, but its efforts exposed its head and three, no four, massively muscled arms. Fascinated as she was by the arms, it was the eyes that caught Kira's attention. It looked at her with silent appeal and she was sure that she could detect a gleam of intelligence behind its feral eyes.

"Why, that's a Vorox," said Queeg.

"A what?"

"Alien. From Li Halan space. Been to their planet once," he said. Kira remembered. Not from any particular service, but she remembered the priest's words: *Among all the aliens, the soul-mirror of the simple and faithful Vorox is the least distorted and reflects the Pancreator's light in a manner most closely to that of man.*

"I've got to save it... him," she said, leaning dangerously far over the railing.

"Are you crazy, girl? If it's not already dead, it'll tear you apart if you go near it. Let it be. I'll call the guild to take care of it in the morning," said Queeg, grabbing her arm. Kira shook free of him and ran down the concrete ramp to the water's edge, tentatively dipping her boot into the water. "Prophet's bones," he snorted. "Don't go in! That water's like acid! It'll eat you alive," he warned. Kira turned back to see Queeg donning his headgear and tightening the waterproof seal. "Damn me. If that monster eats me for supper, you'll have to kill Wang on your own," he grumbled.

Queeg jumped into the water, not with a splash but a sickening "schlorp," and disappeared from view as the debris and black water closed in above him. Kira held her breath. A moment later Queeg resurfaced near the Vorox and pushed it to shore. At the embankment he climbed up and heaved with all his might. No damn good. Too heavy. Donning her gloves Kira ran up to help and, although Queeg didn't hold out much hope for the exercise, he was surprised by her strength. Straining and grunting the two managed to deposit the bedraggled alien on the shore.

A nearby bell tower began to chime out a familiar three-ring toll. "Ah, damn! I forgot; there's a black rain tonight," Queeg cursed. Both of them knew exactly what that meant. The nearby New Novgorod space yards were venting their ceramsteel smelting towers and soon most of the city downwind to the plant would be covered with an acidic, oily black rain that burned eyes, skin and lungs. With renewed desperation the two looked at each other. Queeg ran into his house, returning with a large pull-cart. Together they loaded the Vorox on board and retreated inside.

Despite its location, Kira always liked Queeg's home. It was large and cluttered, but it had personality. Queeg was a tinkerer and his home was filled with oily rags, tools and various components of half finished projects. Old photographs of him from his Charioteer and naval days lined the walls. He was also an avid fan of the magic lantern shows and colorful promotional posters trumpeted such sentiments as: "Antonio Hazat in *The Mask of the Domino*" "Inspector LaVey is *The Crime Vicar*" and "Stupid, Tepid and Vapid: The Bumble Brothers in *Vau Vacation.*"

Queeg grunted and rolled out a large plastic tarp in the center of the living room. Between them the two managed to roll the unconscious beast on to it. They both studied it for a long moment before Queeg spoke.

"Damn, but that's a feral Vorox we've brought in here."

"Feral?"

"Vorox — civilized ones, that is — must have their claws clipped before coming to human worlds. They're poisonous, see? Noble Vorox can keep one claw unclipped to show their rank, but this one hasn't been clipped at all. Legally this creature shouldn't be here and is probably dangerous."

"I wonder how it got here then," mused Kira, changing the subject.

"Damned if I know, but he can't stay here long. The dumb beast will bring all sorts of trouble down on us." Queeg really didn't want it there at all, but he recognized that look on Kira's face and knew there was no point in arguing with her.

"Maybe we should try to clean him up," she said.

They gathered several large basins and Kira went about washing the creature and dressing its wounds. She cleaned first with gum spirits to dissolve the black oil and then soap and water. It was a big job but Kira was persistent, washing the same areas of fur again and again. Queeg kept his distance, keeping watch with a large shotgun he brought from another room. Four hours later, an exhausted Kira viewed her handi-work and Queeg, nursing his eighth drink of the evening, had to admit she had done a good job. Where a bedraggled pile of matted fur lay before, there now slept a stately beast of prey. Despite his trepidation Queeg had to admit that it was an impressive beast and grinned slightly at Kira in congratulations for her efforts. The floor, on the other hand, was a royal mess; he decided not to think about that until tomorrow.

Kira yawned, exhausted by her long day, and Queeg showed her to his bedroom. "Don't worry, girl. I'll keep watch over our guest," he assured her. Kira nodded gratefully and was soon fast asleep. Queeg returned to the living room and poured himself another drink before taking up a watch position in his favorite chair, his shotgun across his lap. He eyed the sleeping beast suspiciously. Kira was a good woman and, if he was only 20 years younger and not such an alcoholic wreck, he would almost admit that he loved her. Unfortunately, she was also soft-hearted and impulsive sometimes. Queeg wasn't going to take any chances with her new pet, however. "Just twitch the wrong way, Mr. Vorox, and all of Sanctuary Aeon won't be able to patch you together." He patted his gun affectionately, took another sip from his drink and was soon asleep.

7:15 CTT

The early morning light filtered through the shuttered windows, painting the room a ghostly gray. Kira yawned and stretched, relieved not to be awakened by a screaming alarm clock. Remembering the pre-vious night's events she donned a robe that Queeg had laid out for her and padded quietly into the living room where she stopped with sur-prise. Queeg still slept in his chair, snoring loudly; the Vorox was gone. Blood, mud and dark clawed footprints told the story of its exit from Queeg's apartment. Kira realized with something of a start that the footprints lead not only to Queeg, where the creature had obviously examined him, but also back into her room before finally leading through the kitchen and out the back door into the building's courtyard. For a "dumb beast," it obviously had little problem with door knobs. Kira shook Queeg, who awoke with a start.

"I'm awake! What?" he exclaimed, snapping to a reasonable approximation of alertness.

"The Vorox left last night, probably through your kitchen. Good job watching, oh great hunter," she teased.

Queeg snorted. "Damn creature stole my gun."

Kira got dressed and splashed some water on her face while Queeg fetched his "back-up" weapon, a nickel plated blaster from his Charioteer days. He grumbled, but decided he should count his blessings. "Could have woken up dead," he reminded himself.

Kira and Queeg followed the Vorox's trail out through the back yard. Queeg's courtyard was choked with weeds and low trees, still heavy with the black residue from last night's rain. The rain that fell now was steady, but at least reasonably clean. Kira welcomed it as cleansing, though she knew that it would be at least two weeks before it managed to wash away the evidence of last night's oily downpour. It was not hard to follow the Vorox, if you knew what you were looking for. Clawed footprints appeared intermittently in the black tar and yellow mud along the roadside, along with the brute carts, automobiles and hundreds of human footprints. Another few hours, though, and its passage would have been completely obliterated. There was heavy morning traffic as people headed to work or went about foraging. The trail lead downhill and Queeg grumbled loudly about this. Downhill meant they were heading even farther into the flooded lowlands near the ocean. The lowest lying areas were populated by the worst sort of human "scum," in Queeg's estimation. They were dangerous at the best of times and were even more so with the recent flooding. Kira wasn't deterred, however, and Queeg followed her silently.

Maxicrete tenements gave way to a shantytown of lumpish turtleshell buildings made from bristlereed and gold mud brick. At its entrance were two squat stone statues of the disciple Hombor, patron of the poor. Their jolly faces seemed almost derisive to Kira, surrounded by such abject poverty. Nevertheless, the totems were dressed with wild swamp flowers by the destitute villagers. Nearby a faded billboard declared: "This is an I.P.A. Village."

The familiar logo of a handsome knight in white ceramsteel armor held aloft a magically glowing sword which illuminated idyllic peasant surroundings. In the background a family of serfs looked at the knight with adoration. The knight's shield sported the I.P.A. symbol, an imperial firebird rampant over the triangular "oceans and dikes" emblem of the Authority guild. The Authority was still the most powerful guild on Byzantium Secundus, but their power did not expand much beyond the capitol planet. Emperor Alexius had made many promises to the people of the planet; one was cheap and reliable electricity to every town and hamlet by the turn of the century. The Authority sought imperial goodwill so that it could increase its off-planet trade position, and so the Imperial Power Authority was born.

Despite the sign's declaration, however, it was obvious that this town had yet to reap the benefits of the imperial mandate. Indeed, Kira guessed that despite the rising floods, the town probably didn't even have a supply of safe drinking water. The road was covered with mud deposited by decades of annual flooding. Half-naked children watched them through hollow eyes and beggars wailed for alms. Kira gave two of them a talon each, but Queeg warned her against further charity.

"They see you have money and some of them may not stop at begging. The city guard don't come down this way unless they have to," he warned. "We're near Amen'ta Island and there's been rumors of a lowland battle over it brewing for weeks now. Besides, you're unemployed yourself right now. Remember?" Kira nodded curtly and put away her purse. She had heard the rumors too. Amen'ta Island was the largest island at the tip of the New Novgorod river delta and was only intermittently inhabited. When other lowland areas flooded, everyone in the immediate area headed there to get above the flood waters. The island was currently held by a local beggar's guild, but an area bravo who called himself "Laird Phebes" had made known his intentions to conquer the wretched muddy sandbar.

The alien's trail ended at a salt marsh where even the most destitute did not live. Marsh birds squawked in the rain and the water in-between the marshy patches of ground was, if anything, more polluted than the canal outside Queeg's residence. Across a narrow stretch of water Kira could barely make out Amen'ta Island in the mist.

"Smart," admitted Queeg. "The creature could live out here for years and not be found. The swamp's so toxic that no one except a Vorox could survive here for long. "That includes us," he added. Kira nodded her acquiescence. The trail was dead.

"Besides," he continued, "you may not be working, but I still have a job and I'm already two hours late. It won't do for both of us to be fired." Kira looked slightly annoyed by the last comment. She had distracted herself with the matter of the Vorox, but his words brought yesterday's unpleasantness back to the fore.

"Don't worry," he amended. "I can ask some questions around the guild; you could do any number of things for the Water-Crafters." Kira nodded, placated, and the two turned back toward town. On the way back through the shanty town they saw a group of five ruffians wearing the tattered tartan scarves of Laird Phebes walking toward Amen'ta Island on a parallel road. They were armed for war with cudgels and short blades. They hollered a challenge to Kira and Queeg, but didn't seem eager to charge them across the stretch of swamp that divided them, especially when they saw Queeg's blaster. Queeg could look damned formidable when he wanted.

They arrived back in town around 11:00 and parted company in the merchants' quarter, agreeing to meet later for a drink at Jando's bar near Kira's place. Kira looked at the stalls and decided that she would enjoy a day of not working. She would go home first, change and then go shopping and spend some money she didn't have.

8:30 CTT

Sitting in his glass-walled observation booth, Chief Wang frowned. He stared at the last month's production quotas (all met and exceeded) and ruminated over how unfair his life was. Ungrateful superiors and surly underlings were just the tip of the iceberg. A crew-chief at the Water-Guild was on the bottom of the shit-list when it came to bonuses and he was barely squeezing enough out of his crew to get any sort of bonus at all, let alone enough to cover the debts from his expensive Vlanii habit —contraband from Velisamil was pricey; one had to compete with nobles for the fine yeasts. If he didn't juggle the books from the receiving department he would have gone under water long ago. To top it all off, his latest review of the figures revealed that he had just fired his most productive worker. He shuffled through the receiving documents, scowled and silently cursed the Pancreator for his unjust ways.

A dry chuckle broke the silence and Wang looked up, startled half out of his wits.

"Troubles, Chief Wang?"

Wang's eyes narrowed on the unwelcome guest who had somehow entered his closed office, unheard and uninvited. The intruder was a tall man, with cold gray eyes and a gaunt bloodless face that reminded Wang of the sewer gulls who scavenged the canals. Distressingly, he had a cleft-pallet which ran from his mouth to his nose, exposing far more tooth and gum than Wang wished to see. The man leaned lightly against Wang's desk. Beside him, near the desk's edge, sat something that looked like an overturned, steel-riveted brass spittoon. The guest had a disconcerting stare that said, to the paranoid Wang, *I know exactly what you are thinking.*

"Can I help you, mister, ah... I am not accustomed to entertaining unannounced guests," said Wang, trying to casually close the incriminating files.

"I am *Director* Corbin from Muster central downtown," pronounced the man crisply. "My card." Wang blanched visibly, heaping yet another silent curse upon the Pancreator's already overburdened shoulders.

"Ah, Director Corbin. My apologies. I was merely reviewing our production manifest from last month. We exceeded our quota by 13% you know," he said obsequiously.

"Yet mysteriously your profitability arose by less than eight," smiled Corbin, revealing a row of perfectly even teeth.

"Well spoken, Mr. Corbin," said the spittoon. Wang blanched again to hear a second voice in the room, as the "spittoon" rounded the desk to reveal its true nature as a brass helmet worn by an evil looking, red-bearded dwarf.

"Why thank you, Mr. Dobbes," Corbin replied with a polite smile.

"To the point, Chief Wang," said the dwarf. "My associate and I do not care what you do with the books in this shop, though five percent strikes me as greedy and unwise. The average percentage corruption for someone in your position is less than two."

"Then what *do* you want?" choked Wang.

"Just this: There is a monster on the loose and we want you to help us capture it."

"A monster?"

"Yes. We have good cause to believe that it was lurking around this building at least as recently as yesterday morning. It is a vicious creature and constitutes a real danger to your employees and to the general population," Corbin said earnestly.

"And what do you want from me?" asked Wang. He was breathing a little easier now and was eager to bargain. "For starters we would like to question your morning staff as to whether they saw anything odd yesterday. No need to tell them what."

"What if they lie? I do not mean to cast aspersions, but many of those in this shop are of a dishonest disposition and may well decide to volunteer false information in the hopes of gaining a reward," said Wang.

"Leave that to us," counseled the dwarf. "Our Mr. Corbin is quite adept at uncovering falsehoods," he said with a significant glance. "In return for your help we will gladly forget the minor clerical errors emanating from this office. That is, *if* your help results in the beast's capture."

"Very well," agreed Wang. "When do you want to start?"

"No time like the present," replied the dwarf.

Wang called in each of his employees in turn, questioning them about the previous morning. True to his prediction several hinted at false information and Wang shot the two investigators a smug look of mock embarrassment. After two hours Corbin decided that none of the workers had the necessary information. "Thank you for your assistance, Wang. I regret, however, that this has been of little aid to us. Good-day, sir."

"Wait!" squeaked Wang. He had not been anxious to mention Kira for a number of reasons. The last thing he needed was the frigid bitch telling a director about his "abuses." Still, she had seemed shaken up about something when she came into work yesterday so maybe she had seen something. In any event, she was now his only hope. "Perhaps there is someone else..."

Half an hour later Wang watched from his office as his tormentors left and sighed with nervous relief as they disappeared into the late morning rain. He had given them Kira's address from his ledger and told them of her departure, casting himself in the best light he could given the circumstances. (Kira was, he maintained, obsessed with him.) In return, Dobbes gave Wang a small pouch of firebirds and a squawker frequency, extracting a promise from him that he would call if he "remembered" any more salient details. As the pair disappeared from one end of the guild courtyard, Wang saw another familiar face enter from the opposite end. It was that drunken brute Queeg, sneaking into work over three hours late! Damned lout was a friend of Kira's and ate lunch with her most of the time. Wang's eyes narrowed on the Water-Crafter and allowed himself a brief smile before closing the blinds.

14:15 CTT

Kira returned home from her shopping expedition shortly after noon. When she had returned there to change clothes earlier that morning, she was — considering the way her luck had been running for the last 28 hours or so — relieved to see it still standing. Not that there had really been any doubt that it would be. It was a sturdy two-story maxicrete box of the sort common in this section of the city. Despite its plainness, Kira had tried hard to make it her own. A small natural waterfall ran down a nearby hill and Kira had spent a lot of time over the last year cultivating a small garden of hardy flowers that could survive the black rains. A gaily colored flag, incongruous against the muddy sky, drooped in the rain. Kira heard the gentle tinkle of her wind chimes as she walked up the pathway. As she approached the front door Kira noticed that there was definitely something out of place. A large rusted basin filled with water sat at her front doorway and around it were strewn wild swamp flowers. Inside the basin swam a large, beautiful blue and gold fish with six eyes. Puzzled only momentarily by the odd gift, Kira had only to see the clawed footprint in her garden bed to realize the identity of her secret admirer. Carefully eradicating any sign of the footprint, Kira quickly brought the basin and her groceries inside.

Kira sat at her kitchen table, contemplating the meaning of the strange gift. Not so much the grand ramifications of the beast's gratitude, but of his intentions in choosing such a gift. She was not sure whether the alien intended for her to keep the fish as an ornament or for her to eat it. She had little doubt which way Queeg would vote if he was here; he would already be heading to the larder for butter and lemon fronds. The alien was like an animal, Queeg would argue, and clearly food would be its most natural expression of gratitude. "But why, then, the flowers?" she countered to the imaginary Queeg. She knew the answer would be another one of his impossible stories about how — on Madoc, Sutek or some other planet — he had seen a race of alien primates behave in a similar nature. "Interesting? Surely. Intelligent? Perhaps. But civilized?" Kira threw her hands up in exasperation at the bull-headed ex-Charioteer. The fish looked quite happy in its basin and she decided that she would let it live. A polite knock interrupted her thoughts and she cautiously answered the door.

The tall man at the door introduced himself as Director Corbin of the Muster and his diminutive associate as Mr. Dobbes. "May we come in for a moment, Associate Kira?" Kira complied without enthusiasm. She did not share most serfs' superstitious fear of the deformed, but there was something about the tall man that made her blood run cold.

"Thank you, Kira," he said with a ghoulish smile. "We shall not take up much of your time. I understand that there was an unfortunate incident at the factory yesterday. I hope that it has not soured you too much on the Muster. Such behavior is something we do not normally condone."

"Ah, no," replied Kira. "Not at all, director."

"Then perhaps we can lure you back to the fold, with a generous increase in pay, if..." he let the word dangle.

"If?"

"If you tell us about what you saw yesterday morning before work. I understand you were quite agitated when you arrived." Kira bit her lip. She was trying to maintain her composure but it was difficult with Corbin's harelip and disconcerting eyes to contend with, not to mention the dwarf circling her legs like a piranha.

"I am sorry I can't help you, director, but I didn't see anything. I was flustered yesterday because I was so late." She didn't feel that she sounded particularly convincing. Even she wasn't sure she would believe herself, but Corbin's face took on a confused and stricken look.

"Are you sure?" he said in a flustered tone. "Not even a six-legged beast with great claws?" Startled by the directness of the question, Kira nevertheless felt that she had somehow gained the upper hand in the conversation. Her thoughts were confirmed by the groan of exasperation from the dwarf at her ankles. She gave the director a puzzled look.

"No, sir. Nothing of the kind. Is there anything else?"

"No," whispered Corbin. "I guess not."

"Well, I am sorry I couldn't help you and that we couldn't come to an arrangement. Perhaps another time?" she hinted, eyeing the door.

"Well, call us if you hear anything," said the confused guilder weakly, handing her an embossed card. Kira closed the door behind him and almost fainted as the blood pounded in her temples.

The dwarf lead his confused colleague down the path and around the corner before speaking. "What in Layalath's name was all that about, Mr. Corbin? 'Not even a six-legged beast with great claws?' Are you nuts? Was she telling us the truth or not?"

"I don't know," protested Corbin. "I couldn't read her. Not at all!"

"What? Has this ever happened before?"

"A few times," Corbin admitted. "That Eskatonic Bishop on Madoc..."

"Well, I don't need to be a mind reader to tell that she was hiding something in spades," said the dwarf, his brusque manner fading. "Don't worry; while you were talking I planted a sub-dermal transmitter on her. She can't go anywhere without us knowing about it."

"A pleasure to work with you as always, Mr. Dobbes," said Corbin, brightening.

"Don't mention it, Mr. Corbin."

"You know, it's about time we called the countess with our status report. Over 34 hours and still no Vorox. I'm not looking forward to this."

"What? You think I am?" replied the dwarf. "Things were a hell of a lot easier back on Bannockburn."

15:30 CTT

The Countess Casmia al-Malik reclined luxuriantly by the pool in her high rise dwelling. The servant who had brought her the squawker a few minutes earlier now returned with it to his richly tiled niche. The skin-crafted buttons that were once his ears made it impossible to overhear what had distressed his mistress; even if he could hear, he was too discreet and wise to ask. Casmia crinkled her lips and nose in the schoolgirl pout that always drove her lover, Marquis Reginus Decados, insane with desire. Unfortunately, this call had little to do with her usual pleasures. Well, no, in fact it had everything to do with them.

Beside her duties as a socialite, which propelled her from party to dreary party, she also had a weakness for big-game hunting. This surprised those who knew her, for she was a small dainty featured woman with long hair that cascaded around her head in reddish-gold ringlets — in opposition to the usual al-Malik black. She had a small beauty mark on her cheek and her slender, girlish figure seemed far more appropriate to the ballroom floor than to the rigors of a safari. Nevertheless, she had spent most of her life learning to hunt. She grew up on Aylon where she hunted the nearly endless variety of terrors which populated that savage world. Here at the Imperial Center there were other hunting challenges, like the great cats of the Tamerlain Veldt. Oddly, some of the best game could be found in the sewers directly under the Harmony lowlands. Whether it was due to a millennium of toxic dumping, Second Republic experiments gone awry or the planet's vast profusion of ley lines, the undercity here teemed with challenging monstrosities of every sort. Casmia smiled sweetly into a nearby mirror held by a servant whose eyeless face was blind to her beauty. She was the most challenging monster of all.

The countess had spent a sizable amount of money to smuggle a feral Vorox all the way to Byzantium Secundus. Even someone with her resources had trouble spiriting such a thing past the watchful eyes of the Li Halan, who blockaded the planet Vorox for their own selfish interests. Even now, she had not yet decided whether she wanted to put the creature on exhibition for her secret following of rich gamblers, or to keep it for her own personal sport. Vorox versus Tranquier? Feral Vorox versus civilized? She new of at least one such creature she could put in the ring against her prize. The possibilities were astounding. Vorox versus Symbiot? Out of the question, at least here on Byzantium Secundus. On the other hand, the idiot Chainers she had hired to watch the Vorox were rapidly taking matters out of her hands. She might have to launch an impromptu safari for the creature after all. It seemed a waste in a way, but she was running out of options. A feral Vorox in a cage was a dream come true, but the same creature on the loose in her city could fast become a nightmare.

In her mind, Casmia briefly counted all the people she would anger if they discovered her little diversion. The Orthodox Church? Yes. The Empire? Also yes. Her gaming clients would be understandably upset if they became exposed with her. Important nobles, guilders and clergy such as they would have much to lose in such a scandal. Who else? The Li Halan? Almost certainly, but then they were always mad at her. Duke Hakim al-Malik? The last thought made her pause. The al-Malik were trying to put their best face forward while the Emperor wooed Lady Theafana al-Malik. A diplomatic upset of this magnitude could interrupt Hakim's desired union and Casmia guessed that the Duke would not be amused.

Casmia clapped her hands, demanding the attention of the two hugely muscled genetic freaks who were cavorting like children in the pool. Their skin bore mottled purple-blue patterns as if someone had bruised every inch of their bodies. Their eager bald faces looked up at her with expectation, but minimal comprehension. Casmia sighed. They were the best the local body-bank could do since she lost her last two bodyguards last month in Tamerlain. They were hugely strong, but short on brains. Still, they had their uses and they did more for her body than just guarding it. Besides, if she didn't like them she could always return them to the bank and have them ground into next year's model. "Get out of the pool, children," she chimed in her lilting musical tone. "Mother Casmia is going hunting tonight."

19:00 CTT

That evening Kira and Queeg met at Jando's to discuss the day's events. Kira told him about the fish and her odd encounter with the Muster. "You know," said Queeg, "I heard Wang was asking some questions about you today at the shop. I'll bet it was that hull rat-bastard who put them on you." On the subject of the fish, Queeg was reassuringly predictable and insisted that the Vorox clearly meant it for eating. After a few drinks the two agreed to keep in touch over the next day or so. They separated for their respective homes, though Queeg warned her that her house wasn't safe. "Sleep over at my place tonight," he offered. "Just because your beastie is bringing you pets or whatever, doesn't mean it won't hurt you if it gets hungry or ticked. And those two visitors..." But Kira insisted that all she really needed was a good night sleep in her own bed and that in the morning everything would look quite different.

23:40 CTT

It was late and raining heavily when Queeg finally turned down the canal to his apartment. He had stopped at another bar after Jando's and was now regretting it mightily. In his 45 years he had experienced every kind of weather, but the last drink had made him disoriented and more than a little dizzy. He had heard at the bar that they were expecting a real bad storm tonight; force three winds, the works. Lightning licked the old temple near his home and the street lights around him flickered and died. "Bloody great," he thought. The block up to his home was

like a wind tunnel and he had to force himself down the narrow courtyard. Fumbling for the keys he unlocked the door and staggered inside.
"Bed," he thought. "For at least a hundred years." Queeg lit an oil lamp
and sank heavily in his favorite chair. "Thank Zebulon this day is done,"
he muttered.

"Oh, don't thank him yet," replied a dry voice from the darkness.
Queeg turned toward the invisible speaker, rising from his chair as he
did so. A tall gaunt man with a cleft pallet emerged from the shadows
and into the dim sphere of light cast by the lamp. Queeg saw a slug
pistol aimed directly at his chest. Instantly guessing the intruder's identity, Queeg scanned the low shadows nearby and was not surprised to
see Dobbes also emerging from the darkness.

"What do you want?" he asked.

"Just a few minutes of your time," assured the thin man. "I understand you and your friend Kira have had a distressing few days and
hoped that you might take this opportunity to share your burden."

"I don't know what you're talking about and, even if I did, I would
have nothing to say at gun point," Queeg said defiantly.

"But I believe you do," said the thin man. "This place is a mess and
you have Vorox prints all over your apartment. What did you do, give it
a bath?" he sneered. The man drew closer and Queeg held his breath,
adrenaline burning off some of the alcohol fog. He just needed to buy
a moment to steady himself. A casual glance at the dwarf gave him his
chance. A strange, stylized chain-link tattoo circled his wrist and Queeg
had been on enough illicit flights in his days as a Charioteer to recognize its significance.

"You're Chainers, aren't you?" said Queeg, changing the subject
and taking a deep breath.

"Only the very best in no-cost, low maintenance human resources
that money can buy," beamed the dwarf with a bow. Queeg nodded his
head, acknowledging the little man's confession. There were few things
in the universe that Queeg hated more than slavers.

As the thin man prepared to speak again, Queeg took his chance.
Two men, one visible gun. The thin man was the threat; he had the gun.
If Queeg could take him down he had little doubt he could intimidate
the dwarf into surrendering. Queeg's massive paw shot out with impressive speed for someone of his size and enveloped the thin man's gun
hand. The man let out a yelp of pain and surprise as Queeg crushed his

gun hand. Queeg followed it up with a punch in the mouth and the man went sprawling. As planned, Corbin's gun neatly remained in Queeg's hand. Queeq was about to pull back and take triumphant control of the situation when he doubled over in pain. The dwarf assaulted his stomach with a flying kick and then followed up with another blow to his knee, almost snapping it. Queeg went down with a bellow and the dwarf was on him. To his surprise there were no additional blows as the small man leapt on his shoulders, just a metallic "snap" around his neck. Queeg tried to dislodge his diminutive tormentor but suddenly couldn't move.

"That is a neural collar," puffed the dwarf. "You will find that you cannot move any of your extremities until I give the command through this control pad. Are you well, Corbin?"

"I'll live," said the thin man, cradling his injured hand. "Though I'm glad we negotiated danger pay for this assignment. It's clods like this who make the job so difficult sometimes," he said, aiming a vicious kick to Queeg's side.

"Now perhaps we should try this again. Where is the Vorox? With Kira? Where!"

"Get spaced, Chauki" grunted Queeg in typical Charioteer fashion. "You may control my body, but my mind is my own."

"Oh?" smiled Corbin.

25:20 CTT

Kira was restless and decided against going immediately home. When she first left Jando's it wasn't raining that hard and she decided to take a little walk. Her trail lead her through the merchant's quarter. The well-lit thoroughfare raised her spirits and she felt exceptionally brave and in control for the first time since — well, she couldn't remember. Without much thought, Kira found herself in an all-night expeditionary shop, buying a fusion torch and a disposable breather. Then, she was walking purposefully downhill toward the swamp.

The rain was coming down much harder and the lights of the merchant quarter lay far behind her as Kira passed into the shanty town. She almost turned back several times, but something urged her onward. Visibility was terrible, which worked against her in some ways and for her in others. She stumbled on the uneven terrain, almost twisting her ankle, and soon became lost in the low dunes. As she wandered she heard a throng of Laird Phebes's men, their voices raised in a loud and drunken war song. The men passed her by unseen in the concealing storm and continued to splash their way toward Amen'ta Island. Kira held her breath as they passed. *As if they could hear you above the storm,* she thought. She exhaled with relief as she watched them go and patted her dagger. It would not have done her much good against such a war party. Indeed, she was not even sure she could bring herself to use it at all. Still, its presence reassured her.

By following the war party, Kira came at last to the edge of the swamp she and Queeg had visited earlier that day. Even through the storm she could vaguely make out Amen'ta Island in the near distance. Intermittent fires punctuated its black surface and Kira was sure that the battle for the miserable mud-flat had begun in earnest. As she surveyed the swamp, Kira found that she was almost enjoying herself. She felt truly alive as the wind and rain lashed her bare face, and felt the giddy flow of adrenaline pumping through her veins. She decided to walk the edge of the swamp, rather than dashing headlong into it. There was an otherworldliness to the area. Frightening forms menaced her from the shadows and then retreated back into the recesses of her imagination. As she passed by a low ridge, Kira sensed a black circular hollow in the dune, darker even than the surrounding night. She aimed her fusion torch toward the dark place and discovered it was a massive sewer pipe, over three meters in diameter. It was overgrown with scrub and a small stream poured from it, cutting a narrow channel in the sand below. Kira turned to go when she saw something else, a pair of eyes glinting from its dark recesses.

Kira's heart leapt into her mouth as she swung in the sewer's direction. Her first thought was one of elation, but it turned into a cold trickle of fear as the twin glints came into better focus. They were not the same eyes! Kira's fusion torch illuminated a brief glimpse of reptilian scale and a flash of movement as whatever it was retreated back into the sewer pipe with a hiss. Kira was about to turn on her heels and run as fast as she could when she herself was suddenly illuminated by a strong beam of light.

"There you are," said Dobbes. "We've been looking everywhere for you."

Kira took an affronted step backward; she didn't like them being here. Corbin casually held his gun in her general direction, as if to

imply that its presence was a mere formality and not meant to consti-
tute a threat. Dobbes stood nearby, holding a fusion torch which he
aimed directly at her. Behind the two Chainers lumbered a dejected
Queeg, wearing a strange metal collar. Kira's friend looked at her and
then his eyes fell to the ground, ashamed. "I'm sorry, Kira. There was
nothing I could do."

"Shut-up, Queeg," spat the tall guilder, obviously nursing a bloodied lip. Dobbes considered his colleague before addressing Kira. "I assure you that Queeg brought us here against his will, Kira. I hope you
won't think any less of him for that. We don't want you or your friend;
it's the Vorox we want. Be reasonable. Help us bring the creature in and
we can all go home and forget this ever happened."

Kira thought for only an instant and then shook her head "no."
The dwarf gave a resigned sigh as Corbin walked briskly toward her, still
holding the gun in his hand. Kira took another step backward, but was
too afraid to run. "Let me make this clear," growled the telepath as he
grabbed a handful of her hair. "You will help us," the man's knee met
her stomach and she doubled over in pain. "You will do so because we
are bound by oaths of loyalty to the same guild!" Kira fell on her belly
in the mud and weakly squirmed to escape. The man's knee was in her
back and he was still viciously yanking at her hair. "You will do so
because the monster is a danger to our guild and others..." Corbin
slammed her head into a rock. "Because we are your superiors and do
not countenance defiance!" Another blow and Kira was aware of rich
blood flowing from an opened artery in her forehead. "And lastly, because if you do not cooperate we will shoot you and your friend and
leave your corpses for the..."

Mud and blood blinded Kira to the cause of the interruption, but
Queeg saw it before anyone. A large shadow detached itself from a
nearby clump of swamp grass and seemed to flow toward Kira and the
angry Chainer. Warned by a sixth-sense, Corbin turned at the last instant and screamed as the Vorox bore down on him. The guilder's energy shield managed to deflect the enraged alien's lethal poisoned claws,
but the Vorox followed up with a two-fisted back hand with its two
right arms. The guilder flew several meters and landed like a rag-doll in
the mud where he slumped with a groan. Kira wiped her eyes and saw
the dwarf pulling out a pistol with his free hand and taking aim at the
great beast. Kira called out a warning, but it was unnecessary. The golden

furred alien dropped from two legs to six, easily avoiding the dwarf's weapon. The Vorox bounded forward and swooped the shrieking dwarf up in his teeth. Dobbes wore a heavy coat of synthetic leather which stiffened under the Vorox's bite, preventing their penetration. The giant alien shook the screaming Chainer like a dog trying to kill a rodent and it was by no means clear that the dwarf would escape a broken neck. The creature looked frustrated by its progress, however, and with a final shake, it flung the dwarf near the semi-conscious telepath.

The Vorox approached its prey, lowering its head and baring its teeth in a vicious grimace. A low growl rolled around the clearing, mingling with the thunder. The dwarf looked up dizzily and screamed, holding up his hands in supplication. The Vorox's intentions were clear and Kira made a rapid decision. Running between the enraged beast and its intended victims she screamed out "no" and pointed her finger defiantly at the creature. To Queeg, standing in his paralyzed front row seat, it was as good as over. Kira looked ridiculously small before the massive creature and its expression gave no sign that it was open to negotiation or pleas for mercy. "It'll kill them all," he thought miserably, "and then save my paralyzed carcass for a snack!" It was, thus, to his great surprise that the Vorox stopped dead in its tracks and sat before Kira like an obedient hound.

Kira seemed almost as surprised by her success as Queeg, but swiftly took advantage of their turn of fortune. Dobbes's control panel lay in a shallow puddle of rain water, its red and blue lights still blinking. Kira fished it out triumphantly. "How do I take it off?' she hissed at Dobbes.

"Three-three-six-blue," stammered the cowering Chainer. Kira punched in the code and heard a reassuring click from the collar. Queeg pulled the collar open with a jerk and almost flung it into the swamp before thinking better of it. The dwarf had delivered several painful neural shocks to him over the past few hours and he was not above some pay back.

"Come here, you little shi..." he started toward the dwarf, but Kira grabbed his arm. "No, this is no time for revenge. We have to decide what to do next. Should we call the city watch?" Queeg stopped and his brow furrowed.

"Maybe the Imperial Guard..." he started, but was interrupted for the second time.

A bolt of white energy flashed through the area, striking the Vorox between its upper shoulder blades. A resounding crack accompanied the bolt and the Vorox let out a high keening noise as it shimmered in the bright glow, its hair standing on end before it collapsed with a grunt in the sand. At first Kira thought that a stray bolt of lightning had struck her companion, but a gun shot kicked up sand at her feet and quickly drew her attention to the bolt's true source. Across a narrow stretch of swamp stood a woman and two men. The men were bald and massively muscled; each carried a heavy rifle. The woman was small, blonde and wore black skin-tight plastic. Leather boots encased her slender legs and thighs, and she wore a circular pair of black goggles. An animal pelt adorned her neck and one shoulder, and was fastened with a pin bearing the solar spiral crest of House al-Malik. Kira's heart sunk to her feet. She stood paralyzed with superstitious fear as she spotted the crest, but then Queeg's voice was in her ear, shouting: "Run! Run!"

Queeg had scooped up the dwarf's revolver and was beckoning for her to follow. The swamp would not do. Their pursuers were too close and could mow them down before they could reach any cover. "There," panted Kira, pointing toward the great drainage pipe. It was less than ten meters to the pipe and every step of the way Kira expected to see her heart explode through her chest from a shot in the back. Two more shots harried her onward, but neither found their mark. Queeg beckoned her from the sewer pipe and as she clambered into it, she was surprised to find the Vorox stumbling drunkenly behind her, shaking its head as it tried to throw off the effects of the blast. "Crazy! She's crazy," panted Queeg. "She let us get to the pipe; I'm sure of it! Dead end, or maybe she just wants a hunt."

Queeg lead the way down the tunnel and then turned abruptly. Kira and the Vorox joined him at the corner where Queeg crouched, covering them from any pursuit. A long second passed and a figure flickered across the end of the pipe. Queeg fired his pistol as Kira crouched near him. The Vorox shambled onward and disappeared into the darkness. "Damn me, but I'm not sure if I hit or not," swore Queeg.

As if in answer to his question a metal canister spun down the tunnel, breaking open on impact. A rolling yellow smoke poured forth, engulfing them both. Queeg hacked and his eyes ran as he got a face full of the noxious fumes. Kira had managed to grab a breath full of fresh air as the canister exploded and reached into her tunic, producing the portable breather. The breather was meant to give a short supply of oxygen to someone trapped underwater (a common enough occurrence on the drowning planet), not a gas attack; it had no eye protection.

Forcing the mask to her friend's face, Kira blindly guided him farther into the tunnels. The gas had spread quickly, however, and as she blindly stumbled forward she could not help but gasp in a breath of the vapors. Her eyes watered ferociously and her lungs felt as if they were about to explode, and then it stopped, just like that. Her eyes filled with tears and the stinging disappeared. The pain in her throat and lungs faded. The passage was still filled with blinding smoke, but she could clearly see the sides of the tunnel. Kira could not imagine to what to attribute this good fortune and decided not to question it, lest it fade through her examination. Queeq was not so lucky, however, and continued to choke and gasp through the mask. Kira pulled him along briskly, scanning foreword and back for any sign of the Vorox or pursuit. Finding neither, she stopped Queeg at a place where rain water poured through a fracture in the tunnel. Guiding her friend underneath the torrent she gently washed his eyes. Queeg bent over and coughed loudly, hacking and spitting with vigor. When he looked back up his eyes were limned with red cracks, but he managed a weak smile.

The two moved swiftly now, going deeper and deeper into the tunnels. The path lead only in one direction, down toward Amen'ta Island; the water grew deeper as they went. Ankle deep at first, the water soon lapped around their knees. At least it was reasonably clean. Queeg had spent much time in the sewers during his stint with the Water-Crafters and knew that this area of the sewers had not actually served to carry waste in decades, perhaps centuries. Kira and Queeg both desperately looked for a path that might branch off from the main tunnel and lead them uphill and into shallower water. The few branches they did find, however, were sealed with maxicrete or metal pressure doors. The water was waste deep as the two came to a great opening where several tunnels joined a central hub. Kira breathed a sigh of relief and started toward a tunnel that looked like it might lead back toward the city, when Queeg gently grabbed her arm. "Not that way," he whispered urgently.

Kira looked at Queeg and then back at the tunnel where her eyes focused on several large humanoid figures hunched over a ledge above the water. In the light of her fusion torch Kira could make out greenish-white amphibian skin with darker markings on their faces. Large saucer plate eyes regarded the intruders and a raucous chittering met Kira's fusion beam as it swept across them. She lowered the torch and desperately looked at Queeg. *Trolls,* she thought with silent despair. "Raechul," muttered Queeg, using the Ur-Ukar name for the sewer dwellers. "Come on. There's no going back that way."

Lady Casmia flashed a provocative smile at the two recovering Chainers, chilling them to the bone. She had given her quarry a five-minute head start and some added incentive with the tear gas. One of her muscle boys had sustained a superficial wound from gunfire at the tunnel's entrance, but they were hard to hurt and fast to heal. "Are you ready to earn your pay?" she asked the Chainers. They entered the tunnel, one of the bodyguards taking point and Dobbes near the rear, examining the pale green oracle screen tied to the tracer in Kira's leg. As the water rose the dwarf found it harder to make his way through than his companions. At last, in concession to the need for speed, Casmia allowed the miserable Mr. Dobbes to clamber onto one of her henchmen's backs.

As the well-armed hunting party reached the central hub, a mere two minutes after Kira and Queeg passed, Casmia spotted the Raech-ul through the ice-blue glow of her goggles. She smiled cruelly as the curious amphibians gathered near the entrance. She had hunted them before and knew that, despite their great size and strength, they were at heart timid creatures. Smiling, she coolly aimed her mini-pistol at the nearest creature and squeezed the trigger. A delicious spark ran through her body as white traceries barked from the rotating cylinders, and her target collapsed with an inhuman scream. The rest of the shapes fled into the recesses of the tunnel with a mournful cry. Casmia walked over to the fallen creature on the ledge, casually turning it over with her boot. It had dark tribal markings on its face and hands, and wore primitive jewelry made from cast off scrap metal. Its breathing came in gurgled fits and starts; its luminescent saucer eyes regarded the countess with terror. Casmia gave the creature a kind smile and shushed soothingly before pulling the trigger of her gun. The gun barked out its fire once again and the creature jerked convulsively as its head disintegrated before the barrage.

Dobbes winced at the countess's sport. "Milady, there are two possible directions they could have taken from here; without tunnel schematics, the tracer can't determine which way they went."

"Split up," hissed the countess.

Kira and Queeg struggled through chest-deep water, hurried on by
the sound of gunfire echoing from the tunnels behind them. Queeg
took the lead, taking care to hold his pistol above water level. They at
last came to another juncture and, without the presence of trolls lurking about the periphery, Kira allowed herself a moment of hope that
they might be able to turn back while avoiding their pursuers. They
sloshed down a promising-looking tunnel and were soon hopelessly lost
in a maze of interconnecting tubes. Kira sobbed out in frustration as
they came to yet another junction, this one deeper than the last.

This juncture was a huge circular structure with multiple tunnels
leading into it from every direction. Most of the tunnels were submerged by water while some were high and dry, but also, unfortunately,
out of reach. A great torrent of water poured from some of the higher
tunnels, creating dangerous currents of white foam in the black and
forbidding liquid. The sound of crashing water echoed wildly around
the cavern's dark recesses. Kira's shoulders slumped.

"That tunnel. I'm sure of it, girl," said Queeg to his disheartened
companion. Kira followed the motion of his finger and could see one
tunnel, higher than the one they had just entered, but still accessible for
someone in the water. A narrow ledge ran around part of the cavern at
their level, but submerged before it reached any of the other tunnels.
The two started across the slippery moss-covered ridge, hugging the
edge as best they could. The ledge sank beneath the water, but they still
followed it as it steadily descended below the black surface. The water
was soon neck deep on Queeg and Kira swam along side him. Queeg
felt the underwater ledge end abruptly below his feet and knew that he
too would have to swim.

Kira sliced through the water toward the tunnel's inviting edge. A
thin stream of water issued from along its bottom, indicating that it was
much shallower than any tunnel that they had seen since first entering
the sewers. Queeg took a deep breath and was about to push himself
from the wall when a great black shape swept at him with the current
from the shadows. Black matted fur and a death like stench assaulted
the Water-Crafter in the darkness. Panicked beyond reason, Queeg bellowed, striking his attacker with all his might. The first blow rebounded

against the unseen shape with little effect, but his second penetrated its fur with a tearing, snapping sound. A putrid stench filled his nostrils as his fist plunged into the cold, dark cavity.

Kira, alerted by her friend's distress, turned back from the ledge and turned her fusion beam on the fracas. She did not know whether to laugh with relief or to vomit. Queeg wrestled with the bloated carcass of a dead brute, its body bobbing sickeningly in the torch light. Suddenly aware of his opponent's true nature, Queeg shoved it away from him with a bilious choke. "It's all right," soothed Kira above the sound of the pouring waterfall. "Let's just get out of here!" Queeg turned to obey her command when he spotted the creature's gapping chest. Its ribs were splayed out at rough angles, recently denuded of flesh and fur. How could a two-ton brute get down here anyway? Kira seemed to share his thoughts as the two looked at each other and then both were desperately thrashing toward the ledge.

Kira reached the tunnel first and was about to clamber out when a light from above revealed a leather boot standing in wait for her. The barrel of a shotgun loomed inches before her eyes and behind it the grim face of Mr. Dobbes. Behind him stood Corbin with a borrowed rifle. "Enough! I see no reason to drag this on further. Surrender and we can walk out of here safely. Resist and I can't be held responsible for your deaths."

All the hope drained from Kira's face. They were trapped and she knew it. She nodded her head weakly in surrender and was about to offer her hand for the dwarf to help her out when Queeg shouted out from beside her. "No!" he boomed, his arm shooting out at Corbin's leg, wrenching the surprised Chainer in a wide arc over his head and into the water behind him with a splash. "Bet you didn't see that one coming," he barked at the flailing airborne telepath. Corbin's gun went flying and the Chainer landed with a splash, conscious but stunned. The memory of a thousand barroom brawls on a dozen alien worlds reared up in Queeg's mind. These men were not going to let them live; if he was sure of one thing ever, he was sure of that. At best, he and Kira could look to finishing out their days as slaves if they surrendered. Painful neural shocks, the tear gas, his enforced helplessness at their hands and the degrading incident with the brute carcass thundered through his blood, driving him toward vengeance against his former captors.

Queeg clambered swiftly onto the ledge, eyeing the startled Dobbes warily. The little cockroach was fast, but this time he was ready for him. Kira, momentarily stunned by the outburst of violence, moved to get out of Queeg's way. As Queeg advanced on the dwarf, one of the two bald walls of muscle she had seen accompanying the al-Malik woman appeared around a near bend in the tunnel. The muscle man moved quickly for his great bulk, aimed his gun at the enraged Water-Crafter and fired. The shotgun crack blended with Kira's scream as Queeg fell like a great tree, blood spurting freely from his chest. As the ground spun up at him through a cloud of red haze, Queeg's last thought was: *You should be getting time and a half for this one, boyo.*

Kira screamed, enraged by her friend's death. Her nails struck out, raking the surprised dwarf's face. The dwarf fell back and the bald giant surged forward, grabbing Kira by the hair and lifting her like a kitten above his head. "That does it, you damned witch," screamed the dwarf. "He can wring yer neck now for all I care!" The giant viewed his shrieking captive; a slow look of mirth entered his vacant eyes and he gave a broad grin revealing two rows of perfect pointed teeth. All reason left Kira as she struck at her friend's killer. She flailed out wildly, hitting the grinning giant once. The giant laughed at her ineffectual blow. Twice. The giant grinned wider and drew her forth. Three times. The giant's head snapped back as though hit by a charging Vorox and he spun twice before falling into the water. The man bobbed face down, floating with the current for a moment before disappearing abruptly below the surface with barely a ripple. Kira crouched on the ledge where the giant had dropped her, observing her fist with slow amazement. She then turned to the dwarf with a darkly triumphant look in her eyes.

Kira advanced on the suddenly frightened Mr. Dobbes, ignoring his drawn gun and cries for her to surrender. As her hand reached out to grab the small man he fired his weapon, catching her squarely in her forearm. A shock from the weapon's concussion tore through Kira's body, but there was no pain. Blood, burnt flesh, twisted metal, sparks and the dwarf's astonished face temporarily became her entire world. Kira stood, immobilized not by pain or fear, but revelation.

Brown robes, blankets of cleansing flame, sparks flying between machinery and her outstretched fingers, and the smell of burning plastic. The lost memories rushed at her in a torrent, blotting out everything else.

"Well I'll be damned, a genuine golem," Dobbes whistled. A look of greed replaced the previous expression of fear on the Chainer's face. One could almost see the Reeves' scales tilting in his eyes. "We've hit the jackpot, Mr. Corbin. Wouldn't you agree?"

"Without a doubt, Mr. Dobbes," gasped the half-drowned Chainer as he clambered onto the ledge. "She's damaged, but still worth a dean's ransom if we can take her without further injury." The man produced a softly glowing sheet of flexible metal from his pocket. "Wet Jacket should do the job nicely. The Vorox for the countess and we'll take Kira as our share of the spoils. She's worth a dozen Vorox and she signed a Muster contract! The new technologies clause makes her our property," gloated the advancing Chainer.

The sheet expanded in contact with the air and Corbin held it like a net as he cautiously approached the strangely docile Kira. Corbin was not as confidant as he sounded; he had seen what the golem did to Casmia's thug. As Corbin stepped over Queeg's prostrate body his expression changed from one balancing fear and elation to sudden surprise. A large boot struck out from the prostrate form and for the second time the surprised telepath went sailing out into the water. Queeg wheezed in agony; the kick had taken everything he had. He had heard what had occurred through a haze and Kira's revelation both startled and frightened him. Golems were blasphemies, he had been taught. Their very existence robbed humans of their sacred place in the cosmos, diminishing and mocking the works of the Pancreator. Golem or not, however, Kira was his friend and the only way through to her was going to be over his dead body.

"Kira! Are you awake? Pull yourself together, girl," he croaked at the prostrate android. With Dobbes still armed and an enraged Corbin swimming back to shore, this was their final chance. Kira did not move and the telepath gained the ledge, staring daggers at the fainting Queeg.

"You are dead, Queeg," the Chainer began, but his words were abruptly cut short. A massive reptilian head broke the surface, its eyes rolled back in its sockets like a shark as its great mouth opened around Corbin's body. Twin guillotines of translucent razor sharp teeth tore into the telepath. The man's deformed mouth emitted a blood curdling shriek as he struggled to free himself from the creature's intractable bite. The water churned with dark crimson foam in the fusion light as Corbin disappeared beneath the surface, his mouth still working, but now silent.

"Saints!" The pistol fell from Dobbes's nerveless fingers as he watched his colleague sink below the water. He stared first at the near dead Queeg and then the silent Kira, still observing her ruined arm. "Shutdown," he thought glumly. "Cut your losses, Dobbes. No point in gaining a great prize if you are not alive to collect it." The dwarf started out along the ledge toward the exit tunnel. The creature was still below the water and Kira on shore. With any luck that would give him enough opportunity to escape. As he started across the ledge he became suddenly aware of a great black shape swooping down on him from above. The monster, its teeth still dripping with the tattered remnant's of Corbin's flesh and gray suit, tore at him from the shadows. "How did it get up there so fast?" The predator's mouth snapped downward toward his face and Dobbes was treated to a slow, spinning view of the monster as it clung like a spider to the cavern wall. It was sleek and had six legs which ended in long tapered claws. Its red-tipped teeth hissed as he passed.

"Decapitated," thought the slaver miserably. "Decapitated and this is the last thing my head will see before it lands in the water and sinks to Gehenne. Pancreator forgive..." The dwarf's spiritual revelation ended as he landed on his behind with a sharp pain that convinced him that he was still quite alive.

Kira was in front of him, casually ignoring the man she had just saved. Her dagger flashed in the fusion light, severing one of the beast's claws with one hack. The creature hissed its fury and retreated up the wall before rearing back to pounce. *One claw down, only five to go*, thought Kira pessimistically. Even with her evidently superior strength she had little hope she could defeat the creature. The reptile hissed its alien spite at her, but its cold eyes betrayed no emotion. Its muscles tensed and it lunged. Even prepared Kira was taken aback by the monster's sheer speed. She could feel its hot breath inches from her face as its front claws plunged into her body, tearing away cloth and flesh. Great jagged tears welled synthetic blood, but the creature's teeth never found their mark. With a rush of motion golden-brown fur replaced scale in her field of vision, followed by a loud splash.

Kira held her damaged side as she watched the Vorox and the great reptile thrash about in the water. The Vorox roared its rage against the six-legged monster who hissed its mad reply. Equally matched in size and speed, each tore at the other with their eleven limbs as they turned over and over in the water. The combatants rolled beneath the surface and then suddenly erupted above it, sending up great whale spouts of water. Kira and the cowering Mr. Dobbes watched as the monsters sank again with grim fascination, knowing that the next few seconds would determine both their fates. The two combatants rose to the surface again, a tangle of limbs, blood and furious sound. Kira thought she could detect the Vorox slowing, however, and a choke caught in her throat. Again the two monsters rose and this time the reptile, though badly injured, clearly had the upper hand. The Vorox tore at it with its poisonous claws, but its blows were a mockery of their former force.

The reptile, sensing its enemy's impending defeat disentangled itself from its foe and broke beneath the water, circling its enemy like a vulture. What happened next was, to Kira, a heartrending series of hit and run attacks. The reptile, clearly in its element, struck at the floundering Vorox again and again. The Vorox bellowed its defiance, but was now little more than an attractive target to the circling predator. Dobbes had recovered his pistol and fired madly into the water at the beast, but his bullets didn't have sufficient power to harm it through the water. What few shots he did land seemed to roll off the creature's armored back like raindrops. Kira prepared to dive into the water with the intention of making one last gesture of defiance. *Maybe it will choke on me,* she thought with gallows' mirth. She crouched to jump as the creature's head surfaced near the Vorox to deliver its death bite. Suddenly the water exploded upward and a concussion hurled Kira to the ground as reptilian legs and entrails rained about the cavern in a red mist. Blinded by the explosion, it took Kira a second to determine its source.

"A pity to destroy such a fine specimen, but it was either that or *my* Vorox," mused the al-Malik woman, eyeing the fallen alien. "Come stand by me, little man," she said to Dobbes in a disapproving tone. Dobbes sullenly took his place at the noblewoman's side, saying nothing to Kira as he passed her. Kira cradled her damaged arm in an attempt to hide her true nature from the woman. Lady Casmia smiled, not unkindly, on Kira before turning to her remaining bodyguard. The man nodded and went about trying to pull the countess's prize from the water.

"I'm sorry, dear," she said to Kira. "This whole business has been most unfortunate... most unfortunate. Unfortunately you are a witness to some — embarrassing information, and I cannot afford to take you at your word that you won't spread vicious rumors about it to my enemies. I hope you understand," she said, her tone suddenly predatory and low. She slowly circled Kira, scraping an orange limned wireblade playfully against the nape of her neck. In Kira's mind the pretty face of the circling al-Malik woman and that of the reptile she had just killed became one. Killing machines without pity or remorse. Kira felt hot blood pour down her neck as the monomolecular blade easily parted her skin.

"You are making a mistake," rasped Kira, her anger finally getting the better of her.

"Oh? And what may that be, pray tell?"

"Only this!" Kira turned ferociously on the black clad noblewoman, both fists joined as one. The woman attempted to dodge, indeed seemed to expect some last ditch effort from the spirited peasant girl, but could not match her opponent's speed or fury. Kira watched as the al-Malik's head snapped back and then rebounded off the nearby wall. The woman slid down the wall into a sitting position, her bruised jaw slumped unconscious to her chest. Kira turned. She was prepared to go after the big man next and Dobbes if necessary, but was surprised to see the dwarf turning to the stooping giant, leveling his gun inches from the big man's bald head. The pistol shot reverberated throughout the corridor as the man fell, dead, into the water.

"Thank you for saving my life," said the dwarf casually in answer to Kira's stunned expression. "Don't be so surprised," he said, eyeing the prostrate countess. "I never really liked her anyway."

It was early morning by the time Kira and her companions reached the surface near the shanty town. Dobbes had helped her patch her friends together and had removed the tracking device from her leg in an attempt to assuage her remaining suspicions. The Vorox was recovering swiftly and limped painfully, carrying the unconscious Queeg on his back. Queeg was not well at all. His pale feverish face sagged and he looked strangely small to the worried Kira. Fires still burned on Amen'ta Island through the early morning mist. The raging storm of the night before had subsided into a hard driving rain and the island had dwindled precipitously during the night. The party saw bandaged members of the beggar's guild in retreat and it appeared that Laird Phebes's men had won the night and the prize, an island that would soon disappear below the waves until the next dry season. Some men passed not too far from

Kira and the rest, but with their recent weapons acquisition from the countess, Kira had little fear that they would dare to impede their progress back to town. On the way back they stopped at Dobbes's rented skimmer.

"What are you going to do with her?" Kira asked Dobbes again, eyeing the bound and furiously squirming Casmia.

"Do not concern yourself overly much with that. I told you I would find her some... rehabilitative employment at a place where she will do no one any harm. Selling off a noble's tricky business and fatal if you're caught, but I see no other way out short of killing her. Besides, I can make a handsome profit with this one," he chuckled, giving the countess a sly wink. "A mind wipe's the first step, then I'll find a place where the al-Malik don't have much power. The Malignatius mines or Kurgan Front, perhaps," assured the dwarf with a wide grin.

Epilogue: Two Weeks Later

Kira sat at the spaceport looking out the window as an Imperial Lekaf slowly lifted and turned 100' above the ground. The ship's rear thrusters burned easily, turning the rain around the ship into great clouds of orange steam before the ship took off with a roar and disappeared in the clouds. A town crier strolled by, shouting out the news of the day and Kira looked down at her luggage, feeling a little guilty. The news of the Countess Casmia al-Malik disappearance had been almost the only topic of conversation for over a week before the cacophony of speculation finally died down to a dull roar. Most people were pleased to assign blame to the area Ur-Ukar, who generally hated the al-Malik, but no one knew for sure. In the end it appeared that few people, except her Decados lover the marquis, who offered a large reward for her return, mourned her disappearance.

Kira looked around and saw Queeg approaching her with a large red-bearded man. Queeg was still walking with a cane and wore a poultice of healing herbs in a pouch around his neck. The Amalthean priestess had done a fine job of patching him up and did not ask many questions. Kira had healed quite well on her own and within two days there had been no sign of her injuries, though she could detect an unfamiliar ripple beneath her skin where Dobbes had shot her. Her super-human strength and speed had also faded shortly after leaving the sewers. She had tried several times since to replicate her previous feats, but without success. She eventually gave up, concluding that she only gained such abilities when her survival was at stake.

"The beastie's all stowed away, if not completely happy about it. I don't think he likes spaceships," Queeg said, nodding toward a strange red segmented ship across the tarmac. It looked a lot like a giant lobster to Kira, but she kept her peace. "This is Captain Jacob Vander Meer, who I told you about. He's an old mate from my Charioteer days and will get you both to Vorox, like you wanted."

The man stepped forward and shook her hand vigorously. "Glad to meet you, Kira. By the time ye get to Vorox with Captain Jacob, ye'll be seeing the universe through a whole new set of eyes. Hot damn!"

Kira nodded, slightly daunted by the captain's obviously Criticorum enthusiasm. It had taken most of the money she had gained fencing Casmia's possessions to the Scravers to book this flight, and now she was having second thoughts.

"Are you still sure you want to go through with this, girl?" asked Queeg. "Vorox is a vicious, miserable excuse for a planet. I know. I got this scar wrestling a Grackle Fox there when I was back in the service," he said, indicating the usual injury. "Besides, I'll miss you if you go," he added sheepishly. His face fell and Kira smiled at him.

"Yes. I will miss you too, but I think it is best. Dobbes may have let things drop back in the sewers, but I still don't trust him not to come after me later. He may be grateful, but he's still a Chainer. Besides, I feel as though I'm tied to the Vorox in a strange way. His appearance helped bring back my memory, at least some of it. I know what I am now, but not why I am. I think I am old, but I don't know how old or why I was built. Maybe I was created to explore or just to experience life as a normal person in one place and then to move on. In any case there are answers I must have, and I'm not going to find them here." Queeg looked prepared to argue, but then nodded his head in understanding.

"No, I suppose not. Be well, Kira."

"Be well, Queeg," she said, hugging him tightly. Queeg's face reddened somewhat and he stiffened with embarrassment.

Queeg watched Kira and the red-suited Charioteer walk through the rain to the red lobster-tailed spaceship. His fingers traced an idle heart-shaped pattern around her in the condensation on the window and then obliterated it with a sweep of his hand. The ship rose up, bending its strangely armored body segment by segment as it faced heavenward. Queeg held his breathe as it rippled into the darkening sky like a great kite, buffeted by the wind and rain.

Less Human Than Human
Brian Campbell

"FIEND!" the black-clad cultist cried.

An Avestite priest towered above me, ominously silhouetted by the leprous illumination of the planet's third moon. As I lay bleeding on the cold ground before him, the nozzle of his ancient flamegun held me at bay, threatening to unleash a punishing conflagration that would eradicate my sins as surely as it immolated my flesh.

My academic career had unquestionably taken a turn for the worse.

Trembling, I rose to my knees. The priest scornfully regarded my stained and torn white robes, immediately recognizing me as a scientist. The Avestites have always harbored contempt for men of erudition — men of my kind. Now their cult had descended on a remote section of Xylac to answer a call of distress... and pass judgment on the survivors.

Vainly, I contemplated some colloquy that might save me from the judgment of my interlocutor. Made captive only a few miles from the Xylac research colony, I submitted my fate to the inquisitor before me — the man who would be my judge, jury and, if necessary, executioner.

Kneeling, as if in penitence, I received his retribution. The butt of his pistol slammed into my forehead, driving me into merciful unconsciousness.

* * *

My name is Professor Lewis Theobaldus, and I have always knelt at the altar of science. For decades, I have been consumed by my work. Once I was an honored professor at the Academy Interatta, the greatest scholarly institution of the age — until academic politics relegated me to a position off-world. My quick tongue and harsh temper resulted in my immediate transfer to the relatively primitive research academy on Xylac, the fifth planet in the Madoc system.

The events of the past few days have led me even further astray. I must bear witness to my last experiment — a singular failure. Several men were killed, forcing me to flee the burning edifice of the Xylac Academy. Screaming in terror, I ran straight into the retribution of the Avestite Inquisition.

A cloaked figure in black found me bleeding in the forest. Moments later, he forced me into submission with his relic flamegun, and my unconscious form was thrown into a containment cell by cultists of the Avestite Church. Three days ago, I sat upright in the brig of their starship. There, I awaited my interrogation.

I had thought that my horror had ended; in truth, it had just begun. As I struggled to regain consciousness, the face of my abductor peered at me through a rectangular aperture in the cell door. Even now, I can still see my tormentor's face.

From the darkness of my prison, I scrutinized his features. His mouth was hidden behind a black strip of cloth singed by the soot of raging fires. His hooked nose extended beneath the mask, giving him a countenance both aristocratic and sinister. The black hood surrounding his face — a garment eerily reminiscent of the executioner's cowl — was there not only to shield his face from the gaze of others, but also to protect it from the heat of flame. Dark eyes blazed from the shadows beneath his cowl — the eyes of a fanatic who seemed to have little regard for scientific truth. Black was not the usual color for Avestite garb; I had fallen into the hands of the most extreme cabal within that order.

"Sinner," he proclaimed, "you must prepare yourself to give witness to the events of your transgressions. You are, I take it, Professor Theobaldus, once Dean of Golem Studies at the Academy Interatta?"

"I am," I professed.

"The self-same *scientist*," he continued, emphasizing the last word with considerable scorn, "who penned that atrocious tome of cybernetic technobabble known as the *Codex Cyberiad*?"

"Though I do not share your evaluation of my scholarly endeavors, I will answer in the affirmative."

"By the Creator, you *are* Professor Theobaldus! I'd recognize that tone of voice anywhere. No one else would compose such torturous statements."

"And I am surprised you have been receptive enough to read my works. Yes, I had ambitions of making my work somewhat more poetic, but I am not ashamed of the usefulness of the *Codex*. "

"Poetic!" he sardonically replied. "I should leave a copy of the Omega Gospels for you to read instead. Maybe you would learn something from them, or perhaps even realize how you will atone for your sin."

"Preposterous! I have no need to atone. You are here to interrogate me, are you not? To learn the origins of the horrors you witnessed in the hallways of the Xylac Academy? I will not hold back in describing the events of the last few days."

"Shocking!" he forcefully exclaimed. "A complete lack of contrition for your actions! Capturing you was more an act of mercy than punishment. Surely, you are mad."

"I tell you with the utmost certainty that *I am not mad*. I am a civilized man, and I have no regret for the experiments I have begun..."

Such shame! I had fallen prey to a common failing of those in my profession. He was clearly inviting me to lecture him on my work, luring me into a confident confession of my deeds. With those words, I began to relate the terrible events of the last few days....

* * *

The Statement of Professor Theobaldus

"I have no regret for the experiments I have begun. You may call me a madman or fool, but I make no apology for my career as a scientist. I have pursued the greatest goal imaginable — the resurrection of ancient cybernetic organisms. Through science, I have reanimated creatures who were never constrained by the limitations of the human race."

"*Blasphemy!*" whispered the Inquisitor.

"Yes! Blasphemy! Glorious, delicious blasphemy! Why should this surprise you? You would condemn the scientific triumphs of the Second Republic, but I consider them works of genius! The men of that age had the power to terraform entire worlds, bring the dying back from death's door, seek out the mysteries of ancient races — blasphemous, yet true! For countless years, I have studied the artificial life forms of their era. You superstitiously call them 'golems,' but I know them as cybernetic wonders!

"A scant five years ago, one of my archaeological expeditions retrieved three such creatures from a distant world. These Companions, as we called them, were originally beings more human than human — thinking, feeling, animate, sentient life coaxed from a matrix of silicon and synthflesh. I sought to take this crude matter, revive it, and possibly even improve upon it. There was but one obstacle to my Holy Grail: the resurrection of their fragile synthetic flesh.

"Our Academy sent expeditions throughout the Known Worlds to retrieve the lost knowledge of our progenitors. At every turn, your agents frustrated these designs. Flames had consigned the written records to oblivion. Degaussing guns had wiped clean much of the magnetically preserved data. The heat from the resulting conflagrations had destroyed their wisdom.

"Time had also ravaged the thousand-year-old 'think machines' of the Second Republic. The millennium after the fall of the Old Republic had taken its toll on all technology, including their computers and cybernetic 'golems.' Data undreamt of by men such as I had devolved into cryptic and corrupted esoterica. Precious knowledge had been lost."

"Knowledge man was not meant to know," responded the cultist.

"Ah, but we *were* meant to know it! Perhaps it was even part of your Pancreator's plan, hmmm? You tried to destroy it all, but you could not. And in our facility provided by the Academy Interatta — the research colony on Xylac — we pieced together enough fragments of lost knowledge to reconstruct the wisdom of the ancients.

"The knowledge I required to resurrect the dead machines was not contained in learned volumes of 'golem science,' as you call them. No, I had come upon a lost file referring to an even more startling discovery, another method of resolving my dilemma. The scientists of that age had begun work on *cybernetic reconstruction at the molecular level.* Nanotechnology, they called it. Microscopic devices that could alter the substance of matter itself!"

"Alchemical nonsense!" blurted the priest. "You do not even know how these demon-spawned horrors function..."

"We would... if enough of the records remained. I do know that nanotechnology was originally developed in hope of restoring human life. With a few simple commands, an army of these 'nanobots' could quickly and efficiently repair any damage to the human corpus. Repairing machines was even easier, and some varieties were specifically designed for that purpose. The science was in its infancy, yet still held remarkable promise.

"The discovery of that lost file was serendipitous, for a colleague of mine, Dr. Arbaghast, had recovered several vials of nanotech media on his last expedition. A few colonies of these microscopic organisms had survived their millennium of containment. They lay dormant, waiting to be reactivated. And my restored file showed how to reanimate them! With the data I recovered, I would resurrect the greatest medical discovery of the Second Republic!

"It was then that I was tempted by a darker revelation. The Companions we had recovered were silicon and electricity, obviously prone to the disintegrations of time. One thought consumed me: If this nanotechology could alter their molecular structure... could we not do more than merely repair their synthetic flesh? Could we, in fact, replace their crude matter with human flesh?

"If we placed these medical nanobites within the machinery of a Companion golem, I theorized, perhaps they would slowly replace the cybernetic analogs with living tissue! Creatures more human than human! Gods resurrected from centuries of torporous dreaming! Ha ha!"

The Avestite priest recoiled in fear. He took a full step backward, retreating into the shadows. At that point, I realized my exposition had sealed my damnation. There was no hope of escape at that point.

If I am to be damned, I thought, *let me be damned for the Truth.* Fervently, I continued to pace in my cell, expounding on the significance of this discovery.

"Yes, now you realize the origin of the horrors your men had witnessed on Annwvyn. In the solitude of my laboratory, I had failed to resurrect the Companion golems... but I could still reactivate the vial of medical nanobots! In exchange for my redeemed files, Arbaghast was willing to sacrifice one of his vials. That very night, I resolved to test my theorem. Reverently, I emptied an entire vial within the remnants of the most promising Companion.

"Consider the marvelous anticipation of that moment! Though my laboratory had been reduced to a deplorable state by lack of funding, I wore my scientist's robes with pride. No longer did I notice the paint peeling on the walls, the wan illumination of gaslight, or the dampness dripping from pipes in the walls. I had been redeemed as well, for now, a millennial-old cybernetic 'golem' stood before me on a dais of wood and metal. Shaking with eagerness, I sent a final charge of electricity through the organism, activating the nanotechnological machines within its shattered synthetic flesh!

"Like a hostile virus, the microscopic homunculi surged through the host body. As its synthflesh skin bubbled and distorted, the cybernetic organism collapsed to the floor. It appeared... dare I say it... feverish in its torment. The engines of resurrection surging within the corpus were no doubt overwhelmed by the disparity between the golem's synthetic flesh and that of a human being.

"My panicked shouting attracted the attention of Dr. Arbaghast — poor ill-fated Dr. Arbaghast. He rushed into the room and watched in paralyzed amazement. Together, we stood in the dampness of my laboratory and witnessed the amazing transformation. Under the gaslight of our primitive institution, the synthflesh of the cyborg surged with newly found life! The experiment was working!

"Scarcely able to contain my enthusiasm, I rushed to the next room to obtain some medium whereby I might record my progress. After triumphantly screaming 'Eureka!' down the hallways — an occurrence that periodically bolsters the courage of our scientific brethren — I seized a quill and a bottle of ink from an adjacent room. My cry, however, was answered by one far more sinister. It was the bloodcurdling scream of an organism not imbued with life, but robbed of it.

"Fearfully, I hurried back to my laboratory. There before me was the sight of a rapidly decomposing amalgam of physiological anomalies. It sprawled across the floor as the nanotech machines went insane trying to repair the horrid deconstruction. I gasped in horror, then bit deeply into my knuckles.

"Such madness! A horror of my own creation! I could hardly recognize the tortured creature writhing on the floor!

"The flesh of the abomination continued to surge and writhe, desperately trying to evolve from its corrupted state. In thirty seconds, I witnessed the *myriad possible paths of human evolution.* The nanobots desperately tried to salvage and improve the organism, but their programming had degraded over centuries into corrupted insanity!

"They had forgotten how to repair human flesh, instead forming fingers into claws... eyes into eyestalks... smooth flesh to rugose scales... sculpting sheer madness in a tangible form! Shaking in fear, I screamed with a forcefulness that would have raised the dead!

"Through the periphery of my vision, I noticed a shadowy form running out of the door behind me. Was it Dr. Arbaghast? Why was he clutching his hand and screaming? Had he been so unnerved by the transformation that he was forced to run shouting in terror through the hallways of the Xylac Academy?

"*Merciful Pancreator!* I thought, *He didn't* touch *it, did he?*

"Fortuitously, I had taken precautions unknown to the other scientists of the academy. In a glass case on the wall, I had secreted a fully charged relic blaster pistol. In this state of emergency, I smashed the case and retrieved the instrument of destruction.

"*Damn it all!* I thought, *it attacked Dr. Arbaghast!*

"Staring down at the genetic abomination that twitched in unspeakable torment on the floor, I sought to put down the monster I had summoned. Screaming in rage and fright, I unloaded several charges of the blaster pistol into the quivering, rugose bestial *thing* violently convulsing on the floor.

"The air was ionized by the blast. Almost instantly, a calm descended on the room. In its death throes, the grotesquerie rattled a singularly curious delusion with halting, gasping breaths...

"'You... fool...' the shambling horror exuded. 'I... am... infected...'

"I was too frightened to consider the import of this remark. To mercifully release the beast from its suffering, I discharged four more shots from the blaster pistol. The pustulent horror shivered, then spoke no more.

"Visibly shaken, I slowly walked back into the hallway. I had wanted to bring a lost creature back into the world, yet in my panic, I had utterly destroyed it. The vial of nanobots had been corrupted over the last millennium, altered like the computer files I had spent countless nights attempting to reconstruct. Once, they would have brought healing, but now, they produced only horror.

"Ashamed, I lowered my head and returned to the hallway to meet the sympathy of my colleagues. Alas! Another failed experiment. As I slowly turned, I saw another curious sight. Dr. Arbaghast stood shaking beside an intern of the Xylac Academy.

"Arbaghast clutched feverishly at his own face. In untold pain, he shivered and screamed! His skin pulsed like the synthflesh of the infected creature in the laboratory! His face bubbled with pustulent sores, the buboes of a nanotechnological plague!

"Emotion overwhelmed me. Tears ran down my face. The mockery of Arbaghast twitched uncontrollably in its torment, lunging at people in the hallway and pleading for succor. I had shared quiet dinners with my colleague many times, but I never thought I would see him rip an intern's ear from the side of his head with such fury.

"'Arbaghast!' I screamed. 'Merciful heavens, *stop eating that intern!*'" Consumed with rage, I once more discharged the blaster pistol. Unfortunately, I am more of a scientist than a marksman — I aimed at the infected, zombified *thing* that had set upon an unwitting innocent, but the full force of the blast shattered the body of the ill-fated intern. Arbaghast shouted imprecations and rushed through the hallway in a red haze of killing frenzy.

"The intern collapsed. The strain of nanotechnological virus instantly infected his flesh. Once more, a twitching, tortured infected body sought out an evolutionary path that would rescue it from the brink of annihilation. Yet in all these forms, it was unable to cope with the sudden burst of ionized energy from my electric pistol. I dared not watch the transmogrification... the surging tentacles... the yawning maw of chittering canine teeth... human flesh caught in myriad paths of evolution! Focusing my will, I averted my gaze and remained focused on the task at hand!

"I disregarded the violated body and chased the demon Arbaghast toward a stairwell. With preternatural speed, the madman vaulted up the stairs, easily avoiding my fusillade of blaster fire. I am old, I profess, and easily winded, so I could do little but watch him escape my field of vision.

"Of course, the scientists of our isolated academy were prepared for such eventualities. We had put certain safety precautions into place. Following these strictures, I ran to an office near the base of the stairs. 'You must charge up the radiophone!' I implored. 'Seal off the exits and sound the alarm! Another specimen is on the rampage!' Having fulfilled the extensive requirements of our security precautions, I rushed to the stairs, nursing the still-warm blaster in my hands.

"The maddened tattoo of a klaxon echoed throughout the building. The gaslights surged to full power. Illuminated by their hideous light, a grisly tableau of carnage awaited me on the second floor. Seven research assistants had been conversing in a hallway. Now rent human viscera coated the walls. The brains of seven scientists... so much blood and flesh... splattered against the crumbling paint of the hallway like the fingerpaints of a demented child!

"Arbaghast crawled out the window, coated in the blood of his colleagues. The genetic rampage in his system was beginning to subside, limiting itself to a few freakish distortions in his tortured face. Convulsing in pain, he began to crawl out of the window at the end of the hallway.

"'Dr. Arbaghast!' I shouted. 'Stop at once!'

"The murderous madman then turned and fixed me with his blazing glare. 'You fool...' replied the killer. 'Arbaghast is DEAD! BUT I... I LIVE!'

"And with that, the demonic assassin leapt from the window and lumbered into the night. I discharged the remaining blaster charges after him, but did little, save to ignite a few of the trees in the forest nearby.

"I have had hours to contemplate the events that followed. Of course, they showed my singular lack of composure. I remember screaming into the radiophone for help... the response of a nearby Avestite ship... gibbering over the intercom of the need for an immediate evacuation... wandering in the forest, foolishly trying to understand what had happened....

"But more than anything else, I remember the shivering, inhuman *thing* that I killed in my laboratory — the abomination whose very flesh quivered and altered in unspeakable ways under the ravages of nanotechnological plague. I recall the pitiless creature that absorbed seven or eight full blasts from my energy pistol.

"'I... am... infected...' it had said. No doubt, in many a nightmare, I will still recall those gasping words, for the thing on the floor was not the cybernetic golem, *but its first victim.*

"The truth is evident to me now. While I was out of the room, my colleague was infected by the virus and fell screaming to the floor. The cyborg, consumed by the overwhelming drive for survival and evolution, *assumed the countenance of its supposed creator, Dr. Arbaghast... replacing the man on the floor I killed mere moments later!*"

* * *

I sobbed in grief, collapsing to the metal floor of my prison.

My abductor gazed upon me with a curious mixture of understanding and relief. I had sealed my doom and now awaited his pronouncement. Already, I could visualize my corpse writhing in the cell, twitching from the punishing conflagration of an Avestite flamegun.

Rising to my knees, I looked up at the priest and bared my guilty soul. "I do not know where the monstrosity is hidden," I confessed, "but I do know that I killed Dr. Arbaghast and unleashed a horrible monster upon the world. Through the protean madness of its infection, the golem can assume a thousand forms. Nonetheless, the shambling berserker will never know its true origins, or why it was created. It can be killed, like any other beast, and your priests can resolve this quickly.

"Do your worst. Through my overwhelming guilt, I already suffer the tortures of the damned."

There was no pity in his eyes as I finished my tale. His blue eyes burned with the same cold fanaticism. Even the mask tightly wrapped across his aquiline nose and square jaw could not conceal his disdain. Carefully, I studied his features again, waiting for some pronouncement of utter doom.

I paused, reeling in a stupor of disbelief. The face in the doorway... it was not the one I had seen earlier. Those eyes... they bore a curious resemblance to... no, it couldn't be! *The Avestite's face had changed!*

Responding instantly to my show of alarm, my interrogator slammed the door's aperture shut and ran off. There was the sound of a scuffle... the distinctive echo of a flame gun's discharge in the corridor.... horrible screams and flickering lights... I passed out from the terror of that moment!

* * *

After several hours, I awoke from the blissful ignorance of unconsciousness. I immediately surveyed my surroundings. The door to my cell was unlocked, for there was no longer electrical power surging through the ship. Cautiously, I ventured forth into the corridor. The scene unveiled before me will be etched upon my memory forever. The ship was unoccupied, save for the dead bodies of five priests *burned by the conflagration of an Avestite flame gun.*

The records within the starship's "think machines," the laborious transcriptions on aged vellum, the carefully documented evidence the Inquisitors had assembled — all of it was gone. Some inhuman creature had slaughtered the inhabitants of the ship, leaving me alive to contemplate the horror of my misdoings.

But that, I fear, is not the most grotesque memory that springs to mind when I recall the fateful results of my forbidden enterprise. No, what unnerves me more than anything else is my remembrance of the face outside my cell, the visage of the *plague-ridden golem who had assumed the likeness of an Avestite priest.*

Now I realize what had occurred, why the final sight of that ghastly golem disturbed me so. Before my interrogation was complete, the monstrous creature had altered its appearance one last time. At the conclusion of the interview, the visage hidden beneath the Avestite's cowl *was my own face.*

My foolish pride has unleashed a thing that should not be. He is my reflection, one that will kill and kill again, for I have created a monster in my own image — a creature less human than human.

Steal Your Face

Chris Wiese

Missive to Bishop Villaro Cortiz:

The following is a complete copy of a scroll brought to my attention by one of the acolytes here at the monastery. According to her report, she found it while cataloging the items of one of our recently deceased brethren. I leave it to you to evaluate its validity and determine any further course of action related to the matter. As for my part, my only comment of relevance is a quote made long ago by one far wiser than myself:

It seems that disaster arrives, much like success, when preparedness and opportunity meet.
— The Forgotten Minstrel
Yours,
Deacon Thara Oolahet

I did not know Sidney Feldspreet very well when this whole affair began. I occasionally went over to the ramshackle tenement he called home, but admittedly, only when necessary. I feel, however, that I came to know him over the past year, and I must say that with his passing, I feel a certain sense of loss.

Although the opportunity never arose for me to ask him if he wished for me to commit his story to paper, I can only hope that he would look kindly upon me for doing so. As for why I have chosen to record for posterity such a strange and sad affair, I shall not deny that, at least in part, I do so to help me sort out a situation that is more than a little disconcerting. Furthermore, whether due to malady or age, it seems that the longer I tarry at the task, the less clearly I remember the details. Perhaps, if I place pen to paper, I can clarify the vague, troubling images that come to me now. Perhaps, once clear, they will torment my sleep no longer.

As I begin, I must say that much of Sid's story cannot be corroborated, for reasons that will soon become apparent. In any case, I have no intentions of releasing this document until after I have gone to the bosom of the Pancreator. Neither Sid's memory, nor my life, deserve the inquisitorial investigation such foolishness would bring.

Here, as best as I remember it, is Sid's story...

For nine years Sid worked for the Muster on the planet Malignatius. "Thinkman" the illiterates called him. "Fool" was his usual retort. Yes Sid often said such things, but never until the "fool" had left the premises. You see, Sidney Feldspreet was not known for his bravery or, for that matter, his looks. Perhaps he could best have been described as a twisted "tech geek" to whom no one in the Muster paid much attention, except when they needed their precious think machines brought back to life. Things had not always been this way. Once, before the accident, Sidney Feldspreet had been more outgoing, more full of life and less full of poison. This is not to say that Sid was ever truly a good man, but now, he very likely could not even recognize one, much less imitate such qualities.

Sid had one driving, gnawing focus to his life — money. When Sid thought about all the firebirds that poured through the scum-coated fingers of his slave-trading employers it made him want to retch. Much of this money was made possible because of Sid's talent with think machines. Because Sid was only an associate, a low-ranking guildsman, the Muster took a large portion of his earnings. This was a slight he never forgave.

In truth, Sid did enjoy tinkering with the arcane machines that came from who-knows-where. In the past, he was able to drown his greed in his work. But this grew more difficult with each passing day. If only the Muster oafs he sweated for would pay him decently, he would still be able to pretend to self worth. As it was, hours passed like weeks, as Sid hid away in his run-down tenement, working with wire and chip. Like the constant droning of bees, his thoughts ate away all other concerns until all that was left for him was seething hatred. Some say there is a reason why boiling pots are never lidded tightly...

Long ago the Muster established itself (albeit quietly) on Malignatius. The gulags here provided a bountiful harvest for slavers. Procuring certain important political prisoners from these locations is difficult but pays handsomely. One of the primary tools used by the Muster for carrying out such tasks is an item known as Moranas Hands. Nitobi Corp designed these rare and valuable gloves during the Second Republic for the express purpose of stealing of a person's fingerprints. Through the years Sid had worked on think machines for the Muster, he had heard stories of these incredible gloves but had never come close to seeing any. Now, he sat looking at a complete set of sourcerunes for making a pair of Moranas Hands gleaned from the storage of a Muster think machine belonging to Etelmar Droos, the "Bookman". Sid had just finished repairing it and was running diagnostics when the plans appeared.

"What to do?" Sid could not just give back this treasure... at least not without first making a copy. Hours passed like minutes as he worked to make a duplicate without leaving electronic prints of his theft. Sid was not worried that he would be caught immediately — oh no, the dimwitted Etelmar who used this think machine for specs was of little concern. He was worried about some other tech redeemer finding his access point sometime in the future and turning him in for unlawful thought access. "It is always best to be twice cautious." Sid muttered the phrase like a mantra as he worked.

The message on his wall squawker would not stop repeating itself in Sid's exhausted brain. "Thinkman, I expect my think machine to be ready by lunchtime today as agreed." For years, the well-heeled Etelmar had brought equipment in to be repaired. Never had he even so much as inquired as to Sid's health. Everything about the Bookman seemed to have a way of annoying Sid. Two things, however, were at the top of the list. The Thinkman couldn't decide which was worse: Etelmar's deep rich voice or his good looks, undeserved in a man fifteen years Sid's senior.

"There is no time for such distracting thoughts!" Sid angrily reminded himself. "Etelmar, or one of his insipid lackeys, will be back for this think machine in less than three hours."

Sweat poured off his scarred and broken nose and ran in trickles past his too-thin, surgically reassembled lips. Sid had to struggle to keep it from dripping into the works of the think machine. Between reconnects he ran nervous fingers through the fringe of greasy yellow strands behind his splayed ears. He had successfully removed the storage from the think machine, placed it in his own box and duped-down the sourcerunes. Now all that remained was finishing the reconnect. The whole process was extremely complicated but necessary to cover his tracks. If done precisely, it would keep the braincore of Etelmar's think machine from knowing that the sourcerunes had even been accessed, much less copied.

Unwashed and unrested for close to seventy hours, Sid worked frantically to reconnect the think machine's nervous system. Struggling to focus, he constantly checked his watch with watery blue eyes; eyes that barely held their color compared to the red web surrounding his pupils.

The door swung open and slammed into the rickety, paper-covered wall as Sid fastened the last outer lock.

"Well, Thinkman, is it ready?" Etelmar's voice practically oozed superiority.

"Oh, quite," was all that Sid could manage. How he despised the brainless buffoon.

"Good, then I'll take it and be on my way." Etelmar said as he strode up to Sid's worktable. At this point Sid's personal stench became more than noticeable. Etelmar shook his head in disbelief. "Good god man, must you insist on smelling worse than you look! Keep the change, I can't bear to wait for you to sort it."

As Etelmar slammed the door, Sid counted the firebirds and whispered, "Indeed, I shall have to do something about my condition, I think. And perhaps you dearest Etelmar can help." With that he put his head down on the sweat-stained table and promptly went to sleep.

Sid stood in swirling, gray mists, feeling cool and comforted. Tiny ridges of fog raced across his palms and fingertips in currents and eddies. Etelmar lay in the dark pool of mist at his feet. Sid could not see them, but he knew that the Bookman's dead hands still quivered — vacant, empty. Cool metal coins feathered across the hypersensitive prints still fresh on the Thinkman's hands. Sid felt the power of his new wealth and turned to stride into the glow of well-deserved reward. He was greeted with smiling faces all around. But they quickly melted into confusion, twisting into horror and hatred until every countenance was smashed just as his was in the oft-remembered explosion, crackling in his own personal flames.

Holding his arms over his head, pressing his tormented visage into the grimy desktop, Sid woke up. Shuddering, soaked, stinking and bone-weary in the darkness, he knew sleep was not worth another attempt.

He began digging in the dusty bins in his back room, looking for various hoarded bits and parts. The tiny window high above sent a bright and lovely morning beam through the ever-growing cloud of dust motes Sid scattered in his efforts. By the time the beam had covered half the room in its daily path, Sid had finished his task and was actually humming to himself in an off-key but obviously happy fashion. In fact, he was actually pleased with himself.

"You know, old fellow, you are positively the best packrat in the business," he said to himself with a smile. "Now that I've got all I need for the job here, I think I'll take the afternoon and actually get a bath. After that, a change of clothes and a bit of a walk; let work wait for the morning." With that he was off to reacquaint himself with his tub.

After a long and definitely needed bath Sid dressed and went to get his razor. Standing in front of his steam-coated mirror, Sid raised his hand and wiped away a portion of the wetness, and stood looking at half of his broken visage. Sensing the darkness welling up inside him and trying desperately to avoid it, Sid dropped the razor back into the rust-stained sink, turned his back on the still half-shrouded mirror, and left the tenement to walk in the afternoon sun.

"There has to be a way to make this work," Sid muttered to himself as he walked. "Plans like these can't have landed in my hands for no reason." He smiled as he caught the pun of his words. "How to use them given my... difficulties? That is the question." Sid continued to walk and keep his own counsel, unmindful of the gathering clouds until the rains were full upon him.

A weathered overhang in front of a closed-down diner offered the best shelter in easy distance. Here Sid figured to just sit and wait out the storm. Half of the windows along the porch had been boarded up and, unconsciously, Sid positioned himself there. His curiosity about the store's contents was not as strong as his desire to avoid reflection. Sid sat staring at the cracked pavement thinking of little and enjoying it.

Presently, Sid found himself looking into a puddle that had formed on the road just beyond his feet. He had not been conscious of it as it grew, but now that it was large enough to reflect his visage he could not stop staring into it. He could not leave it be until the puddle yielded up a clear view of his face. It was splattered with the ever-falling droplets, and he tormented himself with the attempt to bring the hated picture into focus. Finally, there was a brief pause in the deluge and the image crystallized. Shaking his lank hair in disgust, Sid shattered the image with his boot and stalked off into the lightning charged downpour.

"Why did I do that? Why did I make myself continue to look at it? Was it that it seemed worse when it was not clear? I have borne these torments so long, why now are they becoming unbearable just as opportunity is so close?" These questions occupied Sid on his way back home.

The next morning, Sid started organizing all the pieces he had found. About an hour into his task, the squawkbox interrupted him.

"I thought I might mention that I will be moving north to Craggenheld in two weeks." Etelmar's voice held it's usual lofty tones. "Craggenheld is a particularly remote outpost, near a particularly remote gulag, mind you. It is unlikely that they have a tech redeemer there, and I will need one. You are the one I thought of first."

Sid could not believe his ears. Somehow he managed to stammer out his acceptance. In a flash he realized that the opportunity he was waiting for had arrived.

Once he was sure Etelmar had turned off the squawkbox, Sid allowed the wicked plan in his heart to reach his lips. "Fingerprints will give me a new paper trail identity, but if I can find a way to use the tech to steal that great oaf's face, I could be free."

Knowing his proclivity for distraction, Sid constantly reminded himself of the goal and focused his attention on the task at hand. During the next two weeks he would have to do without sleep, but once it was done, if he succeeded, a life of luxury would be his.

Hour after hour, time drained away the frantic energy of the Thinkman at his table. Eating and sleeping became afterthoughts that occurred only when unpreventable. Twenty-hour stints were regular, and forty-hour-long stretches without rest were reached more than once toward the end. Sid could not be sure if he was dreaming of work or actually working. Wires and circuits melded with scars and blood. Visions of Etelmar's face superimposed over his own melded into schematic plans of a wintry gift that would change everything.

Slowly the synth-parka with built-in gloves took shape. Sid would later be unsure how it had been done, but his present for Etelmar was ready in time. He would get the opportunity to show his undying appreciation for the Bookman's "position." Sid's knew Etelmar would keep his perfect gift packed until the two of them were well away from these warmer climes.

The last night, even though he was exhausted, Sid slept fitfully. He would awaken, not knowing why, but feeling strangely unsure of his course of action. These rare twinges served only to aggravate him. By the time the sun was up, Sid had regained his composure. Etelmar came in the door of the tenement wearing the warmest smile Sid had ever seen on the man. It took Sid aback and several awkward minutes passed before he managed to speak. "I have something for you. Call it a token for your kind consideration of me for this position." The words felt strangely painful as they left his mouth. *Why did Etelmar's smile bother him so?*

Etelmar reached out and took the package and proceeded to look even friendlier, if that was possible. "Thank you, Thinkman. Whatever could it be?" With an attitude that was almost childlike the Bookman tore into the brown paper.

Seeing the shiny, synthsilk layered parka in the hands of his victim sent a chill creeping down Sid's back. It was not the sensation he had expected.

Then, to his horror, Sid watched as Etelmar started to put the parka on. Quickly he reached out to stop him. Almost too quickly.

Catching his breath, as Etelmar said, "Well I suppose that it can wait. It is a bit warm to try on such a thick parka just now. I hope you won't mind me waiting to wear this until we are in a more appropriate climate. I would have never expected such a gift. Thank you."

Why did he have to be so happy?

Sid numbly picked up his bag, not feeling the strap in his hand. Like an automaton he closed the door behind him. Etelmar would make the trip on horseback. Sid, however, could not ride a horse, and was therefore relegated to the supply cart for the journey. As they traveled through the forest, Sid could not stop thinking, "What have I done?"

Each morning, as they traveled along the northbound trail, Sid dreaded looking at Etelmar. Dreaded gazing into his face which daily appeared less haughty and more kind. Though it was not yet cold enough to warrant it, Sid found that he shivered frequently, even in the sun. By the end of the first week on the road, Sid could not escape the fact that he was starting to like his quarry. No longer did he seem so stupid; certainly Etelmar was slow in some ways, but far kinder than Sid had ever expected.

He finally reached a conclusion that had been coming for some time: "I must find a way to get that parka back," Sid thought intently, chewing his lip as he sat across the campfire from Etelmar. He could tell that the weather was definitely growing cooler. The problem was how to regain the gift without raising suspicion? He would have to figure things out soon; time was running out.

Sitting there by the fire, Sid found that he was on the verge of blurting out his dark plan when Etelmar suddenly arose and bid Sid a good night, striding off to his tent. Sid was left sitting by the fire with his mouth open to protest, but he never uttered a sound. Hours later, when Sid finally turned to his own smaller tent, he had made his decision. In the morning, he would retrieve the coat while Etelmar took his morning constitutional. He would run off into the woods. Hopefully, Etelmar would think something had happened to him. At this point it did not matter. Sid would find another target, and he promised himself that he would not become attached to this new "face" in such an uncomfortable manner.

Near morning, Sid found himself drowning in sepulchral moans of desperation. Buried in white light thick and cold, numb with fear, Sid screamed himself awake. The moaning did not stop, nor did the shivering numbness. As the fog of nightmare became freezing reality, Sid realized that the thing he had dreaded was upon them.

Ignoring the elements, Sid ripped open his tent and, in his sleepwear, fought through the frozen blast of snow toward Etelmar's tent. He would tell him now. He would not hide anything. Etelmar did not deserve his wrath. "Etelmar!" Sid screamed with a mouth freezing and shrouded in breath-ice. He could barely feel his face as he cried against the wind.

Suddenly, a light burst from Etelmar's tent. Sid was sure that he had made it in time. Etelmar had heard Sid screaming but could not tell what was wrong with the Thinkman. Quickly, he stepped out of his tent, just pausing long enough to zip up his treasured gift. Then all Etelmar knew was darkness and pain. He tried to scream, to breathe, to understand what was happening to him. His lungs raged to draw breath but there was no source.

For a moment the two just stood there, one in physical torment, the other in mental anguish. Colder within than without, Sid watched as Etelmar collapsed to his knees vainly clawing at the bonded face shield of his parka with hands that burned like fire. Something had gone terribly wrong and Sid knew it. The process should have been painless. Nothing should have happened physically to let Etelmar know of his theft.

Quickly he raced across the small expanse between them and tried to free Etelmar from the mask. Etelmar's thrashings made it difficult but Sid eventually uncovered Etelmar's face. At first, Sid could not see the source of the torment. Then, as if in slow motion, Etelmar rolled over, bringing his sealed-smooth eyes into the shaft of light pouring from his tent. Beneath their lashless lids his eyes rolled wildly, looking but not seeing. His jaw worked pitiably trying to rip open the sealed, mouthless face to let in even the smallest amount of life-giving breath. From his throat came muffled moans and muted screams that had no mouth to give them voice.

Etelmar's nose and ears were also closed over by thick new layers of skin. His head was like a hideous mannequin layered in raw, pink smoking flesh. Black veins writhed across the mutated skin. To Sid's horror the crawling veins seemed almost sentient. They acted as if they somehow knew that the air, so desperately needed, was near but unattainable.

Sid could do nothing but look on in horror as the strangled moans and thrashings grew feebler, more pitiful, and more helpless. Then, as the snowstorm sprinkled its last few flakes in dawn's first light, all was still.

Sid remained motionless, still in only his nightclothes. Numbness was all that was left to him. The medtechs might have had some other term for it, like shock, but guilt would have been equally appropriate. Originally, Sid had intended to kill Etelmar at some point after the transfer was accomplished, but that had all changed on the road. In truth, even the old Sid would not have brought such suffering on another person. Now he was grateful for the fine layer of glittering snow that covered the blank face of Etelmar, thankful that he did not have to see what he had stolen by way of trickery and cowardice.

It was not until the sun rose high enough to begin melting away the storm's shroud that Sid stirred. Even then it was with reluctance and only driven by his inability to look at the un-face of Etelmar. Slowly, almost mechanically, Sid searched through the travel gear to find the camp shovel. He then proceeded to wander around looking for a good place to dig a grave.

He found a site some distance from the tent in a small hollow where an area of ground had remained untouched by the snow. There, under an overhang of dirt and roots he began worrying at the ground with the small shovel and found that it would suit his purpose. Turning to fetch Etelmar, he noticed the earthen overhang above. The roots there almost seemed to reach for him, to drag him into that cold hard place, to bury his darkness away from the light. It was only a delusion. He turned and walked back to get Etelmar's cold corpse.

It soon snowed again, soft but constant. Sid resolved to stay in camp and use Etelmar's equipment. It was better quality after all. He could not bring himself, however, to put on the parka. In fact, looking at it made him feel nauseous. Besides, how could he be sure that it would not do something horrible to him instead of making the appropriate alterations? He spent the day burying his tent and all his personal items, not far from Etelmar's grave. Returning to camp, Sid noted that the snow completely hid all signs of his old tent position.

The next day, Sid kicked himself for burying the body in his own coat. He even briefly considered going back and digging up Etelmar to get it. Images of the faceless body soon halted that train of thought. He knew, however, that if he were going to make it through the night he would be forced to put on that accursed thing. Even so, he would not put on the gloves or zip up the face. No, he would not do that.

The following morning, he woke to the sound of voices, muffled across the snow covered hills. Carefully, he opened the flap of Etelmar's tent. *How could I have been so foolish as to stay here?* he cursed to himself. *When they find me, its over, no chance to run and no excuse.* He watched the two Muster hunters as they spotted the camp and turned directly toward him. *They will assume correctly that I have done in Etelmar. After that, it won't take long to torture the body's location out of me.*

Sid let the tent flap close and dropped from his crouch, flat on his back. The thought of what would happen when they saw Etelmar... they would very probably think he was one of those vile demon worshippers — an Antinomist. Death would not come quickly, or cleanly.

He could hear them coming closer. He could see only one option left to him. In desperation, he put on the gloves, waiting for the pain. He felt nothing. Maybe there was still a chance. Maybe they would not malfunction. No longer was he thinking about poor Etelmar, now he was only concerned with saving his own skin. Sid zipped the faceplate closed and white-hot pain hit him like lightning. Then, the Thinkman known as Sidney Feldspreet felt nothing at all.

* * *

Jesmond and Trieff had been sent to find the lost Bookman. A trip that would usually have taken only one short day by horse had taken two full days on foot. It had been a rough two days. In other places the Muster would have just sent in a couple of flitters to search, but not here. The dense trees and snow-fog made an "aerial" in these uplands far too difficult. The two hunters were starting to doubt the chances of their mission coming to a successful conclusion, when they spotted the camp.

"With any luck, the soft city boy won't have gone and died on us, Trieff." Jesmond's mood was already brightening.

"Dead or no, at least he's likely to be here, and even a body proves that we weren't out getting drunk, eh?" Trieff's logic was not lost on his partner. Neither man was in a great hurry as they made their way through the snowdrifts towards the camp.

Inside the tent they found Sid's unconscious body wrapped in a parka. When they removed the faceplate they were confronted with a pink and swollen face.

"Looks like a bit of exposure," Trieff said over his shoulder to Jesmond who was going through an I.D. kit he had found in one of the parka pockets.

"I.D. of Etelmar Droos. This is the fellow we were looking for." Jesmond walked back over and looked down at Sid/Etelmar and compared the pic on the I.D. "The picture is a match, although, he's going to want more than a little salve when he wakes up."

Trieff walked back out of the tent and looked around for a clearing that could hold a flitter. When he found one, he got on his squawker and requested a medium-sized air yacht. He knew that even if the Bookman was alive, he was definitely in need of something better than being dragged through the snow if he was going to make it. They would have to decide what to do with the horses and wagon. It would not be wise to add that much extra load to the yacht. Not long after that, two shots rang out through the icy trees.

Why the Bookman had been so foolish as to try the trek alone was a topic that helped fill the hour and a half the two hunters waited for the yacht to arrive. By the time it landed, Trieff and Jesmond had put it down to the stupidity of cityfolk. Within minutes they had Sid/Etelmar on board, along with his tent and supplies.

* * *

It was some time before Sid felt the soft gauzy realm of sleep slowly ease into barely wakeful senses. Senses blanketed and pillowed in fresh-smelling linen and down. Sid didn't know if he wanted to wake up. Finally, he cracked open an eye and gathered in the rich surroundings. It was the finest room he had ever seen. Deep blue velvet hangings surrounded the posts of the bed; beyond them were darkly polished hardwood walls. He slowly turned toward the window. Heavy layered curtains, barely parted, let light through so bright that it made his head hurt to look. Reaching up, he absently ran his hand through his hair, pushing thick locks out of his face.

Sid then spotted a washstand across the room. Stepping over to it, he washed the half-sleep out of his eyes. Still blinking, he reached for the towel, and looked in the mirror at his murder victim. He screamed.

In moments, a manservant named Furnier appeared at the door. "Are you alright sir?" The smallish fellow asked, looking around the room nervously. "Is there something I can do?"

"No, no, I'm fine, I thought that I saw a rat under the curtain there, but it was just a shadow." Sid's lie was very thin but the skittish little fellow looked quite pleased to hear that nothing was wrong. Satisfied that things remained for the most part as they should, Furnier nodded and quietly closed the door.

Sid dragged a chair in front of the mirror and sat there for many minutes in total disbelief. In every way he looked like the dead man. How the machine had worked so perfectly — even down to the hair on his head, now thick and black — he did not know. What he did know, was that he was not going to let this opportunity slip through his fingers.

Over the next few weeks, Sid managed to pass as Etelmar, by saying little and listening a lot. Everywhere he went Sid consciously worked at maintaining a semblance of Etelmar's deep rich voice. He also covered for himself by carrying on as if he was still suffering the effects of his exposure. As it turned out, very few people were interested in much more than his reports on financial accounts, and that information didn't require a great deal of personality. As far as the information itself, it had not taken the Thinkman long to interpret the Bookman's files sufficiently to deal with the basic reports.

The more detailed matters of the various budgets would not be due for several months. Sid felt sure that he would have them figured out by then.

Wandering through his new home— one that could hold a dozen of the tenement homes in which he used to live — Sid began to notice some of the details. Beautiful statuary, hanging curtains, floor to ceiling mirrors and beautiful furniture filed the house. Evidently, Etelmar had done quite well for himself. "I will make good use of it for you, don't you worry," Sid said to the mirror, as if Etelmar was there with him. Sid found it comforting to talk to his reflection.

Safe in his new and far nicer world, Sid turned to a project that he felt sure would make him very wealthy indeed. The original hardware Sid had put in the parka had fused into an unrecognizable mass of wires and circuits. It was probably a fortunate occurrence. If it had been intact, one of his rescuers might have figured out his crime. Each day after that, Sid went through the process of attempting to "discover" how to make a Moranas Mask. He repeated each procedure that he could remember, but something blocked the final equations needed to complete the system. Eventually, frustrated and in need of funds, Sid decided to work on the more basic model of the Hands themselves. They proved far less difficult to reproduce.

Within a short time, Sid arranged a small production facility. He let the Muster know of his intentions, and they were more than pleased to purchase all the Hands he could produce. Sid had expected the Muster would ask difficult questions of him; he was almost constantly worried about evading peoples' prying interests. With regard to the Muster at least, his worries were unfounded, and in actual fact, only seldom did a topic arise in his other interactions that he couldn't handle or easily avoid. On those rare occasions someone asked him a question he could not answer or evade, he would simply say he could not remember. Perhaps his associates put these lapses down to his exposure of months earlier, or perhaps they did not actually care as much as Sid thought they would. In any case, throughout those early months, nothing ever came of these "lapses."

Sid's star began to rise. The Muster leadership on Malignatius began to invite Sid to more parties. The firebirds poured into his account. He was soon making so much money he could scarcely believe it.

Through it all, he would stop to talk to Etelmar in the full-length mirrors that lined the great halls of his home. He felt that the dead man deserved to hear of their joint success. "Things are going better than expected, dear lost Etelmar. We have done far better than either of us would have alone, my friend."

His servants often wondered at their master talking so animatedly to himself. They found it quite unusual that he talked as if to someone else. This often led to much whispering, but only when old Furnier was not around. "Keep those foolish thoughts in your dust-filled heads and not on your lips!" he would say when he caught them in such gossip. After several such beratings, they kept their own counsel regarding their master's quirks, for none of them wished to risk losing their positions. Privately, old Furnier determined to watch Etelmar more closely. He, too, was concerned for the things he witnessed from behind the thick curtains of the mirrored hall.

The wealth Sid gained allowed him to socialize in ways he had never before considered. It was at one of the many parties he attended that he met Methlea, daughter of one of the directors of the nearby gulag. She was lovely to look at and just a bit shy. For his part, Sid was rather clumsy in his attempts. Perhaps his awkwardness is what made him attractive to her. In any case, they began to see each other from time to time.

Methlea felt from the start that there was something different about the man known as Etelmar. Perhaps she thought there was a truly good person under that stiff exterior. Perhaps it was something more. At dinner one night she got the courage to speak up.

"Etelmar, I just want you to know that I think there is something special about you," Methlea said with a small innocuous smile. She leaned close to him across the table, which always made him a bit nervous. He did not like it when people got too close to him in such well-lit surroundings.

She continued, "I'm certain there is so much more to you than the hard-working man I see." Sid began to shift nervously in his chair. *What did she know?* he thought so loudly he felt certain that his concern must show.

Then she said the words he had feared. "I know that underneath that tough exterior there is another person trying to get out. I would love to get to know the real you."

He almost knocked his chair over as he quickly excused himself, saying that he needed to retire to the facilities. *Was that a look of confusion on her face, or was it something else?* The quick glance over his shoulder as he crossed the room was not enough to be certain. *Has she found me out?* He would not risk another minute in the bright light with her no matter how sweet she seemed.

Once in the facilities, Sid went directly to the sink where he promptly threw up. Standing there shaking, he looked around and was glad that no one else was there to see him like this. *How could she know?* kept running through his brain. Perhaps she was just guessing, but he could not take chances.

He leaned over the sink and washed his face again with the cool water. Sid decided he would leave through the kitchen without seeing Methlea. He would, in fact, never see her again. As he was drying his face he felt something near the back of his ear. A knot, a slight imperfection? It was so small he could not be certain. Sid strained to look, but it was in a place that he could not see without the aid of a second mirror. Whatever it was, he did not remember feeling it before, and this, as much as Methlea's prying words, worried him.

After that Sid stopped going out. He spent a great deal of time trying to determine what the imperfection was, but maddeningly, could not see a thing. The whole process obsessed him. If he had not already developed a team to take care of the production of the Moranas Hands all work would have ceased. People just put the change down to eccentricity. Furnier watched appalled but silent for many nights as his master strained his neck in torturous ways, striving to see something that did not exist.

The old servant had managed on more than one occasion to take a close look at the "spot" that Sid so carefully covered when he thought that servants might be about. There was nothing to be seen except self-inflicted wounds. Finally, when he could come to no other easy explanation, Furnier put the activity down to some sort of ailment involving a pinched nerve. It was not an answer that totally satisfied, but the old servant decided that for now it would have to do.

Sid did not shave after that day in the restaurant. He ranted at the man in the mirror in a loud voice more and more often. Finally, Furnier — and every person within the manor for that matter — heard him scream insanely "You will not so easily escape!" Only Furnier, however, was in the mirrored hall to watch the event play out. Sid took a hammer and smashed every mirror in the room. With each one that gave before his soon blood-soaked fists, he roared things like, "Etelmar, if I cannot see you, you are not there!" and "I curse the day I first saw you!"

Sid could not avoid all contact with the outside world, but whenever possible, he did so by radio. On those occasions when he had to meet with someone face to face (usually a Muster superior), he always wore a hat, a scarf and dark sunglasses no matter the temperature or time of day.

At home, Sid constantly struggled with thoughts of decay and loss. His dreams became more than he could bear. Within weeks, the running of the business was entirely in the hands of his staff. Sid stayed at home with only the single old manservant, Furnier.

The old fellow did not like what had become of his employer, but he just could not bring himself to say or do anything about it. Both of them knew their place, and this allowed the situation to persist. Each day Furnier would bring Sid his food by candlelight. Gone was anything that could possibly cause a reflection. Those things that Furnier spotted that might agitate his master in this way, he quickly dispatched to the shed.

On several occasions, a young girl called trying to get in to see the master, but Sid's instructions had been quite clear. No visitors were to be allowed in, especially not the girl known as Methlea. After each attempt, Furnier could only shake his head in sadness. "She's a pretty thing, such a pity," he would say as he shuffled through the darkened halls.

Perhaps it was unfortunate for Sid that he had become such an important person. If the Muster had not deferred to him, perhaps things would have gone differently. As it was, the story that he concocted for his appearance, his dress and his lack of public presence was accepted. He told the Muster bosses that it was a result of his success with the Moranas Hands. The families of those people that had fingerprints stolen to benefit political prisoners had made him a target. The Muster leadership decided to give him temporary leave. They had an ample supply of the fingerprint-stealing gloves for now. As to Etelmar's condition, it was obvious that the stress of his position was wearing on him, and although he had not shown any real evidence that there were people after him, it was a possibility.

If he was correct and someone managed to get to him, the blame would fall too close for comfort. They were correct in their assumption that each worker in Etelmar's facility got only the smallest amount of information from the think machines that they used. If they did not receive the daily codes necessary for assembly, the work could not continue. As much as the Muster leadership desired to step in and take the lucrative business for itself, they were smart enough to recognize that Etelmar had been very careful to protect his manufacturing process. Without him to re-key the system every six weeks, production would collapse.

The final straw came when Sid saw the armed men standing near every exit of his home. He never considered that they might be guards placed for his protection. Instead, he flew into a panic. "Etelmar, my constant burden, it appears they have found me out!" he said as he raced frantically from window to window drawing the curtains back and dropping them closed again. "It seems likely that it was that wench who said something, but perhaps they don't have enough to do anything just yet." Sid's plans ran mixed with confusion in an already conflicted brain.

Then he hit upon a plan. He would call the treacherous Methlea and pretend interest. Certainly, he would be able to determine what she was up to. When the call went through, her father said that she had moved. The man sounded angry, and hung up after saying, "Methlea will not be forced to look upon your countenance ever again."

"What did that mean? What has happened to my beautiful plan?"

That evening sleep overtook him in spite of his best efforts. Furnier, out of pity, had spiked his tea with a bit of sleeping powder. The old fellow could not stand to look at his exhausted master as he was. "I hope that you will forgive me, sir," he said quietly as he watched Etelmar's shaggy head nodding upon his chest. "You just need a bit of rest. Perhaps it will help you come back to your old self," he muttered as he sat across the dark living room and fell asleep in front of the dying fire.

Something was wrong. Sid was in the fog again; that same fog that he had seen before. Etelmar was choking in the mists and Sid looked down, but this time things became muddled. Suddenly, it was he that was drowning, and Etelmar stood above him wearing Sid's old broken face. Etelmar was laughing at him while he suffocated.

Sid stood up from the couch. He was feeling groggy, but had no idea why. The fire's embers lent a hellish glow to everything around him. He felt like his face was burning. He had been through that once before, years ago. He would not let it happen again.

"Must find water," he said as he staggered toward the basement door. He did not think of the sink; all he could think about was the giant reservoir below the house. In a fit of delirium, he staggered down the narrow stone steps. The manservant had removed all the light bulbs long ago. The only light Sid had was the fusion torch Furnier kept by the door.

Sid staggered, still suffering from the effects of the sleeping powder. There was no water in the reservoir. Sid screamed out his anger at the walls. Spinning about, he saw the water pipes overhead. Sid saw the backpack and tools that had arrived with him long ago. The folding shovel was still there. That would do the job.

Sid set his light down on top of the reservoir wall and turned its beam upward toward the pipes. He reached into the backpack and pulled out the shovel. Swing after swing rang against the pipes overhead, each echoing in a triple ring that grew more and more like that hated name... Et-el-mar. Sweat poured through Sid's beard and soaked his shirt before the first spray of water even touched him. Oblivious to the damage he was doing, Sid kept hacking away.

With considerable effort, he managed to break through several of the pipes. His hold on reality fading, Sid continued to smash away, but now he was attacking anything he could see through the pressurized deluge. He lost his grip on the shovel and it flew across the room to land in water, now two feet deep.

Why did the echoes not stop repeating the name even after he had quit attacking the pipes?

Sid could not see where the shovel had landed and reached out to grab the fusion torch. He turned the light toward the water, and by some trick, the surface shone back at him like a mirror. It was the last thing that Sid ever saw. He screamed until his throat was raw and continued screaming until blood poured from his throat to gurgle in his mouth. Then, as the silence gathered, all that he was, was no longer.

* * *

So ends the tale of Sidney Feldspreet. I have written all that I can remember of his tale. I do not regret the nightmares and visions that have been a part of me since he passed. He was never a kind person. Now, however, in my winter years, as the memories fade from me, there is no doubt that I regret losing him and his knowledge. It is a valid axiom that life is life. All are diminished by the passing of one. The priests here at the Amalthean temple taught me that when I retired from the Muster. I can only hope that, when I pass, those who read this story take care in how it is disseminated.

In the hope of the Pancreator's grace,
Etelmar Droos

Blessed Protection

Andrew Greenberg

Diana flung herself to the ground, throwing her arms over her head as clods of dirt flew high into the air, ripped from the earth by shots from a dozen rifles. Bullets flew by her ears and she pulled herself even closer to the ground. At the first lull in slug gunfire, she twisted her body around, rolling as quickly as possible to the nearest clump of trees and bushes.

Still hugging the ground, Diana inhaled deeply and quietly, filling herself with peace as small arms fire rained down around her. Drawing on her years of Brother Battle training, she cleared her mind of anxiety, bringing in the Pancreator's grace with each breath while exhaling the sins of doubt and fear. Despite the havoc around her, she felt calmness descend on her like a warm blanket.

Renewed, she closed her eyes and listened for her attackers. Vril-Ya's forests provided both ample cover and unknown dangers, while its three tiny moons offered just enough light. Though ostensibly the go-between world for humans and the enigmatic Vau, humans were restricted to one small island — a different island than the one Diana was now on. Here the forests seemed almost primordial. Almost. She could not shake the feeling that each seemingly random growth of plants had been carefully planned and placed.

As one attacker drew close, Diana lashed out with her right leg, sweeping him off his feet. Her compact form concealed muscles of iron, and before he could hit the ground, she swung herself under him, quieting his fall and covering his mouth with her hand. Her other hand grabbed his opposite shoulder and she pulled hard with both hands. As soon as she heard his neck snap she released his body, grabbed his rifle and rolled to another clump of trees.

As far as she knew, she and these cultists were the only humans ever to set foot in these woods. That the Vau had not already interceded and driven them all off amazed her. Vau hostility to trespassers assumed near-biblical proportions, and Diana had made sure to have a priest absolve her of all sins before she sneaked out here.

She took the cultist's rifle in one callused hand and hurled it into a nearby clearing, where it landed with a loud clatter. As she heard footsteps converge on the clearing, she drew her flux sword. Five rapid strokes against a nearby tree cut through it, spraying red sap everywhere. Diana dove for safety as the twisted trunk plummeted to the ground. By the continuing screams she could tell that she had disabled at least two of her attackers, and she turned off her flux sword as she ran to a new place of safety.

She had tracked these cultists from Cadiz, where her superiors within the Brother Battle order had made them her responsibility. When she found she was too late to catch them on Cadiz, she used her contacts with the reptilian Hironem to track them and their leader, a former priest named Emanuel Stek, to Vril-Ya and then deposit her here. She thought she had landed unobserved on the island, but within minutes of touching ground she heard the heavy tromp of their boots. Then the chase began.

She stopped momentarily to drive a spike into a tree at throat level, attach an almost-imperceptible wire to it and a second spike, and drive that second spike into a tree directly across from the first. Seconds after resuming her silent stride she heard a muffled gasp and then two thuds as a body and a head hit the ground separately.

Her masters in the order told her little about these heretics. Of their heretical nature there could be no doubt. Her masters described them as Vau worshippers, and said they had stolen the gauntlets of St. Vnen from their resting place in a Brother Battle monastery on De Moley. St. Vnen, an ancient hero of the order, gained his fame as a missionary. His style remained the model for many in the order. Saving the soul often required destroying the vessel. Thus the command to hunt them down demanded urgency.

Diana slowly looped back around to where she had hung the wire, taking exquisite care to avoid making noise. She saw one of the cultists, a young man in well-worn breeches and rough shirt, leaning on his rifle and vomiting beside the decapitated body. She silently walked behind him, put the hilt of her flux sword behind his head, and activated the energy sword. As the body fell Diana caught it and gently lowered it to the ground.

Her Hironem contacts had confirmed the cultists' obsession with the Vau. "Obsessed with ancient ones they. Much hope to find true favor," one Hironem warrior told Diana. When they brought her to this island they warned her that the Vau might be watching. "Place of energy this. Unfocused, scattered, potent."

Diana picked up the cultist's rifle and quickly swung herself up the nearest tree. A quick scan of the area showed a half-dozen still up and running. She drew a bead on the nearest, squeezed the trigger, and was off to another swaying tree before the body could hit the ground. As she expected, the shot brought them converging on the tree she just left. She shot two more before dropping from the trees and hitting the ground. She rolled into a bush, scrambled to her feet and took off running once more.

Their interest in St. Vnen thus made sense. Just as the Prophet had visited the Vau millennia ago, so to had St. Vnen. Vnen, however, had returned, bring with him tales of wonder and artifacts of fabulous power. Most amazing of all were his fabled gauntlets, which he claimed the Prophet himself had blessed. With these odd shaped gloves on his hands, he battled innumerable pagans and nonbelievers before disease struck him down.

Thirty yards later Diana slowed and began listening for her foes. These three stayed together, travelling in a loose formation with one in front and the other two spread out but keeping within visual range of the first. While the others had fought like amateurs, these three seemed to know what they were doing. Instead of trying to pick them off one by one, she began looking for a good place to ambush the trio.

She finally found a suitable location near two hills. Its heavy growth ensured that her opponents would find bringing their guns to bear a difficult task, while her flux sword would slice through them and the surrounding growth with ease. If things became bad enough, she could either try to escape into the woods again or seek higher footing on one of the hills.

While she had not brought much armor for this mission, planning on using stealth and knavery to recover the artifacts, she had not come unprepared for battle. Her hands and feet were almost as deadly as her flux sword, and an imperceptible energy shield surrounded her body, ready to repel bullets and stop blades. These might not have carried the day if she had faced all the enemy at once, but Diana felt confident that they would prove adequate against three.

She leaned her stolen rifle against one of the alien trees and hid behind another several yards in front of it. For the first time since landing on the island Diana had a chance to survey its odd fauna. The trees bore some resemblance to those she was used to — green leaves, brown bark — but there the similarities ended. Some of the differences were obvious. The branches grew almost as if they had been sculpted, forming odd geometric shapes and patterns. Other differences took some time to become apparent. Only as the three cultists approached did Diana realize that the plants swayed to a non-existent breeze.

As the leading cultist slowly approached the rifle, the other two drew close to where Diana lay hidden. When they drew parallel to her, she erupted from the undergrowth, bring her flux sword up with her. It caught one cultist in the groin and quickly sliced up through his body, finally exiting between his throat and left shoulder. The cultist next to him swung about and managed to get one shot off before Diana was on him.

Diana's energy shield brightened as the slug came into contact with it. Diana did not even feel the impact, for it never touched her flesh. Its energy spent, the slug fell to the ground and Diana's sword hacked through the cultist's upraised rifle. Her back swing collided with his side as he tried to turn and run, sending him crashing into a purple bush. He shuddered and made as if to rise, but then collapsed and lay still as blood gushed from his wound.

Satisfied with the cut, though she had hoped to slice him in two, Diana turned to the final cultist. While the others wore old peasant clothes, this one had a green robe covering his upper body. High leather boots protected his feet. With her sword in the Raised to Heaven, Offered to Stars position, she advanced on him while yelling for him to lay down his pistol.

She couldn't see his face under the hood of his robe as he slid the revolver back into its holster, and she cursed him as he began advancing on her. "Hold your ground, apostate! Advance no farther."

The cultist ignored her commands, moving forward at a slow, regular pace. Diana, hoping to take him prisoner, gave him one last chance to surrender before deciding to kill him. Leaping forward, she swung into Divine Wind, Lightning Shaft, a swirling, powerful cut that spun her around and delivered a blow of incredible power to its victim. Diana hoped the blow would sever the cultist's head and send it flying against the side of the hill.

Instead the cultist raised his arms and caught her energy blade in one gloved hand. Diana's eyes widened in amazement as the plasma stream went out. Off balance, she fell to the ground. She landed on her hands and flipped herself into a squatting position. She again faced the cultist just in time to see his hand, wearing one of St. Vnen's green gauntlets, lash out. She heard her energy shield die with a sputtering hiss as he grabbed her by the throat and lifted her off the ground.

Holding her high over his head, the hood of his robe fell back, and Diana found herself staring into cold, inhuman eyes. The cultist's flattened face broke into a wide grin as he slammed Diana into a tree, and her short blond hair provided no cushioning. Diana lost consciousness while staring at the countenance of a Vau who was not a Vau.

She struggled her way back to awareness once, in time to see the cultist carry her into a small cylindrical building with bizarre alien scenes engraved on its walls. The cultist noticed her stirrings and bashed her head against one stone door, sending her back into oblivion.

When she woke again, several cultists were chaining her spread-eagle to a cold stone floor. Her captor had removed his robe to reveal garments similar to those Diana had seen on Vau travelers. In a calm, distant voice he ordered the cultists away from her and then knelt beside her, thin energy blade in his hand.

Even in the room's sparse light, Diana could now study his face better than she could before. Despite its many similarities to a Vau's, it still retained a distinctly human shape. Some of the cosmetic surgery was still fresh, and she could see where physicks had removed his nose and widened his brow.

"Would you think to use more of your tricks against me? They might have worked on Emanuel Stek. But I am far more than I once was," he sneered. He carefully sliced through Diana's padded shirt, leather belt and reinforced pants, peeling away the fabric as he cut through them. His fingers were unnaturally long and cold, and Diana involuntarily shrank back every time they grazed her now-revealed flesh. Once he sliced all her clothes to ribbons, he directed the cultists to pick up the remains and leave the room. Cupping Diana's face in one armored hand, he again grinned his unnatural grin at her.

"So Brother Battle, you hoped to recover these holy gloves — gloves your kind once stole. Your ancient saint killed for these, you know, killed the Vau mandarin Pakon Tu-Solca and took these from her sanctuary. Your Prophet would not have approved.

"Your Prophet joined the Vau, you know. Oh yes, your Church has worked hard to deny this, claiming he died on his last journey to the Vau. That is not true. He reached a level of perfection, you know, the first human to attain such a level of divine grace. As a result, the Vau let him become one of them, just as they will let me become one as well."

Stek's smile grew wider. "You know, you afford me a perfect vehicle with which to join them. I had hoped that returning these fabled gloves would be enough, but I can offer them you as well." He ran his energy blade along the length of Diana's nude body. "Tonight, when Vril-Ya's three moons are in alignment, I will offer these gauntlets back to the Vau. I will also offer them your soul." With that he rose to his feet and left the room.

Diana passed out again and had no idea how long it took to force herself back awake. She had to take herself through several of her order's pain reduction exercises before she could think clearly. After 30 minutes of this she felt strong enough to effect her escape. She pulled against the chains, only to discover them securely bolted to the floor. The soft light emanating from the ceiling revealed a room empty of anything except similar chains, also bolted to the floor. Thankfully, this was not the first time she had been in such a situation. With but a thought her right index fingertip slid open and a small pick protruded. She twisted her arm and wrist around until she felt it enter the keyhole. It took only a little more work for her to be rewarded with a light click. She pulled her hand free of the manacle and went to work on the other three.

Once free she crept to the door and listened. After a minute of silence she tried the triangular doorknob, and the door swung open. The hallway appeared empty, and Diana carefully put her ear against the closest door and listened. This time footsteps from the corridor forced her hand, and she turned the odd doorknob and bolted into the room.

This small chamber seemed both brighter and darker than the other rooms. The edges of the room felt dark, but as she stepped forward things appeared brighter. Carvings lined the walls, showing Vau in a variety of poses and actions. Fantastic statues filled the room, most representing creatures, animals and plants she had never seen before. At first she thought they were moving, but a closer look showed that they were immobile. Still, Diana could not shake the feeling that they were breathing and undulating.

In the center of the room a green circle danced and pulsed on the floor. At its heart lay a purple cushion, and on it rested St. Vnen's two gauntlets. Diana watched the green circle before daring to step over it. Its lines crept and crawled across the floor, weaving back and forth within what appeared to be a perfect circle. Diana carefully reached out and touched the circle, but other than an odd warmth, she felt nothing.

Trying her best not to touch any of the lines, Diana stepped over them and reached the pillow. She knelt down and lifted up the gauntlets, which almost seemed to jump into her hands. They felt warm and surprisingly light. Still kneeling, Diana offered up a prayer to the Pancreator and then donned the gloves, which fit as though designed for her alone. Immediately confidence flooded into her, and she leaped to her feet. As she purposefully strode toward the door, a voice, quiet and low, made her pause.

"Death," was all she heard, and she almost looked around for the voice before realizing that there had been no sound. Instead the word, and all it embodied, filled her head. A desire to feel death in her hands, to watch it work on other people, ran through her body. She shook herself and again made her way to the door. "Pain," seeped into her head, and Diana felt a physical need to hurt those who had wronged her. The pleasure of causing such agony worked its way through every part of her being.

As she reached for the doorknob, it turned. Diana backed up to avoid getting hit by the opening door. As soon as there was enough room, her hand exploded out in the Close Palm, Reach the Heart attack. She felt a satisfying crack as it connected with her opponent's windpipe. She followed up with Bend Knee, Turn the Page, and her bare foot drove the cultist out of the doorway.

A quick glance into the hallway revealed several cultists milling about, though most of them wore bandages and showed signs of recent wounds. Diana recognized them from her fight in the woods. They all appeared unarmed, and Diana threw herself into their midst with a vengeance. She felt strength and power explode out of her, and she made no effort to dodge the cultists' desperate attempts to grab her. As their hands seized her, wildly reaching for any part of her they could, she tore into them, sending them spinning this way and that.

At first her attacks embodied the pure form of Mantok, Brother Battle's holy ritual of combat and movement. One opponent fell to

Leap Forward, Embrace the Sun, while another collapsed when she Stretched Spine, Spoke the Word. Her attacks soon lost their grace, however, and Diana barely realized that she had picked up the last cultist and was slamming his skull repeatedly into the ceiling until there was nothing left of his head above the neck.

She threw his body into a corner and tried to wipe some of the blood and gore off her chest. "Revel," whispered the voice in her head, and she smiled ecstatically at the bodies lying around her. She confidently made her way down the corridor, wiping the gloves clean. She heard the briefest of noises behind her and swung around, assuming a defensive Raise Arms, Face to Evil stance.

She saw the door to the room she just left close. She charged through the dead bodies, ignoring the limbs giving way under her running feet, and turned the doorknob. The door failed to open, and Diana pushed at it. Feeling it beginning to give way, she slammed the area near the doorknob with the heal of her palm, and the door crashed open.

Inside Stek crouched within the green circle, his old robes replaced by shining ones of definite Vau creation. Diana stormed through the room toward him, knocking statues out of her way and sending them crashing to the floor. As she reached the cult leader, she realized he was actually praying to a small crystalline figure. Diana jerked him to his feet with one hand, and he screamed in fear. The urge to rend his body, to tear it limb from limb, overwhelmed her.

Holding the cult leader still with one hand, she used the other to pull on his arm. Stek's scream turned from one of fear to one of agony as she broke his shoulder. As she continued to rip at him, she slowly became aware of a shimmering filling the air within the green circle.

Stek noticed it as well, and despite his pain, managed a short laugh. "You're too late," he croaked. "He's coming. I've summoned one of Pakon's descendants. He'll deal with you." Diana threw the ex-priest into one of the room's corners, where he collapsed in a heap. Instead of assuming a defensive posture, a basic tenet of Mantok when facing an unknown foe, she prepared to charge forward.

The shimmering quickly coalesced into a Vau, and Diana leapt at him. Inches away from him she stopped, her way blocked by a green ball of energy forming all around her. It held her suspended in mid-air. She pushed it as hard as she could, and her hands slowly sank through it, and they were soon free of the globe. The Vau's black eyes widened and he reached out, plucking the gauntlets from Diana's hands. Immediately she felt the energy globe harden around her hands, trapping them.

The Vau ignored Diana and the gasping Stek, staring instead at the gauntlets. He reached into his robes and pulled out a small wand. He ran it over them and it changed colors repeatedly. Diana also thought she heard it give off a buzzing noise, one which changed in tone and intensity, but she could not be sure. Then the Vau raised his dark eyes, looked at her, and waved his wand about.

Diana suddenly became conscious of her appearance. Naked except for the blood and bits of the cultists she had killed, the enormity of what she had done struck her. Their remains covered her like a thick paint. She remembered stories of St. Vnen's ferocity, and whispered tales of how he tortured heretics and nonbelievers.

The Vau put his wand back into his robes and pulled out a small metal box. He pointed the box at Diana and the globe disappeared. Diana fell to the ground with a thud but immediately rolled into a squatting position from which she could spring forward or back, depending on what the Vau did.

The Vau did not move. Instead his lips began moving, and Diana heard his high-pitched voice wrestling with the Urthish words. "You ... are not what I ... expected." He looked around the room some more before his gaze came to rest on Stek. The cult leader lay moaning, barely aware of anything around him. The Vau made a brief noise which first confused Diana, but which she then interpreted as a laugh.

"He is what I expected. Word of his foolishness reached me. I did want to see it for myself. I think you might have ruined it." Diana looked and saw how her attack had demolished the careful cosmetic surgery. Stek's head seemed ragged and disjointed, and blood flowed from innumerable wounds. The Vau again turned to Diana. "You may leave now," he said.

Diana shook her head in surprise. "But ... the gauntlets? Don't you want revenge for our stealing them?" she asked.

"These?" the Vau asked, weighing the gauntlets in his hand. "Vau did not make them, and I do not care for them. They feel dirty," he said. Then he looked up. "No one ever stole these. They go where they will. I suspect they liked being in the heart of your cathedral."

"Are they ... possessed? Do demons infest them?" she asked.

"Demons?" he responded and then looked at the gauntlets. "Demons," he repeated. "Did you know that some in your ... order ... made these an object of veneration? They sensed that they were special, something more than other objects. They have an ... essence, as do any objects of such energy. Infested? That is not a term I would use, for it implies that something lives within these trinkets, when it is really the gauntlets themselves that exist."

The Vau moved his head in a circle. "I am not being clear for you." Then his lips raised in what looked like a smile. "But that is good," he said, tossing the gauntlets back to her. "Do with them as you will. Now, leave this place. Return to your people. Do not come back again." His hand reached inside his robes, his form shimmered, and he disappeared.

Diana held the gauntlets at arm's length, the blood still wet upon them. Studying them closely, she could almost see their alien form. While before they had fit her perfectly, now they seemed oddly shaped, with fingers of bizarre length and width. Their wrist covers appeared to swell and shrink, writhing and slithering in her grasp. She felt as though they were trying to reach up her arms, to latch onto her as they had before.

She felt doubt and worry creep through her. When she had worn the gloves she had felt neither of those. All she had felt was strong and assured, confident in her actions. Ignoring Stek, who still moaned in the corner, she turned and left the room, reentering the corridor where she had killed the remaining cultists. They could not stop her while she wore the gloves, nor could they escape her. All they could do was fall before her wrath. Diana shuddered at the memory of it.

Suddenly faint, she knelt among their bodies. Her hands twitched and she almost dropped the gauntlets. Clutching them tighter, she thought she heard the voice again, only fainter this time. "Power," it whispered. "Glory."

Diana knelt her head and prayed, beseeching the Pancreator, the Prophet and Saint Mantius, patron of Brother Battle, for guidance. All she heard was the whispering voice. "Fame," came the seductive buzz. "Dominion." Diana had seen pictures of St. Vnen's glorious march among the pagans. His many victories ensured his place in Brother Battle history, and more than a few in the order considered him their patron.

With sudden clarity, Diana saw St. Vnen, battling pagans on some lost world. She saw him tearing through a village, a sword in one hand and a limp body in the other. She saw him hurl the body through the wall of a hut while his sword slashed through its last defender. Then she saw him storm into the hovel, where the sick, elderly and weak huddled in fear. She tried to close her eyes to the sight of him entering that home, but could do nothing but cringe as he laid waste about him. She passed out when she saw his face and the look of righteous fury that lay across it.

When she woke, the gauntlets still lay by her side. She weakly crawled to one of the nearby bodies. She took its garments and wrapped the gauntlets in its shirt as tightly as she could. Then she made her way back to where Stek still lay, unable to move. He flinched as she came near him, and tried to force himself even further back in the corner. Using strips of the dead body's breeches, Diana carefully bandaged his many wounds. Then she picked him up and carried him out. Leaving the temple, she tried to shake the feeling of the Vau's dark eyes following her as she walked toward the shore.

Valukeydir: Shadows and Time

Rustin Quaide

Spring in Vestir was gray and dull, bringing cold rains, and the Ukar prisoner Glam, looking out of the jail, saw the roadway knee deep in red-clay mud. The six window bars glistened like dripping icicles, water droplets falling in slow, disordered patterns, merging and devouring each other, resembling ravished protozoa or rain on ink parchment. Beyond the bars and the mud the chained Ukar (a numb sensation and a skin rash about the clamp on his left leg) could make out the somber edges of tight, smoke hued houses and ashen tree trunks. Cold winds rattled skeletal branches, and the sweet song of a small unseen bird was crushed by dogs barking idiotically down distant streets, and the inane honking of Midian geese, flying from unseen seasons, scattering their mournful, dull cries to the dreary peasant towns below. *Welcome,* a voice whispered in his head between wind gusts, *to the Li Halan Worlds.*

While the rains poured down Glam tried to remember an Ukari childhood song ("One-legged Bwern Crawled to Tont"), or played in a sluggish manner with the heavy chain about his ankle. The damp air, pregnant with spores, produced a musty familiarity, and the rhythmic snoring of the prison guard, Borshka, induced a strangely soothing affect. It was hard to keep time, and Glam surrendered any attempt to mark the chronological divisions which separated darkness from light, time becoming an almost stoic, static thing, holding its breath in the present. In short, he reverted to the timeless, magical present sense of the Ukari and gave up the acquired habit of worrying and marking time the way his human comrades in the Scravers Guild did.

By day he listened to the rain streaming down cut stone gullies, swallowing thought in comforting musical gurgling, as if a musician's notes washed and bubbled against an invisible mountain, old and weatherworn. Then came a waterfall of ascending notes, carving paths on the periphery of sound, lightly mocking the ear's abilities with tiny, diminutive dancing, an elfin sigh destroyed in the soon descending down pour. Those moments, of the light rain singing, briefly lit Glam's mood, but were gone before a smile formed across the Ukar's sullen, downcast face, smashed in heavy torrents of hard rain.

By night, he dreamed, and in his dreams he battled with his ancestors in the mythic times, tooth and sword against the whispering gods and their Obun slaves. The great Ukari heroes were his companions, Thollo the first Nadakira, and invincible Shinris, and Shelkoro the Doomed, who first cursed the race with their shadows, the *ialtach*. Glam beheld great battles, and magnificent cities burned before his dreaming eyes, causing the waking world to seem even more dark and gray. Many-towered Thasfala he saw, and Lidwiant, and gleaming Tinoor'ar, the dream cities so ancient that many despaired that they ever existed, save in storytellers' fancies.

And in his dreams his shadow-self was his friend, tossing him his sword and helmet before the braying horns issued war, or saving him from the fire weapons of the Obun. Comrades they were, fighting alongside the great gods, the Sons of Rillos and One-Eyed Anikrunta, the God of Judgment, whose gouged eye he held above his head, seeing all things in the nine universes while the blood of retribution poured from the wounded socket. Glam tasted the dust kicked up by Anikrunta's gigantic, obsidian legs, when the god appeared in physical form, leading hordes of howling, blood-crazed warriors. And his Shadow urged them ever on, to glory and war unending.

By day, he felt himself the shadow, diminutive, lacking substance, halfheartedly trying to escape, until he would crawl onto his hay bed, where the lice waited, and curl up under his ancient army issue blanket, stamped with the insignia of the Li Halan. Across from his cell the other prisoners, Miho (caught housing a suspected Incarnate priest) and Edson (poaching on Church land) regarded him with superstitious fear, whispering that demons had tattooed his skin, as they did all Ukari.

Glamok nidi Tadwar (his full name) ignored them until he wanted something, and then played the part of the demon-worshipping alien to the hilt, mussing his long white hair and pointing accusingly, saying, "My grandfather on Aylon was a Taudwon who taught me the spells of summoning powerful, thirsty devils and blood-lapping ghosts." They would hand him a portion of their old bread or egg gruel, shaking, eyes downcast. Glam howled, stuffing his face.

Later he prayed, calling on the god of judgment, Anikrunta, to release him. Glam had constructed a crude alter from a lodestone and hay which he tied into a representational figure of the great god. Yet his prayers, while formal, were listless, drowned out by the rains. The heart had gone out of him.

When he was first brought into the Church prison, Glam was an oddity, and people from the town and closer farms came to look at him, crossing themselves with the jumpgate sign, whispering "Ukar Demon-seed," and "Unreflective alien!" Glam reacted vehemently, cursing their patriarch and saints until Borshka would club him, panicking and shaking, fearing for his position as Church jailer, and they would applaud, all idiot grins and "Palamedes be Praised!".

Later, as Borshka lost heart in pounding Glam's sides (a growing sympathy for the prisoner was evident by increased removals of his waste pail) and the routine grew dull, Glam would read fortunes for small tobacco sticks, or bless seeds for local farmers' ale. After three weeks people stopped coming, except for the occasional stranger and the children outside the window, pointing and running, and periodically throwing sharp rocks. Glam grew to respect Borshka's lackadaisical attitude (his grandfather was a jailer, his father was, and so was he), even rolling dice with him, telling him ribald jokes about Criticorum women. Edson, upon hearing Glam was a Scraver, opened up, telling him there was profit in the used tech trade, and began talking commissions. He was waiting for the family matriarch to settle things with the Church quietly, and had a foot in the door of the local parts guild. Edson was from that strange half-caste on Li Halan worlds, the almost nonexistent class of freemen, tilling the land rented from the nobles and Church, mostly poor but fiercely proud of their status.

Miho remained quiet. Her crime was the worse, and the Inquisition would interrogate her before the month was out. She faced possible death, and the presence of death was felt more by her silence, until it seemed that an invisible companion sat by her side, patiently waiting.

At night the wind howled through damp stones, and Glam dreamed that his Shadow was carrying him, injured and bleeding, from the fire arrows of Obun archers, through a city of deep pools, silent and contemplative. Jewels glistened like stars in the far deeps of the turquoise waters, and the stars responded, reflecting fiercely, demiurgic lights dancing to primitive pipe music, mournful and sad.

The music of the fountains reminded him of the primal tears of creation, and when Glam tossed a glance at their reflection in a long, rectangular pool he realized that he cast no reflection, but his trudging, burden-laden shadow did, more real in the dream world now as well, as both dreaming and waking became a fading for Glam. His *ialtach* was long kept in check, and he almost felt that he had placed it in sleep while working with his human guild comrades, except in dreams. Since his imprisonment on Vestir, his dreams grew with frantic intensity. Far off in the somber city, an infant cried and then the stars came crashing down, burning emeralds, causing the great pools to boil.

Borshka's stick tapped him near the kidneys (a sore spot, much bruised). "Wake up then, you got yourself company." In his dreams, the infant cry receded beneath a vanishing purple skyline.

And Glam opened his brown eyes onto the flushed robes of a bishop, looking gaunt and angrily at him behind widened, owlish eyes of sea-gray and a mane of unkempt, snow-white scarecrow hair. Three guards (rich livery causing them to appear like merrily painted puppets against a dark and forlorn wall) covered Glam from all sides with laser guns.

Instinctively grabbing for the piss pot, Glam deflected invisible blows until he heard the bishop's old, brittle voice exclaim, "Glamok nidi Tadwar, you know why you are in here. This is a Church town, on Church land, administered by the Church, so don't apply guild or Li Halan codes here."

"Yeah, I guessed that," Glam said, slowly rising. Why was the bishop addressing him? "Didn't know Li Halan and Church law were much different."

"There are authoritative locations. Vestir is a Church town. Your League friends sent word, but I won't release you yet. You remember your crime?"

Glam nodded. A young Church boy, an Obun, sprinkled vanilla scented leaves at the bishop's feet, clearing the musty air. Glam's eyes bore into the child's, and he retreated tentatively behind the bishop, grabbing onto the old man's robes with fierce strength in his small hands.

"Do not worry, child, he cannot harm you in my presence," the bishop said, and the Obun boy snuck enigmatic peaks at Glam from beyond the bishop's wiry frame. The two cousin races, separated by religion and time, with the old bishop between them, struck Glam as laughably symbolic, and a harsh chuckling shook his throat. You couldn't rub it in more, those who sided with humanity and became their pets, and those who fought them and became their prisoners.

At the sound of his laughter Borshka picked up his iron shock-stick, until the bishop motioned him to stop with a wagging of his index finger. Then he shot an intense, angered glance at Glam that froze the sarcasm bubbling in his throat.

"What do you think, Scraver Glam, that your punishment will be?"

"I thought the Church would just tie me to a whipping post before the town and crack hell on me," Glam said. "I heard you Li Halan bishops are tough."

"An apt response, but no, Ukar Glam, some of us make it to bishop without belonging to the royal family, through what St. Kao Tu called the Reflection of Merit. The world irks me with its variegated void. My name, Glam, is Bishop Mythius Mezenzikes. My bishopric is Zujan province. It is Sanyue, the Season of Rains, in the Year of the Yellow Serpent, an unhappy, churning time, according to the old astrologers. Now, tell me about the incident."

Glam nodded, trying to read the Church man's intent. Why would a bishop from the Universal Church of the Celestial Sun take a personal interest in the affairs of an off-world Ukar? He remembered once, on a hot and balmy day on Criticorum, the blessings of a bishop over the Fifth Dark Legion before they went into battle with Decados-led Stigmata Garrison forces. The Ukari forces were theoretically converted, and the soldiers accepted the blessings as powerful human magic to be added to the protective spells of their tribal and racial gods. When a high Church official asked Duke Hakim al-Malik why he employed so many Ukari in his armed forces, the duke answered that he didn't have any Ukari that he knew of in the military, but there were a peculiar number of armed albino Obun who signed up with his legions.

Honesty is the only thing that will work here, Glam decided. The bishop will discover it if I am lying. Something big is at stake, and he is testing me. Glam cleared his throat and began.

"I had completed a job with my Scraver team on Rampart, and we were told to wait two weeks on Midian for our next assignment. We were in Lyonesse Province — higher tech base, more accepting of off-worlders. Still, even there, I felt uncomfortable, and a woman leading a pig herd through town spat on me and then fled, shrieking. Entertain-

ment proved to be that awful drama the peasant's eat up, "Nobles Also
Weep," and everyone on the magic lanterns looks pale and ceremonial.
A week and I'm bored. Pao and I decide to see Zujan province, for the
local guild pageants they hold here on St. Maya's Eve. They told me not
to go. Lyonesse was dull, but I felt invisible eyes on me, on all of us,
reporting our movements. The off-world section was small, and the Li
Halan army would sweep into town at night, young boys with machine
guns, setting up road blocks. I saw a man shot for being drunk after
curfew, and one evening they came into a bar and beat the owner senseless, in front of us. I was afraid they might kill me on sight, but they
didn't notice me hiding behind the stacked chairs. Military training
doesn't desert you; it becomes habit."

Bishop Mezenzikes nodded, clearly knowing something about the
army sweeps, but saying nothing.

"I wanted peasant life, real life, like where I'm from. Well, you know
how it is. I get here and they start staring at you and pointing, and I
said, well, a drink inside will shake it off, and they cross themselves with
the jumpgate sign and mutter prayers to drive demons out. Pao gets me
drinking, where the old one-armed man, Waigong, serves rice-beer, and
I lose that watched feeling that gnaws at the base of my neck. We see the
parade outside — some village lady singing the miracles of St. Amalthea,
and the Butchers Guild performed the Temptation of Alyward Allmen.
Next, the Market Guild set up Zebulon and the Dragon — what a sight!
But you must have seen it, the clanking, fire breathing mechanical
monster. Now that's religion!" Abruptly Glam's voice broke off.

The bishop's exasperated glance rolled to the ceiling. "Please continue."

"We're drinking and getting ripped, cheering them on, and then...
then... the damned local Baker's Guild comes clanking down on their
mule-drawn cart, with the Martyrdom of St. Glam. St. Glam! I share his
name, though not his outlook. There they are, a bunch of groaning
idiots, painted to look like Ukari, torturing St. Glam. The tattoos are
wrong: no Ukari would recognize those clowns."

One of the guards coughed nervously, his eyes staring intently at
the floor. Another looked at the water patterns on the damp ceiling,
both men expecting a momentary reaction from the bishop. But Bishop
Mezenzikes' face grew flush red, and a strange, crackling sound escaped
his lips. He motioned Glam to continue.

Glam began, hesitantly. "St. Glam was slain when he tried to scare off some clans from an area he cursed so that his traitorous clan could grab the land — the Ukari didn't care shit what he preached! And here they have him yelling about dying for the Pancreator's Truth, which he prays reaches his 'unreflective, demon-haunted brethren.' What crap. I looked at those phoney painted Ukari with their rolling eyes and bad tattoos and spitting tongues and something snapped."

In the dim jail light, the bishop's face glowed red, and his frame began to shake, a thin wind-whacked tree.

"I ran out, over-turned their cart, and went for that phoney Glam's throat. Knocked him unconscious and began wailing on those half-dressed freaks mimicking my people, bloodying those fat bakers up good. The crowd's throwing food at me and then the constable begins beating me with a sticks. I grab it and bash the guy's mouth, but his friend, the one too 'fraid to get near me, strikes me with some electro-gun and my nerves freeze and I fall over, thinking the runt killed me. I woke up here."

Glam smiled, and then laughed exultantly. "It felt good," he whispered.

The guards stepped back during the tale, as Glam's presence engulfed the holding area, and Bishop Mezenzikes' eyes shot into the animated Ukar, who now visibly regained his spirit, crushed on that day nearly a month ago. Then Mezenzikes laid his ashen hand on Glam's shoulder, and a dry uncontrollable force rumbled from his throat, until barking laughter erupted. The guards froze, and the Obun boy jumped from behind the bishop's robes with a sudden fright.

Gasping for breath, his thin arms wailing like wind-tossed branches, Mezenzikes caught himself, clutching his heart. "You're... You're the real thing, aren't you? The real thing!" Uncontrollable laughter again erupted, with tears streaming down the old man's cheeks, until Borshka the jailer brought a tin cup of water for the bishop, who swallowed the offering in one gulp. Next he wiped his eyes with his sleeves, shaking his head in amused disbelief, attempting composure.

"And these buffoons in so much face paint and wigs, howling like fishwives at a mercy coin toss — oh, it kills me," Mezenzikes said, after a final swipe of his liquid eyes. "I've met your people, ministered to them, so I can imagine. Ah, that water, Glam, it hit the spot. You see, I am reminded of a similar incident. I ministered to these remote pagan

communities on Gwynneth, in my ill-spent youth, and they performed
a play about Zebulon, whom they interpreted, primitive fashion, as a
dying and reborn vegetative god. They got this toothless old man dressed
up, and were going to give him a young virgin girl to perform coitus
with, and it was pathetic, a child's game, and I broke up their pageant
with harsh words, until they bowed before Zebulon's representative and
I told them the truth. And that toothless old fake began cursing, because he was all hot and bothered about the girl, looking like one of
those ancient statues to phallus gods, holding his member and imploring the frightened child to embrace him..."

Bishop Mezenzikes laughed again and dried his eyes a final time.
"He went hobbling about, frantically, pleading with her like a horny
mime, eventually begging any of the women, from the oldest hag to the
girl's younger sisters, to minister to his slobbering lust. I ordered him
tossed in the river to cool off, but what a sight. Green leaves were falling
off his crooked crown, and he tore at his vine woven cape, scratching it
to pieces during his anguished moans."

After a distracting convulsion, where all eyes watched the bishop,
too frightened to act, he calmed down. Then, reaching at Glam's prison
garb, a quick diversion to save his dignity, he said "Let me read your
tattoos. You see, I also administered to Ukari on Istakhr in my youth."

Glam rolled up his shirt, trying to minimize the injustice of the
human touching him, reading his life script.

"Hmm, you come from a proud clan. Traditionalists, I'd say,"
Mezenzikes said, reading the upraised pale skin abrasions and intricate
body art, spiraling into ancient code and symbology. "You were a warrior."

"Fifth Dark Legion, attached to Duke Hakim's Command. Beat the
Decados Stigmata Garrison on Criticorum. Twice decorated. Made captain."

A grunt escaped one of the guards. Few Ukari rose that far in
human-controlled Ukari units.

"Family? It's been years. Here. Someone died, here." The bishop's
cold fingers traced a semi spiral around Glam's chest, over his heart.

"That's Symri, my wife, and my daughter Thorta, on the other clan
symbol. The death is my brother, Thardit, slain by fire from the Allied
Clans when they protested the League's attempt to mine Mount
Tenikiklun. Tenikiklun's a holy spot on Kordeth, where the gods sent

emissaries to my people. Over 3,000 deaths, and then our leader, the Nadakira, came, and placed himself in front of the League and traitor clan guns, and they backed down. I was garrisoned on Istakhr then, and word didn't reach me for six months, but I knew something had happened. Symri and I, we connected in our heads. One day, I remember, her song cried in my thought, and I knew. I knew my brother was dead. She's from an ancient clan, Nadont, like my own clan, more powerful before the human conquest. After the Emperor Wars, I kind of drifted. Decommissioned and weary of garrison duty, I found my way to the Scravers Guild, away from my people and their sad history, away from the traitors who reap the wealth of my race. I wanted to start over, and it's hard to settle once you get the taste of other worlds."

"An impressive record, and the Scravers think highly of your skills in artifact hunting," Bishop Mezenzikes said. "Do you know that when you were brought down, one of the town constables says you shot fire into his mind, injuring him? We frown on psionics, alien. What, Ukar, do you know of Zebulon and his mercies?"

A smile flickered across Glam's face, a sly and sophisticated smile, but it was immediately swallowed by the features of a lost and lonely soul. The bishop was testing him still, slowly probing.

"I read the Omega Gospels. I'll tell you honestly, bishop. He was the greatest Taudwon your people produced, and he has power. I benefited from his Epistle to the Warriors. But I think he has not died, nor have great Anikrunta or my gods. But his symbols are dead. Your priests have to breathe life in them, ignore the written word and summon his proud spirit, live in his actions! Ukari gods are alive, but sometimes I think you deaden the very words of Zebulon that should flower in the heart. That's not what you wanted to hear, but I'm tired of sly lies. As for the mind blast, well, we Ukari are blessed with psi, and it may have been my *Ialtach*, or shadow, blasting away. I have no memory of it."

"Yes, I have heard of the *ialtach*, the darkness all Ukari carry in their souls. As a young priest, I was attacked by one of your folk in the grip of the damned thing. Harmless old Zarsha suddenly pouncing and baying like an animal, ripping the Omega Gospels to pieces." Mezenzikes shook his head, reproaching an old memory.

Turning to the guards and other prisoners, the bishop remarked triumphantly in a loud voice, "This is a sign of their fallen state, barely reflective. No sly epistemologies or ecumenical theories of the Libre

Mysticus Thelogia can explain it better than St. C'Slew's warnings, that the Ukari willfully turned from the reflective lights and marched toward darkness, becoming more distant from the Reflective Light of the Pancreator. But there is hope. Your namesake, Glam, was one of Zebulon's priests, and there is still debate in Church circles about Ronga, if he qualifies as Pre-Reflective, like Muhammad, Sakamuni or Christos, whom Zebulon once served."

"Ronga was holy," Glam responded with some pride. "We still have holy priests, only we know it when they are alive. It doesn't take a committee to vote on your status when you're a dead man. Holy priests irritate people, they're supposed to. What did the old religions of Zebulon's day say while he lived? Apostate! False Priest!"

Mezenzikes frowned, and seized the Ukar's white hair, placing his face inches before the former warrior turned Scraver. Glam felt the dry breath strike him, the scent of parchments and old books. "I respect your honesty," Mezenzikes spat, and slapped him hard on the ears, until the world was ringing. "You are coming with me."

Later, one of the guards (Changshi) told him that in seven years of service, he had never seen the bishop laugh once. And older servant said that he had not found humor in anything within her memory. Glam was forgiven much by the ability of bringing mirth into the old man's life. Mezenzikes was called "Zhang Xiang," by his servants, an old term meaning "eldest brother." Later Glam heard that the bishop's hair had gone prematurely white, the results of surviving a devastating Hazat bombing raid during the Emperor Wars. His appearance, like his intentions, remained a mask. The staff knew to be kind to the odd alien, for the bishop trusted him. Glam did not know why.

For a week Glam lived in the bishop's quarters adjacent to the massive Cathedral of Celestial Light, a mammoth church constructed four hundred years ago in the Neo-Regency Gothic style. Eight towers overlooked Vestir from a fortified hill, and Glam gained a vantage sight over the wet streets full of peasant herdsmen and cattle. Within the fortified walls he saw octagonal gardens brimming with floral beauty, aesthetically placed to cover the grounds where priests walked and meditated. Glam worked in the Church stables, grooming the horses and feeding the Church livestock, carefully watched by the staff.

One day, three Church guards took him at laser point to a repair shop on the grounds, and a thin man surrounded by old think machines and electronic parts injected a minuscule tracer into his leg. They gave him fermented Vlanii and liquor to kill the pain, and Glam woke up in his quarters with no memory of how he got there, only a dull headache and the knowledge that now escape was impossible.

After a week, he was unexpectedly removed to a distant monastery, in the semi-arid mountains called the Shanlei, or Thunder Mountain, range, but referred to on the old maps as the Twerrid mountains. The journey by supply truck was long and bumpy, and guards made sure Glam did not look out of the truck's thick canvass sides to gain location. Glam guessed vaguely that they were moving over dirt roads in a southwesterly direction.

He was kept in St. Tanzo's Monastery, where Mezenzikes had a retreat. Thick, white adobe walls looked over high ground of cypress trees and cultivated vineyards down into dusty, semi-arid valleys of stunted oaks and long, dry grasses. The rain was less here then in Vestir, but the scent of the opening Midian flowers reached the monastery, signifying that the brief growing season had begun. St. Tanzo's was an octagon-shaped monastery, with towers, pitched roofs, and high vaults supported by massive piers and columns. Glam was housed in an empty cell down a long hall where faded frescoes of Church fathers greeted him with iconoclastic stares. He saw no sign of guards, but knew, instinctively, that they were out there.

The liturgical chanting, high and beautiful, woke him in the mornings, and he ate at table with the monastic brothers, but had little to do with them again until the night meal and prayers. A few approached him, shy Brother Mednik and Eskild, who cared for the animals, but on the whole he was left to his own devices. Bishop Mezenzikes was present some of the time, but remote, save for their nightly walks outside the monastery.

During the day Glam spoke with Brother Eskild about the animals and life native to the Zujan region, or read in the library what could be gleaned about Midian's geography. At night, for two weeks, Glam walked beneath the stars of Midian, looking at the strange, new constellations before him, a habit he picked up on his journeys. On a new world, get your bearing by the stars, a proverb he lived by. He received permission from Father Tushukan, the head chartophylax, and behind him on his walks, following, were two armed guards in Li Halan livery. Bishop Mezenzikes occasionally joined him, walking with hands clasped behind his back. They walked in silence, listening to the chirping of Midian crickets.

The dreams grew more vivid every night. His shadow appeared in rich garb, wearing the ceremonial armor of mythic days. Glam carried his sword, and his shadow occasionally whispered to him. "Glam, my Glam, they took your brother, but not me. I'm your last companion. Your guild cannot find you here, your clan is too distant. Sly Glam, I will soon carry you." Ahead dream rapids appeared, cascading over a mighty waterfall. "Give your strength to me, Glam," he said, weeping, and Glam embraced his Shadow, asking forgiveness, forgiveness for his swallowed pride, for a race beaten down, for roads of no hope, stretching across the generations.

"Ah, but there is hope, Glam," his Shadow replied. "Sink your survival thoughts into me, that the scarecrow bishop not find them out. The Obun boy is psychic, but not so trained to discover us. And our history, well, you know, Ukari history grows more glorious the more distant you go, leading from the ruined present backward along a long, bloodied road to glory, infinite glory in the past." And then beckoning with his hand, the Shadow pointed to the door of Glam's clan-home, beneath the earth on Kordeth, built from the fungus-like *galisp*. He could hear, faintly, Symri humming a soft tune. Glam's heart raced for his wife's presence. Reaching his hand toward her, the chimerical falls of dream swept him far away.

In the following days the monastery became the scene of much activity. Ships arrived, full of supplies, and Glam saw members of the Brother Battle order disembark and speak with the bishop. Strangely attired Zujan hill-men rode in, on thin and sweating horses, delivering messages. A Li Halan captain was present at the breakfast table one day, seated next to Mezenzikes. The guards about the monastery became more visible, and at night silhouettes of sharp shooters appeared on the rooftops. Glam knew the signs. There would be battle.

One night, during their walks, Glam looked deep into Mezenzikes' pale eyes, and when the large Midian crickets broke ranks in their loud singing, he asked, "What do you want me for?"

"Ah, the question," Bishop Mezenzikes said, smiling. "You think I shall answer why you are useful to me just now? You have no doubt surmised that a military campaign of some sort is coming. And yes, I have a mission selected for you." Mezenzikes grew silent, carefully choosing what he would say next. A large luminous moon moth flapped into his face, and he brushed it aside. The creature fluttered about them, flapping heavily pollinated wings, until Glam crushed it with a quick snatch of his hand.

"An Emperor sits on the throne of the Known Worlds, for the first time in five hundred years, and the tottering Regency days are over," Mezenzikes finally began. "You know, power and politics are a tricky thing, Glam. The Church, in her infallible wisdom, backed Alexius in his drive for the Imperial throne. But the Church needs to display her strength, to show the Emperor we have a stake in this New Empire of his. Glam, for reasons both moral and expedite, the Church, in seven days, is going to destroy a non-guild body-parts factory in Zujan, where they use slave labor. Many of the slaves are local people, peasants. Some are Ukari. That is where you come in, with your abilities. As a representative to your people."

The bishop wrestled with saying more, but decided against it, and held his arm out, motioning Glam to begin their walk back to the monastery.

"Glam," he said, "I am fond of you and your barely salvageable, scarce reflective soul, so I'll issue you a friendly warning. It is wise that you shall restrain from speaking about this conversation, ever, least you wish to incur Inquisition wrath — no idle threat; I have broken your kind before — and keep what transpires here quiet. Believe me, we'll know if the League hears of it. You will sign papers to this effect, over scented tea back at the monastery."

Glam nodded. Flecks of starlight pierced the oak limbs above them. Instinctively, he knew the bishop was lying. A deeper purpose than the military action held him here, but his companion hadn't chosen to reveal it.

That night he dreamed of Symri, in a purple tower he ascended, while his shadow played notes from an invisible flute, serenading the lovers. And his wife was real, her touch, scent, and voice, and she told him, between billowing crimson statues of Ukari heroes, before a silent pool where they made love, "The bishop wants to find Ukari secrets in the sand."

"We were here, you know, on Midian, before," she continued. "The rocks and trees remember us, when the Li Halan defied the worlds with barbaric splendor, and Ukari Taudwon and warriors found welcome in their court, in the days before they converted."

"How is it... how is it you are real? More real than a dream woman?" he asked, fighting back tears at their reunion.

"That, too, is Ukari power, long buried, bridging the gulf between desire, life, and death." And he held her close, while the flute's notes wrapped about them in dark melodious splendor.

Outside Glam's chamber, Mezenzikes heard him call out a name in the corrupted Uryani tongue. Shaking his head, mourning the dark theological linguistics the Ukari spoke, the bishop retired to the monastery library, where an open book on an oak table displayed colored plates of Midian flowers. Beyond, sagging in ghost-dust stacks, were the collected works of unremembered authors, Church works and encyclopedias, the occasional book of Obun poetry, and alone, in a corner, where a single beam from a solar lamp struck, rare pre-Diaspora works celebrating harvest reports and military campaigns ("Li's Lieutenants"). Mezenzikes preferred the heavy, musty scent of the library, and absently browsed from time to time, plucking a tale from Raynor's Book of Martyrs or abstract studies from rare scientific text books on saltwater conversion.

Mezenzikes's major intellectual and theological concern was the purity of language. He regarded language, or Pure Reflective Logos, as the sole criterion of morality, and appointed himself its supreme judge and knight, the sole crusader battling the forces of corruption, exemplified by the lazy writing styles so often found in official reports. Mezenzikes spoke seven tongues — including Uryani — fluently. He both enjoyed and derided Glam's speech, for the Ukar's directness was powerful, but his mother-tongue was beholden to a degenerative spiritual syntax, leading to darkness. Once, long ago, he wrote a report about the spiritual degeneration of the Ukari language. His thesis was that it was corrupt, but not unsalvageable. Enough Ur-Obun concepts from the Proto-Ur tongue left an infusion of Pre-Reflective concepts which were beautiful in the Ukari language, and saved it from complete blasphemy.

He shook his head sadly, contemplating these things, until he drew his attention back to the military action.

He unrolled some large maps, ancient satellite photos displaying the region his forces would attack. On the same day, he knew, the Exoneration of two other small slave factories producing enhanced organs would be attacked by Church forces on Tethys and Grail. These factories fell under the Church's ban on proscribed technology and the Inheritance of Universality, as well as the Doctrine of the Privilege of Martyrs. Theological arguments going back to Horace: 16:12 and Galaxia 5:8 in the Omega Gospels, spoken by the Prophet Zebulon himself, justified the Church's response.

It was hoped that these attacks would display Church power to the new Emperor, and shape policy regarding scientific and exploratory ventures, which so far the Emperor endorsed. Yet there was more, and Mezenzikes rose, holding a cup of warm naja tea in his hands.

His career would receive a boost, no doubt. The politics of his bishopric, the poor and querulous Zujan province, would fall to other hands, and he would rise (eventually) to archbishop. In Metropolitan Marcion Li Halan he found a sympathetic ally. But there was more. Below the grounds of the organ factory, high in the Twerrid hills, were curious labyrinths hiding Preadamite wonders.

They had been explored before, even stripped, by the ancient Li Halan, using Ukari searchers, but something persisted. The local serfs called the region "The Dreaming Hills," or *Shuijiao Shengyin,* and spoke of fantastic visions they saw in the region. There was something there, no doubt, an artifact created by the Ur-races, the Anunnaki, which Glam would find for him. Carefully, Mezenzikes read over the confessions and reports of the local serfs and traders, until the evidence was overwhelming. For three years he had withheld the information he had stumbled on in the recorded confessions of a local priest. Experience had taught him caution, and every organization had factions. He could not draw attention to the search, lest others snatch the artifact. No, the attack on the factory would be a cover, and during it the Ukar would slip into the underground passages, until he recovered the source of the visions.

The bishop had sent two searchers before: one came up empty and the other (an Obun, who should have known better) fell to his death down a subterranean gorge. It was possible that the artifact could mask itself, especially against an Obun's probes. One used what tools fell into one's hands.

The bishop sipped his tea, absently turning the pages of the botanical book before him. It was by pure blind luck that the Ukar ended up in a Church prison weeks before the planned attack. Briefly, he thanked the Pancreator for this miracle, this select treasure searcher, this barely salvageable Ukar. Before this, he had planned to send an old Penitent, Father Gusco, into the depths to perform this psi search. No matter. The recovery of the artifact would increase his reputation, and add to the Church power in the uncertain alliance with the Emperor she was yoked to.

Afterwards, the Ukar could go, back to his Scravers, after an Oath of Silence. Mezenzikes was fond of him in his way and would say the necessary prayers so that Glam could live a superior life, reflective of the Pancreator's graces.

What was it about the Ukar? In a world of servile followers Glam's honesty was refreshing. Mezenzikes even enjoyed the effect of being in the alien's company; it added to his reputation as the tamer of the savage Ukar.

A wave of expectation shot through his stomach, causing him to lie down. He fell onto a dust-covered red couch, and plummeted into deep sleep. In his dreams he was young, walking along the Sea of Galilee, on Old Urth, in pre-Diaspora times. His stomach gurgled and hurt. In a state of divinely morose joy he passed white garbed men, until he rested in the dust of an olive garden, beside the stones of Capernaum. The dry, cloudless blue sky of hungry eternity stretched from west to east, and the noon sun heat bore down. Mezenzikes was reminded of Zebulon's time as a priest in that old church, the pre-reflective one based on the words and deeds of the Christos. Christos was the son of God, Dio, or Dios, from the Greek Zeus, a pre-reflective name for and (partial) un-derstanding of the Pancreator's nature among humanity before Zebulon's Vision.

Presently he beheld a procession, and there was Glam, dressed in white, followed by a richly attired shadow, in Persian colors, rich rings hanging from large fingers. Behind them, a woman carried a bowl of water.

"Olesia!" he called out, recognizing her immediately. There, before him, walked the love of his younger days, who now opened emotions once stilled forever. The woman shook her dark hair, and raised her hand to her eyes, peering in his direction.

"Mythius, it is you?" she said, and rushed to him. Swift arms en-gulfed him, and he heard her crying. Glam turned around, looking, and his Shadow laughed.

"Only Glam can give her to you, for eternity," the harsh voice said. "Beware, bishop, the gods gave you a useful mind, but your plans are not omnipotent."

Glam turned, and displayed a coin with the head of Caesar, absently tossing it to the bishop. "We are getting closer to the source," the Ukar said. "Time is peeling back. Grab onto the Rabbi Christos' words here, because this is the last place of the One God before we enter the time of dreams and legends, when fractious gods ruled."

"Mythius, ignore the shade," Olesia called out. "Listen to Glam's words, really listen," she said, her soft cheek against his own. She had aged, but gracefully, strands of gray in her dark hair, but she displayed the same elfin beauty she possessed in her youth, when their hearts opened to each other. He felt her nails suddenly bite into his hand.

Mezenzikes woke with a start. The quiet books, once friendly, suddenly mocked him. He still felt Olesia's presence, as he had when, as a young man, he fell heedlessly in love with her in Torbrec, Zujan. For a season they loved and laughed, but he was not content to be married, to become a White Priest and languish in local duties. The Red Priesthood beckoned, and doors opened to authority, and on a starlit night he left Olesia in a field smelling of honeysuckle, never to return.

His work became his life: a pile of ecclesiastical papers needed proofing for signs of neo-Orthodox schismatic language; a roster of duties to be checked, questions pertaining to land rights in a border dispute with a neighboring noble. Seen by everyone as a rising master, there was no more faithful servant to work and duty than he. Hence, Bishop Mezenzikes enjoyed his solitude. Until now. The thought of Olesia troubled his dream, and the long latent seed of desire, one he thought forever buried, began shooting up from the black earth of his soul.

Far off, he heard a transport vehicle arrive, and voices carrying in the night, and he was comforted.

The next week was busy, and Glam saw little of the bishop. One night, he beheld the monastery's courtyard full of Li Halan troops, newly arrived, clumped in small groups, while a supply-man handed out weapons from a hastily set up supply tent. The liturgical chanting grew in length, and hymns to victory sung before the bishop. Glam retired to his cell, knowing the day was upon them. Presently, the Obun boy entered, and summoned him to meet the bishop before the monastery.

Walking into the cold night air, Glam saw the bishop conferring with a Brother Battle priest. Serious strings were being pulled, he thought, but kept silent.

"Ah, my Ukar. Come, come," Mezenzikes said, motioning him over. "You know, adept, Ukari are usually trouble, but I found a candidate worthy of reflective contemplation." Looking up, the adept grunted something unintelligible in return. Then, arm over Glam's shoulder, the bishop turned toward a dirt path.

"I have your Scraver equipment in a sack, which you will pick up when we return," he informed Glam. "We have a mission for you. Listen carefully: below the surface of the region, where the synth factory is set up, there are believed to be ancient Anunnaki artifacts, which cause dreams, and may be responsible for the placing of the illegal operation, powering it somehow. You are going in to recover that artifact. I provided maps for you to study."

"What about the Ukari slave labor?" Glam asked, feigning surprise at the sudden change of plans.

"That is on Tethys, and they will be freed," the bishop said. "Preliminary reports indicated some may be on Midian, but this is unconfirmed. We shall drop you off as the attack begins, with a small comm device. Ukari know labyrinths, but call at any sign of trouble. The local peasants believe there is something in the Dreaming Hills, as they call them, and I intend to recover it. Forfeit, and you are dead."

"All covet something excellent and thereby make it common," Glam said. "Once uniqueness loses its rarity, it becomes vulgar and is tossed aside."

The bishop looked long and hard at Glam. "This is no time to speak, and you surprise me, my friend, with your sudden erudite manner, referring to Anunnaki objects so."

"I was speaking of my service to you, unique at the onset," Glam said. "I have studied humans much, and read and learned wisdom from many sources, the proverbs of my people and the dry books of yours. Please reconsider. I am one of the best Scravers, my reputation is that good. But I was also a captain in the al-Malik Fifth Dark Legion, and am used to reconnaissance. Believe me, Bishop Mezenzikes, I can free the slave labor force before the factory foreman turns his ugly butt around. I'm not saying that your Church fighters aren't good, but Ukari are well trained for infiltration and rescue tactics. Give me two experienced Li Halan soldiers and minimal losses incur. What guarantees do I have from you?"

"This pays off your prison debt. After this is over you may return to the Scravers or your people, as your judgment sees fit. I have the papers here. But no, your task is to search for any alien artifacts. We've made arrangements with a Brother Battle company to secure the slaves. But remember, as the ancients said, all social order rests on the executioner. I am a realist enough to see that. Fail me, and the executioner sends your ghost fleeing to the unreflective ice-hells of the damned."

Glam sighed. "I will do my best," he said, his fine speech fleeing him like a wasted ghost. It was plain that little priority was given to the enslaved serfs. He felt now the bishop's Shadow, doing his work while the old man pretended to throw his passion and energy elsewhere. We are too much alike, he decided, Ukar and human, which is why they understood each other better then either did the philosophical Obun.

And the bishop was wrong. The clan kept society together; fear of shaming one's family and friends was a tighter social glue then the executioner's axe. An ousted clan member would often die of shame. Humans make power impersonal, Glam thought, so that it becomes abstract, like mathematics.

Glam spent the night in a troop carrier, packed in with armed men wearing Li Halan and Church battle insignia. Several near him crossed themselves. The priest made a blessing over him. From outside came the whirring of machinery, and the smell of burning fossil fuels and solar generators rotating. The men were armed with Martech Indigo laser rifles.

The Li Halan presence must sanction the Church's use of force, augmenting it with their own, but who knew where the boundaries were in that entangling alliance? Truth was, Glam was too tired to care. He was dressed in his Scraver uniform, with Church insignia sewn on. A tool bag waited at his feet, and he was armed with a short sword (the kraxi) and a Martech Gold laser pistol. He fell asleep listening to two men arguing over logistics and rations, yelling before the heavy sound of hoppers descending into the field beyond the monastery. The man next to him stared into the dim flickering lights illuminating the auxiliary power unit vents and inlets, sweating profusely, nervous about Glam's proximity.

In his dreams he awoke before a jade, jewel-encrusted throne, overlooking a city of bells. Upon the throne his Shadow sat, in kingly attire, a jeweled crown on his head. Beyond the arched windows, the blue shadows of late afternoon enveloped city walls and distant hills.

"Do you know where we are, Glam?" his Shadow said, running his fingers rhythmically over the throne's obsidian arm. Glam shook his head, rising, finding himself in the ancient outfit of a shaman-jester.

"We are in the throne room of Shelkoro the Doomed, the Ukar who bent time and unleashed the first Shadow among you, and the one who cursed your race. Do you know what this is?" he asked, taking the glittering circuit crown off his head. Intense light bathed the room from the crown, emitting from nine sacred jewels, turquoise, amber and blood-red in color.

"The Valukeydir!" Glam exclaimed. Its beauty was beyond the physical, and as he looked into the crown a ripple appeared in reality. There was a liquid, synesthetic quality about the piece, and he found he could smell and taste concepts like grief (bitter, smoky) and joy (morning air, fresh pollen) in its strange proximity. In the shadows, strange shapes danced with savage sensuality, terrifying and beautiful, beckoning him.

"Yes, Shelkoro's greatest achievement," the Shadow said, shifting the crown (and the corresponding shadow shapes) in his hand. "He crafted the crown from the dreams of the gods, some say from the pure, primal note of creation, which caused all to be. And he shaped that note, that pure vibration, into the crown of seasons and time, and forgot that it was a crown of dreams. For Shelkoro, upon unleashing the pure note of creation, purged all evil from his soul in the light and sound of that divine love. The evil that fled Shelkoro regrouped into his *ialtach*, his shadow, and his Shadow came back, to advise him. And he counseled Shelkoro to put parameters on his powerful crown, and give it a name, for once labeled, the unnamed parts would slip from Shelkoro's thoughts. And Shelkoro named it the Valukeydir, the Crown of Seasons and Time."

Rich hues danced about the room, reflections and shadows cast from the unsullied jewels. Glam looked deeply into it, and caught his reflection in an amber jewel, only he was with his wife and daughter, with his clan honoring him.

"You know what happened to Shelkoro and his crown?" the Shadow interrupted, forcing Glam to concentrate. He cast his eye from the jewel's hold, and the daydream was swallowed in the crown's fathomless depths.

"The Shadow became his advisor, and urged him to recreate time more to his liking," Glam said, remembering the ancestral tale from the *Noddavitya.* "Shelkoro became as a god, beloved of that spirit named Teku Arama, goddess of time's secrets. Both the goddess and the Shadow vied for Shelkoro's attention. They caused him to bring into being things that were, and almost were, and half-slumbering things that were not yet, or not to be. But the Shadow grew in power, until he urged Shelkoro to create a breech in the walls of Time, and things came in from the dark universes, long denied entry."

"Yes, the Shadow gets the blame, but a Shadow is attached to the deepest desires of the living, resonant being, only working on unfulfilled suggestion," his Shadow said in contemplation. "But yes, Glam, things did enter, old and forgotten, and the gods themselves rushed to heal the breech in the universe. And Shelkoro, realizing the error, cursed the Shadow, and his race, damning them, and then shattered the great Valukeydir, and the fires destroyed him, his Shadow, and clan Buddar and the land of Mada. For three years the unholy fires burnt in that place, a barren spot still on the lush Obun world. Shelkoro set the Shadows free among your people, closely binding us. And afterwards, the Sons of Rillos came to Mada, and gathered the fragments of the crown, to keep them from the lying gods of the Obun. They scattered the pieces on distant worlds, buried deep, a weapon beyond imagination."

Glam nodded, thinking about his race and their ancient glory. The war of the Ukari and Obun lasted generations, while their gods battled in the heavens. He never doubted the truth of that. Glam also never doubted that the Sons of Rillos removed the Ukari from the Obun world to the harsh planet of Kordeth, to toughen them further.

"Now this human bishop-shaman wants it," the Shadow said, shifting the crown with his fingers. "Doesn't that bother you, Glam?"

Glam didn't know. It was so far beyond him, but he suddenly felt a small shame. He always thought like human factions, like the Merchant League, or nobles or Church, but rarely in Ukari terms, such as clan power, which was limited and under human occupation. What if the Ukari regained the ancient Ur technology?

He looked about, and maidens entered with rich robes, and minstrels came to sing before the Valukeydir. The Shadow smiled, and then screamed, tossing the crown upon the floor, and it shattered in a bril-

liant explosion of color, emitting blue flames. The maidens and minstrels melted into green liquid, limbs and eyes and white hair dissolving
into watery, lumpy flesh, and the walls of the palace warped into grotesque, sinister shapes. Glam awoke with his Shadow's scream ringing in
his ears.

The hopper rose with the whirring of engines, and the Church
security forces braced themselves for battle. Landing lights disappeared
below, and cold air rushed between metal plates. The crackling of radio
read off the flight pattern, and one soldier nervously ran his hands over
his small replica of *Manjushri*, St. Mantius the Soldier's legendary sword.
"Ground hugger," someone cracked, and everyone laughed. The hopper
followed the ground in remote hill country, until after two hours it
dropped at the planned landing site. The Church soldiers rushed out,
silently, and began making for the northeast, to the site of the flesh
synth factories. Glam and the pilot remained, and the hopper took off.

They landed again in a region of harsh rippling hills and steep
cliffs, in the cave country of the Twerrid mountains. Glam picked up
his pack, and jumped off the transport. The pilot hailed him off, and
lifted straight into the blue sky. Making for the cave openings, Glam
tried to clear his head, to use his psi abilities. Jogging to a large opening,
he heard his radio crackle.

"Hello, Glam," came the static-altered voice of Bishop Mezenzikes.
"I trust you are making for the caves."

"Yes, just dropped off."

"Good. This is the area of greatest concentration of visions. Return
communication during the day, and don't think of running. We placed
that implant in your leg, capable of administrating a lethal shock, stopping cardiovascular activity. Do not think of betrayal."

"I've nowhere to run!" Glam shot back, and began cursing. Then,
realizing that the bishop (for a second time) was laughing, he quit in
disgust. The radio crackled off, and Glam felt mercifully alone. Following a small creek he came to a resurgence, where a cave opening pierced
the limestone laden hills.

Below the earth, Glam traveled with the aid of his fusion light,
although darkness did not bother him. He avoided stalagmites, observing a series of calcite ridges. Down a deep ravine his light caught the
remains of an Obun, the one Mezenzikes had sent. They had left his
body, and Glam uttered a few prayers to Sukara, the Keeper of the

Dead. We are both their captives, he thought, and a sudden sympathy developed for his cousin race. At any rate, no one will come for me either, if I fail. Then, with a final bow, he faced the darkness before him.

The cool air refreshed him, and he fought a momentary longing for his home beneath the surface of Kordeth. Glam's guess was that if the Anunnaki left anything here, it was deeper and not in the natural caverns, but in specially carved holding areas he had familiarized himself with in Scraver searches. Anunnaki ruins ran from the uniform to the symmetrically organic; their strange glyphs were mostly unreadable, but in some, a certain precise mathematical beauty displayed itself in the patterns they left behind. Glam halted, and began to concentrate, taking even breaths. If he could summon his psi and investigate the past of these caverns, he would have a clue. He muttered a prayer to aid his psi.

Looking at the stream, he concentrated. Glam felt the dark world begin to fade. Gradually, coruscating stars flashed from the stream, beckoning. Slight impressions of something — faint and ancient-moving upstream, darkened figures, he guessed them to be Ukari. Then his talent faded, and he heard the trickling of dark water against stone, and continued upstream.

The caves here were quieter than on his home world of Kordeth, and their darkness more comforting. It was honest, and did not conceal the traps of rival clans or subterranean beasts, ready to spring. Oh, there was life down here: he could hear the splashing of blind amphibians and knew some sort of insect had colonized these tunnels. But he was safe, and making good progress. The stream lead to a gorge, and Glam put on his climbing gear — rope and stakes, medical bag, flares, and a Ukari hand hammer.

Climbing slowly over wet, smooth rock (and twice losing his grip), he reached an upper chamber where the creek ran to the left, through measureless caverns. To the right a dry river bed lead into caverns of stately chambers, forests of stalactites and stalagmites. Glam followed this way, sensing something. Down small turns and through hidden entrances he crawled, finding a way where none existed. His pate beaded with sweat, and his body itched from small rock scrapes. Glam's eyes adjusted to the familiar darkness. Finally, twisting his torso through a tight crawlspace, he entered a large chamber.

His fusion torch caught something. There, on the wall, was a glyph, a symbol resembling four interlocking horns over two bars. These would correspond (almost) to a Ukari pictogram depicting sacred ground. Ukari and Obun languages were influenced, and perhaps descended, from Anunnaki languages and codes. Glam was on the right track.

Standing, he made out a chamber where nine monolithic stones were placed in equal distances, forming a nine-sided interlaced pattern with a pillar in the center the color of midnight glass. The chamber's ceiling vaulted into darkness. This had to be it, Glam knew. His light traced the pattern over and over, committing it to memory. He looked over the cave walls (cut uniform) for any glyphs or symbols. There were none, save for the first pictogram, but a fine black dust had settled like snow everywhere. Glam took a step into the interlacement. Some dust, stirred by his feet, began to swirl and shape itself, forming into a spinning wind, whipping about the stones, until it settled. As he breathed, he breathed in eons, each intake of air pregnant with mythology and the rich pageantry of his imagination.

"Glam," said a familiar voice, breaking ages in its soft tones.

Symri stood, in her night-robe, looking tired and sullen the way she did when she awoke from sleep to prepare the clan meal. Her white hair was wild, falling in every direction, a tangled forest, and her old robe with its tears and patches sent an ache in his heart, and he remembered her early risings in the dawn of their love. He imagined his daughter crying from a distant room, and found himself unable to speak.

"Glam," she repeated, fixing her eyes upon her husband.

"Symri," he whispered, moving forward, and they embraced. "How's Thorta?"

Her small form became lost in him, her head sunken in his chest, her grip hot and strong. "She asks about you all the time. Her arm was twisted playing with the older children, so we set it, and sent for the healer. She's all right. I miss you so much. It's hard, Glam..."

"I know," he whispered, feeling suddenly ashamed and stupid for being in an occupation which took him so far away from clan and wife.

"Your brother's children are almost too much. I had to punish Krell for misbehaving."

"When he's old enough, I'll see if there's an opening with my guild, to discipline him." Glam sighed.

She heard him. Glam's voice fell into melancholy tones, even when he was trying to keep his courage up. He slowly raised his eyes to meet hers. Symri released herself, and began walking on the glassy, crystallized surface, whispering to herself.

"It's late," she said.

"I... I don't know."

"Listen, Glam, you are in danger. I've seen you in dreams, heard your wild *ialtach* whispering to you. And I know you, you take refuge from your instincts when you work around humans. Don't. I asked Vorpu the Taudwon, and made a pilgrimage to the Nadakira, to give you guidance."

"The Nadakira!" Glam smiled, proud of his wife and regarding her with wonder. The high priest-emperor of their people, in remote Dwestdront.

"Yes," she said coolly. "This is what he said, after drinking from the holy waters. The Valukeydir has power over our desires, Glam. In that sense, I am here, because you want me. But our deeper desires, our *ialtachs*, grow in proximity to it. It will try to kill you, Glam."

Glam wondered what she would say next. Symri grew in reverence in his eyes, which her glance pleaded shelter from. Symri fought her tears, trembling.

"You must name it, Glam. That's what the Nadakira said, reading my finger tips while the incense globes were lit. Name it, and it will awaken to realization."

"What realization?" Glam shouted, but his wife turned with the grace of a descending butterfly in a shaft of light. He reached out, touching her finger tips, then gripping her hands hard. His heart thundered against his chest, and he caught her intense gaze, which said so many things. Then she was gone.

If she had ever been there. Dust particles danced in half-light, and he felt sick and sad, pondering if his desire summoned her here, or their strong bond. She wove her way through the night's howling alleys, through the dark paths between the small suns, to him, on this distant world.

Glam approached the central stone. A small gleaming star lay on its smooth surface, a fragment of the fragment of the Valukeydir. With each step, reality wove into new dreams and desires, and he felt his people's harsh history brush by, yelling and shouting in warrior oaths. Then, looking around the room, he beheld beautiful statues, sacred guardians of the place. Interlocking symbols unveiled before him, revealing a high culture in her prime, with robed ancestral Ukari laughing and singing. They were darker, still tattooed, but not pale; their lives were lived in the open sunlight on Velisamil, the Obun-Ukari homeworld. The language was older, more pure, but Glam understood it, although words reached him from far distances, like sound traveling underwater.

The small fragment glittered before him. It resembled a ruby at first, with an inner green fire. Glam removed it, placing it in his hand.

"See, Glam, your eye, gold-streaking through the myriad fragments," a voice said, and there was his Shadow, attired in traditional Ukari robes, but looking real, a physical presence, a darker version of himself.

"Yes," Glam said. "I'm dreaming this hall, and our people, and you."

"So this is Shelkoro's work," a high clan leader said, and looked at the fragment Glam held up. "He destroyed his clan with it, cursing them, and now our lot is harder because of it. And this sliver looks like beryl." A song of infinite sadness played on the musicians pipes, holy and sorrowful, permeating the air. Two women began singing then, of the loss of men and lands, and the trials of Shinris, their greatest hero.

Little things nibbled at Glam's mind. The rich detail of the tapestries, and the artistic gold straps on the sandals the ancients wore, and the creases in a servant girl's frown, or the rich hair which fell in ringlets from her head; these were too intricate for his imagination. Looking into the fragment, Glam beheld worlds and the vaporous reality of dreams, each interlocking, each a note apart in profundity. Turning the Valukeydir fragment he saw civilizations, robust and strong, reaching their noon and then descending into decadent splendor. The gods displayed themselves in sparkling signs, there the great judge Anikrunta holding his eye up before creation, and here the songs of the Sons of Rillos preparing for war.

Older murmuring from forgotten gods and goddesses whispered secrets through the jewel, and ancestral voices reached Glam from far plutonian shores. He beheld the decline of his race under the human conquerors, which left him feeling an orphan before a rich, tantalizing tapestry. Was he a slave and a tool, leading his Shadow here? Briefly he projected his hidden desires onto the sliver of changing hues. The Old Gods were called back, and the terrified humans and Obun paid tribute to a strong Ukari Empire. In space, great fleets gathered for war, to wrestle with the ancient Vau for rulership of the stars. And Glam laughed, intoxicated, because his Shadow and the court and his vision, the musicians and vibrating colors, were all part of his desire. In a blink of an eye, he wished them away.

He was back in the dark chamber, holding the jewel fragment. The dust danced where the throng had been. Solitude and the comforting familiarity of caves replaced the dream ancestors. His Shadow, however, remained, dark even against the chamber's stygian blackness. It reached out, and grabbed his arm, smiling.

Strong fingers squeezed on his wrist, attempting to pry the crimson splinter. Glam felt the un-space of the Shadow's presence, knowing it was a prelude, and that the struggle must end. The night-darkness grew about them, and only their shuffling footsteps made a sound, as counter-clockwise they warily circled each other. Glam broke free of the dark clutch with a swift jerk of his arm.

At first his shadow moved shapelessly, scarcely recognizable, until their eyes battled, and Glam beheld himself. With a sudden rush of horror he kicked the *ialtach* in the stomach, and heard the Shadow gasp and fall, stirring dust in his nostrils. Then Glam let loose with a psi attack, pushing waves of pain into his double's synaptic receptors, crippling him with an invisible blow. Glam ritually prepared himself for the kill, holding his gun at arms' length, pointed at his fallen rival.

The strangeness before him shielded itself, and then said something unintelligible, uttered by an unfamiliar voice.

"What?" Glam yelled, clutching his gun, and kicking the fallen shape before him.

"Don't," came the pleading voice.

"Get up," Glam ordered, and the Shadow replied, dragging his legs upward, coughing dirt.

"What are you going to do with it?" his doppelganger asked, moving a distance, dancing with wide circular leg motions counter clockwise from Glam's position, regaining strength.

Silence. Glam readied his weapon, tired of discord.

"Give it to the bishop, so the human priests can rule?" the mocking voice asked. "Think! It could be Ukari, our weapon against the jailers. We have a chance here to reclaim our broken people. What would the bishop use it for? Relight their fading suns? Our gods are the gods of darkness, Glam, who shall roll in like ocean waves over the small embers of their stars, and rule forever. Light is bound by time, but the ancient darkness is eternal. Ah, ruin, ruin shall wash over them, obliterating their names and deeds from the memory of the universe. Do you want to save their dying suns, when the Valukeydir is a sign that Anikrunta and his servants shall rule again? Why not devour their world of hypocritical priests and lying nobles in a banquet of ruin and fire?"

Again, silence. The chamber engulfed them, and the shadows from the fusion torch cast fleeing images on the walls. Glam didn't care for saving humanity, only in staying alive, but a small portion of his thought cheered his *ialtach* on.

Then, swift as a cat, the Shadow leapt upon him, and the gun went off. Resounding echoes followed, ghost wailing vanishing to a fixed point beyond the chamber. Impacted by the weight, Glam went down. They rolled in the dirt, clawing and punching, until Glam released his kraxi dagger, and slashed the doppelganger's face below the left eye to the mouth's right corner, and red blood fell onto the ground. Crushing its neck with the other hand, Glam slashed again, and the shadow screamed in his voice, and the echoes created a symphony of pain, howling into the further caverns and corridors of the night cave-world.

"I'm cutting myself," Glam said, and stood up, disengaging. His gaze burned into the bleeding shape below him, disgusted. With dawning realization, Glam spoke. "You don't think I wonder, as every Ukari does, what it would be like if we won the war with the humans? If we ruled? You want to call back the proud gods of blood and shadows, and recreate the old world, before the great spirits removed us from Velisamil. You are an idiot and a dreamer. Something will change, if we call them back, but it won't be the past. You can't recreate what once was," Glam breathed, panting between words, moving his kraxi's thin tip over his Shadow's face down toward the neck, drawing blood.

Then, an inch from cutting into the neck veins, Glam's eyes lit, illuminated with sudden knowledge. "I name you, Shadow, Rivga moro Kadani, Spirit Who Dreams of the Old Gods. But you're also me. Glam. Glamok nidi Tadwar."

"We're hurt," the doppelganger said, eyes regarding Glam with a spark of wonder.

Glam handed his doppelganger a piece of cloth he kept in a side pocket, and watched his darker self wipe the blood from his face.

"This is life, eh? Blood and pain," Glam's Shadow said, breathing hard. "We're still connected, though. Deep down, we know you believe in the Ukari, so far deep you almost forget. The Valukeydir will help us retain our old freedom, maybe lead us to other ruins, other artifacts our gods left, to free us. You see how important this is to keep from them. Your work is undone until you utilize your gifts for the Ukari. But I see now we are brothers. You saved yourself in naming me, damn you. Living or slain, I would have devoured you. Now you set perimeters to my power, and gave me the gift of reflection. A poor exchange, Glam."

"Quiet," Glam said, trying to keep a clear head, pulling out the tiny red fragment. It glowed in his hand like a miniature star, a flower-woven dream sun, and Glam smiled. "The flower of secret desire," he whispered.

Just then he saw his Shadow shift position, and spring. A hard rock struck his head, concealed in the attacker's fist. Glam reeled. Then the rock struck again, but all became calm and silent, and time halted, woven into a slow-moving play which he could observe but not change. His body, heavy and ponderous, went down and all shapes merged into the free-flowing darkness.

*   *   *

The crackling of the radio woke Glam. His doppelganger was gone, and the Valukeydir fragment also. He clutched darkness in his hand, and the sound emitting from the radio hit him like turbulent waves.

"...Contacting Glam. Come in. This is Merchant League Ship Mercury... Contacting Chief Glam..."

"Glam here," he yelled, clutching the device.

"Received your transmission 1100 hours. Pinpointed your location in Zujan province."

"Transmission?" Glam asked, feeling a bump on his head and flakes of dried blood.

"Affirmative. Sending Lyonesse league representative for rendezvous at Vestir in 52 hours."

"Thanks," he answered, and tracked the code numbers. His doppelganger must have contacted the ship. He could have just as easily slain him. Glam discovered all his gear intact, save for a spare light and the dagger. Where his shadow had gone with the shard was a mystery. But something remained. Picking up his bag, Glam began packing it with the fine dust which lined the ruins. Once done, he would send a transmission to Bishop Mezenzikes.

* * *

Above, Bishop Mezenzikes entered the twisted, broken doors of the large body-synth factory, finding a sweat-shop operation in utter chaos. Battle raged about him. Smashed plasma vats and the stink of synthflesh overwhelmed him. His Li Halan guide held him up while vertigo momentarily overwhelmed him. Children and slaves huddled for safety behind large metal containers while soldiers fired at the mold compressors, destroying the bioengineering machinery. In the back of the factory, shots were fired back, at random, two foremen using the heavy assembly machinery for cover. A sharp clicking sound went off in the bishop's vest pocket. Ducking behind an upturned metallic skid, he answered it, hearing Glam's voice. Ricocheting bullets sang in the air.

"Read you, Glam. We're busy here, give me a few minutes." The bishop ended the transmission, and his guide kept him down, raising an arm to fire shots into the corrugated depths of the building.

Swiftly, a team of Brother Battle warriors rushed toward the responding fire, climbing over smashed and partially shattered synth vats. Mezenzikes saw a Brother Battle soldier firing down from his vantage point, point blank, with a Lank Stinger submachine gun. A large man fell, rolling between smashed flesh molders, dying in a strangely comical fit. The other man attempted to surrender, but was swept down in a hail of bullets. Here and there, frustrated men were killing prisoners in cold blood before intervening Church officials could prevent it.

The factory was secured. Mezenzikes and Brother Juao lead the freed slaves out, while swift teams of fighters planted heavy explosives about the plant, timed for twenty minutes. Some of the children screamed — they had implants in their arms which administered lethal shocks if they left the perimeter. When the interior generators blew, they would be safe. Outside, scattered resistance from the third factory continued, until plasma grenades shattered shields, and the survivors swiftly surrendered to the hardened soldiers about them. Deep smoke filled the air, and chaos.

Brother Juao heard confessions from them and administered the Rite of Passing. Some heavily wounded slaves were brought out, caught in the cross fire and used as living shields by the defenders. The Victory Litany was broadcast over the valley as the explosions and great clouds of gray dust engulfed the crumbling tech plants. The soldiers cheered, and the crackling broadcast continued, "O Undying Fire, O Victorious

Sun, the purity of thy cause triumphs..."

The children before Bishop Mezenzikes sat, crying, huddled. One boy ran toward the wounded prisoners, lying on straw beds before a makeshift Amalthean tent. Mezenzikes followed the boy, mentally taking notes, yelling at a soldier to chain the prisoners.

There, before him, the boy held a woman's hand and cried. She was dead, lying flat beneath the sky on a stretcher, her hair hiding her eyes. But it didn't matter. Bishop Mezenzikes knew her.

"Olesia," he whispered, and the wind hissed through the grasses and mocked him. He saw the world blur, and fought back tears. His heart opened, and was alone in this strange region of Zujan.

"She's dead, shot in the left ventricle of the heart while escaping," a small, dark-haired Amalthean woman told him. "We can attempt revival."

"Nothing can be revived," the bishop said, cursing his life's ambitions, and struggling with tears. Tentatively, he touched her son's hair, and the sweet scent of honeysuckle engulfed him. Bishop Mythius Mezenzikes could not move or speak, until the sound of arriving aircraft stirred him. The iridescent eyes of Bishop Mezenzikes looked beyond the ship, far into the deep blue skies of Midian.

* * *

Afternoon fell and Mezenzikes stood guard by Olesia's body, not moving, until they pleaded his attention, and he left her. Duty called, and he was again the servant of the Church. Behind, he left a promise to watch after Olesia's boy. It was his parting gift to her, a final attempt to make amends to one already gone.

That night, after the reconnaissance plane picked him up, Glam approached the bishop's tent, set up beyond the destroyed body-synth factories. Glum prisoners with shackled hands were under lock and guard, and soldiers and priests huddled around small fires, warming their hands. Intense shadows flickered by the makeshift camp, and the scent of smoky meat carried on the strong north wind. Beyond the camp, in the night darkness, the ancient opaque silence breathed, and settled over the small pocket of men, gear and weapons.

"What's this?" Mezenzikes asked, quashing a field report as Glam entered silently, lifting the flap. A small folding table, chair and lamp illuminated the interior, and a comm device crackled by the bishop's ear, giving a continuing commentary through the thick static of body counts and objectives.

"Dust from the ruins," Glam said, producing his bags of rich, dark soil. "It produces dreams and visions."

"I had thought an Ukar Scraver would find more." The bishop frowned. His body slumped, and a listless quality permeated his speech.

"There were ruins, Bishop Mezenzikes. Anunnaki ruins set in a circle of nine monolithic stone pillars with a central stone, forming a ritual nine-point interlaced pattern, a triple trinity of the divine secrets of creation, struggle and—"

"Please, Glam, none of your unenlightened Ukari theology," Mezenzikes sighed.

"Whatever artifact the ruins held is long gone. It was plundered by another long ago. The dust, though, and the minute fragment, are invaluable."

Mezenzikes seemed to be somewhat mollified, although Glam noticed his unusual melancholy. "I do not believe you. Now tell me." The bishop brought up a small hand held device. For a brief moment, the bishop's old arrogance returned. He pressed a button and administered a shock into Glam's leg which sent electric waves shooting into his heart. A scream ripped through Glam's throat, and he fell, clutching at the air like a dying insect. The bishop placed the small device before Glam's eyes, then slowly withdrew it. Guards at the tent flaps rushed in.

"It does not matter," the bishop sighed wistfully, motioning the security away. Clearly, any thoughts of vengeance or interrogation swiftly vanished, swallowed in the bishop's despondent mood. "I could increase the shocks until you would beg to tell me what really happened, but I believe you. You're withholding something, but you performed as best as you could."

The threat folded swiftly with a soft sigh between the bishop's lips, flower petals folding inward at the fading of the sun. Outside, the western wind sang mournfully over the valley.

"I could have used you here earlier, Glam. You were correct. We did not have good enough infiltration to save the peasant laborers. I sent you and we failed here. Too eager. Keep your secrets and dust. It can't bring her back."

Glam's bewilderment broke across his face. Something more had happened here than a battle. An amazing admission of failure from a man who seldom let the mask of his thoughts drop. Something fell from far distances and splashed into subterranean depths, stirring the old man's ice-choked soul. Bishop Mezenzikes looked up, reading the confusion on Glam's features.

"You did your task, Glam. The Scravers are pressing for your return. Two days hence, you will meet their representatives at Vestir. Your service to me is over."

Sighing again, he poured Glam a small glass of wine, and the red liquid sparkled against the intricate grape and vine motif of the glass. Then, with a swift motion, he produced a small coin bag stuffed with firebirds and silver, and moved it to Glam.

"I shall miss you, Ukar. I missed you here today." The bishop's eyes mulled over some event in the long past, ignoring Glam while he accepted the bag and drained the cup.

Glam opened the bag. The scent of myth and history, rich and deep, mingled and struck him. Less than before, Glam noticed, more diminutive, attuned to smaller things.

As Glam exited, he thought he saw a dark-haired woman, wrapped with the night, enter on phantasmal ghost feet from the shadowed corners of the tent, but then discarded the sight from his mind. Two voices rose from the bishop's tent, but Glam was gone.

That night Glam dreamed, sleeping beneath the open stars in a borrowed blanket. He was walking through the fantastic ruins of a vanished civilization. Prodigious, prismatic pillars and stone lead to a dark ocean, where mournful waves crashed against crumbling walls and rainbow glass. Ukari statues, Anunnaki temples and Second Republic marvels felt the fury of the ocean's devouring wrath. And the present civilization, Glam thought, his own, where human nobles, priests and guildsmen held his people down, was wearing, changing, also subject to entropy's surging storms. Yet the Ukari survived, conquered, not dead. A dead people did not produce their sand art, or songs. They would live to see the change. Out from its toppled foundations a newer, younger civilization would arise, maybe harsher, perhaps more life-affirming.

Glam shifted like a child through the colored fragments and thought of his Shadow, and the piece of Shelkoro's crown he bore with him. Where would his *ialtach* take the fantastic relic? To aid his people, or merge with its dreaming secrets, wrapped in the time of legends and splendor? Where would I take it, he thought? Suddenly beyond the waves he saw a glittering star, the future, lighting the east in rich hues. Glam smiled, realizing his terrible and important truth.

He wanted to shout his secret: We are all murderers and saints, but the wind rattled, bringing only soft rain and the scent of honeysuckle.

Alyward Allmen: A Morality Play

Father A, or Mssrs. Quaide & Inabinet (attributed)

Alyward Allmen has long been one of the most popular of the Regency Period (4550 - 4995) morality plays. Originating on the Hawkwood worlds, where it is referred to in various noble, Church and town records, around 4570, its popularity swiftly spread to other worlds. Sir Florvius Torenson, an expert in the study of Church Theater, states that by Alexius's reign at least 23 different versions of the play were in existence. Of these, the best known one, presented here, is arguably the fourth version, believed to be from Cymru, a farming town on Ravenna, and the oldest extant version during the Emperor Wars. The Church historian Suzuki Hahn Li Halan believes that the play had two authors, noting a shift in styles when the demons enter in force, while Torenson believes it is the work of a single priest, whom he identified as Father A.

Religious Drama, under the Universal Church of the Celestial Sun, had its origins in the early Church, and by the Second Republic had become a very sophisticated entertainment involving interactive holograms. After the collapse of the Second Republic, the old technology became rarer, and the new Church dramas grew out of Church liturgies of the 42nd and 43rd centuries. While many forms of theater were suppressed, the Church allowed plays dealing with religious themes and morality to continue.

The Passion Plays, Mystery Cycles and Morality Plays really began in their present form during the New Dark Ages, when the Church presented them to an illiterate peasantry during religious festivals. The Passion Plays often dealt with the theme of Zebulon the Prophet's encounter with the Holy Flame, or other details of the Prophet's life (the healing of Zebulon and casting out of the demons by St. Amalthea being a favorite theme). Other Passion Plays take on other, less elaborated themes from the Omega Gospels, often the lives of the Saints and immediate followers of the Prophet.

The Mystery Cycles came next, and were often a complex series of plays dealing with salvation and the order and nature of the Reflective

Universe. Last, the Morality Plays told allegorical tales of the soul's desire for the Pancreator and the trials the soul endured and suffered when it strayed from the Church's path. *Sorrow's Child* and *Wayward* are two earlier examples, going back to the 4400s, in which allegorical forces ("Death" "Nature" "Science" "Greed") and religious figures and even demons fight for the stake of humanity's soul. These became very popular with the public on feast days, and the Church often let professional acting troupes or local guilds perform them on Church land.

Alyward Allmen was not originally performed by the Entertainment Guilds, but by the local Clothing Guild on the Hawkwood Worlds. The Guilds entered into festive competition on Feast and Holy Days to outdo each other in elaborate sets and design, with the local guilds often going to extreme lengths. *Alyward Allmen*, when performed before the nobility by a powerful guild, would rely on holo-projectors and other technological tools to enhance it, but when performed before the peasantry by local guilds it was done with more primitive, if not ingenious, mechanics.

The similarity between Pre-Reflective morality plays, as well as liturgical musical evolution, was noted by Torenson. However, since few of old Urth works survived save in rare libraries, Torenson merely stated that even in pre-reflective times (admittedly a Golden Age in Church mythology) the old religions displayed moral plays for the people in the best light they could (i.e. having only the pre-reflective truth of Jesuh, Mummaded, Budhi and Mosi and other texts which could not encompass the entirety of Zebulon's vision).

The rhyme scheme of the play is uneven, with the rhyming in the Empyrean heavens representing more of a synthesizing order than the unrhymed speech in the worlds below. Even demons rhyme in heaven, so strong is the desire for Reflective Synthesization present. (This was the subject of a serious Church debate on the spiritual wholeness of the Empyrean realms.) At times demons rhyme, a last flicker of their reflective natures emitted before their souls die the soul-death awaiting those who stray from the reflective Path. The mention of pre-reflective saints ("The Old Urth Fathers") would bring some recognition from references in the Omega Gospels; the figure of Cain would be unrecognizable to most save the most learned, but "old Maya" seems a reference to the Mayan people of Old Urth, whose snake imagery was at least known to the educated, and curiously remembered in common folk-lore.

Dramatis Personae

SAINTS, *especially Saint Maya*
EMPYREAN ANGELS
PERANARGAX, *the Voice of the Pancreator*
ZUTEKUM, *a demon*
ANIKRUNTA, *a spirit of the fallen Ukar*
HERMITHOTH, *a demon*
[Various evil Spirits and Ukari]
DEATH
ETYRI
FATHER CHURCH
CONSTANTIUS
CONSTULTIUS
GALAXY
ALYWARD ALLMEN

> *As the scene opens, the Empyrean Angels are in prayer. A strong light,*
> *coming from above the stage, floods the scene and casts reflections off*
> *numerous mirrors placed behind slowly moving stars and planets.*
> *Zebulon's Saints are seated just below the Empyrean Angels, to the*
> *right.*

SAINTS:
  Ipse caelum fecit et maria;
  Mors ad eius tremit imperia;
  Regni tui non erit terminus!
  Vivat Zebulon in aeternum!

  [Repeat as Angels begin to pray.]

EMPYREAN ANGELS:
  Let us sing the Celestial Psalms
  And give great thanks with our reflective alms;
  For before the Pancreator we are fire,
  Burning with deity's divine desire;
  Before us, about, the Lord of All
  To whom we bow in this holy hall!

> *Peranargax, the Voice of the Pancreator, descends. White wings flap*
> *down, the actor descends on lumnex wire from above, dressed in celes-*

tial white. Peranargax is female, with a bright sword, and hair of fiery
gold (Omega Gospels: Book of St. Horace 23:23)

PERANARGAX:
  With great love beyond the timeless years
  I hear the songs of the Empyrean spheres
  While the Pancreator contemplates the Greater Good
  The Unmoved Mover doing as order should
  With Perfected Forms and Planetary Powers
  The Pancreator's thought concrescening divine hours
  The Light of All and Giver of Reflected Order
  From Zebulon's Vision to the unreflective border
  But who is this? Have I espied aright?
  Who approaches the sacred fire like a thief in the night?

  Enter the serpentine demon, Zutekum, Levayath-Nidhaugg, the Beast
  from the Depths. The Snake Demon bellows brimstone from its nostrils
  and comes through the crowd. Four performers navigate the coils with
  mechanical devices; one uses a hatch to move the jaw and works the
  smoke bellows beneath the nostrils.

ZUTEKUM:
  O Voice of our Luminous Endlessness and glorious lord,
  I ask you stay your wrath, your peace please hold.
  O Peranargax, you are here with your luminous host
  Guarding with divine wrath your appointed post.
  I come and being rustic here, all alone,
  Forget the proper ways to approach the throne.
  From the Lord of Darkness to the Lord of Light
  I come alone from unreflected Night;
  I come to wager, I tire of my usual places
  And desire the light of my old homeland's graces.
  For if setting is good for the soul
  I profit by presence, and collect my toll.

  The Angels begin to toss flaming spears at the demon, which bounce off
  the scales.

PERANARGAX:
  Back, fallen serpent who left the light
  And lead the sixth host into night,
  For in the unreflected realms there is always war;
  No dark spirit rules the unreflected shore.
  All is chaos, fragments fallen from divine law,
  Which feast and devour each other, one demonic maw
  Chewing on itself, plotting, scheming,
  And then contemplating self, lone dreaming,
  Each spirit power thinking "I alone am lord
  Of this unruly, monstrous horde!"
  But each an end: that is I am I;
  A selfish spirit that believes the lie,
  And sees no flame above, will not ascend,
  And hungers for light for selfish end.
  Self glorifies self, until self devours all,
  When madness shatters all memory of divine law.

ZUTEKUM:
  Enough of this talk, it has been years
  Since I came before you beyond the spheres
  Where the great light of the Pancreator guides
  The orbits of stars in heaven's tides;
  For the expatriate of the One Light yearns,
  With an exile's heart which weeps and burns
  Away from colonial imitation,
  To the old source of divination.
  For the Prime Mover must, at times, want rest
  From the presence of the elect and blessed,
  To talk with opposition true and bold
  Of things gone weary in a universe grown old;
  For if you cast your gaze with heart's desire
  You observe all realms far when perched up higher.
  Let us both behold with creative awe
  The constant reflections of Divine Law,
  To see the fruits of your holy cause
  The race of man spread among the stars!

Stars and planets move off stage, revealing below a Church and a Priest, walking in thought.

PERANARGAX:

Still they fight and struggle as before
With engine spirit in strife and lore.
The realm of man is a troubled place
O half divine and unhappy race!
Still, Zebulon led them to the light
From your clutches in the night,
And by the Omega Gospels lit
The Church's Fire on the Holy Writ!

ZUTEKUM:

Zebulon and his saints walked true
But for the rest of the race, too few, too few!
I know the darkness of their hearts;
I mislay them with my darkened arts;
I was an illusion filled with pain;
Before the face of Prereflective God I was the rebel Cain;
I was the demon Saint Amalthea cast out;
I was the abyss of Zebulon's doubt;
I was the snake old Maya called divine;
I was the taste of wisdom on the lips of wine.
Humans are weak and easily stray;
They are the souls on which I prey.

PERANARGAX:

In their allotted years they do great fetes
Which are gnawed by time, which all matter defeats.
The old to the grave, the new to power,
The pieces move, new secrets flower
While the old decays and turns to dust,
Forgotten monuments of fallen rust.
Yet they burn still with holy desire;
In their soul's the Reflective fire
Of the Pancreator's vast eternal flame which marks
Embers from the flame, their souls are reflected sparks.
Do you see, there, Alyward Allmen?

Below, Alyward Allmen approaches the priest

ZUTEKUM:

I do.

PERANARGAX:

Now with him I wager you.

ZUTEKUM:

I wager I shall wean him of the Church's ways
And in the unreflected realm he'll end his days.

PERANARGAX:

I wager that, by order divine,
He will find sanctuary in the Saint's vine,
The living Church which Zebulon planted as seed
For the human race in their collective need.

ZUTEKUM:

If I win, I quench the fire.
The planets die and the stars expire.

PERANARGAX:

If I win, you shall gnaw forever
On the dark abyss, and sever
all contact with the light, eat your tail
Till in repentance you wail
Forgiveness from the source of all,
And send your prayers before the law.

ZUTEKUM:

You have no sense of fun, but I agree;
And we shall both tempt his ear, for words are free.

BOTH:

Let us behold Alyward Allmen's tale
And see the path he will travail.
The planets open, the pageant begins
Blessed with hope and weighed with sins.

*The Angels and Saints Ascend. Zutekum slithers offstage, left, while
Peranargax flies off to the right, smiling down on Alyward Allmen.
Alyward has a staff, and he is looking at the church, while a dog (a
string puppet operated from above) nips at his feet.*

FATHER CHURCH:

Good morrow, Alyward Allmen. This is not a day for sermon, but happy I am to see you approaching the Church doors.

ALLMEN: I seek solace, good father, in the Church, and came today to do good deeds beyond my tithing for the glory of Zebulon's Universal Church.

FATHER CHURCH:

It is good to see a man full of faith gaze not far

And seek his home in his parish and his birth star!

For ill abode thee, my faithful son, to wander from the rays

of the star of your birth which bless and count thy days!

ALLMEN:

If you say so, it is. By Saint Mantius, I pray, protect our Church and her servants this day!

Enter two boys, Constantius and Constultius. Constantius is dressed in respectable white, while Constultius's clothes consist of patchwork, haphazardly hanging off his frame. Constantius comes bearing cheese and bread to Father Church, while Constultius plays with a fiddle stick, and hums while Father Church talks, looking aside at the audience and silently mimicking the priest.

FATHER CHURCH:

Morrow, children. How fare you, Constantius?

CONSTANTIUS: I brought you this offering today, good father.

FATHER CHURCH: May the eightfold vision be praised! And how fare you, Constultius?

CONSTULTIUS: I had a large offering of voo cakes my sister made for you, but it was a long walk and I grew hungry. Certainly the Church would not want to see her faithful servant starve?

FATHER CHURCH:

Thou brat, but the Empyrean angels love thee! I was about to send Allmen upon an errand. Perhaps you boys would like to accompany him?

CONSTANTIUS:

I go where the Church sees best to send me, with a prayer on my lips.

CONSTULTIUS:
Do you wish to purchase sweets for Saint Amalthea Day? I'd best handle the coin purse, I being wisest in such matters.

FATHER CHURCH: No, no, I want you to go into town where a package awaits me, containing the sacred relics of St. Inigo, who died resisting the corrupt charms of the Changed women of Praxti.

ALLMEN: Well, I'm up to the task. Lads?

They follow. The Church is rolled off set, and mountains are rolled onto set. The three travelers climb up a mountain road.

CONSTULTIUS:
I see a lake. Let's notch off some time and go fishing. I know some worm holes and I have twine.

ALLMEN: No, Constultius, we must be true to Father Church's charge. But this trail, it's much longer than I remember.

CONSTANTIUS:
Have faith, Allmen. "For Zebulon charged them with a task, and they went into Cordo, and brought back supplies to his followers, and Zebulon, looking on their faith, said 'I am well pleased.'"

ALLMEN:
That's some memory.

CONSTULTIUS: I bet Zebulon let his Saints take off and go fish, I mean between the verses and books and all.

Enter Galaxy. She is dressed like an Engineer, in provocative clothing, and is enticing.

GALAXY:
Well, well, look here, three men looking for adventure.

ALLMEN: May we help you, young lady?

GALAXY: My poor Guild ship has crashed and needs repair. Repair it and I'll reward thee with my fellowship. Join me in the stars. Let's leave this poor planet and explore the universe, and see the marvels that await. We'll make riches off the ore trade, for 'tis better to sell in material wealth than count invisible spiritual profit.

CONSTULTIUS:
You sure are smart lady, and you sure have a way with words. Could you teach me to speak like that?

ALLMEN: But Father Church said that we were happiest under the sun of our birth.

GALAXY: Yes, but Zebulon himself went adventuring into the outer planets. If all our kin felt the same, certes we'd never have left Holy Terra.

CONSTULTIUS: I like her. Let's sign up into her Guild and sail the stars. We'll be rich, and have a hidden stash of millirice bars.

ALLMEN:
No, Father Church gave us a task. We must take his authority seriously.

An Etyri, the traditional messenger of the Empyrean Powers in folk tales, swoops down on rope-fastened wings.

ETYRI:
Allmen, you stand at the crossway. Listen to Father Church! Ignore false promise of riches. For material gain and Galaxy's wares, technology, lead down the darkened road to Self-Reflective sin, the vilest of crimes, which doomed the Republican longbeards in their electric castles that hummed and sang the thousand songs of sin. Stay away from her, do not go in!

GALAXY: Vile bird! The tools of technology enrich the soul. But certes, technology is not for all, but only the select who are brave enough to seize the Pancreator's secrets, encrypted in electronic wires and broadcast through the cyber ether! I believe Allmen is brave enough, and the Pancreator formed his soul of such clear reflective spirit, that he will learn and understand the lore of the Republican mariners, and absorb the awe of burning synth-gnosis cells, encoded in the living walls of old Republic mansions, since abandoned. And I but hold him for a short while. Thanks, Etyri, but I am not forcing him. Although I'd richly reward a big, strong man like Allmen to help me fly my ship across the stars, and have me for instruction in all things pertaining to deeper understanding of physical and abstract sciences.   [*Galaxy winks at Allmen.*]

ETYRI:

> The Clouds gather, do not sway
> Only evil paths lead her way!

GALAXY: After we are done, Allmen, we'll do the Church's task. Please?

ALLMEN: I cannot refuse such a lady, longing for the distant lights. And Father Church did not place any urgency upon his task. Perhaps the Pancreator meant for us to know his secrets, and master them against the darkening of the stars.

GALAXY:

> My ship is not far. Help me repair it and then return to Father Church's wants. For by helping me you help him. The secrets found afar may help the Church against the darkening of the stars.

CONSTULTIUS:

> I thought he was too stupid to sign on with her. The stars. Can we see the markets on the League World, and the zoos the rich Al Malik keep, full of dream animals and the great cats and oglinines?

GALAXY:

> Of course. Experience and knowledge enrich our souls. The Prereflective saints of old, Jeshu and Budh, Mammed and Mosi, were limited in vision because they never left old Urth. Do you wish your vision to be limited? For Zebulon the prophet explored and found the truth that was profound.

CONSTANTIUS: No! We tithe and give bounteously to the Church. She teaches us that the worship of knowledge, when unchecked, denies the mysteries of spirit and life. Stay strong by her! For the old science has caused the stars to die, and the sin of knowledge kills life and destroys the proper balance. We must be true, like the child martyrs of old, little Saint Roberto and Saint Laja, who did not deny the faith when covered by the rocks of the Ukar on Criticorum!

CONSTULTIUS: We best make a martyr of you then!

> *He throws rocks at Constantius. Allmen follows Galaxy down a dark and gloomy path.*

ETYRI:

> All gone, all vanished, all fled
> Their souls were tempted and now the dread!

From off stage the voices of the Empyrean saints chant:

SAINTS:
Fear the breaking of the College of Ethicals' and Patriarch Anchises' Doctrine of Universal Inheritance, and do not tread upon the holy writ of the Privilege of Martyrs. Doom awaits thee, Allmen, and the Light grows dim, where technology's toys lead to sin. For only the privileged may wield the dangerous gifts, lest they lead the spirit to soul-death down the unreflective path.

The Etyri, having fulfilled his mission, flies off to stage right. Constantius ponders:

CONSTANTIUS:
I'd better keep an eye on them, and not forsake their souls. Surely Father Church would understand!

Scene changes to a dark mountain path descending into blackness. Cold blue fires (symbolized by an ultraviolet lightbulb) are lit below. From the left, three figures emerge, leading Ukari and evil spirits. Zutekum slithers ahead, followed by Anikrunta, an Ukar giant holding a baleful red eye over his head, and Hermithoth the All-Knowing, dressed in a red velvet hood, carrying a chained book.

ANIKRUNTA:
You laid your snares, and now we wait
For Allmen to receive his fate.
ZUTEKUM:
You are lucky, O Ukar spirit foul.
Your folk are fallen, and you do not have to prowl
To seize them, pull them down from illuminated space,
Away from the Pancreator's reflective grace.
HERMITHOTH:
My brethren, quiet, I must think now. Away with rhymes, they are but a code. The mortals are coming. But look who proceeds them. It is Death.

Enter Death, dressed in a crimson shroud, carrying The Hook Of Souls.

ANIKRUNTA:

Away from our realms. Your time is nought.

DEATH:

I come not this day for you, yet none can break free

Of my heavy chains, which bring all lives to me.

HERMITHOTH:

You may be cheated, only the body dies.

But all created crumbles, and is food for flies

DEATH:

As does all wisdom, pride and lies.

ZUTEKUM:

What would you here, O shadowy presence?

DEATH: I come as a sign,

A reminder to those bound in time.

I but watch your snaring, and bide

And behold plots like the turning tide.

I set nought by gold, silver or riches,

Nor by Patriarch, Emperor or Princes.

Were I to take a bribe my riches would flow

And golden vestments would about me glow.

But my custom is clean contrary;

I have a task and I will not tarry.

HERMITHOTH: Can we trust you, then, not to
meddle with our plans?

DEATH:

My task it is but one, no more and no less.

Each soul that I reap, must its own self damn or bless.

ANIKRUNTA: Fair enough.

Now be silent everyone. They are almost here. Begone, imps and dark
brethren of eld, for the sight of you would set our prey afright!

ZUTEKUM:

Aye, and be quick to it! We must take on more common shapes.

> *The Ukari and evil spirits hide behind the mountains. The three de-*
> *mons pull out masks with normal human faces on them. Death steps*
> *back. Enter Allmen with Galaxy and Constultius. Constantius follows*
> *at a distance.*

CONSTULTIUS:
  ... And so the third courtesan says "I thought you said to go down on
  the wharf!"
GALAXY: Ha! What a saucy jest!
ALLMEN: I don't get it.

The demons approach, holding their masks in front of their faces.

ZUTEKUM:
  Halloo, good folk! What brings you to these parts, fellow wayfarers?
ALLMEN:
  This lad and I are helping this fair lady of the guild to find and repair
  her ship, that she might resume her sojourn among the stars.
GALAXY:
  'Tis not far from here, I am certain. If you would join us, your com-
  pany would be most welcome.
CONSTULTIUS: 'Struth! For I like not the way these
  hills huddle close about us.
ZUTEKUM: Aye, this is a dark and cold path we ply.
  Your companionship would be not unwelcome to us as well.
GALAXY:
  Well it is, then. And when we come to my ship, your extra hands will
  make light work of the repairs.

They walk together. Constantius, Death and the horde of lesser demons
all follow, each at a distance.

HERMITHOTH:
  Will you good men be accompanying this merchant lady to the stars,
  then?
ALLMEN:
  Nay, sir. For we are engaged upon a mission for Father Church, which
  we shall take up again once we have seen her on her way.
CONSTULTIUS:
  Speak for yourself, Alyward! My heart is too great to shrink from
  challenge, and I would seek out adventure among the star-lanes, and
  see wondrous sights which are unknown to these parts.

ALLMEN:

Thou art an inconstant and troublesome lad! Remember that we are sworn to our duty.

ANIKRUNTA: Such devotion! What has Father Church given to you, that you should attend him so?

CONSTULTIUS: Precious little, and that's a fact!

ALLMEN:

Enough of you, feckless whelp! (He cuffs the boy's ears.) Good sir, pay no heed to this faithless boy, for he sleeps during sermons, and would steal from the tithe-basket, if he thought none would see him do it. But for myself, I place my faith in Father Church's words, for he is a good and kindly man, made knowledgeable in matters of the spirit through long years spent in study of the holy writ. He has devoted himself to the protection of his flock, he endeavors to reflect the divine light so as to ward off the darkness that threatens to engulf the soul, and he offers his learned guidance in the path of righteousness.

HERMITHOTH:

And in return for such vague intangibles, he has you run and fetch and perform his errands for him. Not to mention taking from you a hefty portion of your hard-won earnings. Is that it?

ALLMEN: What I do for Father Church I do from the gladness of my heart, for the joy of service lies in the doing of it, and not in what rewards might be gained.

HERMITHOTH:

And you two, how stand you on this matter of unrewarded service?

GALAXY:

Oh, charity has its place, I'll hold, for to be seen giving aid to the less fortunate is good for business. But in sooth, exchange is the soul of transaction among equals.

CONSTULTIUS: Aye, you said it, lady. Nobody does anything for nothing.

ALLMEN: Well, so it is with the tithing. For the priest is but a man as others, who cannot do his work on an empty belly. And churches do not build themselves out of thin air. Thus it is right that the flock should donate such wealth as it can afford.

GALAXY:

Hmf! Were I to command prices like that for such weightless wares as words and smiles, I would be Dean of the League, and have enough left over to buy myself a dukedom besides!

CONSTANTIUS: I like these fellows not at all, for they are sowers of strife.

Anikrunta turns behind his mask to speak to the hiding demon hordes.

ANIKRUNTA:

This man is a tough nut to crack. We may need to use more forceful arguments, so stand thou ready to spring at my signal.

CONSTANTIUS: O merciful saints above! They are not men, but foul monsters from Gehenne! I must warn my friends!

Constantius rushes forward from his hiding place, but Anikrunta intercepts him and blasts him off stage left with a brimstone fart.

ALLMEN:

Heardst thou thunder? We had best hasten, as it would go ill for us were we overtaken by a storm in this barren place.

ZUTEKUM: Yes, let us hurry. I think that I saw your downed craft but a little farther ahead there.

CONSTULTIUS:

Did you now? That is certainly lucky for us.

ALLMEN: How is it that you did not tell us this afore?

HERMITHOTH: You certainly show a cynical bent, Allmen, for such a pure heart.

ALLMEN: I do not recall having given you my name. How do you come to know it?

HERMITHOTH: The name of all men is known to me.

ALLMEN: This is passing strange.

GALAXY: Come now, my friend. Would you spoil our good fortune by inspecting too closely this gift-horse's teeth?

ZUTEKUM:

Indeed. Have we not shown to you honest faces?

> [*He indicates his human mask.*]

GALAXY:

Sooth, Allmen! How could you not trust a countenance such as this?

> *Galaxy cups the chin of Zutekum's mask in a playful, almost flirta-*
> *tious manner. In doing so, she accidentally pulls it aside, revealing the*
> *raw horrifying visage of the serpent-demon. Constultius shrieks like a*
> *little girl and faints dead away. Galaxy and Allmen spring back in*
> *horror. Anikrunta and Hermithoth drop their masks. All freeze in*
> *place as the lights quickly go down. A single overhead light now shines*
> *on stage left, where a small chapel set has been wheeled onstage.*
> *Constantius stumbles in, panting and out of breath, and kneels before*
> *the icon of Saint Maya set above the shrine.*

CONSTANTIUS:

O thou most blessed Patron of Justice, hear my humble plea. I tell you that your devout servant in the faith, that Alyward Allmen, has been led astray from his path of service to Father Church, and is now unjustly delivered into the clutches of devils most foul. I beseech thee to intercede on his behalf, for he was lured from the righteous way through no fault of his own, but thought only to perform a boon of charity for a hapless traveler. And hasten, I prithee, for I know not what may have passed since I left his sight.

> *The overhead light becomes brighter, and the voice of Saint Maya is*
> *heard above.*

SAINT MAYA:

Thy prayers hath reached mine ears,
So now, faithful lad, dry your tears.
Rest thou here, and be at ease;
For Saint Maya hearkens to thy pleas.

> *The chapel light dims and the chapel set is wheeled offstage. The regular*
> *lights come back up as Allmen's scene with Galaxy and the demons*
> *resumes.*

HERMITHOTH:

So now you see us as we truly are. We had hoped to play this game out a while longer, but no matter.

ZUTEKUM: See ye now whither your charity hast brought you, Allmen?

ANIKRUNTA: Aye. Your kindliness has led you straightaway into our hands.

ALLMEN: Oh! Woe that I ever strayed from my appointed duty! A pox upon thee, wench, for turning me aside from righteousness!

HERMITHOTH:

Oh, splendid! Mark well, my brethren, how this good man, this kind man, turns to blame the wayward damsel who sought his aid. This is rich sport indeed!

GALAXY: Take heart, good Allmen, and succumb not to superstitious fear! For such things as these cannot be! Science teaches us that devils are but phantasms of a mind in disarray, our own fears writ large upon the world by deceptive sense. Stand ye firm, for they can do us no harm save that which we, in our weakness of will, allow!

ANIKRUNTA:

Yea, heed her pretty words, Allmen. She has not lied to you yet, has she?

HERMITHOTH:

Even so! We are nought but shadows, that can inflict no harm upon a pure soul.

ZUTEKUM: [*Advancing upon Galaxy.*]

As I shall even now demonstrate...

GALAXY: Back, foul shade! You have no power over me!

ALLMEN: Good lady, provoke them not, I prithee! For unless your soul is entirely devoid of sin, you shall surely fall to such as these!

GALAXY: Nay, simple Allmen. Fear not for me. Your concern is founded in nought but the ignorance of the scientifically unenlightened.

Zutekum bears down upon Galaxy, pushing her to the ground, and clamps his jaws around her feet. Allmen rushes forward to grab Galaxy's hand as the serpent demon begins swallowing her legs.

ALLMEN:

Please, I beg of you, repent of your godless ways and confess to the sin of holding to Republican heresies, before you are undone!

HERMITHOTH:

Allmen pleads in vain. Her pride will not admit of error.

ANIKRUNTA:

The serpent-beast shall not be cheated of this succulent appetizer. All guildsmen fall to us in the end.

HERMITHOTH: Even so. Their souls are sweet upon the tongue, but are easily gained and provide little nourishment. Better to feast on the faithful fallen from grace.

ANIKRUNTA: It is my hope that we shall tuck into such hearty fare 'ere our sport here is done.

GALAXY:

[Now engulfed up to the waist, with Allmen tugging at her arm.]
Bestill yourself, my friend. There is no danger here. This is but a play of illusion, a design to cripple us with fright.

ALLMEN: Again I beseech you! Divest yourself of such sophistries, lest your soul sink into the lightless void for all of eternity.

DEATH: *[Stepping forward.]*

Hither and thither and yon again they chase,
But in the end all come to rest in the same place.
A body is but dust; when shed, is dust once more;
The soul unsheathed is free to plummet or soar.
But which? In life alone was made that choice;
For to virtue only the living can give voice.   *[Pointing at audience.]*
So choose, each and all, within your allotted span;
Once I arrive, 'tis too late to change your plan.

Death sweeps his blade down between Allmen and Galaxy, breaking their clasped hands apart. Allmen falls backward and Galaxy disappears down Zutekum's mouth. (The actress portraying Galaxy may either exit secretly through a trapdoor in the stage, or may take a place in the long serpent costume, if space permits.)

GALAXY: *[As the serpent's jaws close over her head.]*
This is not happening...!

ALLMEN:

Oh, fair Galaxy! You are lost! Would that you had heeded the holy words!

HERMITHOTH:

And now to you, Allmen. Have you been paying heed to the holy words?

ANIKRUNTA:

Your lady-friend is devoured, and you are to be next.

HERMITHOTH:

Of what avail are your gospels and platitudes now?

ALLMEN: [*Trembling.*]

I have respected the Church in all things, and lived by the words of the Prophet, and honored the Pancreator in my heart, always.

HERMITHOTH:

You sound none too certain. Could it be that your faith is wavering in this perilous hour?

ANIKRUNTA: [*Pointing at Death.*]

See? The Harvester has not yet left our company. His tally here is not yet complete!

ALLMEN: [*Falling to his knees and clutching at Death's ragged robes.*]

Is that so? Is the end of my days now upon me?

DEATH:

What has been written, none may unwrite.

Prepare thyself now, for darkness...

ALLMEN: [*Shrieking.*]

Darkness? Oh, no!

DEATH: ...Or light.

ANIKRUNTA:

So speak, Allmen. Tell us, before your breath is stolen from you; can you still respect the Church that sent you upon a frivolous errand bringing you to this abysmal place?

HERMITHOTH: Was it not the charity cultivated in your heart by the Prophet's words whereby you lived that caused you to stray into the mouth of doom?

ZUTEKUM: How can you now give honor to a Pancreator that would allow you to fall to this tragic end? Say it now and be quick. If you will renounce this faith which has served you so poorly, and by your own will grant us custody of your soul once it is severed from the mortal clay, then I swear now that you shall live on with us, freed from the confining bonds of time and space, of worlds and years which are wearying to the spirit. Join us, I say, and we shall make known to you true freedom, power beyond measure and majesty beyond compare; we shall take you to the true center of the universe and show you the font of all stars, that original star now fallen in darkness, beside which this Celestial Sun of your Church shall seem but a dull, glittering bauble!

ALLMEN: Can it truly be thus? Have all my prayers, devotion and faith been for nought? What has my servitude to the will divine got me now? Shall I perish, alone and forgotten, in a cold and dark place without comfort or solace? What trust can I now place in a holy power that would forsake me in this fashion? Were the gospels but empty words, the hymns but deafening noise, the tithing but sanctimonious banditry, the righteous service but gilded slavery, the exultation of the spirit but conniving flatteries? What of salvation now?

Death steps forward, pulling back the Hook of Souls in readiness for the fatal blow. The demons gather about him, motioning for him to hold back.

ZUTEKUM:
Stay thy hand for but a moment, Inscrutable One! He is but a breath away from giving himself over to us!
ALLMEN:[*Raising his arms and crying up to the heavens.*]
Nay, I say! I shall not succumb to this darkness of the soul! For it is travails such as these that are the true test of faith, and I swear that mine shall endure! Though the steps I have taken lead me into doom, I'll not forsake the spirit that moved me hence; for 'twas not greed nor vainglory that caused me to choose this path, but kindliness and well-meaning, and by such values I'll yet hold! I'll not foreswear the revealed truth of the gospels, and the Pancreator shall not forsake me! I entrust my fate to the Hand that made me!

The overhead light from the chapel of Saint Maya now shines down upon Allmen at center stage. The voice of Saint Maya rings out from above as she slowly descends on lumnex wire.

SAINT MAYA:

Thou art redeemed, though sorely wert thou tested.

Peace, faithful Allmen; the darkness thou hast bested.

Through the darkness of the soul, beset by tribulation,

Thou hast won entire. So now the jubilation!

Let the glory of the Pancreator resound far and wide;

Man confronts his fate with faith hard by his side.

Upward with thee, pious soul, and be no more distressed.

Upward into th' Empyrean, there to dwell amongst the blessed

As she speaks, Maya grabs Allmen's outstretched hands and begins to ascend, taking him up with her. Death sweeps his blade under Allmen's feet just as they leave the stage. Maya and Allmen disappear into the light above, which then fades away.

ZUTEKUM:

Curses! Foiled again.

HERMITHOTH: That we are, my brother.

ANIKRUNTA: Sometimes I wonder

why we even bother.

But let us not be overmuch dismayed

For there is yet one lean soul before us laid.

Anikrunta kicks at Constultius' still-senseless body. The other demons gather around him, licking their lips.

ZUTEKUM:

Aye, but little nourishment his spirit shall afford;

And to play the tempter's game with him will leave us bored.

DEATH:

Back, benighted ones, his time has not come yet;

He has more annoyances to inflict upon Adam's get. [*Death exits.*]

HERMITHOTH:

To the Morose Harvester's words let us pay heed.

Rootless lads like this one can much better serve our need

As they pursue their own dim course in the world of men.

ANIKRUNTA:

Are you saying we should show him mercy, then?

HERMITHOTH:
  Not at all, my Ukar brother. Just consider thus:
  The lad's common vulgarities can do our work for us!
  Whilst we scheme and plot for years to pluck at a single soul,
  By his casual example can the race damn itself whole.
ZUTEKUM:
  Sooth — he is a lecherous bastard of the worst sort;
  Gazing at carvings of naked angels is his sport.
ANIKRUNTA:
  You are correct. Then let us leave him so
  To burden all goodly folk with petty woe.

> *The overhead light shines down again, and Peranargax descends on*
> *lumnex wire.*

PERANARGAX:
  Not so fast, lying serpent. Mark well who is beckoning.
  'Twas thou who hast wagered, and now comes the reckoning.
ZUTEKUM:
  Stand fast by me, brothers! Together we shall fight!
HERMITHOTH: I think not,
  my friend. Goodnight!
ANIKRUNTA: Yea, goodnight!

> *Hermithoth, Anikrunta and the evil spirits leap off the stage and run*
> *away, menacing the audience as they go. The overhead light becomes*
> *bright enough to eclipse the ultraviolet hellfire below. Zutekum screams*
> *and starts swallowing his tail as, one by one, the players in the serpent*
> *costume climb down through a trapdoor, leaving the empty costume*
> *coiled on the stage. All the lights go out; in the darkness, the church is*
> *wheeled back on stage over the fallen serpent. The Empyrean planets are*
> *lowered to hang in the sky above. While the regular stage lights come*
> *back up, Constultius awakens and stumbles about foolishly. Father*
> *Church and Constantius enter.*

CONSTANTIUS:
  Constultius, my friend! I feared you were dead! Tell us, what has
  become of Alyward and Galaxy?

CONSTULTIUS:

We were set upon by fiends! I fought and fought as hard as I could, but they were too much, even for me! Alas, our companions are lost!

FATHER CHURCH:

O woe, that such a good soul should fall to such an evil end! But he fell in valiant service to the Pancreator. I pray only that he had time to repent of his sins before he died.

Allmen, now wearing a white robe, is lowered on lumnex wire.

ALLMEN:

Fret not, good Father Church, for I managed to affirm my faith in goodly time, and was snatched from the jaws of damnation by the intercession of blessed Saint Maya — may her name be praised! I regret only that I was unable to fetch the relics of Saint Inigo back to you.

FATHER CHURCH:

Trouble thyself not one wit more, Alyward Allmen, for such earthly matters are no longer thy concern. (He turns to audience.) And let it so be for all faithful folk, that they honor the Pancreator, learn the words of the Prophet and heed the teachings of the Universal Church of the Celestial Sun, so as to be taken up at the end of their lives and dwell eternally in the Empyrean heavens!

As Father Church speaks, all the Empyrean Angels and Saints file onto stage.

ANGELS:

Ever and always is it thus:
The souls of the faithful return unto us.
For the Pancreator moves not by wanton whim
But desires that His children shall come back to him.
So heed, one and all, this simple play
And hold steadfast to the one true way
Of devotion, goodwill and earnest piety,
So to gain the shining grace of the deity.
Shun evil ways, give no ear to false words
And your hearts shall take flight like beautiful birds.

Polish now your souls, and of sin have great lack,
The Celestial Sun's light thereby to send back;
Let your actions be an example to all of your race
And rejoice on the sharing of the Luminous Grace!

SAINTS:

Ipse caelum fecit et maria;
Mors ad eius tremit imperia;
Regni tui non erit terminus!
Vivat Zebulon in aeternum!

FATHER CHURCH:

Praise be to the Celestial Sun!

EVERYONE:

Praise be!

The cast bows to the audience, and a hymn is sung as the audience disperses.

The End

Glossary

Amalthea, Saint: Called the "Healer", Amalthea is the saint of compassion and was one of the Prophet's eight disciples.

Amen'ta: Omnivorous alien creatures native to Severus, resembling ratlike armadillos. Also called "hull rats"; a common pest on starships.

Antinomy: Magic that derives its power from malevolent entities.

Anunnaki: Also known as the Preadamites, or the Ur. An ancient spacefaring race (or races) which developed the jumpgates.

Ascorbite: Insectoid alien race, known as "blood-suckers from Severus" (a term also applied to members of House Decados). Their behavior is bewildering to humans, and they seem to possess some form of hive mind. Like many alien races encountered by humans before they attained star-travel on their own, Ascorbites are largely confined to reservations on their homeworld.

Changed, The: The Second Republic produced many experiments in genetic manipulation. Now reviled by the Church, the mutant products of such "sinful" science are hunted and burned by Inquisitors.

Dayside: A jump that moves closer to Byzantium Secundus.

Diaspora: The historical exodus of humanity to the stars.

Doppleganger: The dark side of a psychic's personality, which, if left unchecked, can develop a life of its own. Also called the "Dark Twin."

Etyri: An avian alien race from the planet Grail, often considered regal by Known Worlders.

Gannok: Simianlike aliens renowned for their clownish behavior. Their small size and mechanical aptitude makes them prized starship engineers.

Gargoyle: Ancient creations — sculptures, buildings — believed to have been left by the Ur. The superstitious believe them to be sentient beings of great power.

Horace, Saint: Called the "Learned Man," Horace is the patron saint of the Eskatonic Order and was one of the Prophet's eight disciples.

Jumpgate: A massive alien artifact which allows for interstellar travel.

The inner workings and scientific principles of jumpgates have so far remained unfathomable to Known Worlders.

Keddah, House: A minor noble house, rulers of the planet Grail.

Known Worlds: The planets claimed by the Empire or which have Empire citizens living upon them.

Kurgan Caliphate: An empire of lost worlds ruled by a prophet-king. The caliphate wars with House Hazat over territory.

Leagueheim: Homeworld of the Merchant League, this planet host some of the highest tech wonders still in production, although it is considered a den of sin and villainy by the more extreme members of the Church.

Lost Worlds: Planets which were once part of the Second Republic but whose locations are now unknown.

Mantius, Saint: Called the "Soldier", Mantius is the patron saint of the Brother Battle order and was the Prophet's bodyguard.

Nightside: A jump that moves further away from Byzantium Secundus.

Omega Gospels: The teachings of the Prophet, and the basis for the Universal Church faith.

Philosopher's Stone: Objects of great power from past centuries.

Prophet, The: The man who united humanity with his vision of the Holy Flame. His miracles and the deeds of his saints are treasured by the faithful, who look upon his era with almost Biblical awe.

Psi: Psychic powers, possessed by psychics who — when recognized as such — are treated with distrust and outright fear by most Known Worlders.

Sathraism: The religion that grew up around jumpgate ecstasy, but was squashed by the First Republic. A later revival was crushed by the Universal Church, but adherents are rumored to still exist.

Second Republic: The golden age of human civilization and the peak of technological advancement. Relics from this period are highly valued.

Selchakah: A highly addictive drug known to be manufactured by certain devious Decados.

Shantor: An ungulate race from Shaprut that somewhat resemble earth horses. Treated the worst of all alien races during their first contact with humans, they are still largely confined to reservations and ostracized from Known Worlds society.

Symbiots: Insidious creatures originally born of a bizarre combination of a Xolotl and another plant or animal. Symbiots now breed among unwilling or human aliens. They threaten to invade the Known Worlds.

Theurgy: Church magic. Theurgy rituals are used by the faithful for a variety of spiritual tasks, from blessing a congregation to protecting people from enemies of the Faith.

Trusnikron, House: A minor noble house known for its amazing ability to tame and train creatures of all kinds.

Universal Church: The dominant faith in the Known Worlds, based on the teaching of the Prophet. While there are many recognized sects or orders (Brother Battle, Sanctuary Aeon, Eskatonic Order), most are offshoots of the Orthodox faith.

Ur-Obun: A powerfully psychic alien race known for its dedication to philosophy and learning; its homeworld of Velisamil (called simply "Obun" by most Known Worlders) is claimed by House Hawkwood.

Ur-Ukar: Another race of powerful psychics with highly developed senses, the Ur-Ukar are thought to be violent and savage compared to their Obun cousins. Their homeworld of Kordeth (called simply "Ukar" by most Known Worlders) is claimed by the Merchant League and House al-Malik.

Urth: Also known as Holy Terra or, in ancient texts, Earth. The birthplace of humanity.

Vau: Mysterious aliens who control the high-tech Vau Hegemony, but whose goals and customs remain mysterious to the people of the Known Worlds.

Vorox: Multi-limbed alien creatures; "feral" Vorox retain their highly-poisonous claws, while "civilized" Vorox have them removed.

Vuldrok Star-Nations: A loose confederation of star nations ruled by warlords who often raid Hawkwood worlds. Called "barbarians" by Known Worlders.

Zaibatsu: The First Republic merchants who controlled Urth prior to the discovery of the jumpgate.

KEY

Imperial crest	
House Hawkwood	
House Decados	
The Hazat	
House Li Halan	
House al-Malik	
House Keddah	
Church (Orthodoxy)	
Brother Battle	
Temple Avesti (Avestites)	
Eskatonic Order	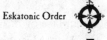
Sanctuary Aeon (Amaltheans)	
Merchant League	
Ur-Obun	
Ur-Ukar	
Vorox	
Vau Hegemony	
Symbiots	

Jumproads of the Known Worlds

The following pages provide a map of Alexius' Empire and its borders. Each world is connected to the others by jumproads — known routes which lead from a system's jumpgate to another system's jumpgate. Many, many other worlds once colonized by humankind exist in space, but their jumpcodes have been lost or their gates locked shut.

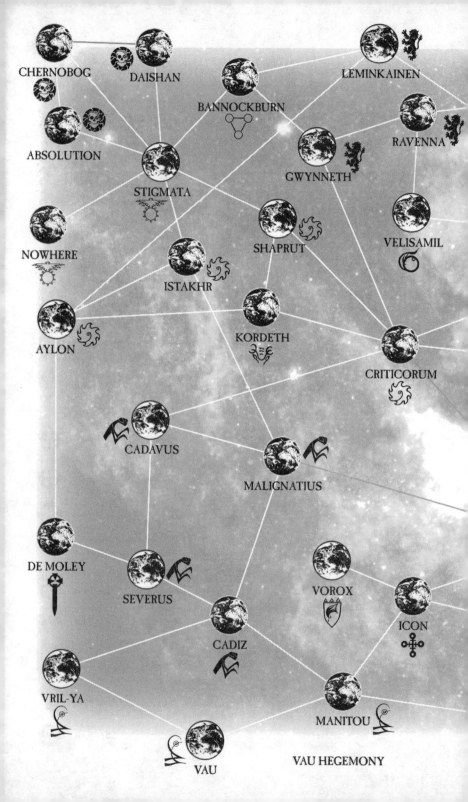

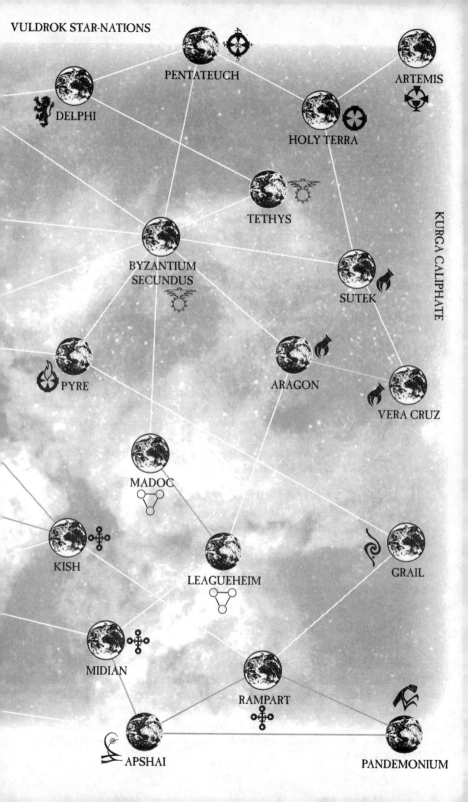

VULDROK STAR-NATIONS

PENTATEUCH

ARTEMIS

DELPHI

HOLY TERRA

TETHYS

BYZANTIUM
SECUNDUS

SUTEK

KURGA CALIPHATE

PYRE

ARAGON

VERA CRUZ

MADOC

KISH

GRAIL

LEAGUEHEIM

MIDIAN

RAMPART

APSHAI

PANDEMONIUM

These **Fading Suns** products are now available:

FADING SUNS: THE ROLEPLAYING GAME

It is the dawn of the sixth millennium after Christ and the skies are darkening, for the suns themselves are fading. Humans reached the stars long ago, building a Republic of high technology and universal emancipation — and then squandered it, fought over it, and finally lost it. A New Dark Age has descended upon humanity, for the greatest of civilizations has fallen and now even the stars are dying. Feudal lords rule the Known Worlds, vying for power with fanatic priests and scheming guilds. Stock #: 200, ISBN: 1-888906-00-6, $25.00

FADING SUNS PLAYERS COMPANION

A valuable expansion to the **Fading Suns** rules, this big book includes new Blessings and Curses, Benefices and Afflictions, skills, occult powers, weapons, equipment and valuable rules expansions. In addition, there are new character roles: Knightly order, Church sects, new religions, guilds, military units, long-awaited details on sentient alien races and the genetically engineered Changed. A must for players and gamemasters! Stock #: 229, ISBN: 1-888906-07-3, $25.00

LORDS OF THE KNOWN WORLDS

Nobles are the unquestioned rulers of the universe. Few are privy to their lifestyles and secrets, and the great unwashed understand little of the perks (and problems) associated with rulership. There are taxes to collect, wars to wage, and rivals to crush. Indeed, as any noble would tell you, the sacrifices they endure more than justify their opulent lifestyles. Not just anybody can be such a martyr; it takes blood privilege. A privilege the nobility protects at all costs, even if it requires deadly duels or declarations of war. Stock #: 226, ISBN: 1-888906-11-1, $18.00

PRIESTS OF THE CELESTIAL SUN

The nobles may rule the secular lives of the Known Worlders, but the Church guards their souls — and in so doing, dictates to the nobility. Few lords dare to defy the will of the Patriarch and his bishops. But the Church's rock is not as stable as it once was — new sects and orders have appeared in the wake of the Emperor Wars, shifting the populace's loyalties and reawakening ancient heresies. While the Church stands united against the powers of the Emperor, the Royal Houses and the Merchant League, they feud within their cathedrals, vying for dominion over the faithful. Stock #: 228, ISBN: 1-888906-06-5, $18.95

MERCHANTS OF THE JUMPWEB

The nobles and the Church may vie for the leadership and minds of the Known Worlders, but the merchants own the stars. Without their high-tech savvy or the loans from their coffers, travel and commerce could not take place. This book details the histories and modus operandi of the Merchant League guilds, from the weird Engineers to the stately Reeves. Stock #231, ISBN: 1-888906-09-X, $20.00

BYZANTIUM SECUNDUS

The first **Fading Suns** setting books details the center of the Known Worlds, the capital and seat of the Empire. There is no more important or intrigue-laden world, for here the fates of millions are determined and the destiny of humanity is in the hands of the royal ambassadors, Church priests, merchant princes, alien envoys and underground conspiracy groups — all vying for the Emperor's attention and favor. Includes new character roles for the Imperial Eye — the Emperor's intergalactic spies. Stock #: 275, ISBN: 1-888906-02-2, $18.00

WEIRD PLACES

Explore some of the varied sites of the **Fading Suns** universe: Roam the strange fields of Pentateuch, a planet terraformed with occult laws. Discover a secret lost world hiding a powerful artifact sought by all. Shop the stalls of the eclectic Istakhr Market, where everything is for sale. Or dock at Barter, a traveling marketplace in space. Ship out to Bannockburn to halt a deadly Symbiot excursion, or search the haunted chapel of Manitou for lost lore. Stock #: 227, ISBN: 1-888906-05-7, $12.95

FORBIDDEN LORE: TECHNOLOGY

The weird world of **Fading Suns** technology is revealed, from starships to ominous psychic artifacts. But beware: the Church claims that such items can endanger the soul, and the Inquisitor's flameguns are ever ready to burn those who dare to use such proscribed and sinful tech. Includes enough equipment lists to choke a Vorox. Stock #: 225, ISBN: 1-888906-03-0, $15.00

THE DARK BETWEEN THE STARS

The Anunnaki left behind many strange devices and their ancient secrets lie buried on many worlds, secrets which can bring salvation — or destruction. But other entities lurk in the void, tempting human and alien alike to enact schemes against the civilized order. An occult book, detailing psychic covens, Sathraists, Antinomists and the many entities and forces involved in the supernatural universe. Stock #: 230, ISBN: 1-888906-08-1, $17.95

CHILDREN OF THE GODS: OBUN & UKAR

One of the earliest sentient alien races humanity discovered was the Ur-Obun — peaceful and wise philosophers. Soon after, humanity met their cousins, the Ur-Ukar — vicious and cruel warriors with a starfaring empire of their own. Humanity has played the two against each other ever since. These two races were gifted by the gods — the ancient Anunnaki jumpgate builders — with unique technology. Xenologists now scour their homes and myths for clues to the riddles of the ancients. But some wonder: How long will the gods permit such transgressions against their children? This book details the histories, cultures and unique powers (theurgic and psychic) of these two races. Stock #: 232, ISBN: 1-888906-10-3, $12.95

SINNERS & SAINTS

Here is a rogues gallery of people and creatures from the Known Worlds and beyond: noble rivals, well-meaning (and not so well-meaning) priests, space pirates, deadly mercenaries, assassins, alien animals (pets and predators), bizarre creatures and more. Each has a story to tell and will lead player characters into intrigue and adventure. Each comes on its own sheet for ease of use by both players and gamemasters. Stock #: 233, ISBN: 1-888906-11-1, $16.95

GAMEMASTERS SCREEN

A sturdy screen with charts and tables to help the **Fading Suns** gamemaster run his stories, with weapons and armor charts, skill lists and more. Includes a fully illustrated Weapons Compendium detailing the wide variety of Known Worlds weaponry, from swords to slug guns to more exotic weapons, such as the Symbiot Element Gun. An additional bonus is a full-color map of the Known Worlds! Stock #: 201, ISBN: 1-888906-01-4, $12.00

NOBLE ARMADA STARSHIP MINIATURES GAME

A starship miniatures game of broadsides and boarding actions in the **Fading Suns** universe. Royal houses vie against rival fleets and pirates for supremacy of the Known Worlds. Command frigates, destroyers or dreadnoughts to carve a fiefdom from the stars! Let loose all guns against your enemies and loot their crippled ships! Includes 32 plastic starship miniatures. Stock #: 500, ISBN: 1-888906-50-2, $55.00

Order from our website (http://www.holistic-design.com) or send check or money order payable to Holistic Design with a list of requested items and costs. Postage fee is $4.00 per order for orders under $50.00. Expect 2-3 weeks shipping time. (International orders: Postage fee is equal to 25% of total purchase price or $10.00, whichever is greater. Expect 4-8 weeks shipping time.)

Product Orders
Holistic Design
5295 Hwy 78
D-337
Stone Mountain, GA 30087

Visit our website at: http://www.holistic-design.com